**To purchase any of these titles in e-book form,
please go to www.baen.com.**

THE CROSSING

THE CROSSING

KEVIN IKENBERRY

THE CROSSING

This is a work of fiction. All the characters and events portrayed in this book are fictional, and any resemblance to real people or incidents is purely coincidental.

A Baen Books Original

Baen Publishing Enterprises
P.O. Box 1403
Riverdale, NY 10471
www.baen.com

ISBN: 978-1-9821-9201-3

Cover art by Kieran Yanner

First printing, August 2022

Distributed by Simon & Schuster
1230 Avenue of the Americas
New York, NY 10020

Library of Congress Cataloging-in-Publication Data

Names: Ikenberry, Kevin, author.
Title: The crossing / Kevin Ikenberry.
Description: Riverdale, NY : Baen, 2022. | Series: Assiti Shard
Identifiers: LCCN 2022019172 (print) | LCCN 2022019173 (ebook) | ISBN
    9781982192013 (hardcover) | ISBN 9781625798718 (ebook)
Subjects: LCSH: Washington, George, 1732-1799—Fiction. | Trenton, Battle
    of, Trenton, N.J., 1776—Fiction. | LCGFT: Alternative histories
    (Fiction) | Science fiction. | Novels.
Classification: LCC PS3609.K46 C76 2022 (print) | LCC PS3609.K46 (ebook)
    | DDC 813/.6—dc23/eng/20220429
LC record available at https://lccn.loc.gov/2022019172
LC ebook record available at https://lccn.loc.gov/2022019173

Pages by Joy Freeman (www.pagesbyjoy.com)
Printed in the United States of America
10 9 8 7 6 5 4 3 2 1

For My Girls

ACKNOWLEDGEMENTS

Back in 2014, at the Superstars Writing Seminar in Colorado Springs, Colorado, I met Eric Flint for the first time. During that seminar, he gave a class in understanding literary contracts that saved my ass on a couple of occasions, but beyond that, I had a dinner with him that changed my life. One of the events at Superstars is an optional dinner where you can sit with the headline guests of the event. I'd chosen Eric because I wanted to learn more about him and his journey, but I also had a burning question in my writer's mind.

"What if the coin George Washington reputedly threw across the Delaware River preceding the Battle of Trenton was a bicentennial quarter?"

Being primarily a science fiction/military science fiction author, I'd never written anything alternate history before and I had no idea if this was even a viable idea. To my utter astonishment, Eric invited me to lunch the following day and we began the plan for this novel. But, as the poet said, the best laid plans often get screwy, and that's exactly what happened.

The week after meeting Eric, I went into the critical unit of my local hospital with a skin-eating bacterial infection that tried (and thankfully failed) to eat my right leg. The next year, Eric survived a scary bout with cancer. In 2017, though, we began work to bring *The Crossing* to life. The path of bringing this book to print faced many challenges over the last few years, but here we are. I'm forever grateful to Eric for his support, mentorship, and friendship.

My thanks also go to the Baen Books team—Toni Weisskopf, Jim Minz, David (DJ) Butler, and everyone behind the scenes—for getting this book together and shepherding it to press. I'd like to say a special thanks to both Chuck Gannon and Alistair Kimble for helping me anticipate challenges along the way.

Finally, and as always, to my family. Being a novelist was never on the menu. I'd wanted to be a good husband, a great father, and everything else above that would be gravy. Since the writing bug bit, though, you've been a constant support system and I am grateful for everything you've given me on this journey. To my girls, and especially my bride, thank you.

Kevin Ikenberry
Colorado Springs, Colorado
2022

THE CROSSING

CHAPTER ONE

November 2008
Fort Dix, New Jersey

I'm lost.

   Again.

   Jameel Mason squinted through the heavy, swirling snow and raised a gloved hand to move a low branch out of his vision. His digitized green Army combat uniform stood out like a sore thumb against the snow-covered ground. In a real situation, an enemy with half a brain and one good eye would have seen the four cadets moving forward a thousand meters out and put them out of their misery with coordinated indirect fire. Training, however, meant that the opposing force of experienced senior cadets usually did their best to slack off, play blind and deaf, and let the underclassmen cadets get close before opening fire. At least they were using blank 5.56mm ammunition instead of yelling "bang bang bang" like they had to do around campus back in Pittsburgh. While the blanks weren't bad, they weren't exactly realistic either. None of it was. In reality, the near blizzard would make both sides hunker down and wait for better weather instead of patrolling around on foot. Mason pushed the thought away and focused. The "suspected enemy bunker" should be a hundred meters downhill from his chosen reconnaissance position. Another ten minutes and they would be done with the final training lane and on their way to a warm bus ride home instead of traipsing around in four inches of fresh snow.

In a year and a half, he'd enter law school and leave the infantry crap to the rest of the Army. Since middle school, he'd wanted to be a judge advocate general's corps officer, like his mother. His Law School Admission Test scores got the attention of Yale, but Mason was holding out for Harvard. He'd take the test again in six weeks with his eyes on a perfect score, better than his mother and father and certainly enough to get Harvard's attention.

Mason shook off the thoughts and got his mind on the squad exercise at hand. Cadets learned and practiced small unit leadership by leading a composite group of nine. Besides the leader, the remaining cadets formed two fire teams, alpha and bravo for a standard infantry squad patrol. All of the cadets in his squad were underclassmen. The juniors held the three leadership positions: squad leader and team leaders. The freshmen and sophomore cadets assumed duties as compass man, paceman, radio telephone operator (RTO), and security. Learning to control the smallest fighting force in the Army order of battle was the perfect place for future leaders to start. At the squad level, success and failure were possible. One happened more often than the other.

Displacing a tree branch in front of him shook fresh fallen snow down his arm. In the craterlike depression below was nothing. He strained to hear against the muffled impacts of the snow. All around him, the forest was quiet. To his left, one of the sophomore cadets whispered.

"Nothing there."

Footsteps crunched the snow behind them. Mason saw a tan, rough-sided boot in the corner of his vision. A slightly louder voice said, "Mason? What's going on?"

Their evaluator for the lane, Cadet Porter, was also the cadet battalion commander and a graduating senior. Already selected for a regular Army commission in the infantry, he'd successfully pushed every one of Mason's buttons for months. Having a reputation as the wannabe lawyer who didn't want to serve in the field only made it worse for Mason. "I'm reconning the objective, sir."

Mason stared down into the depression again. The snow blotted out the brown bed of leaves in all directions. An hour before, there had been nothing. The OPFOR should have been easy to see. *Was it Myers down there hiding as usual? Or Compton asleep against a tree and not playing fair again?*

"Are you sure this is the objective?"

Mason nodded. "Stratton, take Martinez and move over there. Twenty meters that way. Behind that tree. See if you can get eyes on the OPFOR."

"Yeah." Stratton smiled. He turned away from Mason and crawled two meters to Martinez and gestured toward the position. Mason alternately watched them crawl and turned back to the objective. Most of the time, the seniors playing the enemy would show themselves or do something very unrealistic to help the cadets learn. Into the spring, they'd get sneaky and difficult. In a snowstorm, they'd want to go home as badly as Mason did.

Stratton and Martinez reached their position. Mason stared as Stratton broke into a smile and laughed. The smaller, blond junior turned toward Mason and shook his head.

"Damn it," Mason whispered. He motioned Stratton to return. They would try the other way. Maybe then they could—

"Are you sure this is the objective, Mason?"

Annoyed, Mason rolled to face Porter. "Yes. That's the depression right there. The OPFOR is hiding and—"

Porter raised his voice. "ENDEX, everyone. Back to your assembly area."

The end-of-exercise call resulted in everyone but Mason jumping to their feet and brushing off the rapidly accumulating snow. Mason rolled to one side and met Porter's eyes. "Why now? The weather?"

Porter squatted down. "You're nowhere near the objective, Mason."

"That's it down there," he said and jerked his chin toward the depression.

"No, it's not. You are a hundred meters off. Your azimuth out of the patrol base was supposed to be what?"

Mason replied, "Zero four five. Due northeast."

"You were fine for about fifty meters," Porter said. "Then you ducked around a bunch of low brush and started off at zero six five. That's enough to get you off course on a four-hundred-meter lane."

Mason looked down. The compass had been Murphy's responsibility. A goofy kid from Missouri who never took anything seriously. No wonder they were off course. He stared at his own wrist compass, purchased by his mother so he'd always have a backup. The hands were frozen at due northeast, forty-five degrees. He'd never bothered to check himself or Murphy's navigation. He failed the situation training lane for the fourth time in five weeks. Two weeks earlier, back at the University of Pittsburgh, he'd failed his third straight lane before barely passing a standard ambush.

Porter continued. "Your plan was solid this time. Everyone understood the mission and their role, unlike last time. But, your navigation skills suck. You need work, Mason, or you're not going to pass LDAC."

The Leader Development and Assessment served as the capstone event for Army officers commissioning through the Reserve Officers' Training Corps (ROTC) programs across the country. Cadets between their junior and senior years converged on Fort Lewis, Washington, for six weeks of constant observation and machinated leadership experiences. Leadership, though, took a backseat to technical and tactical proficiency. With variables like peer assessments thrown into the mix, LDAC took on some vestiges of a popularity contest. Being good with a map, compass, and rifle weren't enough. Having all the requisite soldier skills and not being able to lead, or follow, would catch the glare of the instructors. That meant low scores in the overall order of merit list. With every LDAC graduate numbered from 1-n based on their performance in school and the six-week course, slots in the active army were hard to come by. Being accepted to Harvard was no guarantee that Mason would gain a coveted JAG position. His future depended on passing the summer tactical course with flying colors. With seven months to go, the mountain in front of him appeared unclimbable.

There wasn't time to practice all of the things that Porter and the Army cadre wanted and maintain a high grade point average and job at the university recreation center. Something had to give.

"Mason?" Porter's inflection changed and snapped his thoughts like a twig.

"What?"

"Get up out of the snow." The senior extended a hand. "You're gonna be fine. Just keep working."

Mason wanted to say something, but the look on Porter's face was something he'd not seen in two years with the ROTC battalion. The senior put a hand on his shoulder and smiled.

"We've all fucked up a few lanes, okay?"

Mason returned the smile genuinely. "Thanks, Porter."

Like all cadets, they used only last names. Technically, Porter was a cadet lieutenant colonel and Mason was a cadet staff sergeant. Protocol in "CadetLand" meant he should have said "sir," but Porter would have shrugged it off. They were cadets, after all. There would be a time and a place for actual rank and real responsibility.

"Get your squad and head to the road. We'll debrief on the way to the bus."

The snow fell harder as Mason and his small team of four met the other five members of the squad. The bravo team leader, Ashley Higgs, was the only one to meet his eyes. The pretty, shy blonde frowned at him, disappointment all over her face. Not only had he let himself down, but her and the others.

"Everybody ready?" Mason asked.

"All up. Kennedy is using the B&W." The "bushes and woods" were the equivalent of a field latrine in Higgs' midwestern parlance. It brought a smile to Mason's face as always.

"Again? The kid's got a small bladder."

Higgs giggled. "Tiny tank."

Mason smiled and reached down for his rucksack. The large, digital-patterned rucksack weighed roughly thirty pounds with a standard load for cadets on a weekend training exercise. A uniform change, extra set of boots, underwear, physical training clothes and shoes (for wear in the barracks), extended cold weather modular sleep system, and personal hygiene items filled the space quite nicely. As he slipped his shoulders into the straps and pulled the rucksack on, the sky flashed and a tremendous sound came down on them. The ground came up at once and threw them all down.

Mason closed his eyes and covered his head. *Did Porter throw an artillery simulator?* He looked up and saw Porter stumble to his feet, looking skyward.

"Is everybody all right?" Higgs looked at the collected cadets, her eyes wide and frightened. "What was that?"

"Thundersnow!" Porter yelled. "Let's get going, people! Get your rucks on!"

Mason turned to the collected group and opened his mouth to yell for Kennedy to hurry up. Instead, there was a bloodcurdling scream and then silence. "Kennedy?"

Higgs yelled as well, with no response.

"It stopped snowing," the other junior in the squad, Mark Stratton, said with a laugh. "How about that!"

"Kennedy!" Mason yelled again. He turned toward Stratton. "Get him back here."

"He's not my problem," Stratton said. "You want him, you go get him."

Mason spun on his heels. "Kennedy is your soldier right now, Stratton, and I'm still in charge of this mission. Get Kennedy and get ready to move."

"Whatever," Stratton said, but he moved toward the wood line Higgs indicated. He looked over his shoulder to glare, and Mason knew why. They hadn't liked each other as freshmen. Mason won the Superior Cadet award their freshman year, and Stratton took the award their sophomore year. A coveted opportunity to attend the Army's basic parachutist course at Fort Benning the previous summer came down to their physical fitness test scores, with Stratton winning out. Given the chance, he loved calling the other cadets "legs," the airborne derogatory term for those unqualified to jump from a perfectly good airplane. Which meant Mason and ninety-five percent of the rest of the cadets in the battalion.

"Medic!" Cadet Martinez, Kennedy's battle buddy, screamed. "Higgs! Get over here!"

The young woman dropped her rucksack, opened it, and removed a Combat Life Saver bag. The squad carried two of them, and Higgs always managed to grab one. Mason teased her about always wanting the lighter-weight bags versus the tactical radios, until he'd learned she was an emergency medical technician when she'd sewn up a fellow cadet the previous year. Mason watched her jog toward Martinez. The freshman's face was pale as the snow on the ground around them.

"Hurry!"

The blizzard had stopped. Stratton had said something, but it hadn't registered until that moment. Not even a trace of snow fell from the sky. The solid ceiling of gray clouds appeared broken amidst a cool yellow western sky. His stomach twisted on itself. Something else had gone wrong. He jogged after Higgs. Behind the frozen remains of a thicket, they found Kennedy lying facedown in the snow. The tall kid's pants were down around his ankles, and he lay motionless. Higgs gasped at the amount of blood on the snow. It made no sense.

"What the hell—" Mason said. A loud crack sounded to the right. For a split second, he could hear a whistling sound before the bark of a nearby tree exploded. The group all dove into the snow. Mason looked into Kennedy's motionless blue eyes. Voices screamed from the clearing in an unintelligible language. Mason shifted to his elbows and looked low over Kennedy's helmet. In the clearing to the north, three men in green jackets and funny plumed hats sprinted away.

One of them had Kennedy's rucksack. Another had his M16A2 rifle.

Porter's voice spurred them to action. "Hey! Stop right now!"

The three men looked over the shoulders and kept running. After a moment, one of them slowed and spun. He knelt in the snow and aimed a long rifle back toward the cadets.

"Take cover!" Mason yelled and flung himself into the snow. The rifle cracked and a shot whistled low above their heads. Mason waited for another shot, but it did not come.

"Come on!" Porter yelled and got to his feet. Mason looked up to see the senior tearing through the snow toward the retreating men. Stratton and Murphy followed. The Warrior Ethos, the model for behavior in combat, said to never leave a fallen comrade.

"Help me flip him over," Higgs directed. When he didn't respond, she yelled. "Mason! Help me flip him over!"

Grabbing the freshman's shoulders, Mason did as he was told. The boy's eyes stared unseeing into the distance. Blood covered his abdomen and soaked through the thin combat uniform shirt and trousers. Higgs touched Kennedy's neck for a long minute.

"No pulse. He's not breathing." She pulled up the shirt and grimaced. "Gunshot wound left lower abdomen. Puncture wound at the solar plexus." She touched Kennedy's soaked trousers and announced, "Another one at the femoral artery."

"What happened?" Mason looked up at the receding cadets in chase. Higgs worked quickly and cut away Kennedy's pants leg. The amount of blood turned Mason's stomach to the point he had to turn away before his lunch made a second appearance. "Do we need to start CPR?"

"No. He's dead, Mason. He bled out." Higgs wiped her right eye with the back of her bloody hands. "What do you want me to do?"

"Bled out? From what?" Mason shook his head. "Get him up so we can get out of here."

Higgs held up her hands. "He's dead, Mason. Didn't you hear me? Those assholes"—she gestured toward the fleeing men in the funny white costumes—"stabbed him twice and took his gear."

He could hear Stratton and Porter screaming. One of them fired six or seven shots of blank ammunition. They were out of the training range. The whole mission had gone into the toilet. Kennedy was dead, the cadets were running around without any leadership, and the rifle was missing. *Focus*, he told himself. *Pick one thing and deal with it.*

"Higgs, get the cadre on the radio. Call in the emergency." Mason licked his lips and looked at the collected cadets. "Koch, you come with me. The rest of you stay here until the cadre come."

"There's nothing but static." Higgs shrugged.

"Keep trying. Call them on a cell phone if you have to." As the directions came out, Mason calmed and focused. "Koch and I are going after Stratton and the others to get the rifle. Stay here and maintain positive accountability. If anything else happens, call me on the radio. Same will happen for me. I'll be back in ten minutes."

Mason shrugged out of his rucksack and let it fall to the snow. He heard Higgs calling into the radio, "Charlie Two Four, this is X-ray Two One, November November November. I say again, November November November. We have an emergency situation."

There was no immediate response. *Go! Get the rest of them before this whole thing gets worse!* "The rest of you stay here and don't move. Let's go, Koch."

The big kid from Indiana got to his feet and started toward the clearing and Mason followed. In the flattened winter grass, they began to run.

"What the fuck is going on?" Koch asked.

Mason shook his head. "Don't know. Let's just get that rifle back before this gets any worse."

"Roger that."

Koch wasn't much of a runner and Mason began to pull away from him. After a hundred meters, the snow faded abruptly into a light powder on the ground. Mason accelerated like a gazelle and began to close the gap on Porter and the others. Another crack echoed through the valley. For the first time, Mason wondered if they were some kind of terrorists. Who else would trespass on a military reservation with live ammunition? Mason closed on the tree line and found Porter and the three other cadets lying behind trees for cover.

A two-story wood-sided cabin sat inside the trees, off-center in a circular clearing. The front steps did not have a porch, just a weathered brown door. Small windows adorned each side roughly a meter from each corner. A longer, thinner building abutted the taller main house. Two horses grazed in a wooden-fenced paddock. Wood smoke trailed out of the central rock chimney with the smell of bread cooking.

Stratton glanced over his shoulder at Mason. "They went inside."

"What is this place? A movie set?" Mason looked toward Porter. The senior ripped open a foil packet and removed a field dressing. Murphy's right arm was a bloody mess. "He okay?"

"They're shooting at us and Murphy's hit. What the hell do you think, Mason?" Porter asked. "You call the cadre?"

Mason nodded. "We did. Nothing but static."

Porter ripped open the Velcro pocket on his left sleeve and removed a smartphone. He stared at it for a moment. "That's odd."

"What?" Mason asked.

"No service."

Voices drifted on the wind. A scream rang out from inside the cabin. A woman's scream. Porter tied the dressing on Murphy's arm. "You with me?"

Mason blinked. "What are you talking about? We don't have any ammunition."

"Five versus three and they're using muskets. Single-shot. We can get in there and stop them before someone else gets hurt."

"Muskets?" Mason shook his head. "We need to wait for the cadre. They stole a rifle. That's government property."

Porter nodded, chewing on his bottom lip. He looked at Mason for a long moment. "What if the cadre isn't coming, Mason? It's up to us to get that rifle back."

"What do you mean?" Mason blinked. None of it made any sense. The weather change. Less snowfall on the ground. Three men who obviously killed Kennedy and ran into the woods and were holed up in a shack.

"I'll explain later." Porter looked up at Stratton huddled behind a tree fifteen meters closer to the door.

"Let's go," Stratton whispered. "We can take them!"

Porter licked his lips and looked at Mason. "You ready?"

Stratton jumped to his feet. "Come on!" he hissed at them and ran at a crouch to the side of the cabin. Koch, Porter, Murphy, and Mason lined up against the wall behind him to stack against the door. The stack was a standard formation to clear a room. The point man would kick down the door and the rest would follow him into the room, each with a given sector of fire. The idea was to get inside the room quickly, identify the enemies, and bring them down. As a group, they'd practiced room clearing exactly once.

Stratton held up his rifle and flipped the safety off. He rotated the switch past the semiautomatic setting to full automatic. Everyone else did the same. Without a grenade or any actual weapons to use, they'd have to use their blank ammunition to startle the men. Finger to his lips, Stratton motioned them to creep along the wall toward the cabin's front door.

Mason lined up as the last man, behind Murphy. "Your arm okay?"

"Yeah," Murphy said. "Hurts but I'll make it."

Another scream came from inside followed by more incoherent language. "Is that German?" Mason whispered to Murphy, who nodded.

"Sounds like it."

Stratton looked back at them. "Shut the fuck up, you two. Something's wrong in there. Let's go."

Porter moved first, telling Stratton with hand gestures that he would lead the assault. With the accomplished senior leading, Mason felt a bit better. Porter would know just what to do, like always. There were three armed men inside versus five unarmed cadets.

They shuffled toward the door as quietly as they could. Stratton stepped out and kicked the middle of the door near its jamb. Wood flew in all directions as the flimsy door slammed inward. In one move, Koch ran inside firing his weapon on full automatic. Not that the blank ammunition would do anything other than maybe scare the attackers or stun them to inaction. Five against three was pretty good odds.

Porter went left, Murphy went right, and Mason looked high and checked the corners. Stratton came through last and froze in the middle of the room. All of them squeezed off multiple shots, filling the tight room with noise and a small amount of blue smoke. Three men in strange white clothing and green felt jackets stood in the cabin. Two were armed and one lay astride a pretty blonde girl on the kitchen table. His intentions were immediately clear. One of his hands covered her mouth while the other stopped trying to open his belt. Another man lay on the floor bleeding from a head wound. He moaned but did not move.

The girl locked eyes with Mason for a moment and then Porter. She closed her eyes and bit down on the hand across her mouth. The fat man howled and brought his other hand up and slapped the girl viciously.

"Hey!" Porter screamed and gestured with the barrel of his rifle. "Put down your weapons and get down on the floor!"

As if time slowed down, Mason saw it was all wrong. These people, whoever they were, did *not* dress or live as modern people did. The cabin looked like something he'd seen as a boy on a family vacation in the south. A working colonial farm with old women dressed much like the pretty young woman thrashing at the fat man attempting to rape her. Cooking utensils mixed with tools on the hearth, making the fireplace a combination workbench and kitchen. A heavy cast-iron pot hung above the smoldering logs. Some type of stew simmered by the smell. The fat man barked an order in German, snapping Mason's thoughts.

"Tote sie alle!" he roared and pushed himself away from the girl with a grunt and his penis flopping absurdly in his hand.

The two others looked at each other for a moment. The one with a hawk's face held his rifle at the waist and spun toward the cadets. The glint of a bayonet caught Mason's eye. Blood covered the slim metal blade. Mason wondered if the rifle could fire with the bayonet attached.

"Put it down on the ground," Porter ordered. He took a step toward the two men. "Now!"

The man sneered and pulled the trigger. Mason blinked at the intensity of the burst. Sulfurous smoke filled the cabin, its stench overwhelming the breathable air. Coughing and sputtering, Mason waved at the smoke with one hand in a desperate attempt to see something, anything.

Can't see! What the hell?

The smoke swirled and cleared as the chimney did its work and pulled the remnants up and away from the cabin. The two men shouted at each other, but the ringing in his ears muffled everything. Something moved on the floor and Mason recognized the brown rough-out boots of his friends. He knelt toward them and moved up the legs. Eyes looking up into the smoke, Mason felt something slick and moist on his hands and looked down for the briefest of moments.

Porter lay crumpled on the ground, a black-and-red stain spreading across his abdomen. Eyes wide, he looked up at Mason and raised a bloodied hand. Blood trickled from both sides of his mouth as he struggled toward Mason. "Take charge," Porter whispered. "Mason. Take . . . charge."

CHAPTER TWO

Koch was the first to move. Vaulting past Mason, the big blond barreled into the shooter and drove him across the small room and into the rough wall. Mason came up screaming and followed Koch's lead while Stratton went straight for the bastard with his pants undone. The tall, skinny German's eyes widened as Mason charged and swung the butt of his rifle. The sickening crack shook Mason's arms and the man went down to the floor without another sound. He spun to see Stratton flung to the floor by the larger man. The fat bastard stared at Mason and glanced to Mason's right and stopped. Another crash sounded and Mason flinched. The fat man's head disappeared in a cloud of blood and tissue.

The girl lowered a musket and began to reload. Koch screamed over and over as he pummeled the man who'd shot Porter. The man's head lolled from side to side with every blow. Koch clutched him by the neck and hit him repeatedly. Tears ran down Koch's face.

Mason stepped over. "Koch!"

Raging blue eyes turned to Mason and softened. He let go of the bloodied man's neck. The German collapsed to the floor like a sack of rice. The big man huffed and puffed, finally putting his hands on his knees. As Mason watched, Koch knelt by the man and pressed bare fingers to the wounded man's neck.

"Anything?" Mason asked.

Koch shook his head. Stratton stepped in and clapped the sophomore on the back. "Hell, yeah! You put that motherfucker down!"

Koch did not smile. Instead he looked down at the man

and his own bloody hands. He was extraordinarily strong but not given to brutality, and was obviously shaken by the lethal results of his fury.

Stratton stepped around to the girl. "Are you all right?"

She did not look up. Instead she rammed a ball into the barrel of her musket and pounded it down. "Is my father dead?"

Her accent caught Mason's attention. He turned to the man lying across from Porter. The man moaned and stirred. "No, he's not."

Porter. Mason stepped back toward the senior. Porter's face was gray and his breathing erratic. On the left chest of Porter's load-bearing vest was the personal first aid pouch. Mason ripped it open and withdrew the plastic-wrapped field dressing. Tearing it open with his teeth, Mason withdrew the green-and-white bandage. The white dressing was designed to absorb and expand to hold twice its weight in fluids. On either side of the dressing were twenty-four-inch woven green straps that tied to secure the dressing in place. Mason unzipped Porter's ACU top and gently pulled the sand-colored undershirt away from the gaping wound. He pressed the dressing onto the wound and leaned down.

"You're gonna be—" Hands shoved Mason roughly to the floor. The first man scrambled past Mason and rummaged the long table before he darted out the door. As the door swung shut, Mason saw Kennedy's rifle in the man's hands. "Stratton! He's got the rifle!"

"I got him," Stratton said and moved toward the door. "Come on, Murphy!"

They opened the door and Mason heard the tinkling of glass breaking. He looked in that direction and saw the young woman extend the barrel of the musket through one of the small rectangular panes. She took a breath, held it and let it out slowly.

Through the open door, Mason watched the man sprint down the wide lane in the gathering darkness. Against the dark trees, the man's white-stocking-clad legs flashed. He took off his green jacket and slung it to the ground. The fallen snow would camouflage him if he got much farther. Mason looked back at the girl just as she pulled the trigger. The deafening noise slammed into Mason's ears and a thick cloud of smoke filled the cabin's kitchen in an instant. Mason stepped forward to the window next to the young woman and pressed his nose to the glass.

In the distance, a good hundred yards away, the man stumbled and fell into the snow. After a moment, he scrambled to his feet and Mason could see a spreading stain across his back. The man stumbled and picked up the rifle before stepping into the forest.

"Nice shot," Mason said. The girl paid no attention to him. She was already loading another round.

Outside, Stratton and Murphy were running into the darkness. They'd be out of control in a matter of seconds. Mason looked at Porter and then at Koch still kneeling over the dead man. The rest of the squad were still out in the snow with Kennedy's body.

Mason moved around the kitchen table and raced to the cabin's door. "Stratton! Stop!"

The two cadets skidded to a stop a hundred yards or so away. Stratton spun angrily. "We need to get that rifle!"

"Go back and get Higgs and the others. Bring Kennedy's body here before it gets dark," Mason shouted. He stepped out into the cold and began to close the distance. Stratton did not move. "Come on. We need to get the squad back together and figure out what's going on."

"What about that rifle?"

"We have the serial number and can report it missing. The cadre will notify the local authorities. Right now, we have one dead, two injured, and half our folks are out there in the snow. Go bring them back. Take Koch with you."

Stratton's nose flared for a moment as if he was about to argue; instead, he started walking toward Mason. As they passed, he said, "Just how lost did you get us, Mason? Come on, Koch. Let's go get the others."

Mason watched Stratton and Koch break in a slow jog in the direction of where Higgs and the others waited. The setting sun turned the western sky to a bright gold through the clouds. Sunset was maybe thirty minutes away. As Murphy approached, Mason pulled out his own cell phone. No service.

"You're not going to get a signal, Mason," Murphy said. He swung his rifle strap over his good shoulder.

Mason shook his head. "Must be some kind of dead zone."

Murphy glanced at him for a long moment. "There's something you should see."

"Where? In the museum?"

Murphy squinted and shook his head. "In the house. Those people's home."

"That's not a home," Mason said with a chuckle. Murphy grew up in New York City. Unless he had a side of the family like Mason's, who were dirt poor and living in squalor in the sticks of Mississippi, he had no idea about backwoods life. "I've seen too many historical places, you know, living farms and that kind of thing. Same thing here. Some kind of museum just off post, I guess. We can use their phone to get the MPs out here."

They walked silently, Murphy dabbing a hand at his wounded arm twice and checking for blood. Mason said nothing and the silence felt like a vice around his head. The cadre would be coming through the woods behind the cabin any moment. A cadet was dead, a rifle had disappeared, and any chance he had of earning his lieutenant's bars vanished. *Why do we even do this field bullshit?* The guys who want to go in combat arms should do it, but not somebody who planned to be a lawyer. The day when soldiers turned to the wannabe lawyers for tactical expertise was right up there with hell freezing over.

The brownish-red door opened. The costumed girl looked them over and locked eyes with Murphy. "Did you get the Hessian?"

Hessian? Mason spoke, "No. I told the others to get the rest of our people and bring them here. We'll call for help and figure out what happened."

"Help? From whom? Washington?"

Mason shook his head. "No. Our leaders. They'll know what to do."

"Your leaders?" She folded her arms across the white apron front of her dress. "And just who are your leaders? And what is that emblem on your shoulder?"

Mason looked at his right shoulder, the one typically reserved for combat action unit patches. Cadets wore the emblem of their university. "My school."

"The flag," the girl said, again looking at Murphy.

"Yeah? It's an American flag."

"Not our flag," the girl said. She stepped down onto the moist ground and walked up to Murphy. "You mind telling me just who you are?"

Murphy nodded at the open door. "We should check on your husband."

The girl scowled at him. "He's my father, not my husband." She turned toward the door. "How many others are with you?"

Mason started to speak but Murphy grabbed his elbow. "There are nine of us total. One of our men is dead in the forest back there."

"Bastards. They are worse than the Sassenach." She spat and shook her head.

Mason squinted at Murphy, who shrugged his shoulders. "What's a Sassenach?"

The girl gaped at him. "His Majesty's army? The bloody red-coats. Who did you think I was talking about?"

Mason didn't know what to say. Murphy spoke for him. "It's a long story, miss."

The girl looked over their shoulders, scanning the wood line and surrounding forest. "Get inside. There may be more of them."

They stepped into the cabin. The foyer they'd burst through was tiny by comparison to the rest of the home. A large fireplace with multiple hearths dominated the center of the structure and poured heat and light into the dim spaces. The girl moved to her father as he rolled to his back and started to sit up. The head wound was nasty, likely concussive, but he'd be okay. They'd managed to save both of them at a terrible cost.

Mason knelt next to Porter. The senior barely breathed and his pulse was weak. Mason slid his hand up to Porter's shoulder and squeezed gently. "Help is on the way, man. Just hang in there."

Porter did not respond.

Chin on his chest, Mason closed his eyes intending to pray. Instead, his failures over the past several hours played back like a horror movie. In his worst nightmares, he could not have imagined any of this. He would be drummed out of ROTC within a week. Having already signed a contract for entry into the services, he could expect basic training and years of being a lower enlisted soldier instead of law school and an automatic promotion to captain. All of it because he couldn't find a simple tactical objective. It was stupid and frustrating. Not every person in the army had to carry a rifle. The army needed lawyers, too.

"Mason?" Murphy asked. He knelt next to the man with the bloodied head. "How's Porter?"

There wasn't an answer that he wanted to face. Blood covered the senior's torso and waist areas. A fresh pool spread across the rough-hewn flooring. The shoddy craftsmanship distracted Mason's thoughts for a moment. These strange, savage people had gone to extremes to make this museum-home authentic. Shaking the errant thoughts away, he leaned down to Porter's ear.

"Hang on, Porter. Help is on the way." He grasped the senior's left hand, gazed at the bloodied wedding ring, and froze. Like most of the cadets, he'd been there when Porter proposed to Janet at Three Rivers Stadium during the World Series. They'd provided the color guard for the pregame ceremonies and then spent Game One in the Pirates owner's box. Fourteen months married, with a little boy named David.

God, what do I tell her?

He looked at his watch and frowned. Stratton should be back with Higgs soon. Maybe there was something she could do with Porter's wound until the cadre evacuated them. The senior's eyes were open now and frantically looking around.

"Janet?" he choked out. "Janet?"

Mason leaned closer. "She's coming, Porter. Hang on."

Porter turned his head slowly and looked at Mason for a long moment. "All this."

"What?"

Porter swallowed and coughed. Mason felt moisture hit the side of his face as he leaned in closer. "All this."

Mason looked at Porter's face. The senior's breathing hitched and he struggled to get the words out.

"Grantville." Porter's eyes closed and his head thumped against the rough floor boards. After ten agonizing seconds, he took a shallow breath and then another.

"Let me look at your arm," a new voice said. Mason spun to see the bloodied man sitting up at the long table with his hands untying the field dressing.

"Don't undo that," Mason said.

The man glared at him. "I do what I want, boy."

Mason stood up. "Boy?"

Murphy looked at him. "Mason? You need to see something."

The bloodied man turned back to Murphy and untied the dressing. "As long as it missed the bone, you'll be fine."

"I said, don't untie that dressing." Mason stepped toward them. Murphy stood up and put his good arm between them. "Get out of the way, Murphy. No one talks to me like that."

Murphy turned toward the table and picked up a floppy book.

"Look at this, Mason." The rough-edged booklet with stylized writing had a familiar title. "This is what I was talking about."

"*Common Sense.* Yeah, I've read it." Mason shook his head. "I don't need a history lesson, man. This muse shit ain't going to help Porter and Kennedy."

"This is a brand-new copy, Mason. At least it looks like the one from the museum I remember, except it's almost new."

Mason sighed and stood. "So what if it's brand-new, Murphy?"

Murphy squinted but did not say anything. "Sir?"

The bloodied man dabbed at his wound with a disgusted look on his face. "Yes?"

"Would you mind telling my friend today's date?"

The man shook his head. "December the twenty-first."

Mason glanced at Murphy. "It's November—"

"The year?" Murphy asked. "What year is it?"

The girl frowned. "Seventeen seventy-six, of course. What is wrong with the two of you?"

Grantville. Hadn't Porter whispered that? Oh, no.

A knock at the door stopped them. Mason stepped to the door and heard Stratton whisper, "Let us in."

"Sir, may our friends come in?"

The man looked up and stared at Murphy's right shoulder and the American flag. "Your friends? Are you our friends, son?"

Murphy nodded. "We'll explain. We have some medical supplies that might help our friend and dress your wound."

The man nodded. "My name is Daniels. Vernon Daniels. This is my daughter, Emily. You're wearing a flag like ours."

Mason nodded. "It is."

"More stars," the man said. He stood and half staggered to one of the Hessian bodies. He began stripping the man's clothes away. "Help me with the other one. We have to get them out of here."

Mason looked at Murphy. "Grantville. That's what Porter said."

Murphy nodded. "I had a cousin there, Mason. That's what I was trying to tell you."

"What are we going to tell the others?"

Murphy shrugged. "What's to tell?"

Mason nodded. "We don't know what happened."

"But we're sure of where we are." They stripped the fat Hessian's body and piled the clothes and belongings near the fireplace. "We're southeast of Trenton in the days before—"

"Northwest," Daniels said. "We're northwest of Trenton."

Murphy shook his head and nodded. "Right. That's what I meant." He looked up at Mason for a long moment, and Mason understood. If it was December 1776, they were on the wrong side of the Delaware River. Washington would attack on Christmas Day. The attack would change the entire scope of the war. Mason's stomach turned. They'd lost a modern assault rifle in the midst of a war. And the wrong side had it.

"We have to get that rifle."

Murphy shrugged. "It's dark and we don't have a good grasp of the terrain. We can search him out in the morning. He's wounded. We can track him."

Mason laughed. "You a hunter, Murphy?"

"Eagle Scout. I can do almost anything."

Daniels spoke. "Are you a freedman? Is that why you're listening to him?"

Murphy looked at Mason but said nothing. Mason met the man's eyes. "I'm not a freedman, Mister Daniels. I'm from Pennsylvania."

"Why did they listen to you?"

Mason took a breath. "They are my squad. I'm the squad leader."

"Squad?" Daniels shook his head. "Where are you from? Are you with the rebels or the Sassenach?"

"The what?" Mason asked.

Daniels frowned deeper. "The British, boy! Are you with them?"

"No. We're Americans."

"Where are you from? Who sent you?"

Mason took a deep breath and exhaled slowly. He reached into his front left pocket and pulled out a group of coins. He looked at the quarter and smiled. He flipped it to its unique rear side and handed it to Daniels.

"That's where we are from."

Daniels studied the coin and looked up. "Bicentennial? America is two hundred years old where you are from?"

Murphy smiled. "More than that."

Daniels handed the quarter back to them. "We'll discuss this later. Help me get these bodies out of here or the Hessians will come and burn this all to the ground."

"There's another body out in the big clearing behind the house," Murphy said. "One of our friends."

Daniels nodded. "We'll take them into the woods to the east, down toward the Princeton Road. There's a hole that the Hessians won't think to check until spring. Emily, you get the mess here cleaned up."

"Yes, Father." The girl's wide brown eyes were steady.

Murphy piped in. "Our folks will help."

"How many of you are there?" Daniels asked. The scowl on his face darkened.

Mason did the math. "There will be eight of us now, sir."

Daniels nodded and for the first time looked at Mason's weapon. "May I see that?"

As he handed the rifle over, Mason looked at the far wall. Several muskets and implements caught his eye. "This is an M16 rifle. All we have is blank ammunition."

"How do you load it?"

Mason twisted the rifle in Daniels' hands and pushed the magazine ejection button. The slim, metal rectangle slid easily out of the rifle. The crimped brass rounds gleamed in the firelight. Mason waited for some incredulous outburst, watching Daniels' face for shock, but there was nothing for almost two full minutes as the man picked up and twirled a brass cartridge in his fingers.

"Noisemakers?" Daniels chuckled. "What kind of soldiers are you?"

Murphy said, "Cadets. Officers in training."

Daniels ran his hands over the rifle from butt to muzzle. "You know how to work this? With real ammunition?"

"Yes," Mason said. "We do."

"I've never seen anything like this. They are exactly the same? All of its parts?"

"Yes," Mason said. *When did the concept of interchangeable parts start?* He couldn't remember. Instead, he thought of one of the old Star Trek movies where the crew convinced a modern-day metallurgist to make transparent aluminum.

Daniels handed the rifle back. "I'll see about that ammunition later."

"You can make it work?"

"I'm a weaponsmith." He smiled for the first time. Daniels took a breath and shifted in his chair. "I can make any musket or long rifle better. But, you're going to have to tell me the God's honest truth, boy. Who are you and where are you from?"

☆   ☆   ☆

On the Princeton Road, a mile northeast of Trenton, three men in green jackets and plumed hats stamped their feet against the cold. The patrol's leader tugged at the long mustache hair along the corners of his mouth and frowned.

"Late again." His voice was a low growl. "Wonder where Essen found a bottle this time?"

The others blew into their hands and said nothing. For weeks, their commanders had given them free rein over the countryside. Anything they found was theirs. Food. Drink. Women. Children, even. They'd all taken whatever fancied them. Filling their pockets and emptying their balls often occurred at the same places. Amongst the dumb colonists, nothing mattered. The only thing good about them was their propensity for strong drink.

"We should join them," one of the young Hessians said. A few others huffed their agreement as they hunched against the cold.

"Did you hear the shot?" asked another jaeger. "Maybe they found something to eat?"

"Wrong direction," the leader said. He turned and looked to the west where the single shot had resonated from a few moments before. He thought about investigation, walking farther away from Trenton to find a drunkard and his patrol.

"What if they were captured?"

"Not our problem."

"Quiet," the leader said, but the cold air seeping through his boots made the want of a fire and a drink too strong. "Let's go. Essen and his idiots can stay out here all night for what I care."

They turned as a group, slung their muskets over their shoulders, and hiked back toward Trenton. Heads down, hands stuffed under the jackets for warmth, they moved silently toward comfort oblivious to a wounded man scrambling for help in the distant wood line.

CHAPTER THREE

The first time Ashley Higgs saw a dead body, she'd been twelve years old on a family vacation in rural Georgia. A scenic route turned into carnage as they came upon the remains of two cars strewn across the two-lane road. She'd recognized the blue car. Full of teenagers, it had blasted past her family's sedan a good twenty miles before. The blue sports car lay crumpled on its side. The other vehicle, a black diesel truck, sat across the center line with a crumpled front end. The smoking sports car looked to catch fire in a widening pool of spilled fuel. Her father jumped out of the car and took two steps before leaping to one side.

"Sonuvabitch!" He'd stepped on a severed forearm.

The three teenagers were strewn and mangled across the road. The driver's side door of the truck had opened and the driver, a thick man in overalls, staggered and fell onto the road. Blood poured from his nose. Ashley and her mother grabbed the first aid kit and started for the man. The mangled limb caught her eye and she froze. It was the last time she could remember not knowing what to do in an emergency situation. She'd never seen anything like Kennedy's wounds.

"Higgs?"

She looked up into the soft, round face of Mike Martinez. The freshman cadet was well over three hundred pounds and would never finish the ROTC program because of an ongoing Adderall prescription. It was too bad. The kid had heart for miles. He never stopped shuffling through physical fitness training. He'd cried on their first ruck march in the early-morning humidity, too, but he'd never quit. He looked at her face and not the carnage that was Kennedy's body.

"I can't reach anyone on the radio." He shrugged. "I've tried my cell phone, too. Nothing."

Higgs nodded and looked back at Kennedy. Most of Kennedy's rib cage on the left side was exposed. The shot, whatever it had been, had killed him instantly. His left lung shredded and aorta cleanly severed, the gangly freshman had been dead before he'd been stabbed twice and crumpled into the snow. "I've never seen anything like this."

Martinez knelt next to her on the snow-covered grass. "You've been an EMT for a while, too."

She chuckled slightly. "I've seen two GSWs—sorry, gunshot wounds. Neither of them were anything like this."

Martinez did not look at Kennedy's body. Higgs realized he was trying not to vomit. He coughed and asked, "What do we do?"

"Yeah!" a new voice came from over Martinez's shoulder. Higgs bit the inside of her lip. Diana Dunaway was the antithesis of Martinez. She never wanted to do anything and complained constantly. Twice a week, she'd collapse during physical training. The first couple of times had been scary, the cadre yelling at each other and calling the ambulance. When it kept happening, and her antics increased, everyone would collect her off the football field and sit her down until the rest of the battalion completed their exercises. Somehow, she passed the physical fitness tests and stayed a cadet. Higgs knew that Dunaway only stayed in the program because of her parents. Both of them retired as full colonels and wanted the same for her. She said she wanted to go into the finance corps and was studying to be an accountant. When she wasn't trying to major in theater, too. The nickname of Drama Queen was all too perfect. "I'm cold."

Higgs looked over her shoulder and locked eyes with the girl. "Do some push-ups. You'll stay warm."

Dunaway sneered but said nothing. Higgs looked at Martinez and then at Booker—a quiet sophomore cadet who'd been in ROTC for a year. No one knew him well—except that he spent every weekend at home in Chicago rather than at school. She'd almost forgotten he was there. "Get Kennedy's poncho out of his ruck. We'll make a litter and get him out of here."

"You want us to carry his body? There's like four of us?" Dunaway whined.

Higgs whirled on her. "Yes, Dunaway. That's exactly what we're going to do. Never leave a fallen comrade! Got it?"

Dunaway nodded and looked away. "Yeah. I guess."

"You guess?" Higgs stood up and stepped over to her. "Until we figure out what's going on, you're in my fire team. That means you do what I tell you to do. Got it?"

"Yeah," Dunaway said. "I got it."

Martinez shook out Kennedy's poncho. "How do we do this?"

The ground was open field with a few trees. They could drag Kennedy if they had to. "Lay it down next to him. We'll roll him onto the poncho and drag him. It's easier than building a field expedient stretcher."

Martinez did as directed. As he did so, he looked up at Dunaway. After a few seconds, she shrugged out of her rucksack and set her rifle atop it. Together, they spread the poncho. Martinez barked a little laugh. "Why are the ponchos woodland camouflage and everything else the digital ACU pattern?"

Higgs looked at him. "Lowest bidder." They glanced at each other and continued their work. She repacked the Combat Life Saver bag. Better than a traditional first aid kit, it could handle everything up to minor surgery. "Ready?"

Martinez grabbed Kennedy's body on the right side and rolled him onto the left. Something wet smacked into the ground and Dunaway choked. Higgs reached down with her gloved hands and tucked the loose intestine back into Kennedy's abdominal cavity. Booker turned away. Distinctly pale, Martinez swallowed and looked at Dunaway. "Come on, Dunaway. We can do this."

"Grab his legs, Dunaway," Higgs directed. "On three we'll roll him onto the poncho. Ready? One, two, three."

They moved in unison and settled Kennedy onto the poncho. "Now what?" Martinez asked.

"Get him into the center of the poncho, if we can. Grab his shirt at the shoulders. We'll grab the corners and move him together. It will be awkward, but the poncho slides better than his clothes or boots will."

Martinez blinked. "Where are we moving him to?"

Higgs put her hands on her hips and took a deep breath. She hadn't thought that far ahead. Tactically, they should wait for their friends to return and move as a group. But, what if they didn't come back? The radio sputtered and crackled, but there were no voices. Emergency signals of vehicle horns and star clusters—handheld flares—were nowhere to be seen. Darkness and the temperature fell at the same time. "If we don't hear from anybody in the next fifteen minutes, we'll head toward the road we came in on. We'll find somebody."

Martinez nodded and knelt on one knee. "Might as well rest a bit, Dunaway. Take a knee." The young woman did and Higgs joined them. Booker remained standing.

"Both of you turn around and face out. Let's keep some security, okay?" They shuffled on their knees until they each faced the wilderness with a hundred and twenty degrees of vision. "Keep your eyes peeled."

"What are we looking for?" Dunaway sniffled.

Higgs closed her eyes. *Oh, just shut up.* There were four females in the whole Panther Battalion. One, a senior who spent more on makeup than Higgs spent on her off-campus apartment and another freshman like Dunaway except she barely spoke. Either of them would have been an improvement. Whatever Dunaway's parents held over her, it was strong enough to keep her in a program she wanted nothing to do with. Unlike Higgs.

Since her older brother died in Afghanistan five years before, serving in the military was all Higgs wanted to do. She wanted to rectify the poor treatment that killed her brother. The words "if only" stung. If only they'd recognized the infection. If only they'd evacuated him in time. If only they hadn't mistaken the symptoms for malaria for three days. If only.

The breeze freshened and the cold stung her eyes. She wiped them with the back of her gloved hand as two figures emerged from the far tree line. "Contact."

Martinez shifted on his knee. "Stratton and Koch."

Higgs watched for a moment. Koch's familiar stride was easy to spot. The guy walked like a robot. That his idol was Arnold Schwarzenegger was no surprise. Despite his penchant for bad cigars and three-hour gym sessions, Koch had a serious girlfriend. They were high school sweethearts and the two of them were cute together. Stratton, on the other hand, had no real social life and walked like he'd been born with a rifle in his hands. Weaponry fetishes had to be real, at least that's what it seemed like. Stratton had more weapons in his apartment than anyone she'd ever met, including ridiculous throwing knives he tossed at a ratty dartboard all hours of the day.

Stratton and Koch approached quickly. Higgs stood up. "What's going on?"

Koch stopped but would not look her in the eyes. Stratton brushed past her, walking in the direction they'd come out of the woods.

"Stratton?" Higgs asked. He kept walking quickly and disappeared into the tree line near where Kennedy had died. She turned to Koch and saw tears streaming down his reddened cheeks. "Koch?"

The big sophomore said nothing and wiped his nose on the sleeve of his uniform. There was blood on his sleeves. A lot of it. Fresh tears pooled in his eyes and fell like the others.

"Koch? Talk to me. What happened? Where's Porter and the others?"

When he didn't respond again, she walked over and tapped his shoulder. His eyes turned to her with a combination of rage and guilt. He opened his mouth and a choked sob escaped. He looked up over her shoulder.

"Ruck up! Let's get the hell out of here," Stratton hissed.

Higgs faced him. "And go where? We need to wait for the cadre."

Stratton closed the distance. "They aren't coming, Higgs. Now get your shit together and follow me. We're not in Kansas anymore."

"We need to wait here, Stratton." Higgs turned and looked up at him.

"Didn't you hear me? The cadre aren't coming, Higgs! You stupid bitch—"

She didn't hear anything after that as she swung her right fist and connected with the side of Stratton's sneering mouth. He staggered backward into the snow and dabbed at his mouth, smiling at her viciously.

"You done? Grab the extra rucks and get your ass moving." Stratton pointed down at Kennedy. "What the fuck is this?"

"We were ready to move him," Higgs said.

"Leave him here."

Higgs shook her head. "Not a chance. Never leave a fallen comrade, Stratton. Does that ring a bell?"

The Warrior Ethos was a moral construct the Army instated during the Global War on Terrorism. That they'd had to construct a device to teach their soldier about teamwork and persistence was not lost on Higgs or most of the other cadets. The four points of the Ethos invoked great passion, but the harsh reality was that it had to be taught at all.

I will always place the mission first.

I will never accept defeat.

I will never quit.

I will never leave a fallen comrade.

"Don't lecture me, Higgs." Stratton spat into the grass and snow. There was some pink tinge still from where she'd bloodied his mouth. It felt strangely good to know she'd hurt Stratton at least a little for all the shit he dealt.

"We move Kennedy with us."

"Fine. We'll need his gear anyway."

What? Higgs blinked as Stratton continued giving orders. "Pick up the extra rucks, too. Let's get to the cabin."

"What cabin?" Higgs asked. There was no response. "What's going on, Stratton?"

"Keep your goddamn voice down!" he hissed. "It's time to go! Come on, Martinez. Koch. Let's get moving."

Dunaway interrupted. "I can't carry two rucks."

Stratton whirled on her. "You want to end up like Kennedy? Pick up another ruck and start walking."

Martinez looked at her and then picked up an extra ruck. Pulling the shoulder straps on, the rucksack rested on his chest in a mirror image of the one on his back.

Booker did the same and spoke for the first time that afternoon. "I'll take this side."

Koch moved slowly, but did the same. Higgs caught his eyes and tried to smile, but the big kid looked away. She turned and saw Dunaway trying to figure out whose rucksack weighed less. "Just pick one up, Dunaway," she said and did the same. Getting it set on her chest took a moment, but soon they were all ready and standing around Kennedy's body.

Stratton stood at Kennedy's head. "I've got the shoulders. Martinez and Koch, you take the front corners. Booker, you've got the feet. You two"—he gestured at Higgs and Dunaway—"just try to keep up." The smile on his face made Higgs want to hit him again. And again.

They picked up Kennedy by the poncho litter and started

to move. Higgs grabbed Kennedy's belt with her left hand. *God, he's heavy.*

"Grab the other side, Dunaway," Higgs said.

Within a minute, they were all breathing hard. Martinez kept talking and trying to motivate them.

"Come on!" he panted. "We're closer to the trees."

"Shut up, Martinez," Stratton huffed.

Dunaway let go of Kennedy's belt and the whole group shuddered and stopped. "Sorry! My hands hurt!"

"Pick him up, Dunaway!" Stratton and Higgs said at the same time. The freshman did, and almost immediately starting sniffling. They shuffled and walked slowly, so much so that as Higgs looked up and saw the outline of the cabin in the distance, soft light coming from its windows, she was surprised.

"We're here," Stratton said.

Higgs looked past Martinez's arm at the front of the cabin. A horse-drawn carriage sat in the mud. Mason and a shabbily dressed man shuffled out of the cabin's door carrying a naked body. In the back of the carriage were two others like it. They lifted the body into the bed of the wagon.

Porter.

Higgs dropped Kennedy's belt and stepped around Martinez. Mason was already walking toward them. "Strip Kennedy's clothes and boots, then get your gear and get inside."

Higgs put up her hands and hit Mason in the chest. "What happened to Porter? What in the hell are you doing, Mason?"

His dark face was drawn and tight. "Look, Higgs. We're in trouble."

"Yes, we are! We should be back there waiting for the cadre and trying to make contact with the—"

"The cadre aren't coming, Higgs. Nobody is."

Hands still on his chest, she shook him by his load-carrying vest. *We're not in Kansas anymore,* Stratton had said. "What's going on?"

Mason took a breath and spoke softly. "As near as we can tell, we're back in time."

"What?"

Mason took a breath and shook his head. "Grantville? Alexander Correctional Facility?"

Everyone knew of the Grantville incident, and the Alexander

Correctional Facility had been a more recent unexplained disappearance. The difference in weather after the flash made sense. The lack of snow beyond their rally point in the forest reminded her of the differences found in vegetation in Grantville and Alexander. *It wasn't possible, was it?*

"You mean we're *back* in time?"

"December 21, 1776. We're north of Trenton, New Jersey," Mason said.

Higgs shook her head. "The Revolutionary War?"

"Yeah," Mason grunted. "And we're in British-occupied territory."

"Oh, shit." Her mind spun as she tried to remember the shreds of history she'd had in high school and college. Washington would attack Trenton in a couple of days, and win. That would turn the war in American favor. "What do we do?"

He whispered, "Go inside and get warmed up. This is Mister Daniels and his daughter's place. He's a gunsmith. We found the three Hessians who killed Kennedy beating them. The daughter, Emily, was about to get raped." Mason took a breath. "They shot Porter. Koch beat one of them to death, Emily Daniels killed another one, and the third got away. Well, Emily shot him too, but he escaped into the forest."

"Emily? The daughter?"

"Yeah. Go in and talk to her. Try to figure out anything you can do to help."

"What are you doing?" She tilted her head toward the cart where Koch and Martinez had just loaded Kennedy's naked body.

"Ditching the bodies in a sinkhole a mile or so away. When I get back, we need to talk. Plan. Shit, I don't know what to do. Stratton wants to go after the guy that got away. I think we have to figure out the big picture."

"You think the guy will bring back reinforcements?"

"Maybe. I'm more concerned that he has Kennedy's rifle."

Higgs opened her mouth, but stopped. *The rifle.* Were it to find British hands, it would change the course of history. "We're changing history."

"Yeah," Mason said. "Really managed to fuck this up, huh?"

Higgs looked at him and released his vest. "I'll get everyone taken care of here. You do what you need to do."

"If something happens and I don't come back, you take charge. Don't let Stratton bully you."

Her fist hurt, but she knew she'd do it again if she had to. "I won't."

"Have everyone drop their gear in the parlor, to the right. I'll be back in an hour or so."

Daniels called, "Mason? You ready?"

"Coming." He looked at Higgs a final time. "Help me figure this out."

"You got it." As he walked away, grabbing Martinez and Booker to join them, he told them to drop their weapons. Martinez jogged them over to Higgs.

"Be careful," she said.

"You going to tell us what's going on?" Martinez asked.

Higgs nodded. "As soon as you get back, if Mason doesn't tell you himself."

"Roger that." The big freshman jogged back to the wagon and climbed aboard. Mister Daniels handed him and Booker long muskets before snapping the horses' reins. They plodded off into the darkness.

Higgs turned to Dunaway and Koch. "Let's get the gear inside. The room to the right. We'll warm up and figure out what's going on."

"Not going back inside," Koch said.

Higgs looked at him. "Yes, you are. We are all going inside and figure out what's going on."

Koch stared. "I can't."

"You have to, Koch. I know what happened, okay? Mason told me. You did what you should have done."

Tears appeared in his eyes. "You really believe that, Higgs? That I should have killed that man?"

Higgs nodded. "You just contracted, Koch. You were going into the Army. What do soldiers have to do? Be trained to kill in defense of their country. Their values and the lives of the people close to them. You did exactly what you should have done."

Koch nodded slowly. "Okay."

"It's getting cold and we need to eat something. Where's Stratton?"

Dunaway pointed. "He went inside as soon as we got here."

Higgs frowned. "Fine. Let's get everybody's gear inside and warm up."

☆   ☆   ☆

Ghosts. The ghosts followed them out of the woods. Stumbling in the darkness, the cold seeping through the wound in his back, the Hessian clutched the strange rifle by its handle and blindly sought the Trenton Road. Darkness falling, he rested against a tree for a moment and felt his body growing weaker. If he did not find the road soon, he would die. The colonel needed to see this weapon. Needed to know about the ghosts in their midst. Hiding in the middle of their territory and unseen. Huge things that looked like men but fought like demons. Poor Essen beaten to death after shooting one at close range. They did not scatter like the rebels did. They stayed together. Fought like demons.

The colonel must know.

Go, he told himself. *Keep moving.* Instead of north, he headed south and then southwest past the gunsmith's cabin toward the Delaware River. The night cold and dark, he struggled to see anything. Bare branches in the low, thick brush stabbed at him from a thousand places at once. Tearing through the remains of a summer thicket, he looked up into the sky for a star to navigate by, but there were none visible through the low, thick clouds. Head down, breathing ragged, he pushed into the night toward what had to be the Pennington Road. There would be patrols there. He could warn the colonel before the surgeon pushed the schnapps into his hand to dull the pain.

Go.

Deeper into the full darkness, his wobbling legs threatened to collapse at every other step. He came to the bank of a creek, but could not stop himself and tumbled into the icy water. Fighting to the surface, he clawed to the far bank and crawled until his body was out of the water. Shivering madly, he stumbled to his feet and pressed on for a few minutes before his weakened legs gave out. Barely twenty feet from the road, he fell to his knees. His addled mind dropped toward a confused shock, but he took the heaviness in his limbs as fatigue.

Rest. A few moments and I'll get to the road. He took a deep, heaving breath and closed his eyes.

He tumbled forward to the forest floor, the odd, cold rifle in his grasp. It did not take long for the cold to sap his remaining strength and leave him dead in the underbrush.

CHAPTER FOUR

The sun peeking through the late afternoon clouds gave the illusion of warmth as Captain Victor Sutton stepped outside his quarters into a quiet, subdued Trenton. Hessian soldiers ducked in and out of buildings, their green blazers and tall headgear oddly out of place in a colonial town that seemed dipped in mud and snow. A few children played their way home making Sutton think for a moment of his nephews in England. Christmas was a few days away now. Hope that his brother's family had received his gifts held strong in the career captain's heart. He'd purchased his commission six years ago, following in his older brother's footsteps, before the colonial uprising that brought him to a faraway land. Truth be told, he had not minded the colonies making their case for independence and the like until his brother died at the disastrous Bunker Hill. After Roger's death, Sutton wanted nothing more than to return home until his previous regimental nemesis, Bannister Tarleton, managed to capture General Charles Lee not two weeks before. The subsequent elevation of Tarleton to hero status burned in Sutton's stomach.

Lee had been General George Washington's second-in-command and was more feared than the rebel commanding general by both General James Grant and Lord General William Howe. Lee's capture sent a ripple of hope through the British army. They might not end this insufferable war before Christmas, but they could certainly be home for Easter. The rebels, under sufficient control from His Majesty King George III, could have this cold, untamed land and all the trouble that came with it.

Unfortunately, those troubles were still Sutton's as a part of His Majesty's army at war. Months of boorish behavior by the Hessians against the colonists, regardless of their affiliation, dwindled support for the British army dangerously. As winter set in, with the Hessians in their posts along the Delaware to watch for Washington, Sutton found himself called to speak with Lord Cornwallis personally. The older man looked down his nose at Sutton and told him in no uncertain terms that reporting on the conduct of the Hessian garrison at Trenton was his personal responsibility. There would be no more transgressions against any colonists that went unreported. Cornwallis had said specifically that anything Sutton could do to stifle the ravenous appetites of Von Donop's men would be rewarded. Smelling a promotion, Sutton accepted the task and rode out with his company of dragoons to spend the winter amongst the Hessians and plan a way to make major before the next Christmas came along. Finding Washington's rabble and leading the British army to extinguish the colonial rebellion would certainly do that and make the world forget Bannister Tarleton.

Sutton's reverie had been interrupted by a tremendous clap of thunder, enough to propel him away from the fire and into his uniform for a last check of the stables and the situation. The skies were barely clouded and there was nothing to suggest anything bombastic in the atmosphere.

Washington?

He shook off the thought. More likely, the explosion was the result of Hessian incompetence with either their munitions or the rebels gallivanting around the countryside in complete disregard for Lord General Howe's orders. For a long moment, he strained to hear the distant sounds of early battle, but there was nothing in the chilly breeze to suggest action. Washington and his ragtag army were in no condition for action if the British spies were to be believed. The old man would sit across the Delaware and try to reconstitute what he could and leave the harassment of the Hessian garrison to others.

Around him, the Hessians went about their business as normal, though there was a clearly disguised panic on some faces. The last several nights passed sleeplessly for the Hessian infantrymen after countless alarms and maneuvers. Whatever the cause, the explosion or thunder hadn't raised any concern in the sleepy town of Trenton.

Maybe the explosion destroyed the band? Sutton snorted at the thought and decided it was time to move off the stoop.

He stepped down from the doorway of the flat-fronted home of the widow Christensen and her son, Ian. Their quarters gave him proximity to the stables and his dragoons, but he had chosen them as much as for the pretty, dark-haired woman of the house. Unfortunately, he'd learned early that she wanted nothing to do with him beyond the minimum required by her duties as his hostess. Her discomfort was not unexpected; no colonist appreciated having soldiers billeted in their homes. Yet they did their duty in quartering and feeding him. Among the loyal colonists, Sutton was something of a celebrity being the only British officer in a town filled with Hessians and their card-playing drunkard of a commander.

Colonel Johann Rall seemed like a competent commander to the passing, noncritical eye. Sutton doubted the man would have lasted more than a week as a British regular officer, no matter how wealthy he was. More annoying than Rall's evening ritual of card playing and disgusting German wine was his obsession with parades and his damnable band. From the sound, they were somewhere in the orchards east of town again, marching through the naked trees and blaring their instruments in some German processional that Sutton never wished to hear again. Shaking his head, Sutton strode across the frozen mud of King Street and caught sight of a single Hessian officer at the edge of town, some two hundred yards distant. From the man's fidgeting and nervous staring into the rapidly growing darkness north of town, Sutton knew it was Lieutenant Sturm and that one of his patrols had again failed to return on time.

Through the street, most of the Hessian soldiers avoided his eyes. The colonists smiled openly and bowed or nodded as he walked through. Most of them saw him and his dragoons as a vestige of the monarchy on the continent. They lavished respect openly and while he kept his face still, he relished it. The town itself stood mostly deserted. Fearful colonists, both those favoring His Majesty's rule and those opposed to it, fled to other parts of the countryside when Washington's army approached. Sutton believed that they were forecasting the inevitable future. Washington would eventually be brought to face the full might of the British army and would fail spectacularly.

Sutton walked carefully at the edge of the street, away from the deep troughs of mud tracked by supply wagons and the contrary flow of horses. Passing what he considered to be barely livable homes, Sutton occasionally caught the scent of dinner from the inhabited houses. Candles were lit in lanterns outside the tavern doors as he passed. By appearances, it was quiet there for a change and Sutton chastised himself for not going to the stables and finishing the day's tasks. But, he relished the chance to put junior officers in their place on a regular basis.

He stepped lightly in the mud, drawing behind Sturm without so much as a sound. "Lieutenant? Have you lost something?"

The younger man with the harsh, pockmarked face turned. His eyes wide, Sturm turned and nervously fingered the scar on his left cheek. For some, a scarred face gave their countenance an air of seriousness, dignity, and even respect. In Sturm's face, it accentuated his bluster and incompetence.

"Sir," Sturm blurted in heavily accented English and looked down the Princeton Road in the gathering darkness. "Waiting for my last patrol to check in, that's all."

Gray hair fell out of Sturm's helmet over his ears, belying the man's age. Sutton wondered if he'd been ranked higher and been demoted before wiping the thought away. The man was lucky not to be a private.

"Who is it this time, Lieutenant? Essen? Or maybe Gutros?" Sutton smiled only with his mouth. "Which one of your miscreants is wandering the countryside doing things I'll have to explain to Lord Cornwallis? How many of them are still unaccounted for, sir?"

Sturm swallowed. "Three men, Captain Sutton. With Essen leading."

Sutton allowed his grin to show teeth. "And where did you send him this time?"

"North, sir."

Sutton nodded. "And the noise a few moments ago? What might that have been?"

Sturm looked at the clouds. "Thunder, perhaps?"

"Perhaps," Sutton said. "Are you certain it's not Washington?"

Sturm shook his head. "I sent four patrols north, sir. All of them reported no sightings of the rebels. They scoured the countryside from the river to the Princeton Road. There was nothing of consequence."

"You haven't answered my question about the noise. It upset the townspeople, I'm certain." Sutton smiled. He'd seen nothing of the sort, but an inkling of fear was a powerful ally. "Artillery? A close attack?"

Sturm squinted and shook his head. "One blast, not artillery. Maybe something exploded. No attack based on my reports, sir."

"And yet you're missing a patrol, Lieutenant."

Sturm looked down the Princeton Road for a long moment before turning back to Sutton and nodding. "I am, sir."

"Where was Essen supposed to search?"

"Along the Scotch Road, sir."

"That would be where the thunder came from, no?"

Sturm shrugged. "Seemed to come from everywhere at once, Captain Sutton."

"Quite," Sutton said. The more he thought of it, the more the blast seemed to not have a particular direction of origin. It had seemed to be rather on top of them in the town. "Was it something else? Munitions? A magazine detonating?"

Sturm shook his head. "Colonel Rall did not say. He ordered the garrison to full alert but said nothing regarding the noise or the missing patrol, sir."

"Well, why don't you let me know when you find them?" Sutton leaned in. "I'm sure you'll figure out what they've done in the morning when they don't return. You can send out more patrols to find out where they've drunken themselves into unconsciousness and done Lord knows what else. Then, we'll see just how lost your men and your command are, won't we, Lieutenant?"

That a Hessian patrol, again, was missing was not something to report to Cornwallis, but it was not something to be ignored. Later, after a meal and a glass of brandy, perhaps, he'd summon Sturm and demand an answer. There would be none, of course, and come morning he'd order his dragoons to mount their horses and scour the countryside. Finding Hessians intoxicated beyond comprehension in various states of disrobing had become the norm despite the orders to behave and not further incite the populace. Sutton's own reports went unanswered or acknowledged as the generals in Princeton and New York settled into their winter revelry, leaving him alone in the cold of his solitary duty.

Of course, riding the countryside had certain advantages. Away from the headquarters, Sutton thrived. His men would do anything he asked them to with ruthless efficiency. This gave him free time. Since the widow Christensen was uninterested in any sort of relationship beyond quartering him, Sutton looked elsewhere for a potential confidante and someone to share a warm winter's bed. In Trenton itself, the choices were scant, but the countryside around the small town provided at least one suitable candidate. The gunsmith's daughter, Emily, had potential. Her father's work was adequate, but the scenery made every trip worth the time on horseback in the brutal cold.

The explosion had been in that general direction. For a moment, he considered fetching his horse from the stable and riding out. A swell of breeze stopped the thought in its tracks. With the sun almost down, that warm fire was more attractive than a smile from the gunsmith's daughter. Still, there were appearances to keep.

Of course, the townspeople's smiles were largely to be believed. Lord Howe told Sutton, the first and only time they'd met in person, that Trenton was the kind of town that the rebels loathed and loved at the same time. Its inhabitants true to the Crown when the mood suited them, or as long as money flowed into the town. An army needed goods and services, even the deplorable Hessians. At least Lord Howe, and more likely his brother Admiral Lord Howe, proved able to stop their pillaging across the countryside. There was nothing worse than loyalist towns and villages being picked apart and torn asunder by awful men deigned to be allies.

Sutton frowned as he stepped across the muddy street toward the stables. His men, dutiful to the last, milled inside the stables at the completion of their duties. Tack cleaned and hung to dry, the men brushed and cleaned their horses quietly and without the superfluous commentary that every Hessian seemed to enjoy. The damnable mercenaries never stopped talking. Sutton stepped into the stables and nodded at the young sergeant at arms.

"Carry on, Mister Jenkins."

"Sir!" Jenkins said with a nod and a slight smile. "All mounts are ready for the evening. An extra serving of oats for the holder for Christmas, with your permission."

Sutton smiled. *Oh yes, Christmas. How quaint*, he thought. "After tomorrow's patrols and inspections, we'll see about those oats. Won't we?"

"Indeed, sir." Jenkins nodded and stepped away. "I was about to release the men. The officers have departed for the mess."

Sutton nodded. "If you feel the men have completed their work for the day, to the standards His Majesty would accept, then by all means release them."

Jenkins looked around the stable for a long, hesitating moment. "Perhaps a bit more, sir."

Sutton turned away from the stable and walked back through the doorway and into the muddy streets. The cold seeped through his boots, and with a tug of his waistcoat, he marched down the thoroughfare of Queen Street in the late-evening sun.

"*Hauptmann Sutton!*" a heavily accented voice called from his right, up a side street. "Colonel Rall is expecting you for dinner. Promptly at six. You will not be late again, will you?"

The laughter in the deep voice made Sutton smile. At least one of the Hessians had an appropriate sense of duty and honor. One without the brass bells and drums of Rall's awful band. "Major Hesse, sir, I would not miss a moment of required amusement for the world."

"I almost believe you." Hesse grinned. They shook hands briefly. Hesse was taller, thicker, and a bit rotund. His ginger beard and bright eyes were always full of mirth. Sutton wondered why the man was a professional soldier and not an entertainer of sorts. Given his protruding stomach, he obviously went where the money was good and the challenge nil. "There will be much card playing and maybe a little food."

"As usual, *Herr Oberst*?" Sutton chuckled and almost allowed himself a genuine smile. "I shall not be late. A change of accoutrement, perhaps, and I will be there."

Hesse's eyes twinkled. "From the widow Christensen? A change, indeed."

The large man laughed and Sutton wanted to join him, but there was nothing to laugh about. The woman of his house, her husband long dead in the service of the Crown, barely looked at him when they were together. Selena Christensen and her son wanted nothing to do with him. Perhaps they would before the horrid winter was over. His friends and colleagues enjoyed the parties and warmth of Boston while he and a measly company of dragoons were to spend the winter in the company of wretched men under a charlatan of a commander.

"Alas, I know that my boots will be dried and readied for the morning. As for the rest, I cannot report success."

Hesse nodded. "Much can be said for choosing the right house to laager for the winter, my friend. I'm afraid you've chosen poorly."

Sutton laughed. "We'll see, *Herr Oberst*. By your leave, sir? I will see you at the commander's this evening."

Hesse's smile faded. "Of course, Captain. Good evening."

"*Guten nachte.*"

The sun fully set along the western horizon, the evening chill touched his face with icy fingers. He swore silently against the cold and stomped across the muddy street to his quarters. Halfway there, he looked up to see Selena Christensen looking at him from partially behind the open door of her home. The look in her eyes was one of apprehension and uncertainty. For the briefest of moments, she held his gaze before ducking back into the meager house and closing the door in front of her.

Darkness fell around them as the wagon plodded deeper into the woods. Mason rode alongside Daniels, the gunsmith quietly scanning the road and the tight forest ahead. Booker and Martinez sat a few feet away, each taking a side of the wagon and providing security. Looking over his shoulder, Mason tried not to look at the naked forms of Porter and Kennedy jumbled with the equally naked Hessian soldiers. A pool of blood, black in the fading night, stood out against the worn and bleached floor of the wagon. There was no delineating whose was whose. Daniels' gruff whisper, barely audible above the screeching and knocking of the wagon, jostled his thoughts away.

"Now, Mason. You were going to tell me where you're from before your friends arrived."

Mason looked at the older man. There was a trace of a smile on his lips, but his eyes were anything but friendly. With a nod, Mason tapped his right shoulder, showing the reversed American flag. "We're Americans, like you."

Daniels stared at the patch. "Not the same one Washington's army flies."

"No, it's not," Mason said. "More stars."

"More states."

Mason didn't know if it was a question or a statement until Daniels spoke again.

"There can't be more states," Daniels said. "And you act like a citizen, not even a freedman."

Here we go, Mason thought. "I told you before, sir, I'm not a freedman. I grew up in Pennsylvania. My parents are lawyers in New York, but not your New York."

"I gathered that from your coin."

Mason shrugged. "Look, Mister Daniels, we're not from your time."

"The future." Daniels shook his head. "Can't say I believe you, Mason."

There wasn't a good way to say it, and Mason considered not saying a thing. The idea that he could let it go and find a way to get his squad out of the farmhouse and out of the march of history surfaced again, but he didn't take it. "We were on a field exercise at Fort Dix, just northwest of Trenton. There was a big clap of thunder and we found ourselves just over the hill from your house. The year was 2008 in our time, Mister Daniels. Not 1776."

"That's more than the two hundred years on your coin." Daniels' voice, still a whisper, echoed off the nearby trees. After a moment of silence, he shook his head. "I read that right, didn't I? It said bicentennial. And your flag with more stars? That means we win?"

Mason nodded but said no more. There was nothing wrong with giving the man some hope.

"There's no way we win this war, Mason," Daniels chuckled. "Washington is ready to surrender, we hear. The army is in disarray and the Congress"—he laughed, a harsh staccato burst—"they'd fled south to Virginia. It's a matter of time before the British roll them up like a winter blanket."

Mason bit his lip as the wagon rolled through a darker section of forest. Daniels tensed in his seat. In the tight bend of the road, Mason felt as if he heard every single sound the wagon made. He turned and met Booker's wide eyes. Mason took his first two fingers, made a "V" and pointed them at his own eyes and then into the woods. His intent was clear—eyes out there. Booker spun back to the woods and stared into the darkness. Mason decided to do the same.

"The hole is just at the end of these trees," Daniels whispered.

Great place for an ambush, Mason thought as the wagon agonizingly passed through the dark spot and into the last bit of twilight. The hole was a sinkhole as wide as the length of a basketball court. Over time, it had devoured part of the tree line and the half-eaten trees looked like ragged teeth on one side of the hole. The bottom was dark and appeared only partially frozen. Mason barely suppressed a shiver at the evil sight. Daniels worked the wagon around to the side of the hole that received the most sun, where the liquid water was, and stopped.

"Quickly," he hissed. The three cadets vaulted out of the wagon, set their muskets aside, and dragged the first Hessian out of the wagon by the naked corpse's limp arms and legs. Martinez and Booker swung the body between them and grunted through a count to three before throwing it into the sinkhole. A splash greeted them as they worked to get Kennedy's body into the hole and then the last two Hessians. Mason looked into the wagon, at Porter, and hesitated. Something needed to be said. It didn't seem right to just throw such a person, naked, into a sinkhole.

"Come on, Mason," Martinez said.

Booker grunted as he worked a grip on Porter's ankles. "He'd do the same for you."

Mason nodded and they tossed Porter like they'd done for the others. There was another splash and Mason looked down into the hole, unsure that the bodies wouldn't be found come morning.

Daniels appeared at his side. "The ice has been thinning for a few days. The pond will freeze again tonight. If the weather holds for a few days, it will be solid enough to last the winter. We can come out and check it tomorrow or the day after, but there's nothing to worry about."

Mason wasn't so sure. He looked at Martinez and Booker. "You guys okay?"

Booker shook his head. "No, and you ain't either."

"No, I'm not," Mason conceded. They were all lost in time, with blood on their hands, and surrounded by an enemy bent on destroying their country before it even took its first breaths. Outside of whatever had thrown them two hundred years into the past, fault for their predicament was his. Had he navigated the STX lane correctly, they would be in their own time and taking a bus home. The thought of a warm, comfortable bus ride seemed to drive the rapidly chilling air in between the layers of his ACUs.

Daniels shuffled around them and climbed into the wagon. "Let's get home. There are patrols about."

They climbed aboard, resuming their posts and security, and trundled north and back, finally, to the east. Riding in silence, eyes and ears focused into the night, made the trip much longer than it had seemed. Mason's stomach gurgled. Daniels stopped to light a small lantern that did little more than light the horse's ass in front of them, but it was enough that the gunsmith could navigate. Before long, the familiar cabin came into view. Light peeked through the closed shutters just enough to light their way. Daniels moved the wagon into the barn before they dismounted and walked back to the cabin. They'd not said a word for more than half an hour.

Daniels turned to Mason. "Two hundred years?"

"Yes, sir."

"And we win." It was a statement with a measure of finality. Mason liked hearing it. "In the morning, we'll need to clean the wagon and figure out what to do with you and your friends. You can stay here for tonight."

Mason nodded. "Thank you, sir."

"Don't thank me yet, Mason," the gunsmith said with a frown. "There's quite a bit you and your friends don't know. We have a great deal to talk about."

Captain Jeff Branson stopped dead and blinked against the blowing snow. Ahead, the wide dirt road ended abruptly. Trees crossed the road in a stand no more than thirty meters wide. Through the empty winter branches, he could see the trail on the other side. He walked to the end of the road and looked down. The road ended with a clear edge, as if the whole road had been sliced out and the stand of trees deposited in its place. There was a faint tinge of ozone in the air and a faint smell of smoke. The whole area appeared nearly barren, missing the six inches of fresh snow that had collected in the last hour. He glanced back to the last vestiges of footprints in the snow before they crossed the line into the strange tree line.

Fuck, it's like they disappeared.

"Panther 3, Panther 6. SITREP. Now."

Branson rubbed the back of his neck with one hand and brought the handheld radio to his face with the other. "Boss, there's no trace of them. I followed their footprints and there's a big barren area up here. You need to get up here."

"What's your grid?" the battalion commander, a career light infantryman, growled into the radio.

Branson looked at his handheld Garmin global positioning unit. While the power was on, the unit reported no satellites in view, which he knew was impossible. "I can't give you a grid, sir. My GPS is fried. I'm on the tank trail adjacent to lane four near the assembly area."

"Roger. I'm on my way. Get on the radio and notify range control that we've had an incident and request assistance. As soon as I get the rest of the cadets rounded up, I'll be there."

"Roger, Panther 6." Branson grabbed the handset for the AN/PRC-77 radio. The ancient UHF system, like the cadet's field gear, had been standard issue during the Vietnam War. Supply lines hadn't quite caught up to the training command, though it was promised that state-of-the-art radios were coming. Branson readied to push the transmit button and paused. He looked over the ragged trees and saw that the ones on his side of the line were singed cleanly off. There was nothing on the ground where the limbs should have fallen. The footprints off to the south rapidly disappeared.

Branson looked at the black radio handset and shook his head. "What the fuck do I tell them?"

CHAPTER FIVE

The cabin was warm, and over the pungent odor of wood smoke, Mason could smell stew and his mouth watered. Gone were the thoughts of a quiet bus ride home to Pittsburgh and listening to Jay-Z on his headphones. His duffel bag and headphones were two hundred some years in the future and never to be used again. Stratton jostled past and hunched over his rucksack in a corner of the Danielses' pantry. There wouldn't be enough room for them all to sleep in the room, Mason knew. They'd spread into the kitchen and dining area with the central fireplace keeping them all warm through the night. His first thought was to separate them, leave the upperclassmen the kitchen area. They needed time to think and plan. If there really wasn't a way home...

The possibility stopped him for a second. Seeing Murphy and Martinez helping themselves to steaming bowls of the Danielses' food triggered something else. "Hey! We've got our rations, man. Don't eat their food!"

Martinez looked at him and shrugged. "Emily invited us, Mason."

Murphy smiled. "Venison stew, bro. It's amazing."

"I'm not your fucking bro," Mason said. "These people need their food to survive the winter. A bunch more mouths to feed is going to hurt their stock."

Emily turned a head over her shoulder. "It's fine. We have plenty."

Mason watched the cadets spreading out their sleeping bags

and realized that there was nothing he could do. One of his instructors at Fort Knox, a crusty old drill sergeant named Perez, had compared soldiers to horses heading home to the barn. He'd been right, of course. With a warm roof over the heads, they'd shut off any measure of security in their quest for comfort.

Mason shook his head. "Booker. Koch. Pick a window and keep watch. We'll spell you for food."

Booker bristled. "There ain't nothing out there, man."

"We're in hostile territory, Booker. Behind enemy lines. You get it?" Mason pointed out the door. "We don't know what's out there. Until we do, we keep watch. They killed Porter and Kennedy and they'll kill us if they find us. Set perimeter security. We'll put a schedule together."

"You're overreacting—"

"Hey!" Higgs snapped. "Mason is the squad leader. Get your asses to the windows."

"But—"

Higgs stood up from the table and stepped toward Booker with her finger raised. "Security, Booker."

Booker grabbed a loaded musket and slapped it into his left hand. "C'mon, Koch. Get your ass on a window."

Koch put down his bowl of stew without a word and moved through the kitchen toward the pantry. Mason noticed him look back into the kitchen as he did, but the big kid did what he was told without a complaint. Security set, Mason made sure that Higgs and Stratton ate first before grabbing a bowl. Midway through his dinner, Higgs sent Murphy and Dunaway to replace Booker and Koch on security. They'd have to keep it up all night, Mason realized. He didn't know if he could sleep at all given their situation and the guilt bearing down on his shoulders.

Higgs moved her bowl next to him and sat down. Stratton sat across from them. For a long moment, no one said anything. Mason realized there wasn't a better time.

"We need to set security all night. Higgs, make up a schedule for it. We can't do range fans or dead space—" Mason shoveled a final bite of stew into his mouth. The venison was tough and the stew was bland. "Stratton? You start with priorities of work. Inventory all of our gear. Figure out what we have with us."

Higgs lowered her voice. "What about going home?"

Mason shrugged. "I'm not sure we can."

Stratton nodded. "We can get to Washington's army in a day or so. All we have to do is cross the—"

"No. Not yet." Mason said. "Mister Daniels said there were a lot of things we don't know. We need to figure it out and—"

"Hell, Mason!" Stratton whispered and hit him on the shoulder. "We know what happens on Christmas Day. We can be there!"

"Shut up." Mason pointed at Stratton, who flinched backward. "The less we tell people, the less we affect history. We need to disappear. Fast."

"Where do you think we can go?" Stratton asked. "We're already behind British lines, Mason. It's not like we can waltz out of New Jersey. If you want to run west, then we have to cross the Delaware. That means we should try to join Washington's army. It's the simplest solution."

Higgs shook her head. "The simplest thing to do is recreate what happened today. We have to try to go home again. Same time tomorrow, same place. Maybe it will work."

Mason shrugged and no one said anything for a moment. He hadn't considered the same-time aspect. "It's a good idea."

"It's not going to work," Stratton said. "They've got one of our weapons, Mason. Every minute that they have it, provides an advantage."

"They can't make it work. It only has blanks in it." Martinez shook his head. "But maybe we should try and get home."

"They can take that weapon and reverse engineer it. A rifle like that moves weapons technology ahead a few hundred years in no time at all. If they do that, and we go home, what if everything is different? Go back into a world where the British won the war?" Stratton waved his hands by his head. "That's a great idea! Let's fuck up all of history by doing nothing. What a good idea. We have to get that rifle and—"

Booker burst through the door from the parlor area. Tears glistened in his eyes. "We gotta go home, Mason."

There was a cell phone in the young man's hand. "Put that thing away."

"My mom...she texted while we were..." Booker wiped at his face. "My brother got shot."

Mason drew in a sharp breath. Booker's family was in Chicago and for most of the year the big kid had been driving back and forth on weekends, ten hours each way, to help out. They were hopeful of moving out of the city around Christmas. The kid had been a train wreck from day one of the semester. "What did your mom say?"

"Come home. Wes was shot and is in the hospital." Booker sniffed. "That's all I got. We gotta go home, Mason."

"We're going to try." Mason looked at Stratton's scowling face as he spoke. "We have nothing to lose and one day isn't going to start the Industrial Revolution."

Stratton snorted. "We can try, but it's not going to work. We're stuck here."

"Don't say that, man," Booker whined. "We gotta go home. We gotta go right now."

Mason looked at Higgs and she took the hint. She stood and grabbed Booker's arm. "We're going to try, okay?"

"We can't do anything tonight," Stratton said.

"We got flashlights! We can—" Booker started. His tears flashed into anger. "What's wrong with you? We have to go home! We have to go home!"

Mason stood up and closed the distance to Booker. His voice was a harsh whisper. "Knock it off, Booker. You want to get the whole goddamned British army here and let them kill us before we can try? Shut it down, okay? I said we'll try to get home, but we can't right now and you know that as well as I do."

Booker took a breath and visibly relaxed. "Okay. But we have to try. As many times as it takes."

Mason nodded. "We'll try. Now, do me a favor and get everyone in here and get back to your window. We need to talk as a group and get our shit together."

"Dunaway is already asleep." Booker sniffled, but his eyes were clear and serious again. He was fine for the moment.

Mason sighed. "I don't care. Get everyone in here. We need to talk."

More than Dunaway had been asleep in the sleeping bags on the Danielses' floor and it took Higgs some time to get everyone roused and back to the table. The gunsmith and his daughter had volunteered to stay by the windows and keep watch while the cadets talked. Once everyone was settled at the table, Mason stood at the head of the table and spoke softly. "Look, I can't explain what happened. None of us can. We have a pretty good idea of where and when we are. That's the good news. We have a lot to learn about what's going on outside this cabin, but that doesn't change where we're at. We're here and we need to figure out what to do."

All of their eyes were on him expectantly and with the exception of Stratton's mocking half smile, they were ready to listen. He took a deep breath and continued.

"Here's the situation." For a moment he faltered, but then all of the training they'd done on operations orders and planning came back to mind. He chuckled. "We'll do this the Army way. Enemy forces. From what the Danielses have told us, we're behind British lines four days before the Battle of Trenton, 1776. Our location is about four miles to the north-northwest of Trenton. This territory is occupied by Hessians and some British regulars. They're pretty much surrounding us as we speak and—" Murphy raised his hand. "What?"

Murphy cleared his throat. His face was serious, not the usual happy-go-lucky one he wore. "I did a report on this just a few weeks ago."

Mason blinked. "New Jersey?"

"The run-up to the Battle of Trenton and the battle itself. For my military history class."

Mason realized that he'd had the same class, an ROTC requirement, the year before. He'd focused on the Continental Congress and their relative inaction during the winter of 1776 instead of an actual battle, earning him a C. "And?"

"There's a lot more going on here—this side of the river—than we were taught in school," Murphy said. "A lot more."

Mason made a come-on gesture. "So, what do we need to know?"

"Washington had a lot of help getting ready for Trenton. Seriously, this was the fascinating stuff I learned. There's so much about this time period that we didn't hear about in school I had to dig deep for Dr. Cole's class, man."

"Murphy? Come on," Higgs said. "We need to hear this, fascinating or not."

Murphy replied, "Sorry, guys. This is just weird, you know? Anyway, tonight is December 21. Across the river to the south of Trenton, there is a General Ewing who is sending boats across the Delaware to burn houses along the shore in Trenton. Think of it like an insurgent attack against the Hessians. They're really riling up the garrison—pretty much to the point of stress and failure. Washington will keep this up for days and the Hessian commander, Colonel Rall, pretty much runs his regiment ragged."

"What about the British? Where are they?"

"The closest real threat is Princeton—about eight miles away to the northeast. There are a few thousand British regulars there. Most are spread out along the New Jersey frontier now. They've just recently determined that the war is basically paused for the winter. The main army garrison is in New York and while they still believe they can find and destroy Washington before 1777 starts, the leadership has pretty much decided that Washington is on the run and ending the rebellion can wait until spring." Murphy looked at the group, cleared his throat, and continued. "There are some British forces in Trenton. Less than fifty dragoons, I think. There are about two thousand Hessians, give or take, in Trenton. The real concern we have right now is that there are a lot of friendlies operating around us. The Hunterdon raids stopped yesterday, but they are still around us. Ewing's men won't come inland, and that's fine, but there are skirmish parties roaming around. If we're found by them, they'll shoot first and ask questions later."

"Hunterdon raids?" Stratton asked. "What are those?"

"Long and fascinating story," Murphy said. "Again, think insurgency. There are a lot of friendlies out there harassing the Hessians and the British all over New Jersey. They're pretty upset with how the British and the Hessians have treated them in the last couple of months. It's crazy out there."

Mason nodded and looked at Booker. "That's why we're not going out with flashlights. Plus, we really didn't get a good look at the terrain. Getting lost in the cold is not something I want to do."

"Plus, we have a bigger problem," Stratton said. "We lost a weapon. That should scare the shit of out all of us."

Dunaway yawned. "Why? It's a rifle."

Higgs leaned in, her eyes blazing at the younger woman. "Modern technology. The whole concept of interchangeable parts. The Industrial Revolution. All of it. If the British get the rifle, they'll be able to move all of that along faster. Maybe even expand their empire."

"If we're stuck here, we'll be dead by then. Big deal." Dunaway rolled her eyes.

"It is a big deal." Higgs glared. "We could change the course of history!"

Koch leaned forward and his arms jostled the rough-hewn table. "Look, time doesn't work like that."

Stratton laughed. "You're a farm boy. What do you know about time?"

"My uncle's farm ain't far from where the Alexander Correctional Facility was. It disappeared, right? The area filled up with all kinds of stuff from sixty-five million years before. If what happened to us is what happened to the prison, what we do won't change anything."

"That's bullshit," Stratton said. "How can you—"

Koch raised a hand. "Our timeline wasn't affected. There's been no evidence of humans going back that far."

"Maybe they all died or got dropped into a volcano!"

"Or maybe," Koch said, "they didn't and created their own version of history. A parallel universe. That's one possible explanation. Not saying that it's something else, but we're back in time and shit's kinda fucked up, okay?"

Mason shook his suddenly throbbing head. "Look, whether we're in our timeline or a completely new one doesn't matter. We have to have a plan. Tomorrow, we're going back to where we came in—same time and all. We'll see what happens. If we get back, great. Awesome story. If we don't, then we've got to figure out our options. I see we have two."

Murphy looked up at Stratton and then to Mason. "And they are?"

"We move west, find a place to hide. That's option one." Mason took a breath. "Option two is we find General Washington, and tell him our story. Either course of action has us crossing the Delaware. Or we try to find a place to hide out here until spring. I don't think that's smart for us or for the Danielses."

Murphy sighed. "We are a liability to them. Unless we all suddenly learn to act like them, dress like them, and talk like them, we're going to be easily found out. We can't stay here. It's too dangerous."

"All of our choices are dangerous, Murphy," Koch said. His voice was little more than a whisper.

Stratton brightened. "What we know is as dangerous as our weapons and our gear, guys."

Mason nodded. It was true. Knowledge was power and all that. "But, there's a lot we don't know. Look around you. None of us have ever lived like this. We have to learn quick and be careful doing it. Getting caught, or killed, isn't an option."

Higgs looked at her hands. "We've had enough of that for a while."

Her tone troubled Mason for a split second. "Understand, everybody. We're at war and because we're different"—he paused and looked at Booker—"we're in danger from both sides. Everybody here is going to think that Booker and I are freed men or escaped slaves. That's trouble for us and any allies we gain are going to assume that Higgs and Dunaway can't do anything soldierly. One look at us and they know we're something very different and a threat."

Higgs looked up at them. "We have to take care of each other."

Booker snorted. "Nah. We gotta go home."

Mason nodded. "We're going to try, yes. But if we don't make it, Higgs is right. Our first priority is to take care of each other."

"And the second?" Stratton asked. "Join Washington's army?"

"Not immediately," Mason said.

"Why not? We'd be generals in a week!" Stratton slapped Murphy's shoulder and grinned.

Higgs rolled her eyes. "He'd see through your bullshit way before then, Stratton."

"Whatever. You'd make a great camp follower, Higgs."

"Shut up," Higgs said. She looked up at Mason with a "can you believe this asshole" look on her face.

Koch said softly, "We gotta find that weapon. Emily... she shot that last Hessian. The one that ran into the woods. Maybe we can track the blood. When it gets light."

Mason nodded. Finally, a good idea. "Would give us something to do in the morning before we head out to where we came in."

Even Stratton nodded his head. Mason decided to press his minuscule advantage. "We're going to keep watch all night—I'll take the first and last one as the squad leader. Higgs has the schedule. Try to get some sleep, no electronics. Just get some rest and we can figure this out in the morning."

He watched the underclassmen get up and move into the parlor. Stratton, Higgs, and Booker hadn't moved, which neither surprised nor scared him. The four of them were going to either find a way out of this mess or not.

There was a little more stew, so Mason and Stratton had another bowl while Higgs and Booker made sure the younger cadets were asleep or pulling security. They were quiet, leaving Mason to wonder what his counterpart was thinking the entire time. Joining Washington's army sounded great in theory. Their knowledge could change the war and speed up independence. But there was great risk involved. Death and disease were constant threats. Of course, he rationalized they could be killed by wild animals or Native Americans as they traveled west, too. The more he thought about it, the more his head hurt. Everything was different here and if they could not get home, they had to adapt quickly. More importantly, if they failed to get home the next afternoon, they needed to move away from the Danielses.

Maybe going to Washington isn't such a bad idea?

"You okay?" Stratton asked.

"What?"

"I asked if you were okay. You stopped eating and stared off into space."

Mason snorted and ate the bite of stew on his hanging spoon. "Yeah, I'm good. Just thinking things through."

Stratton chuckled. "And how's that going for you?"

Mason sighed. He wanted to say it was overwhelming or something to that effect, but Stratton would see that as a sign of weakness. Any opportunity to control the situation and the squad was an opening that Stratton could capitalize upon. If he'd been in charge, they would be marching through the night to Washington's army. Something dangerous and stupid was not what Mason was willing to do. Joining Washington's army was the last possibility Mason intended to pursue. There were always other options.

Except for the rifle, I believe that.

"We have to get the rifle. Or at least try," Mason said. "Any luck and we'll find it in the woods tomorrow before we head back to where we came in."

"And if we don't, we have to assume the Hessians have it. And that they'll pass it to the British." Stratton dropped his spoon into the bowl. "That could spell doom for America in this timeline."

Mason nodded. "Lots of possibilities."

"None of them good." Stratton shrugged. "Our knowledge, though, could change that."

Of course it could, Mason thought. There was a lot their knowledge could do. Changing the world wasn't something Mason was prepared to do.

Booker joined them at the table. His eyes were a million miles away. Brown eyes puffy from silent tears, Mason knew his friend was hurting but didn't have a clue what to say. They shared the same skin color but had very different upbringings.

"You okay?" Mason asked.

Booker nodded but said nothing. His fingers traced the wood grains on the table in front of him. If they could not go home, Mason wondered if Booker would ever function. He and his younger brother were inseparable. Not knowing if his brother survived the shooting, or the circumstances around it, had to be miserable. Mason was an only child, so knowing that bond of kinship was as alien as their current surroundings.

They sat quietly until Higgs joined them. She sat down and brushed her dirty-blonde hair away from her face. "Martinez and Murphy have the first watch. I know you said you'd take it, Mason, but we need to talk."

She thinks of everything. Mason nodded, suddenly down on himself. *Maybe Higgs should be the squad leader now.*

"Thanks." He looked at the group. "Where are the Danielses?"

"Emily is upstairs. Mister Daniels went outside a few minutes ago," Booker said. "He's over by the barn."

Mason nodded and lowered his voice. "We have to have a plan. In the morning, we need to gather all of our gear and get out of here."

"You said we were—" Booker started.

"We are going to look for the rifle and try to go home. If it doesn't work, we don't need to come back here. Every moment we're here puts them at risk," Mason said. "If someone came, we can't defend ourselves or them. We need to move into the woods or someplace that's been abandoned."

"We could move into the barn," Stratton said.

"No," Mason said. "We need to be a little distance from here and close to the spot we arrived at. I'll ask Daniels what he thinks, but we can't stay here."

Higgs nodded. "It's too dangerous, I agree."

"We'll need some kind of shelter. The winter is about to get brutal," Stratton said. "I remember that much from my history classes. The winter of 1776 to '77 was awful."

"Staying outside is something we can't do for long. Better gear or not," Higgs said. Mason agreed. Two hundred years of materiel development would help them over their now-modern compatriots, but it was not something he wanted to do any more than necessary.

"Don't matter," Booker said. "We're going home tomorrow."

"We don't know that," Mason said.

"And we don't know we ain't gonna end up right back in 2008, Mason," Booker said. "I say we forget the rifle and go straight back there soon as it's light. We wait all damned day if we have to. Get home. That's what we gotta do."

The confrontational tone, even in a hushed voice, couldn't be missed. Mason gestured at Booker to get his attention. "We're going to try, Booker. We're going to see about finding the rifle. I don't want to go home to a different world, if that's how this shit works, all right?"

"We have to try, Booker," Higgs said. "And no matter what happens, we're going to take care of each other."

Mason sighed. "Okay, in the morning we have a couple of things to do. Stratton—you're in charge of inventorying our gear. Take Kennedy's and Porter's gear and split it between everyone. Higgs—once we find a place to hole up, you're in charge of priorities of work. Cover and concealment—all of that kind of stuff. Booker—after tonight, our security is your responsibility. Make sure we maintain security all the time. You know how Sergeant Sheets talks about situational awareness? That's your thing now. Keep us focused, all right?"

All three nodded at him. Stratton even looked somewhat impressed.

"What else?" Higgs said.

Mason nodded. "Murphy said he did a paper on Trenton this semester. I think he needs to draw up a sand table or something and brief us what he knows. Knowledge is power, but we have to know what we're dealing with out here. We gotta understand the situation more than we think we know from high school. I know I didn't pay that close of attention."

He got the chuckle he was looking for and it filled him with a little hope instead of dread. Higgs looked at him. "If we can't find that rifle, and we can't get home, what then?"

"I think Stratton may be right about getting to Washington, but I don't want to rush it—especially trying to cross the river. He's coming to us on the day after Christmas. That's a good starting point unless the situation changes. For now, though, let's get some sleep. Long day tomorrow and we have to be sharp. Sharper than we've ever been in training. Our lives are going to depend on it."

No one moved for a long moment. Higgs finally leaned close over the table. "We need to get the full lay down on what's out there. From Daniels and everything that Murphy can remember, Mason."

Mason nodded. "Tell Murphy I want to see him at the end of his watch."

Higgs frowned. "You need to sleep, Mason. You're the squad leader and we need you sharp tomorrow, too."

"I'll be fine. I'll need to talk to Mister Daniels before I rack out anyway."

CHAPTER SIX

The soft light of his headquarters washed the adjacent trees with a faint yellow glow. In the darkness, remnants of recent snows hung close to the north sides of the houses as a reminder that winter was only just getting started. His shadow moved across the neighboring house until he passed by and stood looking across the wide, cold Delaware River toward New Jersey. In the darkness, he could see the pinpoints of small fires of the Hessian pickets warming themselves along the roads north of Trenton. The retreat, if he could call it that, of the British regulars to New York should have eased his anxiety, but it did not. General Howe left New Jersey in the hands of a few scattered British units and the wholly unpredictable Hessians.

Reports surged across the river daily of Hessian barbarism. Weary citizens had been seen on the roads fleeing New Jersey and the Hessian scourge that pillaged their homes and endangered their families. The reports turned Washington's stomach. Even those citizens who pledged their support to the Crown were not spared. Hessian aggression knew no bounds. As winter came, the violent mercenaries had calmed some. Whether the break in activity had been ordered by General Howe or was simply the common sense of winter preparation, Washington did not know. The Hessians were no longer plundering the countryside. Their commander in Trenton, Rall, even paraded his men once a day with accompaniment of a band. He seemed too caught up in ceremony to have actually decided to end their terrorism of New Jersey. Not that it mattered. New Jersey slowly began to fight back, and Washington yearned to hear more from his commanders bent on making Rall's life miserable.

Footsteps approached from behind. A long, shuffling gait Washington knew from years of experience to be done with purpose by his personal assistant. Washington half turned his head. "Mister Lee? A fresh report from our friends across the river, per chance?"

"Begging the general's pardon." The gruff, deep voice closed the distance and stood at Washington's shoulder looking into the darkness. The older, former slave had been his constant companion for more than twenty years. Of his friends and fellow patriots, only two he held in as much esteem as Mister Lee. Without Franklin's wit or Jefferson's intellect to stimulate the conversation, honesty was the best salve he could want. Lee would tell him what his commanders might be afraid of saying, though Washington wondered if the situation could get worse. Enlistments would expire in ten days' time and his army would wither and die without a miracle.

"Would the general care for his coat? New Jersey's a touch colder than Mount Vernon."

Washington snorted even as a fresh, lonely pain stabbed at his heart. Martha would be sitting down after dinner, knitting or writing letters until her hands ached. He blinked the clear vision away. "I'm fine, Mister Lee. Just a breath of fresh air to clear my head. Do you have our numbers for the day?" Desertions were rising.

"Sixty-two today, sir."

Washington nodded, but said nothing. Sixty-two was better than the hundred per day they'd been losing for the better part of a month. "Is there any more news from across the river?"

Lee shuffled his feet at Washington's shoulder. "The Hessians have scheduled a Christmas feast in Trenton. Rall has made his band practice twice a day. Their colonel in the south has a love interest and is spending a lot of time at parties and not with his troops."

Washington smiled. "A merry widow with good friends and better intentions. I'm well aware of her situation, and I learned about the band earlier."

Lee lowered his voice. "You're worried about not knowing all that you think you should again, aren't you, sir?"

Washington took a deep breath. The gathering of intelligence steadily improved, but there were too many things he did not know. Things to which he would think and plan, but never with the surety of knowledge. "I'd like to know more. I hear about the big pieces, Lee—the bands and merry widows. I want to know the little things. Seeing how Rall handles them provides an insight to whether or not..." His voice trailed off.

"You think we should attack them?" Lee asked gently. He knew Washington's labors were not on something trivial like a Christmas feast. "Rall is convinced that's what will happen."

"Yes, I know," Washington replied with a wave of his hand. "He's requested help from Howe several times now and never been taken seriously. He's either scared to death and wants reinforcements or he seems to care nothing about his command or the town he is in charge of."

Lee nodded solemnly. "There was a report of a Hessian patrol not returning to Trenton by evening assembly."

Washington's eyebrows rose slightly. Hessians were prompt, if anything. "What came from it? Any increase in patrols? Greater security?"

Lee shook his head. "Our people reported no changes. Rall seemed to dismiss it. No one on that side of the river seems to know where they've gone."

"And the British forces? Did they investigate?" Washington could picture the British dragoons left in Rall's care thundering through the countryside pursuing leads and harassing citizens much like the Hessians.

"Nothing as of yet. We'll see what they do at first light."

Washington nodded and clapped a hand on Lee's shoulder. "Those are the kinds of things I need to know, Mister Lee. Now, we'll see how Colonel Rall takes care of his command. Surely we can have some insight into whether his plundering bastard soldiers either take wholly to a garrison lifestyle or can be agitated into uncertainty after sitting for so long."

"You're planning to do more than that, sir. Don't sell yourself short."

Washington chuckled softly. "Has there been any word from General Ewing?"

"His men will launch within the hour, sir. There are scouts posted along the river to report as soon as the attack takes place."

Washington nodded to the darkness. "Rall's forces have been alerted almost every day?"

"From what we've seen and heard, yes, sir."

The key to agitating an enemy was constant concern. While fear would have been preferred, the inability to see and control every aspect of the fight worked to Washington's advantage. Rall wasn't afraid to alert his forces and step up patrols in the local countryside. Most certainly, he was communicating back to General Grant in Princeton for additional support after the Hunterdon raids. Von Donop wouldn't listen and, Washington smiled, would have more pressing concerns in the very near future. A small uprising to the south presented a unique opening that could be stretched wider by tiring out the Hessian forces and splintering command relationships. All it took was a little fear.

"We've had enough of that for the last six months," Washington whispered to the wind. "It's time to let them fear us for a change."

"Sir?" Lee leaned toward him.

Washington turned to his longtime companion and let a small smile crawl across his features. "Just thinking aloud, Mister Lee."

They stood silently for a few moments. Washington heard the muted sounds of an army at night. There was no singing and cajoling in the camp. The few fires lit surrounded by men and boys trying to stay warm were mostly silent affairs. Surely there was talk, and there were likely plans to desert or questions about their contracts ending in ten days' time, but no one was loud. The main body of the army was several miles to the north near McKonkey's Ferry and well out of sight from prying eyes. A mostly hidden army was one of the few keys to raising British fear. The other was doing the unthinkable at the right time and place. A breeze freshened through the darkness. The cold increased, seeping under his uniform tunic and getting to his skin. Washington turned toward the warm light of his headquarters and felt the immense weight of paperwork and leadership setting around his shoulders again.

"It's time to lead the army again, Mister Lee."

"Can I get you anything, sir?"

"Please summon General Greene, with my compliments. I'd like to discuss our options." The young general was more than a competent commander. As Washington's army shrunk around them, Greene was a friend and developing confidant as well as a skilled tactician. They could do good work as they waited for reports from the river's edge.

Lee disappeared into the darkness, leaving Washington to his own thoughts for a moment. He looked up into the ragged clouds and saw a few stars poking through with dim, flickering light. He thought of Martha on the lawn at Mount Vernon and forced himself to shake away the thought and get back to work. Momentum, he knew, could be capitalized upon as it swung his way. With Rall and his forces in a state of panic and Von Donop moving south, a window was open. Greene would help him determine if the window was adequate to risk the army's dwindling strength.

Washington walked with his shoulders back and his chest out, both calm and decisive at once. Knowledge, no matter how slight or seemingly unimpressive, painted pictures. With the right collection of pictures, deciding to attack Trenton would be easier than he originally hoped. Their unease struck the right chords, but Washington could not cross the Delaware on Hessian anxiety alone. He needed an advantage. Be it weather, actionable intelligence, or plain luck, he needed something more.

Sutton sat before the small hearth in Selena Christensen's home with his uniform tunic undone and his feet propped onto the hearth beside his slowly drying boots. The small glass of brandy in his hand served to warm his stomach nicely, and his extremities would come around given time. He glanced at his watch, a gift from his fallen brother, and frowned. The officer's call would start in another fifteen minutes and while the fire, more brandy, and sleep would be better activities than socializing with the Hessian officers, Sutton took it upon himself to gain intelligence on them for General Howe. The Hessians did not live up to the general's trust, of that he was certain. The only way to prove it was to get to know them and learn their weaknesses before they cost General Howe more than the measly village of Trenton.

"Captain Sutton," Selena's voice came from behind him. "You asked to be reminded when—"

He sat forward and turned around the chair's curved highback to smile at her. "Thank you."

She twisted a towel in her hands. "There's some dinner, if you'd care for some."

He raised a hand and gently shook it. "Not tonight, thank you. I'll be dining at Colonel Rall's this evening."

"Shall I wait up for you?" Her lips were a thin white line. There was no interest in him. She simply wanted him to go.

"No, madam. I shall not be late this evening."

Selena ducked away as quietly as she'd first appeared and Sutton returned his attention to the fire. Reaching for his boots, he ran a hand over the worn, fire-warmed leather. While not completely dry, they would suffice for his walk across the town and a couple of hours of cards and the horrible liquor they called schnapps. He tugged them on and buttoned his tunic as he stood and stretched before the fire. The last swallow of brandy warmed his throat and stomach on the way down and he smiled. Perhaps the holiday in Trenton wouldn't be as bad as he'd feared. There was endless entertainment around should he look for it. He found his coat and pulled in on, eschewing his sword and ornamental helmet, gathering instead a traditional tricorne hat for the short walk.

As he stepped down into the mud of King Street, four young Hessians trotted past and turned the corner to the north. Colonel Rall's constant adjustment of his forces to every rumor from the countryside played hell on the men's nerves and drove what few citizens remained in the town behind closed doors when the sun set. As such, men shuffled through the night from post to post and the streets were nearly deserted. Even the tavern, which by colonial standards was more than decent, seemed subdued and anxious. The latest rumor maintained that Washington and his men were looking for the right moment to surprise Rall's forces from every direction at once. Sutton, of course, had laughed in the face of it just as the Hessian officers did. His men and their mounted patrols clearly proved that Washington was on the far side of the Delaware and that there was no viable pocket of resistance large enough to assist him on the New Jersey side. Rall didn't believe an attack imminent, but a scattering of musket fire in the distance would cause him to rouse and alert the entire garrison for hours on end. Still, the Hessian commander's anxiety was at least a passable measure of leadership.

Behind the daily parades, the god-awful band, and his evening card games, Rall seemed frightened. Letters and requests for support flew from his headquarters to New York several times a day. Despite two other regiments within a dozen miles of his headquarters, Rall felt alone. He wasn't incompetent or lazy.

His men were reasonably well trained, but they were starting to show strain. The kind of strain that starts from leadership and trickles down in grumbles and curses. He'd seen it before, but on the colonial side. Washington's men always looked tired and disgruntled. That they'd fought as well as they had and still survived was nothing short of amazing.

Rall's headquarters gleamed in the night. A half dozen men were visible around the front of the house with two messenger's horses. Either Rall was about to send another message or he'd received something. Sutton quickened his pace and stepped into the light of the porch lanterns as one messenger came out of the house hurriedly, mounted his horse, and galloped into the night toward Bordentown to the south.

Colonel Von Donop had either answered a silly request or told Rall to be calm. *Again*, Sutton thought with a barely concealed smile. Either the good commander had buttoned up his pants long enough to actually lead his regiment or, more likely, Rall demanded news, intelligence, and support from his allied forces. The man wanted to know everything, but kept it at arm's length. It was easier to play cards and parade his troops than focus on an enemy that was everywhere and nowhere at the same time.

No one else is going to fight your war, old man. Should the rebels be bold enough to strike, it will be your responsibility to stop them. Sutton cleared the mud from his soles with the boot strop mounted on the stairs. Satisfied, he nodded to the door guards and stepped inside the headquarters. The house was warm and crowded. Junior Hessian officers stood in the foyer eating bowls of sauerkraut and huddling over mugs of tea or more powerful drink. All of them ignored his entrance and their conversations didn't waver. There were only a handful of British officers in Trenton and most of them were transient and had the good sense to stay away from Rall's headquarters in the evening hours, but gaining intelligence on their allies was too promising of a venture. While not as grand and fortuitous an assignment as Tarleton's capture of Charles Lee, his mission was valuable and worthy.

Sutton solely wanted to find Washington's army. With their known position and strength he could convince the British leadership to pull the garrisons out of the winter hiatus and attack. He would give them the keys to crushing this rebellion. Stepping deeper into Rall's headquarters, between smelly men and hushed conversations in their own language, Sutton knew he could take something from Rall and gain his British commanders' favor. It was a matter of time before he would gain the intelligence needed to find and defeat Washington and his army. Or, if Washington came to call with his ragtag band of farmers and blacksmiths, Sutton believed he could put them down once and for all.

Trouble was that Rall spoke exclusively German with a rough, soldier's language tempered further by his Hessian dialect. Von Donop, at least, could converse fluently in French, but the senior commander's distance from Rall made it impossible for Sutton to chat with the man regularly. He rather liked Von Donop—they were cut from the same cloth. Harsh, direct, and willing to do anything to advance their station. Von Donop's weakness for the fairer sex was well known, but Sutton preferred his conquests to be private, thorough affair. For a moment, he thought of returning to his quarters but he caught the eye of Lieutenant Sturm. The young officer sat at the right hand of Rall, whose flushed face told of more drinking at an earlier hour than Sutton thought possible.

Sturm gestured to him, and Sutton pushed through the crowd of officers around Rall's table. He sat opposite of Sturm in a position Rall normally kept open for one of his brigade commanders. The older man squinted at him but said nothing.

Sturm leaned across the table. "The colonel has asked for you. The loss of our patrol troubles him and he requests your dragoons patrol the roads north of town tomorrow and search for them."

It was a struggle to maintain a straight face. Sturm's translation was rough and accented. Rall was more than troubled, but at the same time he seemed strongly resolute. Engineers wanted to secure and defend the city until Rall shushed them down. From what Sutton knew, Rall had gone back to General Grant saying the town was indefensible and that Washington's rebels were on the verge of attacking on a moment's notice. Rall was troubled by the loss of a patrol. *What did Von Donop say?*

"Tell the colonel my dragoons will patrol at first light." Sutton blinked and smiled. "The rider? Was that dealing with this troubling loss?"

Sturm looked at Rall, who roughly grabbed the arm of a passing lieutenant and ordered a drink. The opening was enough for him to say, "Von Donop rides south to Mount Holly to confront rebels in the morning. He knows nothing of the lost patrol."

Sutton nodded. A glass of wine found its way in front of him and Rall. The colonel held up his glass expectantly as if to toast.

Rall roared at the collected officers in broken and barely coherent English. "To victory!"

Dutifully, Sutton felt, the officers cheered for a moment before drinking from their glasses. The wine was sweet, but good and it almost warmed Sutton's chest. The collected officers returned to their hushed conversations around the fireplace and left the main table in near silence. Rall began to speak, and Sturm nodded his head and glanced several times at Sutton.

"The colonel asks if you will attend the Christmas dinner, and if you will have a guest?"

Sutton felt his eyebrows raise involuntarily. The dinner was a form of mandatory amusement where he assumed his participation was required. The opportunity to bring a guest was a unique opportunity. Immediately his mind went to task and quickly dispatched any thought of Selena Christensen holding his arm and looking miserable. The gunsmith's daughter, she of the pretty face and quick smile, could be a possibility. Emily Daniels was young and poised enough to hold his arm and turn every head when they walked in the door. Her father had a dozen of their muskets for repairs. A visit would provide a chance to check on their function and ask her to be his guest.

"I most certainly am attending, Colonel." Sutton nodded and smiled at Rall, who blinked and then returned the gesture. "As for if I will have a lady on my arm? I shall do my best. I'm afraid the choices here in Trenton are fairly meager."

Sturm finished the translation with obvious embellishment and Rall roared with laughter. Sutton leaned across the table to ask what specifically the young lieutenant had said and saw runners approaching through the tavern's windows. Muted outside voices became urgent shouts as they closed the distance.

"*Feuer! Feuer!* We are under attack!" The calls echoed through the town in rough German.

Rall's red face paled as he pushed back from the table. Sturm looked at Sutton. "Washington?"

Sutton almost laughed. "Doubtful, sir. The rebels do not attack at night."

Rall stood and bellowed. "*Raus!*"

The collected officers scattered like rats into the night. As

Sutton stepped into the muddy street, he saw the orange glow from fires over the rooftops. Several structures along the riverfront burned. Making his way toward the light, aware of the Hessian band striking up the familiar call to muster, he paced slowly, in constant control of his bearing, toward the river. In the distance, he could see boats paddling away and drifting south with the current. Jubilant rebels with blackened faces laughed and called out to the Hessians in unintelligible voices. Beyond them, there was nothing. Sutton strained to hear anything else in the chaos around him, but there was no indication of an attack. Hessian cannons were drug into position, but Sutton could already see that they would be unsuccessful in targeting, much less engaging, the receding boats. The rebels had successfully riled up the Hessians for a third time in five nights.

A young boy ran past and Sutton caught him by the jacket. "You're Jackson's son. Yes?"

The boy nodded and swallowed.

"Go to the livery. Tell my dragoons to stand down. There is no attack. Go now, or I come for your father. Is that clear?"

"Yes, sir." The boy sprinted toward the British garrison. Content with the boy following his orders out of fear for his father's life, Sutton walked slowly toward the riverbank. Two cabins and a fairly large barn burned intensely. *Another raid*, he thought. *Rall's fears burn higher every day.*

Hessian commanders barked at their soldiers. A few fired muskets at the rapidly receding boats. Their errant shots met with yells and curses from the rebels. Men formed a line of buckets in an attempt to quench the rising flames. Sutton watched them slowly form their lines and relay water from the river as the fires roared.

Sturm appeared at his side. "Watches have been doubled. The colonel insists your men patrol at first light."

"I promised they would," Sutton said slowly. Sturm's eyes darted away from his own and betrayed the man's fear. The effect on Sutton was far better than words could describe. "I believe your men were mistaken about Washington's intent."

Sturm nodded and looked out across the river. "If he comes, we are vulnerable and undefended. Doubling the guard doesn't help."

Sutton chuckled. "You believe Washington will come?" The

roof of one cabin collapsed into its own burning walls. "His broken, ragtag army?"

Sturm said nothing for a long moment. "When the river freezes—"

"When it freezes, we will cross it and find them."

"Colonel Rall would never allow that. He would—"

Sutton grabbed Sturm's arm and turned the young officer toward him. "Quite right, Lieutenant. But I will. Once I find him, General Grant will relieve your incompetent commanders and attack with the full force of this army. By summer, we'll be home and the rebellion will be a distant memory."

Sturm freed himself from Sutton's grip and staggered backward. "I do not share your enthusiasm, sir."

Of course you don't, Sutton wanted to say aloud but did not. He turned loose the young man's arm and walked toward his quarters. Watching the fires made him cold and the small fireplace of his quarters, and the promise of brandy and rest, called him away from the scene.

CHAPTER SEVEN

By the light of a single candle, Mason sat at the Danielses' table staring at his hands. His fingertips traced the raised lines in the old, worn wooden surface as if searching for something. The longer he looked, the less he felt there was an answer. If he hadn't been lost none of it would have happened, or so he told himself. Sitting alone in his guilt, he wondered about the cadre and his parents. Would they be upset? Would they secretly be relieved that he wouldn't get his commission and serve in the army? He snorted at the sudden thought of missed homework for his psychology class. None of that seemed to matter anymore. The only thing that mattered was survival, especially if they could not make it home. Nothing of his life up to that afternoon would matter a thing. He'd stepped back in history as a black man in charge of a squad of cadets who had no real concept of war. Everything he did from now on had a consequence. Every single thing he did now would affect something in the future. More troubling was that everything he did from now on could get himself or one of his friends killed. Doing nothing and letting history roll by would be easiest. He didn't believe in parallel timelines, no matter what Koch and the others thought. They might be in a parallel universe, but what if they weren't and their presence fucked up the entire history of the United States? Not wanting to screw up the future was motivation to do nothing.

Except for the rifle.

Mason closed his eyes and tried to push away a wave of despair as his brain worked out possibilities. Reverse engineering the rifle would take years, if not decades. Studying the weapon could yield other gains. Iron sights, for example, and the concept of magazines and spring reloading. The metallurgy of the weapon could lead to other changes, too. Some of the advances, particularly the magazine cartridges and semiautomatic firing were less than one hundred years away. Whether or not that timeline would change based on one lost rifle, Mason couldn't say. Whether or not it would lead to a different future seemed unanswerable as well, except he knew they'd have to do something. If they could track the injured Hessian and recover the rifle, that would be perfect. Otherwise, Stratton would be right and they'd have to report to General Washington. Mason felt his face warm with shame as he looked around the room in the low light. If facing his cadre of officers at the university was a challenge, owning up to his failures with George Washington seemed too daunting to consider.

A half dozen muskets leaned against the far wall where Daniels obviously plied his trade. Another dozen leaned in the corner. Even in the low light, Mason could tell they were very different. From his pocket, he pulled out a LED keychain light and shone it into the dark corners. Seeing his dormitory room key and his car keys almost jogged him out of his search. He'd never need them again, after all. Curious, he stood and quietly walked across the floor to inspect them.

The wooden ceiling creaked above him and he heard Daniels' heavy footfalls descend the stairs. The older man pushed through the door into the kitchen and stopped. With a nod, he stepped around the end of the table and stood opposite Mason. He ran a hand through his thinning black-and-silver hair and then rubbed his unshaven face.

"What are you doing?"

Mason shrugged. "Looking around."

"I think I can make your rifles work."

Mason nodded. "Is that before or after you turn these over to the Hessians? Or are you planning on turning us over, too?" He pointed to a musket with a fancy silver buckle on the shoulder strap and words etched into the wood of the shoulder stock. The words were very clearly German. Another pile bore a familiar sigil on their straps. "Or the British?"

Daniels sighed. "It's not like that, Mason."

"Then what's it like, Mister Daniels?" Mason squared his shoulders to the man and tried to imagine his first move if the gunsmith went for a rifle. After a long moment, the older man sat down heavily in a chair and gestured to Mason to do the same.

"If I fix their rifles, they stay away from us. From Emily, primarily," Daniels said. "Until today, they've kept their word. Sassenach bastards."

Mason sat down and folded his hands. "Are you a Tory, Mister Daniels?"

"No." The man looked into Mason's eyes intently. "I am a gunsmith, Mason. Both sides want my services and they pay well."

"You're on the wrong side of the river."

Daniels chuckled. "Remember when I told you that there was a lot you didn't know? That's part of it. There are rebels on this side of the river and they're constantly toying with the Hessians. All through the state, people are rising against the Hessians. I made a deal to keep them away from my daughter. Today, that changed."

Mason nodded. The older man's eyed blazed with hatred. "And what about your deal? How can you conduct business with them now?"

Daniels squinted at him. "Mason, your boys killed two of those men. If the third gets back to the Hessian garrison, they'll be coming for us all."

Mason blinked. "And if he doesn't, they'll come looking for their patrol."

Daniels nodded. "I think it may be best if you and your squad move on. Find some other place from where to fight or make your decisions."

"We're going to try and go home tomorrow." Mason sighed. "I don't think we can."

"Whatever magic it was, I hope for your sakes that it works," Daniels said. "Washington and his army continue to retreat. Word is that they are losing men every day to disease and desertion. Come springtime, there might not be a rebellion to speak of."

Mason stared at the man. *Here it comes*, he thought. *He's going to want to know everything and I don't know what I can tell him.*

"What happens?"

Mason shook his head. "Sorry. I can't tell you anything. It could mess up the future."

Daniels leaned across the table and his voice was a harsh

stage whisper. "Tell me what you know, boy."

"I am not a boy, Mister Daniels." Mason seethed. "And I'm not sure you're not a traitor or a British spy. Until you prove me otherwise, I'm not telling you a damned thing."

Daniels sat back. "But you know."

"Of course I do," Mason said. "I showed you a coin that said the United States of America and 1976 on it."

"So we win," Daniels said again. "But you won't tell me how or why?"

"No," Mason said. "Everything I said could affect how our future unfolds. I can't take that risk, Mister Daniels. And, I don't trust you."

Daniels smiled and pointed at Mason's uniform. "That's unlike anything I've seen, and I want to believe you, Mason. You saved our lives, but that doesn't make trusting you and your people any easier."

Mason thought he understood. New Jersey was occupied territory and because Washington and the rebel army were not a total construct of a federal government, they weren't trusted much more than the Hessians and British were. Daniels and others like him had simply wanted to eke out a living and be left alone by both sides until the war played out in their backyard. Mason wondered if it would get worse before it got better.

"We were talking about rebels on this side of the river," Mason said. "What about the Hessians and British? What do we need to know?" He hoped the question sounded innocuous. He could always verify with Murphy in the morning.

"The rebels have lots of small parties under Colonel Hunterdon skirmishing with Hessian outposts and disrupting British supply caravans. There have been raids across the river into Trenton and reports from Bordentown and farther south that large bands of resistance were challenging Hessian positions there. Because no one has been caught, the Hessians are wary of everything. Especially in Trenton. Word is that Colonel Rall, the commanding officer, has asked repeatedly for help from the British and received nothing. While other commanders have fortified their towns and defenses, Trenton is mostly undefended save for the Hessian outposts. Rall boasts about being able to defeat the rebels at every turn but rejects every suggestion given to him by his officers regarding the defense of Trenton."

Mason rubbed his eyes. Fatigue was setting in, but he needed to know more. *Focus, dammit.*

"You said they've raped and pillaged? The citizens in Trenton can't be happy with them."

Daniels cocked his head to one side. "Almost everyone is gone, Mason. There are a few Loyalists there, sure, and others like me who've made deals to support them in the hope of some type of protection, but the reality is that Trenton was a ghost town when the Hessians moved in. There's only a thousand of them and a few British dragoons."

"Dragoons?"

"Horse infantry," Daniels said. "You don't have horses in your time?"

Discussing cars and industrial revolution was not a path Mason wanted to tread just yet. "We do, just not familiar with the term. We call it cavalry. I have a lot to learn."

"And I can help you."

Mason met the man's eyes. "How? Our rifles?"

"That's one possibility. Making your ammunition work is certainly something I can try. Whether I'll be successful, I can't say." Daniels opened his hands. "You'll need information. And, you'll need a way to General Washington."

"Again, what's going to stop you from turning us in—"

Daniels interrupted him with a sternly pointed finger. "Because you saved our lives. And because I need you out of here because the British commander or the Hessian quartermaster will be by tomorrow to see about the rifles. I told them they would be ready on the twenty-second, and so they are. They'll come for them and you and your people have to go."

"We can't risk the river crossing without trying to get home."

Daniels shook his head. "Once you leave here, you can't come back. The Hessians will step up patrols. They're already out here at dawn most days."

"We'll need shelter. Our gear is good, but we can't last in the elements for a long time."

Daniels rubbed his eyes with his index fingers. "The Simmonses' place—they left a couple of months ago. Half of the house burned, but there's enough structure there to keep the wind off of you. Just don't make a big fire 'less you want people to know you're there."

"Won't any of those rebel parties or anyone else use it?"

"Always a chance," Daniels said. "It's better than nothing and keeps you out of sight but close enough if something happens."

"How close?"

"A half mile, give or take." Daniels sighed. "Best get some sleep and be ready to take your friends out before the sun comes up." He stood up and padded out of the kitchen without another word.

Mason scratched at his left shoulder, his fingers brushing up against a small, bulky package tucked into the pocket there. He tore open the Velcro closure and dug inside. Inside a plastic sandwich bag was a dog-eared copy of a blue-covered Army training pamphlet. The Ranger Handbook was a concise guide to tactical operations. His father's copy had been through the excruciating Ranger course in the early 1980s. When Mason joined ROTC, his father presented the copy with a quiet kind of reverence.

"There's a lot of knowledge here, Mason," he'd said. "Most of the best is on the first couple pages."

Mason worked the copy free of its bag and flipped open the old blue cover. By candlelight, he read "Rogers' Rules for Rangers" for the hundredth time, but really understood them for the first time.

1. *All Rangers are to be subject to the rules and articles of war; to appear at roll-call every evening, on their own parade, equipped, each with a Firelock, sixty rounds of powder and ball, and a hatchet, at which time an officer from each company is to inspect the same, to see they are in order, so as to be ready on any emergency to march at a minute's warning; and before they are dismissed, the necessary guards are to be draughted, and scouts for the next day appointed.*

The rules dated back to the French and Indian War. If Mason remembered his history correctly, Major Robert Rogers had drafted them somewhere in the Hudson River Valley in 1757 or maybe 1758.

2. *Whenever you are ordered out to the enemies forts or frontiers for discoveries, if your number be small, march in a single file, keeping at such a distance from each other*

as to prevent one shot from killing two men, sending one man, or more, forward, and the like on each side, at the distance of twenty yards from the main body, if the ground you march over will admit of it, to give the signal to the officer of the approach of an enemy, and of their number,

3. *If you march over marshes or soft ground, change your position, and march abreast of each other to prevent the enemy from tracking you (as they would do if you marched in a single file) till you get over such ground...*

Almost two centuries later, Lt. Colonel William Darby had presented the rules to the 1st Ranger Battalion prior to action during World War II. A modified version was still used to the present day in Ranger training.

He skipped to the end of the text. There were twenty-eight rules in all, in Rogers' original version.

28. *If you cannot satisfy yourself as to the enemy's number and strength, from their fire, conceal your boats at some distance, and ascertain their number by a reconnoitering party, when they embark, or march, in the morning, marking the course they steer, when you may pursue, ambush, and attack them, or let them pass, as prudence shall direct you. In general, however, that you may not be discovered by the enemy upon the lakes and rivers at a great distance, it is safest to lay by, with your boats and party concealed all day, without noise or shew; and to pursue your intended route by night; and whether you go by land or water, give out parole and countersigns, in order to know one another in the dark, and likewise appoint a station every man to repair to, in case of any accident that may separate you.*

Mason closed the cover and slipped the book into his shoulder pocket without a word. He sat with his eyes following the flickering candle flame for a very long time before he knew what he would do given the possibilities they would face in the morning.

CHAPTER EIGHT

Darkness fell on Fort Dix, but the search gained steam. More than a thousand soldiers from various units filled the training range complex and walked in the darkness with white flashlights. Lieutenant Colonel Sam Graves stood at the break in the vehicle trail with the commanding general of Fort Dix and the garrison commander. The search command post was little more than a few vehicles and about ten officers. Graves leaned over the hood of a Humvee and stared at a topographical map of the area. Outside of the perimeter fencing, there wasn't much of an area where a search would need to take place. Local police forces were already looking for the cadets in the off chance that they'd somehow left the installation. Graves frowned. Cadet Porter wouldn't have let that happen.

For a moment, he considered calling the senior again, but there was no answer and the voicemail box was full. Not wanting his frustration to show, he turned away and looked at the strange forest where the road had been. None of it made sense.

"Something the matter, Colonel?" the commanding general said behind him. Graves turned to meet Major General Cuthbert's gaze.

"This wasn't here during our recon, sir."

"What wasn't?"

Graves pointed at the road. "The road stops here and picks

up over there. This group of trees wasn't here—it was a road. That's one thing. Look at the trees, sir. Those branches are cleanly sheared off. None of this fits."

Cuthbert shook his head. "We've been through this. I've relayed the situation to the provost marshal and he's notifying Federal authorities to aid in the search."

A helicopter flew overhead drowning out conversation for a moment. A searchlight flashed on and traversed the length of the strange wood line as the helicopter hovered a hundred feet above the trees. The rotor wash kicked up snow and blew it around. Graves shielded his face but watched the helicopter pivot and move to the east and start to land in a nearby clearing.

"See who that is," Cuthbert directed his garrison commander. When the other man moved away, Cuthbert wiped his face and looked at Graves for a long moment. "Are they good kids?"

Graves blinked. "They are, sir."

"Your cadet in charge? What was his name?"

"Porter," Graves replied. "Selectee for regular Army and branched infantry, sir. Married with a young son."

"Not the kind to run off in the middle of a snowstorm?"

Graves shook his head. "Definitely not, sir. He's as good as they come."

Cuthbert nodded but said nothing for a moment. Graves watched the general study the cut of trees and the sheared branches above lit by artificial light poles from a construction battalion. The general sighed and curled one side of his mouth under. His face filled with trouble, Cuthbert avoided eye contact and stared into the forest that shouldn't have been there. The helicopter touched down, its engines spooling down quickly. His eyes darted in that direction. Graves glanced but couldn't see what was happening there. Cuthbert spoke slowly, "We're going to keep searching through the night. I want you to move along their direction of travel, to the north. Once the search parties reach you, pivot them along the perimeter fencing. You have my phone number—stay in contact every thirty minutes. Clear?"

Graves nodded even as his face betrayed him. "Yes, sir."

"Is that a problem?" Cuthbert leaned closer.

"Begging the general's pardon, but shouldn't I remain here?"

Cuthbert frowned. "No, Colonel. Move out and take charge of the search along the fence. Find your cadets."

Graves walked into the darkness, heading north. He turned over his shoulder and saw two men in dark suits leave the garrison commander's Hummer and walk up to General Cuthbert. One of them carried a briefcase and the other a hardened laptop computer. Graves looked away and moved north. The perimeter fence was a mere two kilometers ahead. Another helicopter moved in that direction, sweeping its light back and forth. As he walked, thankful that the snow had stopped, Graves had the difficult thought that his cadets were dead. He tried to brush it away, and mostly succeeded save for a more disquieting thought about the agents he'd seen with Cuthbert.

What in the hell is going on?

December 22, 1776

At first light, Mason looked over the sleeping forms of his squad and let his eyes fall on the extra rucksack of Kennedy's against the far wall of the Danielses' parlor. The green nylon rucksack sat on top of Kennedy's load-bearing vest and the clothing they'd gathered from his and Porter's bodies before committing them to the sinkhole. He tugged open a chest pocket and pulled out two sheets of paper that Higgs had laid on his gear the night before. Their inventory. Amidst the list of gear was the standard Cadet Command garbage. Everyone had an extra change of their green-digitalized camouflage Army Combat Uniforms, and an extra pair of boots, underwear, Army Physical Fitness Uniform components and running shoes, and personal items. Higgs smartly labeled all of those on a separate sheet of paper.

All of them carried smartphones and a few had their headphones. Two of them had separate music players. Four of them brought textbooks but there wasn't a subject listed for the entry. He'd have to address that later. Having a history book would be both a huge help and a risky undertaking. Kennedy carried an iPad tablet in his gear, along with a solar charging station. The computer science engineering student, no surprise, had been a huge techno-geek.

Mason snorted. *If we can't get home, we'll end up fighting over who can charge their phones.* At the bottom of the list were the two ancient AN/PRC-77 radios and their extra batteries, just under two thousand rounds of blank ammunition, two artillery simulators, and a red star cluster signaling device. The pyrotechnics had been in Porter's vest. The artillery simulators were essentially large cherry bombs and the red star cluster was a hand-operated firework/flare. All of them could come in handy if they couldn't get home.

At precisely 0530, Mason crept across the room and nudged Higgs awake. She sat up, ran her fingers through her hair and rubbed her eyes.

"When do we want to move?" she asked with a yawn.

"Soon as we can," Mason said. "We can eat, shave, and do whatever else we need at the farmhouse. Right now, we just need to un-ass this place."

Higgs nodded. "They're in danger the longer we stay here."

"Right. We can easily get back to our site from there, too." Mason stepped over to Stratton and relayed the same message. Instead of intelligent questions, Mason got smirks and barely respectful nods. "You done, Stratton?"

Stratton laughed. "You think you can lead us, Mason? You couldn't lead Girl Scouts to a bake sale."

"I'm the squad leader. You got it?"

"Yeah. Whatever." Stratton turned away. For a moment, Mason didn't believe he'd actually do anything, but the other man packed his gear and leaned over to wake up Koch. After another moment, he moved to Booker and did the same. Mason watched him for a moment more, thinking that they'd have to have it out at some point. Within minutes, his fireteam leaders had woken up everyone.

"We do this quietly," Mason stage-whispered to the group as they milled about. "Murphy? You, Booker, and Koch split up the extra gear. We're not leaving anything behind."

He turned to securing his own gear. By 0545, he was ready to go. Another ten minutes and everyone in the squad was ready except for Dunaway.

The dark-haired freshman huffed and struggled with her layered sleeping system. Designed to simply stuff into a cinchable sack, Dunaway was dutifully rolling her sleeping bag and looked around with pleading eyes. Thumping footsteps on the stairs caught Mason's attention. He pointed at Murphy to assist Dunaway as he stepped into the small hallway where the stairs were and saw Mister Daniels descending toward him.

"You leaving?"

Mason nodded. "We don't want you to be in danger any longer than we have to."

"You going to try and go home?"

Mason nodded. "First thing we do is to get to that burned-out farmhouse. From there, it's not far to our . . . site. Then we'll see what happens."

"If you can't, then what?"

The million-dollar question. He sighed. "I have no idea."

For a moment, Daniels chewed his lip. His contorted face again made Mason feel the man did not fully trust him, or any of them. "If you can't get home, come back tonight and let me know. I'll see what news I can get from in town. Maybe there will be a way to get you to General Washington."

I'd really rather run, he thought and said nothing. "Thank you, Mister Daniels. Do you want us to cover any tracks outside?"

"Ground's frozen solid. It will be fine." Daniels slipped past Mason and opened the front door to peer into the predawn light. "Cold and quiet."

Mason nodded and stepped back into the parlor. Dunaway was ready to go. All of them had weapons at the ready and their rucks on. He stared at Dunaway for a moment as if he was going to say something and then shook his head. "Come on, let's go."

Mason shrugged into his rucksack and stepped back into the narrow hallway. Daniels met him and held up a single 5.56mm round. "You want me to try and reload this?"

"No." Mason held out his hand and Daniels gave back the round. "If we can't get back, I might. But right now, no evidence we were even here."

Daniels stuck out a hand. "Good luck, Mason."

They shook and Mason said, "Thank you, Mister Daniels. Sorry for any trouble."

Daniels smiled. "Somehow, Mason, I think you're about to *be* trouble."

Outside the house, Mason directed them into a Ranger file. Spread five meters apart, they walked in a single file line away from the Daniels home. As the daylight grew, they could move into a standard wedge formation, but in the predawn twilight they needed to move as fast as possible. Martinez started as the point man with Koch right behind to watch the compass azimuth and keep them headed west-northwest toward the Danielses' former neighbors. From his position in the middle of the squad, Mason looked behind him, all the way to Booker bringing up the rear. The lanky sophomore kept turning as they walked to check for anyone or anything coming up from behind exactly as he was supposed to do.

Content, Mason looked around the forest while they walked. Thick brush gave way to lighter, easier forest about two hundred meters out. As they came through, Mason made a "psst" sound to Higgs in front of him and then again to Stratton behind him. He gave the hand and arm signal to increase intervals and each cadet slowed down and allowed ten to fifteen meters before following the person in front. With early-morning twilight, something his father referred to as BMNT—before morning nautical twilight—dawning around them, he could make out individual trees in the semidarkness.

Martinez raised a gloved fist, the signal for freeze, and everyone stood still. Martinez took a knee and gave the signal for "danger area" by acting as if slitting his own throat with his fingers. Koch and the others passed it back, but Mason was already moving toward the front of the patrol. He tapped Higgs on the shoulder as he passed. When they reached Martinez, the heavy cadet wiped his face and pointed ahead.

"Looks like a road," Martinez said. "What do we do?"

Mason's first thought was to practice a tactical road crossing, complete with security on both sides, but common sense took over. "Go quickly across it. Move out." He gestured to the squad to stand and then gave them a signal to "double time" by pumping his fist vertically. Everyone shuffled across the road and down the slight hill beyond it before Mason was able to tell everyone to slow down. Out of view from the road, Mason called a halt and brought everyone in to a circular perimeter. Once the squad was set, he knelt in the middle of the circle with Higgs and Stratton.

"What the fuck was that?" Stratton asked. "That's not how we cross roads."

Mason shook his head. "We needed to get across fast. I'd rather do it that way. Even with security posted, we've got nothing to shoot back, Stratton."

"We're just gonna keep running, huh?" Stratton spat.

Here we go.

Mason made to argue, but Higgs raised her hands to both of them. "Shut up. Both of you."

Stratton shook his head. "Let's get moving to the farmhouse, or do you want to just keep running all day?"

Mason stared at him. "Your team has point. Should be four hundred meters northwest. Got it?"

"I can find that in my sleep." Stratton turned away and said over his shoulder, "Unlike you."

Heat flushed in Mason's face, but he said nothing. The squad was up and moving within a minute, taking care not to step in any remaining deposits of snow. Mason walked in silence, stewing in the memory of his failure when the squad halted as they climbed a small slope. The outline of the farmhouse was visible through the trees ahead. Mason gestured them back down the hillside for cover and concealment. As Stratton worked his way back to the middle of the squad, Mason's mind raced about how to secure the house.

Stratton grinned. "Told you."

Mason motioned for Higgs to come forward and whispered. "Good job. Now let's secure it."

Higgs came forward. "What's the plan?"

Mason pointed at her. "Your team stays here. I'll go with Stratton's team to circle the house and then go inside." He looked at Stratton. "You know stacking and breaching better than I do. You lead the assault team and we'll secure the house."

Stratton beamed. "Fine. Let's go."

The band started playing some traditional German march long before Sutton and his dragoons closed the distance to the parade ground. His mount, a white gelding named Jack, shook his head as the brass section of the band brayed to life.

"Easy, Jack," Sutton laughed. "I hate that shit, too, old friend."

Turning the corner onto Queen Street, his dragoons trailing behind in parade line, Sutton saw that Rall's command had turned out entirely, including the alert forces, for the morning muster. Sutton motioned for his men to form up and take their position to the extreme right of the formation. He rode into position, saluted, and glanced over his shoulder to ensure his dragoons stood ready. The march came to an agonizing, off-tune end and Rall began to bark in his Hessian-inflected German. Sutton caught a few words here and there. Things about duty and fear and winning. Something about foolish Washington came through, and there were a few muffled comments from Knyphausen's brigade nearest to Sutton. It sounded like one of the soldiers, maybe more than one, laughed openly at the commander and his fears.

They don't believe Washington is coming, either. He snorted and felt a cold grin cross his features. There was no better time to pursue Washington himself. He would increase the distance his dragoons would travel on their daily patrols by two or three times. They needed the additional time in the saddle to perfect their abilities. Intelligence was everything.

But there will be challenges. He chewed on the inside of his cheek. The Hunterdon men, the shadows of New Jersey, were out there, too. Defending Washington's spies and the trails the old weasel had carefully constructed to hide his movements and cover his transgressions. They would not matter in the end. He could hunt them down just as easily.

Rall abruptly ended the formation and walked away from his post. The confused soldiers stirred until their immediate commanders started barking orders. Patrols left hastily, alert forces rushed to their posts, and the garrison soldiers, the ones charged with supplies and logistics, stood mute in their formation. Sturm, the young lieutenant, looked at Sutton with a bemused smile and released his troops before walking to Sutton's side.

"Good morning, Captain," Sturm said.

"Good morning," Sutton replied without looking down from his mount at the young lieutenant. The scrambling Hessians made good theater. "Tell me, are you still short three men?"

Sturm nodded. "Yes, sir. They have not returned."

"Then I suppose it's time my men and I find them."

"Colonel Rall's instructions were to leave them out there to their fate. That we have to defend this town against Washington's imminent attack. He believes that Washington will attack any day." Sutton felt a grin form on his face as Sturm's face screwed in concentration. "You don't believe Washington is coming?"

Sutton looked down and smiled with pity on the young lieutenant. "No, I do not. You and I, however, are going to find Washington and bring the wrath of the British army in New York down upon him. Mayhap by the new year."

"Pardon my question, sir, but how do you intend to do that?"

Sutton leaned down over the pommel of his saddle. "My dragoons will patrol the perimeter roads from the river east to Maidenhead. You will arrange several vantage points with three-man patrols and place them where I tell you based upon what my men find. Using our eyes and ears are the key to finding Washington. If we cannot pinpoint his location, we can at least learn where he would cross given the best opportunity. When he does, the entire British army would be waiting and not just the paltry forces left in New Jersey."

"Colonel Von Donop has marched south to defend Borden-town against militias numbering a thousand men. Are those not Washington's men?"

Sutton shrugged. "You mean acting because of Washington's orders? I think not. But, given the direction of their attacks, it would be wise to assume, for example, that Washington lies farther south than we believed."

"But we don't know that for sure."

"Precisely," Sutton grinned. "That's why we're going to lever-age our ability to observe and report, Lieutenant. We can find Washington and defeat those who're trying to cover his movements in one fell swoop. There are men supporting him on this side of the river. We will find them."

Sturm stepped closer. Interested. "I can provide a platoon's strength, sir, but no more lest Colonel Rall suspect something."

"Let our dear colonel suspect what he wants." Sutton laughed. "Though I'm posted here, General Grant is my commander, and yours. He would appreciate our efforts as would General Corn-wallis and even Lord General Howe. Washington lies across the Delaware, that much we know. But his plan to attack or defend Philadelphia? We'll find out for certain. Once we do, General Grant will certainly want to know."

Truthfully, Grant wouldn't do anything. The fat bastard was too far removed from his troops to see anything other than opportunities for his own promotions and rewards. Even if Sutton were to write for approval, Grant wouldn't bother to respond. Asking forgiveness in the pursuit of an advantage was always more desirable than requesting permission from the uninterested. Finding Washington, though, would raise the notice of Lord General Howe. That would be something spectacular.

Sutton looked at Sturm for a moment. The young lieutenant's

interest to do more was intriguing. How far the Hessian would go could tell Sutton just how frustrated these mercenaries were with their abhorrent commander. "Have your men ready to leave by noon. I will have a route for them to patrol and see about finding more rebels."

"Where exactly, sir?"

"I'm not sure yet. This morning I'm riding out to the gunsmith's home to check on rifle repairs. There may be someplace out there that bears watching. Your patrol disappeared in that area, so it is a good place to start."

Sturm shook his head. "We're not sure the patrol went to the gunsmith's home, sir. It was a mile farther than their planned route."

"Stranger things have happened, Lieutenant. There are many places out there for a three-man patrol to be captured or even killed," Sutton said, motioning for his troops to prepare for movement. "Be ready when I return and we'll set our plan in motion. We'll find your men or someone who'll talk."

Sturm saluted in the British manner, which filled Sutton with an almost perverse pride. Surprising himself, Sutton returned the salute smartly. He spun his horse toward his men.

"First section. You will patrol the Princeton Road and west to the river from Trenton to Maidenhead. Second section, you will patrol the Bordentown Road and west to the river. Return to Trenton by noon. Third and Fourth sections will remain here and you'll take over the patrol routes in the afternoon. First and Second sections, move out."

The five-man sections wheeled about and trotted away, half to the stables and the others to their routes. Watching them move with determination and precision, compared to the barking scrambling Hessians, made Sutton appreciate his position. Purchasing his commission, in a time of war, had been an excruciating exercise in determination in its own right. Rising to the rank of captain without a nobility or privileged upbringing was highly unlikely. Rising as fast as he had to a captain of the dragoons was unheard of. Still, success didn't matter to those above him. He was unlike them, a commoner with a commission, and as such he would remain outside the circles that would take him places.

Unless he did something that no one else seemed prepared or motivated to do. In the dead of the coming winter, with his superiors having sought warmer places to shelter away from any possible battle, he could change the outcome of the war. The very idea seemed to vibrate his soul. He could end the war and even earn a cherished title from His Majesty. Washington was no more than twenty miles away, maybe much less, and on the other side of a river the rebels navigated freely. If he could find the rebels, Admiral Lord Howe would send his own forces up the river to secure it and give passage to His Majesty's army and this farce of a rebellion would be quelled.

Sutton shook off the imagined pleasure and took a long, deep breath of the cold air to clear his mind. *One thing at a time*, he told himself. The first order of business was to reclaim the rifles he'd sent for repairs to the local gunsmith. The man's daughter was as pretty as she was sympathetic to their cause. She would be a fine guest for the Christmas festivities with Colonel Rall. His stomach gurgled and he thought of breakfast instead of an immediate patrol.

Sutton adjusted his hat and nudged Jack back toward his quarters. At the crossroads of King and Queen Streets, he turned east. After a good meal, he would ride past the outer defensive line manned by cold, huddled Hessians. With their rifles repaired by a skilled craftsman and better intelligence of the local area, Washington would soon be his. Moreover, he would get what he wanted and none of the silver-mouthed bastards above him would take his success away.

CHAPTER NINE

The farmhouse was severely damaged, but livable. One side of the simple one-floor cabin had burned and partially collapsed leaving one large room open with access to the somewhat collapsed, but still workable fireplace. On the un-collapsed side the roof appeared intact enough to keep off the weather, but whatever provisions or usable items had been in the house were long stolen.

Mason pushed through the still working door and looked into the room. Despite smelling of wet, burnt wood, the room appeared dry and large enough for them. Satisfied it was safe, he stepped inside and looked around. A small table stood against the far wall along with what looked like the frame for a bed now broken into pieces. Mason couldn't see any animal droppings, which was a plus. Mainly the room was dry and while it would be tight, it would provide them a break from the wind and precipitation. Two cracked and smoke-smeared windows looked out into the forest on opposing sides of the far corner. With a person at the door, they could almost see a full three hundred and sixty degrees for security. While not ideal, they could work with it.

"Stratton?"

"Yeah?" his counterpart called from outside the home.

"Get the squad and move them up here. Now." Mason shrugged out of his ruck and set it on the floor. His watch read 0830. They could set up security, eat, and plan their way back to the site. Weapon in hand, Mason stepped to the door and cracked it ajar two inches. He could clearly see Stratton's fireteam moving back through the forest to Higgs. He watched them, the gray-green-suited figures clearly standing against the dark, moist ground, getting their rucks on, and moving through the forest all the way to the door. Mason pushed it open and waved them inside one by one.

"Higgs? Stratton?" They turned toward Mason. "Set fifty percent security. Everyone get a bite to eat. Fifty percent security on thirty-minute rotations while we eat, change socks, and get the lay of the land. Move."

Higgs stepped away and Stratton even managed to nod. Within a few minutes, half of the squad positioned themselves near the two doors and one window on the undamaged side. Koch crawled under the partially collapsed roof and watched from the other side of the cabin. Content that they had three hundred and sixty degrees of security, Mason settled into the center of the cabin, opened a canteen, and again consulted the inventory list Higgs had collected. Between the eight of them were twenty Meals, Ready to Eat or MREs. They'd each consume one for the morning meal, leaving twelve.

If we don't go home, that's twelve. We can't survive on that. He debated not eating one of his meals for a moment before opening one of the exterior pockets. Using his multi-tool knife, he opened the package labeled Pesto Pasta with Chicken and sorted through the file packets. Every single of one of them was a finite, perishable resource. Right down to the artificial coffee creamer, never mind the miniature bottle of Tabasco sauce. If they did not get home, it would be a reminder of a world they would never see again.

Mason shook off the thought. "Focus," he said softly to himself and rubbed his eyes.

Footsteps clomped on the floor next to him. Higgs took off her rucksack and sat on it across from him. "You okay?"

"Yeah," Mason said. "Just trying to stay focused."

Higgs drank from her canteen. She leaned closer. "You're thinking we're not going home."

Mason met her eyes but did not move his head. He knew that he didn't have to. Ashley Higgs was incredibly smart. As a freshman, she'd beaten out all of the other cadets in the program for a slot to the U.S. Army Basic Parachutist Course. The next summer, when her classmates planned their beach trips and vacations, she spent two summer sessions studying Pashto, one of the tribal languages of Afghanistan. She was everything Mason knew a leader should be, and most everything that he wasn't.

"Don't give up, Mason."

He grunted and tore open his plastic spoon and main entree. "I'm not, Higgs."

"We have to think like we're going back." She sat her canteen on the floor. "If we don't then we can deal with it."

"We have to have a plan, Higgs."

She nodded. "I'm not saying we don't have to. You need to have faith, Mason. If not in the situation, then have it in yourself. You made the right call with this place. You're going to make a lot of right calls."

"Thanks, Higgs." He took a bite of pasta and chewed. The simple act of eating helped to clear his mind and focus it on the simple things. Mission first and people always were the key touchstones of the Cadet Creed. It was a perfect place to start.

"Once everybody has eaten, we go to one hundred percent security so you, Stratton, Booker, and I can plan this afternoon. I'm not talking an operations order or anything like that. We just need to get back to where we came in and see what happens."

Higgs nodded as she chewed her spaghetti meal. "Koch thinks we need to be there at the same time of day to make it work, or ..." She paused and wiped her mouth with the back of her left hand. "Or that it will be in a year from yesterday if it even works at all. He's not convinced it will."

"A year?" Mason almost choked on his pasta. "We don't have the supplies to last a year here, Higgs."

"If we stay here, we can't run."

I was afraid you were going to say that. Mason sighed and kept eating. The trouble was that he knew she was right. What they had, what they knew, and what they believed could change the course of the American Revolution. The battle of Trenton would turn the tide of the war, but there would be several more years of bloodshed and turmoil. He tried to remember the details of the years after Trenton but could not. "Murphy wrote a paper on this thing, right?"

"That's what he said."

"Then I need to talk to him. We need a full brief on what happens in Trenton and the days after."

Higgs nodded. "Why just a few days?"

Mason grinned with one side of his mouth. "If we can't go back, all we can do is live a few days in the future, Higgs. Any further than that are things we can't control." He chuckled. "We have to get back, because if we don't, Kennedy and Porter won't be the last of us to die, Higgs. Whether it's in battle, or from disease, the odds are against us."

"We need to know everything Murphy knows or thinks he can remember"—she gestured to the group—"and everything we all know. Knowledge is power, Mason."

"What if it's trouble, too?"

Higgs nodded and the conversation lulled. Mason knew he was right. There were too many variables in play and way too many things that could go wrong. As he ate, he opened the Ranger handbook and reviewed the Standing Orders for Rogers' Rangers. Rogers was out there, somewhere in the strange new world, right now with his Rangers making trouble for Washington's army. As he read, Mason noted with pride that they'd posted sentries before eating and were planning to run on fifty percent security for the next several hours. He'd also gotten up before dawn. No sooner had he thought about it than he heard his father's voice telling him to focus on the present. That he could pat himself on the back later. That people were going to die because he'd eventually screw up. Mason choked down his remaining pride with a bite of pasta and a splash of cold water from his canteen. The icy swallow triggered a thought and he looked at Higgs.

"We need to find a water source."

Higgs nodded. "After everyone eats, I'll take my team and do a quick box around the house and see what we can find. If nothing else, we get a lay of the land and see where an enemy could hide."

Mason nodded and ate another spoonful. *I should've thought of that.*

Dammit.

He decided to play it cool and collected and replied, "That sounds good. We'll also need to identify food sources."

Higgs looked at him. "After this meal, we ration. One MRE per person per day. That buys us time to reach Washington's army, if we can't get home."

"We could hunt," he shrugged. By the look on her face, he

knew it was a wrong answer. "But, yeah, we might call attention to ourselves. That won't work very well, huh?"

Higgs chewed slowly through a bite of spaghetti. While she chewed, she added a few sprinkles of hot sauce and stirred the remainder inside its foil pouch. She looked up at him. "We have food for two days, Mason. Water for one. If we can't get home, that's our first priority."

Mason nodded. "We can find water, I'm sure of that. The food we can forage for if we..." He trailed off and realized that his impossible thought of running west would be harder, infinitely harder, than actually joining Washington's army after all.

"We have to get home," he said more to himself than to his friend.

She frowned. "Mason? If we can't, we have to have a plan."

He sighed and met her eyes. "I know."

"But you don't want to think that far ahead." Higgs frowned deeply enough he could see the lines in her face in the low light of the room.

"No." He looked away. "No, I don't want to think that far ahead."

Higgs rolled her eyes. "You sound just like Sergeant Sheets. Mason? There's a lot more than worrying about who's going to die when you're in command. How about thinking, maybe just a little, about everyone who's going to live? What happens when they're looking to you for leadership? That's a bigger problem you can affect than who's going to die. You could walk out that door, trip on the steps, and break your neck. It is highly unlikely, but it's possible. What's more possible is that you skin your elbows or your knees and everyone laughs at you. Which one do you plan for?"

Mason shrugged. He'd never thought of it that way. Leadership, especially leading soldiers in a combat situation, was like a heavy yoke around his neck. The burden was simply too much to bear. "You can't plan for either."

"Right. So stop thinking in absolutes beyond taking care of your people." She pointed at him with her fork. "Taking care of *us*."

"But if I fuck up, Higgs," Mason huffed. "I mean—"

Higgs nodded. "Yes, people will die. Your job is to do your best to mitigate that. Every squad leader in history has wanted one thing for their people—to bring them home alive with all of their fingers and toes. You can try to do that, but you may not succeed. Winning battles and wars should be the farthest thing from your mind. Yeah, we can change the world and all that"—Higgs rolled her eyes and gestured wildly with her hands—"but, the reality is pretty simple. If we all die tomorrow, we can't change anything. If we stay alive, every day is an opportunity to change history. You have to give us that opportunity."

She stood up and tucked her half-eaten foil pouch into her armpit carefully so it wouldn't spill. "Where are you going?" Mason asked.

"Taking care of my people. The faster they can eat, the better." She smiled at him. "It's the little things, Mason. Try to remember that."

She moved away and Mason found himself eating a little faster. There were too many things to do and the day was wasting.

Sutton opened the Christensens' front door and nearly swooned at the smell of fresh sausage coming from the kitchen. The widow Christensen, he believed, must have caught a vestige of the Christmas spirit and traded with the passing hunters of the day before. He'd seen the rough, dirty men approach the town with their catches that the Hessian quartermasters took en masse with barely a second thought. As he'd watched the men—an older father and a younger son, Sutton surmised—he'd waited patiently to see something in their tired, desperate eyes that bordered on something like subterfuge. Had they looked up, glanced around, or taken more of an interest in their surroundings than the actual transaction of trade, he would have gathered them up in a heartbeat and tortured them for information. Countering Washington's growing nest of espionage was of great importance to General Lord Howe and his staff, but in the wilderness of New Jersey, Sutton seldom knew who was friend or foe in those he passed along the muddy streets of Trenton. Farther outside the all but deserted town, he didn't know what to expect.

The man, Daniels, he remembered, seemed to occupy a clever niche between the armies at war. He repaired any rifle or weapon brought to him for a fair price. Lieutenant Sturm's early report of finding colonial muskets along Daniels' walls were hardly troublesome. The man's dealings were simply to protect him and his young, pretty daughter in the face of any threat from any side. However, by taking no side, he'd isolated himself and his family. The time would likely come when protection would be necessary, from the rebels most likely, and Sutton was prepared to offer that and more, particularly where the daughter was concerned.

Selena Christensen was simply not interested in him. Like the gunsmith, she'd simply aligned herself in a way to protect herself and her boy. Unlike Daniels, Selena recognized that the British and Hessian armies were better equipped, despite the Hessian savagery, to protect her interests. Ultimately, it did not matter. She would have nothing of social interaction or his gentlemanly, or other, intentions. Only once he'd considered forcing himself upon her only to walk away and find solace in a wineglass at the tavern. Simply taking what he wanted wasn't exciting anymore. Taking what no other man thought he should, however, had promise.

The gunsmith's daughter, for example.

Rall's Christmas-dinner invitation would be lost on Selena Christensen. Sutton decided to ask the pretty brown-haired girl instead. Maybe he could spark some resemblance of jealousy in the widow who barely spoke to him or even marked his existence with a passing glance. The predawn cold outside drove home the point that his own existence in this awful place was vacant and alone. He'd thought of going to Selena so many times, but had never even attempted it. The smell of cooking sausage suggested a gift of some type, but it didn't matter. His mind was made up before he walked into the kitchen. Seeing Selena with her back to him, he flushed with warm excitement for the first time in weeks.

"Good morning," she said without looking at him. "Would you care for some breakfast?"

"Yes," he said and stepped through the door. He moved to the table quickly, sitting down just as Selena turned with a plate of a fried egg and sausage. "I believe you traded for this yesterday, did you not?"

Her dark eyes glinted in the low light of the kitchen as she smiled. "I trade nearly every day, Captain. You're well aware of that."

Her smile did not falter as he grinned up at her. His eyes flitted over her chest, hidden behind the blue dress and black knitted shawl she wore over her shoulders against the chill. "Indeed, and sausage? You've outdone yourself, madam."

A touch of color appeared in her cheeks. "Thank you, sir."

"You're quite welcome."

She moved back to the fireplace. "There'll be some tea shortly."

With a speed that surprised him, Sutton tore into the plate of food. If anything, Selena was a more than decent cook. He watched her for a moment and realized that she was much more civil than in recent memory. She pushed through the kitchen door toward the parlor, leaving him alone. He made quick work of the eggs and the sausage, finishing them just as she stepped into the kitchen with her young son Ian behind her. The boy took his customary place behind her legs and squinted out at him distrustfully.

"Good morning, Ian," Sutton smiled. The little brat ducked behind his mother fully.

"Now, Ian. Don't be rude." Selena looked up at him with a sad smile.

"It's quite all right," Sutton said as he stood. "I must get going anyway."

"You won't stay for tea?" She asked with a hopeful expression that almost made him change his mind about the Daniels girl.

"I'm afraid there are long patrols to the north today," Sutton replied. "I must get going."

Selena actually smiled at him. "Be safe then and we will see you this evening."

Sutton flushed in sudden embarrassment at his thoughts of the young girl compared to the sudden interest of the beautiful widow. "Yes, of course." He nodded at them and rushed through the cabin to the front door and into the cold morning with a broad smile on his face. The day showed promise for a change. If the Daniels girl would entertain his offer, then he could surely inflame Selena Christensen's newfound interest through jealousy. So much was his preoccupation with the idea of playing a young, beautiful girl against the equally beautiful widow, that he barely noticed the intense cold and the freshening breeze from the west. The four-mile ride to the gunsmith's place would be an agonizing crawl in below-freezing temperatures. Still, his excitement never wavered. He turned from Trenton with his head bowed into the high collar of his coat and a smile on his chilled face.

Frost gave the drooping forest branches the glint of jewels in the sunrise. High, thin clouds dominated the skyline to the west and foretold of heavier weather in the week to come. The breeze came up gently, like a frigid kiss on his cheek and Jack nickered under him.

"Easy, boy," Sutton said and patted the horse's thick neck. They'd been through a lot together in the last several months, but the sturdy gelding never wavered under fire. Jack tossed his head and looked side to side as they plodded through the mud toward the gunsmith's home. Rider and horse were well matched: both anxious and looking for a fight. Sutton clicked his tongue and pulled back on the reins gently and they stopped at the muddy intersection. For a moment, Sutton listened and closed his eyes to adjust to the sounds of the wilderness. He removed his helm and let the breeze cool the top of his head for a moment while he concentrated on the stillness around him. Far enough from Trenton that Rall's damned band practices could not be heard, Sutton believed himself to be ready for anything that might meet him. Pistol loaded and sword at the ready, he replaced his helm and nudged Jack down the Princeton Road and what he hoped to be a great prize for the taking.

CHAPTER TEN

Like most nights, Washington could not sleep. In the early days of the rebellion, Martha and the farm at Mount Vernon were top-of-mind concerns that haunted his early-morning hours. Once the union declared an open rebellion against the Crown, Washington had reasoned out their diplomatic and operational responses with an almost uncanny success rate. Not that Admiral Lord Howe, and his brother General Lord Howe, were predictable in their occupation of the Colonies, but Washington reckoned correctly that the British would simply try to squeeze a rebellion against the limited resources of the frontier until they broke and came crawling back for mercy. The British admiralty, regardless of the Crown's meddling in colonial affairs, believed that the colonial settlers would simply acquiesce to being ruled from afar like so many thousands had for millennia before them. The Howe brothers tried both to rule the public by fear, circulating rolls of obedience to the Crown for colonials to sign, and by an iron fist against any who would attack a soldier of the Crown in the performance of their duties. A declaration that any attacker would be considered an assassin and put to death on the spot had recently filtered down through Washington's intelligence network. The Howe brothers believed they were safe for the winter in New York with their garrisons securing the tenuous frontier.

Washington knew otherwise.

Laying in the early morning's near darkness, he could see the candlelight flickering in his outer sanctuary where Mister

Lee and the other staff officers worked through the night gathering intelligence dispatches. He'd lain down at three o'clock with the knowledge that General Ewing's planned harassment of the Hessian positions at Trenton had gone exceedingly well. Reports converged from several credible sources that Colonel Rall placed two-thirds of his troops on guard through the night for the third consecutive evening. The Hessians were tired and edgy, which played directly into his hands. But, there was more.

Reports filtered through his staff that organized militia to the south of Mount Holly were riling the Hessian's ire as well to the point that Colonel Von Donop had organized his regiments for a morning march to the south from Bordentown to dispel the rebel militia. With the nearest support to Rall at Princeton, eight miles to the north, a move south by Von Donop would open a unique situation. Trenton would be held by a force of nearly equal strength to his own army. Rall would be open between his main reinforcements, provided his own forces could attack the captured town.

Perhaps a window has opened?

The thought struck him enough that he opened his eyes and blinked in the near darkness. His army stood in ragged shoes with bloody feet. Their supplies from Philadelphia were unorganized and ill-aligned to the army's needs no matter how much he pleaded with the recently recessed Congress. There was hardly a reason to attack now. With the British army in garrison from Princeton to New York and the British fleet making preparations to send several blockading vessels home for the holiday season, now appeared to be the time for pause. Yet, his own army would find their enlistments completed at the end of the year and because of the inadequate support from the Congress, most would walk away without some kind of momentum to drive them forward.

But what if we attacked Trenton? And what if it was successful?

His mind whirled around the consequences of a successful attack. The Hessians represented the scourge of everything the Rebellions fought against. A deft strike at them, removing their most critical position along the banks of the Delaware River, would send a message to the British army. A counterattack would be imminent, within a day or two at best. The army could be ready for that. He envisioned the British coming upon vacated campsites and burning fires while his army retreated north for the winter. Closer to supplies and farther across a treacherous river, it would be a fine place to loiter and plan the spring's march. A successful attack would persuade many of his soldiers to stay—believing the momentum would carry them forward another year or so.

Would a simple attack be enough?

Washington took a long, deep breath and closed his eyes. Sleep would not come no matter how hard he tried. His mind played out the course of his decisions. The tactician would not succumb to the need for sleep until the problem had been wrung out and solved from every possible end. He opened his eyes and stared into the rafters for a long moment.

The brothers Howe would do one of three things. The first possibility, the one Washington considered the least serious, was that the Howes would do nothing at all. With the Hessians paid handsomely from His Majesty's coffers, any loss the mercenaries suffered could disappear like water off a duck's back. Their reputations and deeds preceding them, Washington wondered if the loss of a few thousand Hessians would be a blessing to the British army.

He snorted in the darkness. No, Howe would not let New Jersey fall. The Delaware River posed a perfect boundary, especially for those thousands of miles away. Howe would ensure, whatever happened, that New Jersey would remain under his command. He would counterattack with a large enough force to leave behind a stronger garrison in place of whatever the Hessians lost. This was certainly the most likely situation to develop were the Continental Army to risk a crossing of the Delaware River and attack at Trenton.

More problematic was the river itself. If the river froze, as it was apt to do, there was nothing stopping Howe from marching the entirety of the British army out of their warm barracks in New York and across the Delaware. Nothing would stop them short of Philadelphia. That, he decided, was unacceptable. His army in rags, with their enlistments rapidly ending, Washington needed a bold stroke to bolster recruiting, if not his own spirits. He thought of Martha waiting at Mount Vernon and immediately tried to blink the vision away. He would only return to the sanguine plantation life if independence was successful. If his army faltered, he and the members of the Continental Congress would be paraded through the streets and shot for treason against the king.

At half past eight, there was a knock at the door, quiet as if testing his restfulness. For a moment, he considered saying nothing but his insecurity about the decision worked his mouth open before he could stop it. "Yes?"

A crack of light appeared, silhouetting the familiar head of Mister Lee. "General? You asleep?"

"Not anymore, Mister Lee." He smiled. His staff, once again, had seen to it that he rest. The days of warm beds and late-morning dozing were few and far between. "What is it?"

"A rider, sir. Message from Colonel Reed for you." His tone was urgent, but not panicked in any way. "You want to see it, sir?"

Reed. Colonel Joseph Reed served in the tenuous position of Washington's adjutant. Rarely did the two men seem to get along, but Washington knew that Reed's perennial stubbornness in the matters of the army was second only to his ability to gather and analyze intelligence. Reed had taken up a winter position to the south in Bristol, Pennsylvania, on the Delaware. His frequent reports on the Hunterdon uprising and General Ewing's raids brought key intelligence to Washington's headquarters after every successful raid. The agitated state of the Hessian command was well known through Reed's reports, and yet his position to the west of Burlington, New Jersey, provided Washington with more insight into the activities of Griffin's militia and the prospective march of Von Donop's regiment.

Washington sat up and pushed the rough blankets down. Lee stepped into the room with a lantern and the general's spectacles. "Tea?"

"Brewing some now, sir. The good ones and not that swill Lieutenant Jenkins tried to poison you with." Lee smiled.

Washington chuckled. "Thank you, Mister Lee."

The older man handed Washington his glasses and the wax-sealed note and shuffled from the room as Washington turned the letter in his hands. Reed might be a thorn in his side for the operation of the army, but he knew his job and his network of personal contacts on the New Jersey side of the river impressed even the most scornful of Washington's generals. Washington broke the wax seal with his thumb and unfolded the simple letter.

As he read, Washington's mind worked. The militia in southern New Jersey were giving the Hessians fits. Colonel Griffin had advanced his six hundred militia toward Mount Holly and clearly had the Hessians' attention. Colonel Von Donop, the Hessian commander, at this very hour was marching toward Mount Holly to defend their positions against the ragtag militiamen. In Trenton, Rall's men were exhausted to the point of illness, and tempers flared. Reed urged Washington to consider either supporting the militia efforts with a reinforcing attack or to attempt a diversionary attack—or more—at Trenton. The passion of Reed's words took Washington's breath away.

He's right, Washington realized with a start. *The door is open and we must kick it down.*

Lee returned with a steaming cup of tea. "Good news, General?"

Washington looked up and smiled with one side of his mouth. "Indeed, old friend. Put the word out to my commanders."

"What word is that, sir?" Lee lowered his chin. "Are we going to fight?"

"Summon a council of war at one o'clock today." Washington waved the folded letter. "We have an opportunity. One not to be missed."

At noon, Mason gathered the cadets and all of their gear for the journey to their entrance site. The open woodlands were quiet and without a breath of wind in the air, almost warm. Two hundred meters out from the abandoned farmhouse, Mason called a halt and brought them into a small perimeter. All of them were hot in their thermal wear and proceeded to shed at least one inner layer. Mason stepped over to Murphy, who had the duty of compass man.

"You've got an azimuth?"

Murphy reached into his pocket. "Made a waypoint on my phone and—"

"GPS won't work for more than two hundred years, Murphy."

Murphy shook his head. "I have a map, Mason. It shows key terrain like creeks. I can get us back there—or pretty close. It would be easier if we went back to Mister Daniels' house. From there it was almost straight west. I'm guessing southwest for us. Azimuth of two hundred twenty-five for five hundred more meters."

"Put the phone away, Murphy. I don't want you distracted and us getting off course." Mason frowned even as he said it. Murphy snorted.

"I didn't get you lost on that lane, Mason."

"I didn't say you did." Mason shook it off. "Just get us back to the site, okay?"

"Yeah." Murphy turned his head and eyes out to the southeast and said nothing more.

Higgs gave him a silent thumbs-up, which Stratton echoed. They were ready to move. Mason gave a gentle whistle and the squad stood and moved out to the southeast in a single-file line with Koch in the lead.

Two hundred meters later, climbing a small knoll filled with dormant thickets, Koch raised a gloved fist—the signal to freeze. As quickly as he gave it, he dropped to his knees and then into the prone position, frantically waving all of them to do the same. Mason went to the ground staring at Koch. For several heartbeats, the big sophomore did nothing except strain to look over the low summit of the hill. Whatever Koch had seen, the thickets and higher terrain appeared to have obscured him and the rest of the squad. Koch turned his head back to the squad and raised his hand to touch the front of his ballistic helmet—the silent signal for the platoon leader.

Mason shook his head. The proper signal would have been for Koch to touch his sleeve, because squad leaders were NCOs and still wore their rank on their dress-uniform sleeves. Officers wore their rank on the front of their helmet. For a split second, a sad, empty feeling filled Mason. If they couldn't get back, he'd never see officer rank on his head. If they couldn't get back, he'd be a young black man in a time where people owned slaves and would fight viciously for that privilege in less than a hundred years.

I'm as good as anybody else. There would be time for dealing with that later. He got to his knees silently and crept forward in a low crouch. Higgs caught his eyes, fear evident in her face. Mason kept moving, saying nothing and staying as low as he could with the weight of his rucksack. At Koch's feet, Mason went to his hands and knees and crawled up alongside the big sophomore. He saw Koch's hands shaking.

"What is it?" Mason asked.

Koch licked his lips but did not meet Mason's eyes. "A road and—"

There was a burst of laughter and several voices speaking a harsh-sounding language. There were people nearby. Mason strained to look over the hill through a bottom of a thicket but could not make out anything. "What did you see?"

"Four, maybe five. All dressed like...the ones we killed yesterday. The ones that got Kennedy."

"Hessians."

Koch nodded. "What do we do?"

"Sit tight. If they're patrolling that road, they'll move along. After they—"

Another voice barked at the group and the happy bantering stopped. Mason fought a smile—the voice of an NCO hadn't changed in more than two hundred years independent of the language. They heard a rustle of gear being collected and a voice calling a soft cadence. The sound faded quickly. Mason edged up to the crest of the hill and saw the Hessians moving away from them, toward the Delaware River. He turned and made eye contact with Higgs and Stratton. With his left hand, he made an imaginary gun, turned it upside down, and pointed in the direction the Hessians moved. Higgs and Stratton relayed the signal to their teams. Enemy nearby.

Mason watched the squad silently pass the signal. He added a closed fist for emphasis and mouthed back "Nobody move."

Lying still, the cold seeped through his thin combat uniform and worked at his inner layers. Moving had been warm and easy. Lying still was not. Against the brown forest floor and the occasional patches of old snowfall, the squad stood out like sore thumbs in their modern uniforms. Mason tugged at the sleeve of his thermal undershirt and pulled it down closer to his gloves. The cadre called it "snivel gear" and, at first, Mason hated their derision as false bravado. None of them wore it and they gleefully chastised the cadets who did. Later, in the second semester of his freshman year, he'd seen their battalion executive officer, Major Guest, carefully concealing this own snivel gear under his uniform. At that point, Mason understood that it was a matter of show, but also a measure of self-care.

No longer hearing the Hessians, Mason edged forward in the high-crawl, elbows and knees propelling him forward to the top of the hill and an open spot in the thickets. The road below was no more than a muddy smear, barely two meters wide. Mason waited two full minutes before crawling back to Koch and turning to the expectant faces of his squad. He waved them to their feet and gave the signal for a Ranger file again, his hand like a knife blade raised between his eyes.

Without a word, the squad moved into a single-file line. Mason blinked at the recognition of following one of Rogers' Rangers rules. Moving single file would make it difficult for an interested party to track them and minimize the footprints on the muddy road. Crossing the road would be faster that way, but the woodland on the other side was much more open and exposing.

Higgs was the first cadet to reach him. "What is it?"

"Danger area—small road crossing. Double-time across and keep a five-meter interval. Don't stop running until we reach the far hill and can take cover."

"How far is it?"

Mason shrugged. "A couple of hundred meters."

"Then we'll be at our site on the edge of the fields, right? The thickets where Kennedy was killed?"

Mason nodded. "Yeah. Follow me."

The field just west of the Daniels home was empty and cold. In the forest, Mason and his squad found their entrance spot because of the snow remaining on the ground being thicker than anywhere else, but it was melting. Already lost was the bloody snow where Kennedy fell. The rest would be gone in a matter of days. As Mason was about to whistle the group to stop, Koch raised an open hand and took a knee. He'd realized where they were, too.

Mason called softly to the group. "If you've got a radio, turn it on."

Booker and Martinez dug into their rucksacks and fumbled for the switches on the ancient AN-PRC 77 radios. Mason watched them hold the receivers to their ears.

"Nothing," Booker said.

Martinez keyed his radio. "Pittsburgh cadre, this is 2nd Squad."

There was no response as Booker also attempted. "Any station, any station, this is 2nd Squad, University of Pittsburgh. Over."

They waited thirty seconds. Mason shook his head. "Spread farther out. We can—"

"No," Stratton said. "Stay tight here and send out heart-and-box method patrols."

It was a good idea. "Stratton, your team does a box method along the way we came in. Higgs, two-man heart method toward the field. Stay in the wood line. See if you can find anything. Booker, stay with me."

The fireteam leaders moved off with their cadets. Stratton would split his team and walk a giant box shape to see if they could find anything. His elements would meet in the middle at the far side of the box and work back through the middle of their route. Higgs and Koch would do a similar method in a heart shape in the opposite direction.

Mason looked at Booker. "Keep trying the radio. Every minute."

"Yeah," Booker said. His eyes were soft and far away.

Mason leaned over. "You with me, or not?"

"What do you mean?"

"Right here, right now," Mason said. "Need you focused on the present. There's nothing we can do otherwise."

Booker grunted and looked away. Mason kept his eyes on Stratton's patrol in case they suddenly disappeared. "Watch Higgs."

"Doing it," Booker said. He then whispered into the radio. "Any station, this is 2nd Squad. Come in."

Mason followed Stratton's progress intently, even failing to hear Booker call twice more with no response. As Stratton turned back toward Mason with a grin on his face, Booker stood straight up behind him.

Mason whirled around to face him. "What are you doing? Get down!"

"We gotta try—"

Mason stood up and grabbed his friend by the load-bearing vest. He dragged the taller cadet back to a kneeling position. "Sit tight, Booker. We're trying. Keep trying the radio."

"Yeah."

Mason kept watch for Stratton and heard Booker half-heartedly transmit on the radio every minute. Time slowed down to a crawl and Mason wondered if something else had happened as Stratton and his team completed the patrol and returned at a slow jog. "Let's get the fuck out of here. We're exposed and we're not going home."

Booker stood up again. "Try again."

Stratton bowed up on Booker. Mason stepped in and pushed Stratton backward. "Knock it off, all of you!" Mason hissed.

"Get your hands off me," Stratton snarled at Mason. He slapped away Mason's hands. "We can't stay out here like this, Mason."

Stratton was right. Booker stepped forward and pointed at Stratton's chest. His eyes were wide and blazed with fury. Mason grabbed at his friend's shoulder to stop him, but Booker had other ideas and went for Stratton.

CRACK!

Mason and Stratton snapped their heads to Higgs standing behind them. A tendril of smoke curled away from the bright red muzzle adapter of her M16.

"What the fuck are you doing?" Stratton growled.

Higgs stepped closer. "Knock it off, Booker. You're all acting like a bunch of toddlers. Get your shit together before we all get killed. You're the squad leader, Mason. You're in charge. Stratton? You're a team leader. That means you do whatever the fuck Mason says. You got that?"

Neither of them said a word. Higgs turned to Booker.

"And you!" she hissed. "We can't get home. There's nothing we can do about it. We tried, just like we said we would and it didn't fucking work! Standing here and fighting just makes us a—"

A solitary burst of rifle fire echoed through the forest. They froze.

Murphy said, "Not near us, but they had to hear all the noise."

"Get your rucks on," Mason demanded. "Let's get the fuck out of here."

"Where?" Koch asked.

"Our farmhouse," Mason said. "We need to have a plan."

There was another rifle shot in the distance, followed by another a few seconds later. These were behind them.

The Danielses.

Stratton whirled at Mason. "We've got to go help them! Come on!"

Mason grabbed at Stratton's vest and made contact. "No! We do this my way!"

Stratton grabbed at his arm. "What if they're in danger? We have to help them!"

"We don't know that!" Mason struggled. "You want to end up like Porter?"

Recognition dawned in Stratton's eyes. "No. We have to move fast, though."

He was right, whether it was guilt or not that welled up in Mason's chest.

"Yeah." Mason let go of Stratton's vest. He turned to the rest of the squad. "Move out through the wood line—stay out of the field." Mason pointed slightly west of the Daniels home. "We'll backtrack into their barn, assess the situation, and do what needs to be done."

"With what? We don't have any—"

"We didn't need them last time. We don't need them now. We have surprise and synchronicity. Now get your shit together, people!" Mason said. Fire burned in his stomach. Their friends, the only ones who'd taken any type of pity on him and his squad, were in danger.

They started moving, Higgs with her fireteam in the front of the Ranger file. Mason took his position in the center, aware that Stratton was only a few feet away and staring holes in his back. The last thing the squad needed was a power struggle, and unless Mason did something, they'd continue to fight. With no cadre and a harsh world around them, one of them could end up dead. Mason shook off the thoughts and gave the double-time motion to Koch at the front of the column.

"Move, people!"

CHAPTER ELEVEN

Sutton lowered the musket from his shoulder and couldn't help smiling. Corporal England's weapon hadn't fired reliably in more than three months. Whatever the gunsmith had done to repair it was admirable work. He set the stock on the ground and held out a hand. "Reload."

Daniels, the gunsmith with the puffing, red cheeks and ragged facial hair, stepped forward with a paper-wrapped cartridge and placed it into Sutton's hand. For a moment, Sutton stared at the man with what he knew was a thin smile that could mean many things, none of them pleasant.

"A good load?"

Daniels nodded. "Should hit a target at seventy yards. Maybe more in the hands of a good shot."

Sutton allowed his smile to widen. *A challenge?*

He looked across the field toward the skeleton of a half-collapsed farmhouse just visible through the naked trees. "How far to that house?"

"Half mile, give or take."

"Too bad," Sutton said. He found a tall, ragged oak whose trunk split into a thick V twenty feet above the ground. It looked to be within range. "How far to that big tree?" he nodded as he withdrew the plunging rod and prepared to load the musket.

Daniels looked into the distance. "About that far. Seventy yards."

"Right," Sutton said. He poured the powder into the barrel and gently rolled the ball in his fingers before dropping it into the smooth tube. With the tamping rod, he tapped the ball into the powder to pack it tightly. Ramming it home would produce a greater ignition and propel the ball farther with greater accuracy. Satisfied, he checked the flint and found it satisfactory. He raised the rifle to his shoulder and paused.

"Could you hit that tree, Mister Daniels?" The smile again creased his face.

Daniels shrugged. "Been some time since I shot a ball."

"You don't test your work?"

"I don't have to. My repairs will work every time."

Sutton nodded. The man knew the right things to say. Perhaps his loyalties were well placed. "You've repaired the worst rifle in my platoon, Mister Daniels. I'd like to see if it's more accurate than when it came from His Majesty's armorer in Boston. I'd like you to fire as well."

"I believe you'll do far better than I will, Captain Sutton."

Sutton nodded. "Perhaps, but I need to see the gunsmith fire a weapon. Then I'll know if you truly understand what His Majesty wants from your services."

Daniels turned to the stack of muskets and selected one. Like Sutton, he went through the ritual of loading the musket with practiced ease. "I've fired thousands of shots, Captain Sutton. In the service of His Majesty against the French while you were toddling around England in diapers."

A veteran? Sutton smiled. "Then I'd have to assume you'll fire it as well as I will."

Daniels smiled with one side of his mouth. "I'll hit the tree, but I'm not sure what point it makes for you."

Sutton laughed and clapped the gunsmith on the shoulder. "The point is that you can shoot, Mister Daniels. And by verifying that"—his smile faded and he stared into the older man's face—"you'll be able to fire upon any rebels that seek out your services."

Daniels snorted, but did not look away. A sign of strength. "Any man could be a rebel and there are a hundred farmers and hunters nearby who've had me look at their guns. Nary a regular soldier, sir. But if my friends and customers are rebels, I know not. Nor do I care. I don't need another war. One is enough."

The man's words were true, Sutton decided in an instant. A man's eyes were an indicator not of who they were, but the culmination of the things they'd seen. Daniels had the look of a man tired of war. A man who'd likely seen too much and made his living taking care of the weapons of others. For the moment, he even appeared to be a man loyal to the Crown.

"Very well. Shall we?" Sutton said. "A yard below the notch, then?"

"Yes," Daniels said and raised the musket to his shoulder. Sutton watched him sight the barrel, inhale sharply and let it out slowly. So intent was he on the gunsmith's process that he almost flinched when the shot rang out. A fist-sized chunk of bark flew from the trunk of the distant tree.

"Well done," Sutton said. Raising the musket to his shoulder quickly, he performed the same ritual from His Majesty's manual of arms and fired. A similar piece of bark fell toward the ground. "Splendid. Very nice work, Mister Daniels."

"Thank you, sir."

Sutton lowered the musket and set the stock to the ground again. He leaned on it casually. "His Majesty thanks you for your loyalty and your services, now and during the war."

Daniels nodded, but his eyes were down and away. "What else can I do for you, sir?"

Emily must be inside, he thought. "Are you as talented in the repair of pistols?"

"I am." Daniels looked down at the weapon at Sutton's side. "Giving you trouble?"

Sutton laughed. "Reliability isn't its strongest asset, no."

Daniels gestured to the house. "Come inside then. I'll look at it and have my daughter serve tea." His neck ticked to one side. "A bit cold today."

Sutton nodded, his thoughts now on the pretty young woman he'd snuck glances at during summer-market days in Trenton. Daniels was already moving to the house. Sutton slung his musket on his left shoulder and walked after him. Geese descended across the field toward the far wood line.

Daniels pushed through the modest door and stepped into the darkened interior. "Come in, Captain."

"Thank you."

They passed through the tight foyer to the kitchen and Daniels held out a hand. "May I?"

Sutton nodded. "Certainly."

No sooner had he turned over the pistol than Daniels' lovely daughter entered the room. Her hair was up but not covered by a traditional kerchief or bonnet. In the light from the solitary window and the fireplace, it glowed. Sutton let his eyes linger over the swell of her bust and the curve of her waist.

"Emily? Would you make a cup of tea for the captain?" Daniels asked. "I'll be in the workshop for a moment."

"Yes, Father." Emily nodded and stepped toward the hearth. A kettle rested to one side. Sutton noticed a stack of rifles in the opposite corner and stepped in that direction. Inspecting them, he found two Hessian ones and a curious rabble of muskets in terrible condition.

"Your father is repairing these rifles?"

Emily did not look up from the kettle. "Yes, sir. Those are ones he hasn't completed yet. He's been hard at work on yours, Captain."

She looked up at him and smiled, except her eyes were those of a frightened rabbit. Perfect.

"You're much prettier than I remember from your trips to the local market," Sutton said. He moved to stand in front of her and raised a hand to her face. Fingertips against her skin, he flushed with sudden, rampant desire. The girl's fear filled his nostrils and threatened to make him shake. He reached down and grabbed her arm. "You'll be my guest for the Christmas Ball."

"I-I think not," she said and flinched away. He tightened his grip.

"Those rifles, not the Hessian ones. They belong to Washington's rebels, don't they?" he hissed at her.

"I don't—"

He jerked her close. "Quiet!" His voice was a harsh whisper. The girl whimpered in his grasp. "Tell me."

"No! They're not anything of the sort."

Sutton grinned. "You're certain."

She nodded. "Please let me go. You're hurting me."

He relaxed his grip, but did not let go of her arm. "Traitors are to be shot, Miss Daniels. Unless you're my guest, that is."

"Please—"

A scuffling sound came from the attached workshop. Sutton dropped the girl's arm and placed the practiced, charming smile on his face. The gunsmith appeared in the doorway with his pistol.

"Good news?" Sutton asked.

Daniels shrugged. "Nothing seems to be wrong with it." He placed the pistol and a pistol cartridge into Sutton's hands.

"Good," Sutton said. "I was just telling your beautiful daughter that this curious collection of rifles makes me believe you're supplying services to Washington and his rebels. Treason equals death."

Daniels did not move. "I told you outside, Captain. Farmers and hunters. Men without money who need their weapons to put food on the table. They're the—"

"Are they Hunterdon men?" Sutton asked. Across the northern New Jersey countryside, citizens friendly to the rebel cause had rallied under a man named Dickinson and called themselves the Hunterdon men, causing havoc along British and Hessian supply routes.

"I don't know."

Sutton turned toward the man, squaring his shoulders. He ripped open the cartridge and began to load the pistol with slow, deliberate movements. "If they were, and information could be exchanged, you would be in the favor of His Majesty, Mister Daniels. I'd hate to believe my initial impression of you was favorable if you were withholding information on the rebel army's whereabouts."

"They're farmers. If they're Hunterdon men I can't say," Daniels said. "They're to come by the day after Christmas."

Sutton pushed the ball into the pistol's barrel. "I see."

He rammed the ball home with the smaller rod from his belt and raised the pistol, inspecting it in the dim light. Satisfied at the pistol's appearance, and the fear streaming across the daughter's face, he held the weapon aloft for a moment, studying the barrel before he holstered the weapon. "Very well, Mister Daniels. A patrol of dragoons will collect our weapons, and theirs, this afternoon or tomorrow at the latest. If you wish to enjoy His Majesty's protection, you'll turn away other customers. Is that clear? If you fail to—"

"I'll go." Emily stepped forward. "I'll go to your ball, sir, just don't threaten us anymore."

For a split second, Sutton heard blood rushing through his ears. The threat died on his lips. "Of course. Christmas Eve then. Be ready at sundown. I'll send a wagon with escort for you."

He stomped to the kitchen door and turned back to the gun-smith. "Remember our arrangement, Mister Daniels. Turn over everything or face an official inquiry."

Daniels nodded. The man's face was impassive and as much as it infuriated Sutton's drive to demean and dehumanize civil-ians, it was impressive to see. "You'll have those weapons, and the Hessian ones I'll finish today."

At the end of the lane, where the thin road into the Dan-ielses' property met the Trenton-Princeton Road, Sutton paused. Midafternoon sunlight streamed through breaks in the low cloud cover. There was no warmth on his face as he sat and looked back up the road. As he nudged his mount toward the garrison, Sut-ton determined that Daniels was worth watching. If the farmers were Hunterdon men or not didn't really matter. Christmas Day, he'd capture them and gain more intelligence he could choose to give to Rall or take directly to Lord General Howe. Perhaps there would be an advantage.

But what if Daniels lied?

The thought stopped him for a moment, but he realized that Rall was a buffoon but his troops had some usefulness. The gun-smith bore watching and the hapless mercenaries were good at surveillance because it took little effort.

From the relative warmth of Daniels' barn, Mason peeked through the door as the British soldier rode away. Murphy lay next to him. "Who do you think that was?"

"Officer. See that one epaulet on his shoulder? He's a captain, and a dragoon, too."

Mason squinted his eyes. "That's what the helmet is for, right?"

"Think light cavalry." Murphy stared out through the crack. "There was a platoon or so of them left in Trenton by the Brit-ish. I could never find out much about them. There wasn't much in the history books. Maybe twenty of them at the time of the battle. They run for Princeton over the Assunpink Creek bridge, I think."

"The what creek?"

Murphy smiled. "Assunpink Creek. No shit."

Mason shrugged. "You think Daniels is helping the British?"

Murphy shrugged. "I don't think so, but it's hard to say, Mason. There were a lot of duplicitous people who walked a very thin line of treason against their newfound Republic or the Crown that still claimed them. I suspect that Mister Daniels is the only gunsmith in the area and is good at what he does. He probably has rifles for both sides in his workshop."

Mason shook his head. "You think he can get us to Washington?"

"If he can't, I can navigate us there. I mean, I think I have a pretty good idea of where we are. We just need to get to McKonkey's Ferry. Colonel Glover and his Durham boats will be there tomorrow night. He can get us across and escort us to Washington."

"Without an introduction? We're likely to get shot, Murphy."

Murphy chuckled. "You got any other ideas?"

"Not really." Mason watched the dragoon officer ride away slowly. As the officer moved out of sight from the door, Mason crept to other cracks in the siding to watch the man depart. Just as Mason prepared to move the squad toward the Daniels home, the red-coated officer stopped at the road junction and waited.

"Come on," Mason breathed. If the man would get farther down the Trenton Road, they could move. After what felt like an eternity, the officer rode into the distance at a slow trot. Mason waited three minutes before turning to the squad. They were spread through the small barn, peering out of cracks and keeping security by appearance, but he knew their minds were elsewhere.

"Psst," he whispered at them all. As they turned their heads, he waved them in to the middle of the barn silently. Stratton came last, a visible shiner under his left eye. He shuffled into the loose circle opposite of Mason, his face impassive.

Mason cleared his throat. *What the hell can I possibly say to them?*

Higgs rescued his pause. "What's the plan, Mason?"

"Yeah," he said. "We're stuck here. At least that's how it looks. We have two options. We can run and find someplace out west to hide or we can go to General Washington."

Higgs shook her head. "No, Mason. We have only one option. We have to go to Washington. If the British get that rifle, the entire Industrial Revolution gets accelerated. If we go, we can help win the war faster and set America on a faster course to match the British. What we know is more powerful than if we're on the battlefield."

"Field conditions for us suck," Murphy said. "For the Continental Army, they're deadly and getting worse every day. Dysentery, mainly."

Koch rumbled to life. "We can help that, too. Simple things like hygiene, right? Washing hands?"

Higgs nodded. "There's a lot we can do, guys. It's a simple choice."

"We should put it to a vote," Dunaway said. All eyes turned to her. The freshman had been silent for the better part of twenty-four hours.

Stratton smiled at her. "Sorry, Dunaway. This isn't a choice. It's a decision. Mason's in charge and we follow his lead, you get it?" He looked up at Mason and nodded.

Mason cleared his throat to cover his surprise at Stratton's words. "We get to Washington. First, we find out what the fuck just happened here and if we can really trust Mister Daniels."

Mason knocked twice on the door and flinched backward as the door flung open and Emily stepped into his face.

"You! Where were you? That redcoat bastard was here in our home!" She stammered, red-faced and breathless. "He—He threatened us! Why didn't you kill him?"

Mason pointed at the parlor. "Can we come inside before we're seen?"

Emily stepped back, flustered. "Yes, of course."

Mason stepped aside and waved Higgs and her team inside. The two young women said hello as the squad filed past with Stratton checking their rear security. Relative darkness in the inside of the cabin made it hard for Mason to see. He stepped inside and closed the door behind them. He turned to Emily. "Are you both okay? We heard gunfire."

"Captain Sutton," she said with clear distaste. "The leader of the dragoons in Trenton. Father is repairing their weapons. The good captain came by to test them and our loyalties."

Mason squinted at her. "What does that mean?"

"He threatened us. Father is to stop working on any weapon other than the British and Hessian ones. If he doesn't, he has to provide information on the rebel soldiers who come by to have their weapons repaired." Emily moved toward the kitchen away from the rest of the squad in the parlor. Mason followed.

Mental pieces began to come together. "Your father is providing information to Washington, isn't he? And he's obviously willing to provide information to the British, too."

Emily moved to the fireplace, her back to Mason. "You don't understand. We're trapped here. Any error will cost us our lives."

"Yeah, I do understand." Mason stepped around the table. The pile of white summer linens caught his eye again. "We can't get back, Miss Daniels. We have to find our way to—"

"Emily." She turned and half-smiled at him. "Is Mason your first name?"

Mason blinked. "Last name. Surname. My first name is Jameel."

She nodded. "Now, we can speak as friends."

Mason froze for a moment and then smiled as she did. "I hope so. We need some real friends here."

She nodded her head. "We are your friends, Jameel. You asked if my father was providing information to Washington and the British. The answer is yes, but it depends on what you call information to which side."

"Deception?" Mason asked. "He's lying to both sides?"

There was a scuff and Daniels stepped into the room with a musket held at his waist, barrel pointing away from them. What Mason knew as the "low ready" position. He shook his head. "Half-truths to get by, Mason."

"This isn't a game," Mason said. "You're in danger."

Daniels laughed. "You're damned right we are, Mason."

Higgs and Stratton appeared in the doorway and he waved them inside. Daniels didn't move. Emily stood by the fire with her hands at her waist, frozen. Her father cradled the musket in his arms and appeared to be relaxed, but with his shoulders square and hands at the ready, Mason couldn't be sure. For a split second, Mason thought of the decisive moment in every cowboy movie, where the combatants looked at each other and ultimately decided how to go for their guns faster than the other.

"You're trying to decide if you can trust me, aren't you?" Daniels asked.

Mason nodded. "Yeah, something like that."

"I fought for the British in the Indian Wars, Mason. When the Continental Congress started this mess for freedom and independence, I was against every part of it. My commanding officer in the Indian Wars was for it. I'd follow that man to the very gates of Hell itself." He paused. "I knew he was right, Mason."

"You served with Washington, then?" Higgs asked.

Daniels nodded. "And I still serve with him, but I tread lightly on the British side, Mason. Since they've come to our land, we have to. You understand that?"

"You have British and Hessian rifles in your workshop, don't you?" Mason asked.

"Twenty-two of them," Daniels said. "Fourteen for farmers friendly to the cause, as well. There are forty-two muskets in the barn. Those are for General Washington's cousin. His men should be by tomorrow to get them. You probably were sitting on them without even noticing them."

Mason looked at Higgs. Her blue eyes were wide, but she exuded confidence. Stratton gaped. "*You* can get us to Washington?" he asked. "Within the next twenty-four hours?"

Daniels nodded. "Faster than that. There should be a way."

"McKonkey's Ferry?" Mason asked, remembering his conversation with Murphy. "Colonel Glover, right? He'll be in position tomorrow night."

"How do you know that, Mason?" Daniels said. "You know it all, don't you? I think it's time you share your information, and I'll do the same. Is that fair enough for you?"

Mason could not help but smile. "Higgs? Will you ask Murphy to come in here?" He looked at the pile of white linens and the idea clicked into reality like the tumblers of a lock. Murphy said that storms were coming and the last thing they needed to do was to stand out like sore thumbs.

Emily squinted. "What is it, Mason?"

"You need to know the truth," he said. "But, can we borrow those sheets?"

CHAPTER TWELVE

No sooner had he reached the outer pickets of Trenton, with the Hessian regulars stamping their feet in the cold around tiny fires, when Sutton decided that a simple increase in patrols around the Daniels homestead would not do. Patrol frequency he could manipulate without consulting the Hessian commander. Constant surveillance would undoubtedly rile Colonel Rall, but it was necessary for Sutton to gain the upper hand he craved. By the looks on the haggard Hessian faces, Rall had them on constant alert for yet another day. Inside the friendly area, Sutton was no less concerned with his security. His eyes swept the terrain in front of him constantly. Washington was, if anything, a gentleman and he would attack like a gentleman. The roads and wide spaces around Trenton were covered with Hessian patrols and guard posts. His personal intensity burned regardless. He found himself staring down the Pennington Road as he crossed it as if willing the Continental Army to come dressed for battle.

Sutton grinned at the thought and his mind went through a common exercise, asking himself what he would do if in command. How would he defend Trenton? The city itself was indefensible, even with the redoubts the Hessian engineers wanted to emplace. No, the keys to Trenton were the avenues of approach. The roads and the river itself.

The cold, gray water looked impassive in the afternoon sunlight. Maybe Washington waited for the river to freeze—to cross it in the night like his minions had done—

"Hauptmann Sutton," a familiar voice snapped him away from his thoughts. Sturm, red-faced and breathing hard from running, slid to a stop next to Sutton's horse. "Colonel Rall would see you, presently."

Would he?

Sutton looked again at the river, decided that Washington wouldn't risk his troops to thin, moving sheets of ice, and turned slowly back to Sturm. "And the nature of the colonel's request would be what, Lieutenant?"

"The colonel demands that you see him at once. Your patrols are too short and do nothing to uncover the whereabouts of the enemy."

He wanted to laugh, but kept his face calm. "Return to the good colonel and tell him that I'll be there shortly, once my horse and men are taken care of. The enemy is on the far side of the river. What we face here is nothing more than..." He let the words slip away. General Grant would undoubtedly agree that the Hessian commander was incompetent. There was no reason to blatantly call Colonel Rall or any of his subordinate commanders idiots to their faces just yet. There would be a time in the very near future, and he would restrain himself until that moment.

"Tell your colonel I will be there after my horse and my men are prepared for tomorrow. Dismissed, Lieutenant."

Sturm saluted and trotted away. *Let Rall stew and fumble in his anxiety. The man knows nothing of war. Washington and his men are not coming.* There, he'd thought it. The citizens in revolt to their south were, rightly, upset with the conduct of the Hessian troops over the previous months. The Hessian occupation was more pillaging than peaceful interaction with the colonists. Whether they were loyal to the Crown or not was of little concern to the Hessians as they stole, raped, and burned their way to the Delaware. The rise in violence from insurgents was to be expected. Von Donop would put them down handily, and quickly. Until then, Rall commanded Trenton unchecked and unbalanced. The thought soured his stomach.

And here they are, the mess I've been left to tend.

His orders, tucked gently inside his tunic, were signed by Lord General Howe himself and had been given by hand through General Cornwallis with explicit instructions to support Rall's operations but report extensively to the British garrison under the command of General Grant. His platoon of twenty dragoons were the closest British unit to the likely position of Washington's forces. From here, he could develop the situation and see if the presentation of a softer target lured the old fox out of the hole he'd prepared on the far side of the Delaware.

Sutton made his way lazily down Queen Street and turned for the dragoon's stables and his men's quarters when Sturm again came running behind him in the mud. The Hessian lieutenant fell noisily in the slop a good thirty yards behind Sutton, but the sound was as if the young man dove into the muck beside Sutton's mount.

"Captain Sutton!" Sturm called from the mud, slinging it off his hands in a disgusted gesture. "Colonel Rall demands to see you. Immediately."

"I gave you direction, Lieutenant. Did you misunderstand my intent?"

"Colonel Rall is my commander, sir. His rank and authority outweigh yours in the present events." Sturm stood in the muck with his shoulders erect and square. The mousy little lieutenant wanted to hide behind the orders of his commander. Fine.

"Very well." Sutton gestured to Sturm. "You will take my mount to the stable and—"

Sturm sputtered in German and then in his accented English, "S-sir! My orders are—"

"I don't care what your orders are!" Sutton roared and jumped from the saddle in one smooth move. With his mount's reins in hand, he stomped back to Sturm and slapped the younger man in the chest with them. "Do what I say, Lieutenant! I am a captain of His Majesty's army and you will damned sure follow my orders to the letter. Is that clear?"

The nearly deserted street was silent around them; Sutton knew everyone that was there watched them intently. Aware of his flushed face, Sutton forced himself to take a breath and he leaned closer to Sturm. "Get out of my sight, Sturm. Do not bother me again unless Washington crosses the river. I'll take whatever orders I am to receive from Colonel Rall himself."

"But, you'll need a translator." Sturm's voice was a whisper.

Sutton laughed. "A translator? You misunderstand your precious commander and a trained officer like myself, Sturm! War is very simple. I put my troops here, he puts his troops there."

"But Washington—"

"Damn that man!" Sutton roared, not caring who heard him. "If I were in command we would have already crossed the god-damned river and ended this bloody war. Do you understand?"

Sturm's widened eyes were not on his face. Sutton grabbed his ruffled collar and yanked the younger man closer. The stench of cabbage came with it. "Colonel Rall. He is approaching."

Rage was not a common emotion. Only once had he struck another officer and that had been for cowardice in the face of the enemy. With the portly colonel stomping up the muddy street and cursing in his guttural tongue, Sutton knew the source of his rage was not young Sturm, nor Washington as he'd initially believed.

Sutton turned and saluted with his inner cheek firmly clenched between his teeth. "Good afternoon, Herr Colonel."

Rall glanced at Sturm and gave a curt nod. His portly frame and red cheeks reminded Sutton of something from his childhood, but he couldn't place it. He raised the thick finger at Sutton's face and began to sputter in a deep, thick accent that sounded like he was trying to cough out his lungs every third or fourth syllable.

Sturm finally began the translation. "Colonel Rall wants to know where your men are. Specifically, the two patrols he requested on the Princeton and Pennington Roads. Reports are rampant of musket fire and armed incursions to the north."

Sutton wanted to laugh and covered the smile threatening to crease his face by clearing his throat. "There is nothing going on to the north. I was on the Pennington Road myself this morning, alone. Our concerns should be south, with Colonel Von Donop, sir." He waited as Sturm translated and fresh red color crept upward from Rall's ornate collar into his face with every word. Was that a hint of alcohol on the colonel's breath?

Rall erupted with a harsh sentence that Sutton understood only through repetition. "Washington is coming."

Every day. He raised a hand to keep Sturm from blabbering. "The only thing out there are disgruntled farmers who think they can help Washington by harassing us at every turn. I will take care of them by Christmas Day."

Rall hardly waited for Sturm to finish the translation before launching into his reply. Sturm translated, "He says you don't understand the situation. Your headquarters does not support us. General Grant refuses to even accept correspondence from anyone but Colonel Von Donop."

"Does Von Donop agree with the assessment that Washington's arrival is imminent?"

A troubled look passed over Rall's face. "What Colonel Von Donop believes is irrelevant. General Grant is prepared to sacrifice our forces."

No great loss.

Sutton cleared his throat again. "I don't think that's the case—"

"You are ordered to increase patrol frequency, day and night until the situation quiets. Your men will follow Colonel Rall's regimental duty schedule to the letter," Sturm said, his eyes nowhere close to Sutton's.

"Respectfully, Colonel," Sutton nodded solemnly, "I don't take my orders from you."

Rall barked a short laugh and withdrew a paper from his jacket. The familiar red wax of General Grant's seal said otherwise. Sutton knew what it said before Rall began to read. His Majesty's army would not be bullied or coerced into supporting the Hessians or anyone else.

They are placating him by assigning my men to his fruitless and perpetual alerts.

"You do now," Sturm said and translated the order. "Captain Sutton, His Majesty's dragoons, is to put his men at the colonel's every service until this situation has quieted. Within a week, at most, we'll expect Captain Sutton in Princeton to make his full report."

Sutton took a long breath through his nose. The air bit and smelled of venison. "Very well," he said, trying not to sound amused by the whole spectacle in his utter and complete rage. The wobbly colonel now away from his precious band and standing in a muddy street to pass his orders to His Majesty's dragoons was almost laughable. "Tell the colonel we will patrol along the river and the main roads to Trenton. You may also tell him that I expect to find nothing of consequence and would recommend, respectfully, that your attention be diverted to the south and what Colonel Von Donop faces. Unless the river freezes tonight, Washington will not dare to cross it."

"You really believe that, sir?" Sturm stared wide-eyed at him.

"I do. My commanders in Princeton understand the situation

far better and their guidance is much clearer, Lieutenant. His Majesty's army is in winter garrison and has asked your commander to secure this frontier. Colonel Von Donop understands that and has decided to take action rather than wait for a coward without the fortitude or the soldiers to attack this position until spring. If ever."

Sturm relayed his words and Rall turned on a heel and stomped away in the mud. Sturm followed a few seconds later and Sutton watched them gingerly work through the mud of Queen Street as they headed for Rall's headquarters and the shelter of good alcohol and a game of cards. The young captain of the dragoons clutched his stomach and barely contained the laughter threatening to erupt from his mouth as he watched the Hessian commander retreat into his constant fear. All the man needed was the band playing to make it a perfectly abysmal scene.

December 23, 1776

They'd waited out a long, full day at the Simmons farmhouse. Without a large fire, the day had been cold, but they'd been able to rest and stay inside their sleeping bags to rest. At fifty percent security, Mason encouraged them to sleep as much as possible before moving through the night. McKonkey's Ferry, where Colonel Glover would be in position with his fleet of Durham boats, was a little over two and a half miles from their objective rally point position on an azimuth of three hundred ten degrees. They'd start moving an hour after sunset. At the ferry, they'd wait for a boat to cross the river carrying Daniels. His wagon would have one lantern lit if the passage was off. If two lanterns were lit, the squad would leave their position in the wood line above the ferry and board the boat across the Delaware.

As the sun set to the west, Mason rousted everyone who'd been able to sleep their last shift. Pre-combat checks and inspections would be the second item after making sure everyone had eaten and replenished their water supplies. Higgs had found a spring a few hundred meters away and they'd filled their canteens a few times over relishing the sweet, pure water. As they ate in relative silence, Murphy looked up at Mason with his eyes wide and bright.

"Holy shit, man." Murphy chuckled.

"What is it, Murphy?"

The sophomore laughed. "If we pull this movement off, we're going to do something every kid in America has wanted to do since they started school."

"Meet George Washington," Martinez said around a mouthful of pasta. "See if he cannot tell a lie."

Murphy chuckled and shook his head. "Ask him if he really chopped down a cherry tree."

"You won't even be able to speak, much less make a comment like that." Koch crumpled up an envelope that had held crackers and threw it across their loose circle as the group laughed nervously. "You'll just be grinning like little kids when we meet him. Guaranteed."

"Doesn't seem real," Dunaway said. Her voice was quiet, but firmer than Mason could remember. The shell appeared to crack a little more every day.

"Yeah," Booker snorted. "We should have tried to go back today."

"We tried yesterday, Booker." Mason met his friend's eyes with a hard stare. "It didn't work."

"And it might've worked today, Mason."

Mason shook his head. "We've been through this, man. We tried. It's a done deal."

Koch cleared his throat. "Unless it only works on that day? Or when the planet's in the same position?"

"Wait a year?" Booker asked.

"If we make it through this, we'll come back here in a year, Booker. You have my word."

"But a year might go by back home."

"Or it might be ten seconds, man." Mason gestured with his hands wide. "None of us understand what happened. We have no idea what might work, okay?"

Booker looked down into his MRE for a long moment before he dabbed at his nose and looked up again. "You promise?"

"A year," Mason nodded.

"Deal."

Good, Mason thought. He took a deep breath. "Murphy? You want to tell us what's going on right now?"

"Not much," Murphy said. "Colonel Von Donop, the senior Hessian commander, engaged a large group of rebel sympathizers, not the army, south of Trenton this afternoon. He'll decide to stay there a couple of days. His troops get blind drunk tonight and the good colonel finds comfort in the arms of a beautiful widow, so the story goes."

Mason smiled. Fresh research and a photographic memory would serve Murphy well. All Mason had to do was keep him alive. *Shit, all of them.* He blinked away the thought. "What about Washington?"

"If I remember right, Washington received a message yesterday from his adjutant down at Bristol. I can't remember his name but he sees a clear advantage and begs Washington to attack. They're basically laying out the plan today and preparing to do the shaping activities. They'll decide to launch an attack tonight but keep the operation a secret from the men until the last possible moment."

"And tomorrow?"

Murphy shrugged. "Pretty sure that Christmas Eve and Christmas Day are mainly spent preparing. Christmas Day is fairly quiet, except a group of Hunterdon men engage Rall's outer security. Rall thinks that's Washington's long-overdue attack. As soon as it's over, Rall believes Washington retreated in fear and he gets overconfident."

"That opens the way for Washington's attack," Stratton said.

Murphy grinned. "Somewhat. Washington is committed, and the decision to hit Trenton on the twenty-sixth gives his army enough time to prepare and get any last-minute intelligence. The weather is a huge factor, too."

"Like this? Clear and cold?" Higgs asked.

"No," Murphy grinned. "A huge nor'easter rolls in while Washington is on the march. I mean it gets really shitty and fast. Like wicked bad. They come out of the snow and surprise the Hessians."

Mason sat upright. "What don't we know? What doesn't Washington know?"

Murphy leaned forward and pointed at the floor. He quickly scratched a long Y shape in the dirt. "Washington is here and Trenton is here. His attack plan has three prongs. General Ewing, the same guy whose been fucking with the Hessians for a week, is supposed to cross at the Trenton ferry. Farther south, a prong under General Cadwalader is supposed to attack near Mount Holly to keep Hessian forces there from responding. Neither Ewing nor Cadwalader get across the river because of the ice that stacks up on the night of the attack."

"There was no effect on Washington's crossing though, right? I mean the weather and surprise worked to Washington's favor and the Hessians didn't put up much of a fight being drunk and all." Stratton grinned.

Murphy wagged a finger at Stratton. "What you learned in school is all wrong, man. The Hessians aren't drunk at all. Most of them are exhausted, but they're not drunk. That's a myth. And the Hessians don't immediately strike their colors and surrender. They try to counterattack. A couple of times. That's when Colonel Rall is killed."

"No shit?" Mason said. "That doesn't match anything I learned in school."

"I know, right?" Murphy said. "So, Washington is facing a good enemy force that is simply tired and without good communication in poor weather conditions, surprise takes the field. The Hessians capitulate fairly easily and with minimal casualties to the friendlies."

Koch spoke up. "What about the British? The dragoons?"

"It's a platoon or so. Roughly twenty men, I think. Since they have horses, they escape over the Assunpink Creek bridge before Washington's forces can get to them." Murphy took a bite of crackers and peanut butter. As he chewed, he said, "Presumably, they notify the British garrison at Princeton. The Brits counterattack on January 2."

Mason took a deep breath and looked at his watch. "We've got to get going. Look, I'm gonna be honest with you, this isn't going to be easy. Yes, the terrain is okay and we only have a couple of miles to go, but we've got to be silent and slow. There's no telling what's out there."

Stratton tapped the musket leaning against his rucksack. Daniels supplied them with ten rounds of ammunition apiece. "Good thing we have these and know how to fire them."

Mason took a breath but didn't answer. They all had one round loaded, and in the dark, under fire, there was no way in hell they'd be able to get off a second shot. "Let's make sure it doesn't come to that."

For a moment, all of them looked at him and he knew it was

time to say something memorable. Or something that, at the very least, would assuage their fears. Nothing came to mind. After a moment, he spread his palms to them.

"Let's just do everything like our lives depend on it tonight. Once we get across that river, to Washington, things will be a little better. We'll be on friendly ground and can figure out our next move. We're a few miles and a boat ride from there. Daniels is supposed to cross at midnight, if all goes well. Let's make sure we're there to meet him."

Higgs closed her MRE and stood in the growing darkness. "Bravo team, finish up. Break down your M16s and stuff them into your rucks. Make sure everything is strapped down tight and silent. I've got some tape if you need it."

"Alpha team"—Stratton stood—"same thing. We're leaving here in fifteen minutes. Murphy, you're on point. Koch, you've got the compass. I'll take pace count."

Mason watched his friends, his fellow cadets, get to their feet without a word. They were solemn and serious. Were they ready for combat? He didn't know, nor did he want to think about it.

Miles to go before I sleep, he thought and mentally winced. His mother loved Robert Frost's poetry. *I can't think about you right now, Mom. Just not right now.* But the thoughts didn't immediately fade.

Do you even know that I'm gone?

Mason shook off the thoughts by packing his gear and getting ready to move. There would be time enough for confronting his demons after Trenton, if he lived that long. If not, the least he could do was make a difference in this new republic. The thought cheered him almost immediately. Not many others would ever have the chance he would. He reached into his pocket and felt the bicentennial quarter there. Putting it into George Washington's hands would rival anything he would have ever done in his own time, that was for certain.

CHAPTER THIRTEEN

November 2008
Fort Dix, New Jersey

Sam Graves stood silently next to the commanding general of Fort Dix, Major General James Cuthbert, as the general briefed the families of his missing cadets. Two days had passed since their last radio transmission. Ground and aerial searches had revealed nothing but a ragged oblong of dry, empty forest surrounded by the deep snow of the last twenty-four hours. There was extensive tree damage on all sides of the area as well, but no one wanted to talk about it openly. A variety of three-letter agencies were on the ground studying the area, but it was abundantly clear that the cadets were nowhere to be found.

"It's been two days, General." Vivian Mason leaned forward in her theater chair and pointed at him. "Fort Dix isn't that large and you can't find them? There has to be some explanation!"

Cuthbert took a deep breath, removed his glasses, and rubbed the inside corners of his eyes. "No, Colonel Mason, there's not. We'll continue looking for your son and the rest of the cadets at first light. We've exhausted the training area where they were last seen, and we're working out from there in waves. I have soldiers walking shoulder to shoulder through those training ranges right now. The local authorities outside the installation are also looking for your children." The use of Mrs. Mason's retired rank should have been respectful, but Graves thought it sounded insincere from the general. Obviously, colonel-retired Mason wasn't going to be satisfied with his answer, and rightly so.

"What about their cellphones? Have you had any pings from them?"

Cuthbert shook his head. "No. None of the phones with the cadets are activating when called."

Colonel-retired Mason looked at Graves. "You've been calling them?"

"Yes, ma'am. We've tried every single one of them more than a dozen times. There's been no response," Graves said. "We'll keep trying and—"

"We'll find them. Thank you for your patience," Cuthbert interrupted. With a curt nod at his provost marshal, Cuthbert walked out of the auditorium. After a moment of awkward silence, the families all watching him and speechless for the first time as a field-grade officer, Graves followed the general and met him in the foyer. Outside were a growing collection of media that he obviously did not want to engage. He looked at Sam. "Get the families to lodging and be at the 0600 update brief, Colonel."

"Sir, what aren't you telling them?"

Cuthbert frowned. "You have your orders, Colonel. Do I make myself clear?"

Graves nodded. "At 0600, what are you going to tell them, sir?"

"Don't make this more difficult on yourself, Graves. I'd suggest you find your cadets before I do." Cuthbert waggled a finger in front of his face and walked through the doors and into the media circus. In the incessant flashes of camera and the stark brightness of the television cameras, Graves understood. They weren't going to find the cadets and he was going to take the fall. Left with his orders, he moved back to the families and got them moving through the back door of the theater to their waiting transportation.

Moving the families to the dedicated vans was easier than he'd imagined, but once they were on board, he moved to his rental car to follow them to the Marriott in nearby Trenton. As he turned the ignition, the satellite radio news channel was talking about the strange disappearance and relating it to a terrorist incident. Graves snapped the radio knob to OFF and left the base in silence.

This doesn't make any fucking sense.

His hands gripped the steering wheel tightly. Porter, especially, would never do anything of the sort. The rest of them were good, young kids. Any idea for all of them to suddenly go AWOL for more than two days made no sense at all. The possibility that maybe they were captured by someone grew stronger, save for the fact that this was New Jersey and—

Just outside the main gate, his cell phone rang from the interior of the center console. He'd left it in the car all day. The number was from Minnesota, and not familiar. Probably more press. He pushed the talk button. "Lieutenant Colonel Graves. I have no comment on the situation."

"That's a shame," a man laughed. His British accent was smooth and friendly. "Colonel, my name is Doctor Malcolm O'Connell. I'd like to have a word with you, if you have time tonight."

"I really have no comment, sir." Graves made the turn onto the I-95. The man's name was familiar. *From graduate school?*

"You're staying in the Marriott downtown, correct?"

Graves nearly froze. The location of the families was a closely guarded secret, at least until the press eventually caught wind of it. "I am, how did you know that?"

"It's a long story. The VIP lounge on the concierge floor. I'll be the guy at the bar who looks like a college professor."

"I'm not at liberty to discuss the situation, Doctor O'Connell."

"You're not going to find them, but I think I know where they are. I'll be in the bar in ten minutes." The line clicked off and Graves fingered the keypad for a moment and considered calling the commanding general, or even 911, but hesitated. The name Malcolm O'Connell triggered a response from his memory, finally. If Graves was right, Malcolm O'Connell was a theoretical mathematician, and a fairly distinguished one at that. During Graves' graduate work at Michigan, he'd read a paper written by O'Connell on time manipulation. Most of it hadn't made immediate sense to Graves, but the concepts stayed with him enough to read several books on time and logic in what spare time he had.

How did he get my number?

Shit, what do I do now?

As Graves put the phone down he made up his mind to meet the man. He wasn't going to get answers from General Cuthbert and whoever came to the disappearance site. Graves finished the drive to the hotel debating whether or not to check in with his wife. After deciding not to—the kids would be starting bedtime routines—he parked and boarded the elevator. He and the rest of the families were on the concierge floor where armed soldiers guarded the elevator. The two buck sergeants snapped to attention as he exited the elevator.

"Good evening, sir."

"Evening."

"There's a gentleman in the bar asking for you," a young female soldier whose name tag read Johnson said. "He's cleared. We've swept the bar, as well."

What the hell?

"Is anyone else in the bar right now?"

"Just the bartender, sir. We'll ask him to step out."

Graves squinted. "You said he's cleared. Cleared by whom?"

"Our company commander has the order, sir, but the guy is cleared by the SECDEF."

Holy shit. If the secretary of defense was involved, there was no telling how bad things were going to get. For a split second, he wondered about calling General Cuthbert but decided against it. Something stunk, and like he'd seen more and more in the later years of his career, it appeared to be the Army.

"Thanks," Graves said and walked down to the private bar. Sure enough, a guy with salt-and-pepper hair, a corduroy jacket with elbow patches, and a thick beard sat at the bar.

"Joey? Get the colonel whatever he'd like on my tab and then would you excuse us for a second?"

Graves looked at the clean-cut young man and decided he was probably in on whatever this was, too. He had that look. Piercing blue eyes, and friendly, benign smile, but he clearly was military and probably special operations. "Bourbon, water back. Please."

"Sam? Malcom O'Connell."

The drink came immediately, with a small glass of water on the side. Graves slid onto the stool next to O'Connell and shook the man's outstretched hand. "Nice to meet you, Doctor O'Connell."

"Malcolm, please. It's nice to meet you, Sam."

"You, too. What's going on? How did you get my number?"

O'Connell smiled. "One thing at a time, deal?"

Graves snorted. "Sure."

"Brian Lance gave me your number. He said you were a

better than average student at Michigan. That's pretty much the highest praise he gives."

Graves smiled. Lance's courses were the toughest of his graduate studies in mathematics. "Getting a B from that guy was the hardest thing I've ever done."

O'Connell smiled. "He's a bastard. You can say that—I won't tell him."

"He's a solid-gold bastard." Graves smiled. "Now, what's going on?"

O'Connell glanced around the bar quickly. His voice was low, but clear. "Grantville, West Virginia and Alexander Correctional Facility in Illinois. Do you know what they have in common?"

"Terrorist incidents." Graves narrowed his eyes.

O'Connell shook his head. "That's the usual official account, Sam, although if you look closely it's always hedged with qualifiers. There's much more to the story."

"I don't do conspiracy theories—"

O'Connell laughed and raised a hand in a supplicating gesture. "Nothing like that at all. The public, though, wouldn't understand, hence the subterfuge. Blaming the unknown on terrorism does a few things. The public stops asking questions and the military industrial complex keeps rolling forward faster than the caissons. Of course, the conspiracy theorists have latched onto these events, too. They're closer than you might think to the actual events."

Graves blinked. "So what happened? Where are my cadets?"

O'Connell sipped from his own whiskey. "I asked your thesis advisor about you before I came here. He gave you high praise and I figured that you're a better than average mathematician. When I discovered that we had a mutual acquaintance, I knew I wanted to speak with you. You have the head for what I'm about to tell you."

Graves looked around. "Does what you're going to tell me exceed the security classification of this bar? I assume it does."

"I've taken care of that, Sam." O'Connell shook his head. "Where your cadets are? I've got a pretty good idea. The question is when."

"What did you say?" Graves realized his mouth hung open and he closed it with a snap.

"The Reader's Digest condensed version is simple. After Grantville, scientists around the world noticed some strange readings on equipment designed to detect neutrinos. A bunch of us came together and started what we call The Project. We're headquartered in a lab deep underground in Minnesota. It's in the middle of an iron mine and was built to study proton decay in the 1980s. We took the data from Grantville and started studying it. We started unraveling it. Grantville disappeared in what we're calling a chronoletic event. There was an instantaneous exchange of mass between two time periods. Given what we found in its place, and what we determined through our data, we think the entire town of Grantville reappeared in central Europe some time in the 1600s. Probably in the first half of that century."

Holy shit.

Graves took a stiff swallow of bourbon as his mind started to process the concept. "On purpose or coincidental?"

"Data supports coincidence, though Alexander was something unlike anything we've observed. Instead of one transfer, there were several at different points in history. Alexander Correctional Facility ended up in the past somewhere between seventy and about a hundred and thirty million years ago, along with anything in the area in four different time periods. Those things were mixed in that new existence and other mass from those time periods found their way to our present."

"You have proof of this? Physical proof?"

O'Connell smiled. "We have proof, Sam. The kind of proof that will blow your mind and make Steven Spielberg jealous."

Graves nodded absently, his mind working through the possibilities and accepting the offered proof without dissent. "If this was a time event, and it went both ways like you're saying, why hasn't there been an effect to our history? You're saying that the event has created a parallel universe, then."

"Precisely."

"Grantville is in Europe during the 1600s. A geographical switch, too? What about Alexander Correctional Facility? Do you think it is in the same place?"

"No," O'Connell said. "With that one we think it's fairly close to its original position, just moved backward in time."

"Jesus Christ," Graves said. "That's impossible to believe."

"I can show you the data, once you retire and come to work with us. Consider that the only job offer you'll get from me." O'Connell smiled. "Your cadets are much more recent, but they're in trouble most likely. The data suggests they're not that far from here geographically, but they're somewhere in the Revolutionary War. I'm guessing 1776 to 1777."

Graves blinked. "Behind enemy lines?"

"Most likely." O'Connell took a drink. "Your cadets that were nearby, what did they see? Hear?"

"A bright flash of light, a quick tremor, and a really loud clap of thunder. That was it."

"Was there anything out of place where the missing cadets were?"

"Snow," Graves said. "There was a spot of no snow. The surrounding forest was five to six inches deep by the end of the day. That oblong piece, maybe a hundred meters by fifty meters, was completely clear."

O'Connell nodded. "There was considerable snow outside Trenton in 1776, especially between December 1776 and February of 1777, save for the warmest parts right before Christmas. Based on your observation of bare ground, I think that's when they are, and likely behind enemy lines."

Graves shook his head and looked at their faces in his memory. "They're good kids. Young and dumb, but they're good. General Cuthbert asked me that. Do you think he knows where what's happened?"

O'Connell shook his head. "I think they have some ideas, especially with the idiots in the Special Investigations Branch feeding different theories around. They're not as close to the data as we are. There are a lot of scientists working this, Sam."

"Outside the knowledge of the federal government."

"We're officially a private organization, Sam, although we now have very close relations with several government agencies. We started as a bunch of antiestablishment folks who didn't believe the bullshit our government was putting out initially. We've come a long way."

"Once the exchange happened, they could have all dropped into the Delaware River or the middle of a British camp, right?"

"Anything is possible. I am statistically certain that the actual time exchange didn't kill them, Sam. They are back in 1776. What happened after they got there, I cannot say."

"If they're together, they have a chance."

O'Connell nodded. "I hope you're right. The most likely

scenario for them would be seeking out General Washington and trying to find a place in his army. I suspect they'll end the war much faster and set their new America on a very different path."

Graves took another drink and tried to wrap his mind around the idea of Kyle Porter, Ashley Higgs, Jameel Mason, and Mike Martinez, among others, making their way in colonial America. He swallowed and the thought crystallized. "They'll be fine. Assuming they live through the war."

"And if they make it?"

"They'll change that world."

O'Connell grinned. "Doctor Lance told me you were the right man to help me with what I call my Elrond math. How soon do you retire?"

"My plan is a year and a half from now," Graves said. "Does this sort of thing happen a lot?"

"No," O'Connell said. "But they're happening more frequently. I think Grantville was just the start, Sam. If we're right, we can get to almost predicting these things. And if we can manage it, one day we'll be able to replicate the effect and go there ourselves."

Graves sat back and steadied himself on the bar. "You're talking time travel? And you want me to come work for you? Is this a DoD contracted thing?"

"No. Again, we're a private corporation, like I said, but this is something that won't get a lot of press until we make some leaps forward," O'Connell said.

"Why keep publicizing these things as terrorist events?"

O'Connell shrugged and ran a hand along his beard. "We're desensitized to terror, Sam. This is a different situation, though. We have a smaller group of people to satisfy. They'll take the news eventually. I'm sure my colleagues in the Beltway will find a way to package it. But, I wanted you to know what happened and that I want you to work with us starting immediately as you finish your retirement."

"I'm still the Professor of Military Science. The Battalion Commander—"

"Cadet Command is going to relieve you," O'Connell said. "They'll call it an early transition, but a relief for cause OER is in your future. It's part of the storyline. You know that I'm right. For what it's worth, we'll pay you a lot more than you'd make as a retired full-bird colonel and you'll have a lot more fun.

That active duty retirement can be your extra savings account or something."

Graves fingered the glass of bourbon with a whirlwind raging in his mind. "The families can't know, but you wanted me to know so I'd be okay with it. Be vested in what you're trying to do?"

"Yes," O'Connell said. "General Cuthbert and his team aren't going to fare very well in the aftermath of something like this. He's got all the three-letter agencies spun up about this and they don't have a clue what's really going on. I do. Our project could use a guy with your credentials, Sam. Personally, I think you deserve better than what the Army intends to give you."

Me too.

Graves raised his glass and held it out to O'Connell in a toast. "Then, I accept your offer. How do we get started?"

The bulk of Washington's room was the large table he'd overtaken with correspondence, maps, and intelligence of all sorts. The fading light of the day reminded him that he should eat and try to rest a bit. Working later than normal on the final adjustments to the attack plan required him to be sharp even long after his army bedded down for the night. Leaning against the table, Washington met the eye of Nathanael Greene with a tired smile.

"It's a good plan, General. I do believe that Colonel Glover is correct that Trenton is the right place to attack with the full might of our army," Greene said. His features were sharp but his smile was warm. There was no other general Washington trusted so fiercely. Since the arrest of Charles Lee, the army's dissension with Washington's policies and plans dwindled to nothing. Yet, Washington knew their trust in him was simply from a position of singularity. He was their leader and despite his most able general's assurances, Washington was anything but pleased.

"There's so much riding on Ewing and Cadwalader." Washington sighed. "I fear Cadwalader will decide against crossing for fear of engagement and I fear Ewing will attack without us."

Greene rubbed a hand across his chin. "Ewing will wait. Cadwalader would be facing the bulk of the Hessian garrison, provided Von Donop doesn't march to Trenton tomorrow."

Washington nodded. "I've sent Reed to Cadwalader tonight. Tomorrow, he'll present an exchange opportunity to the ranking officer in Mount Holly. At that point, we'll know if Von Donop has returned his regiment to Trenton or not."

"Wise plan." Greene smiled. "Very crafty."

They looked at each other for a long moment, smiling, before chuckling together. Washington gestured to a small bottle of brandy. "Join me?"

"Of course, sir."

Washington poured a small amount into the two pewter cups at the table side and handed one to Greene. "I've asked you to stay for good reason, my friend. A gentleman in our employ is coming with information that he insisted was to be delivered personally."

Greene's eyebrows rose. He gestured to Washington with the cup of brandy. "If not tomorrow, then today. And a job well done."

"Indeed." Washington sipped at the brandy and pushed away a clear vision of his servants carefully distilling it every summer. The last of the past summer's batch had to be savored. "I'm intrigued as to this visit. Especially so close to our attack."

"Has this man misled you?"

"Never." Washington shook his head. "If anything, his reports are more sporadic, but just as detailed as Mister Culper up north."

"Then, you're worried he's bringing word of a British march or something similar?" Greene's eyebrows rose.

Washington shrugged. "Possibly. It's hard to say."

"What's your fear, sir?" Greene sipped again. "If this gentleman provides good information, what could he report that would change the plan?"

Washington shook his head. At this point, there was nothing short of a complete British army recall from garrison and order to march on Trenton that would change his plan. "Nothing, I suppose." He looked up at Greene and smiled with one corner of his mouth. "Thank you, Nathanael."

"You're welcome, sir."

A firm knock came from the closed door. Greene stepped over and opened the door. Washington's companion Mister Lee stood there with a portly, bearded man.

Lee nodded. "General. This is Mister Daniels. He'd like to have a word with the general."

"He's been checked for weapons?" asked Greene.

Lee cocked his head to one side but said nothing else. Washington covered a smile with a sip of brandy. As good as Greene was, he never gave anyone the benefit of the doubt. Besides his natural leadership ability and affable nature, Nathanael Greene was a bulldog in the highest sense of the word.

"Mister Daniels, do come in," Washington said. He stood and closed the distance to the shorter man and extended a hand. "Now, what's this news you have for me?"

Daniels took a breath and put his hand into his pocket. "General, I've seen many things in my time. From the time we served against the French until now, I've done my best to keep my ear to the ground. Nothing has really surprised me until now. Two days ago, sir."

Washington sat on one side of the table and gestured Daniels to sit. Greene sidled up to the side opposite Washington, his eyes intent on Daniels. "You served together? In the British army?"

"A long time ago," Daniels said.

Washington nodded. "I've known this man for more than twenty years, Nathanael. He is a friend and fellow patriot. And, one of the finest gunsmiths in the colonies."

Greene visibly relaxed. "Really? Then, I believe we're all ears, Mister Daniels."

Daniels bobbed his head, licked his lips, and spoke. "Three days ago, just before sunset, a patrol of Hessian regulars burst into our home bloodied and carrying some gear I'd never seen before. They gave me this mark on my head and held me down while one of them tried to rape my daughter, Emily." He looked at Greene. "She's seventeen. Her mother died of fever a few years back."

"What happened?"

Daniels swallowed. "I thought they were going to kill us right then and there. But, the door burst open and four young men came in. The Hessians killed one of them, but they beat two of the Hessians to death. The third grabbed...a rifle...and escaped. Emily hit him with a musket round, but we couldn't find him. The Hessians had come upon these young men in the woods and killed one by surprise. They fled to our house and thankfully the boys came after them."

Washington nodded. The rest of the story was coming, of that he was sure. "Who were these boys?"

"There's eight of them now, sir. Six young men and two women. They're soldiers."

"Women?" Greene squinted at Washington. "And soldiers? Of whose army?"

Daniels looked at Washington. "This is where it gets a little difficult, sir. They appear to be from the future."

"What?" Washington gaped and immediately caught himself. "What do you mean, 'future'?"

Daniels shrugged. "They look and talk differently, General. They're wearing flags on their shoulders like colonial ones, but very different. They're dressed in incredible uniforms. Like nothing I've ever seen. And the one in charge is a colored man—which the others don't seem to find unusual."

"What else?" Greene asked, frowning. "If they come from a year in the future, what do they know about this war?"

"Everything, General." Daniels sighed. "They know what you're planning and how it turns out."

Washington felt a ripple of paralyzing fear run down his spine. "They know? Only a dozen men know, Vernon. Did they tell you?"

"They did, sir."

Greene clapped a hand over his mouth. "We have a spy, General."

Daniels shook his head. "That's not what I said. These young soldiers are from the future." He brought out his hand and unfolded the curled fingers. A single silver coin rested in his palm. "They gave me this."

Washington turned the ribbed edge of the coin in his fingers. One side was clearly his profile and the other showed a minuteman. "The bicentennial of the United States of America. 1776 to 1976."

"May I see that?" Greene asked.

Washington handed over the coin. "It's convincing, Vernon. But, I'm not quite sure I believe it. I'll need to talk to them, but I don't really have the time—"

"They're on their way here now. I'll meet them at McKonkey's Ferry at midnight. With your permission, I'll have them brought across with all of their gear," Daniels said. "They say the attack is successful, General. That it changes the course of the war and makes people believe we can win. You are planning to attack, aren't you?"

"Vernon, I . . ." He trailed off. This man had been a great ally and fellow soldier. "Yes, Vernon. We plan to attack."

Daniels nodded. "Then talk to them, sir. They'll be here 'round midnight."

Washington looked at Greene for a long moment. There were no words between them and Washington felt there shouldn't have been. "We win," Washington held out his hand for the coin.

"It would appear so," Greene said. "Mister Daniels is right, sir. They should have an audience with you. They should be escorted from the Ferry, though. With someone we trust implicitly but whose absence from their unit area wouldn't be suspicious to the men. Nothing travels faster than rumor amongst the infantry. I believe your cousin fits the bill, sir."

Washington thought for a moment and realized that Greene was correct. "Have him mustered with a group of twenty to march in an hour. I want them in position when these young soldiers cross the river. I will accept no risks, Vernon."

"You'll have none, sir," Daniels said. "What they know could change the war, sir. But there's something else that's troubling. Wherever they came from, they brought rifles like nothing I've ever seen come from an armory even like His Majesty's."

"Rifles? Better than our muskets?"

Daniels nodded. "Incredibly different, sir. Capable of things I've never seen."

"That could be good," Greene said.

"It could be, sir." Daniels licked his lips again. "Except that the Hessian who escaped has one of these future rifles. Sergeant Mason and his squad, that's what they call themselves, believe if the English get their hands on it that the war will end differently than from their history. Our history. That's why they're on their way here, sir. To convince you to attack Trenton and get back that rifle."

"But we would have their rifles," Greene said. "We could keep pace with any advance in technology."

Washington nodded. "But, what if we had the clear advantage? Going forward, we could not only win this war but protect ourselves from attack from sheer deterrence."

He let the thought trail off. His army numbered maybe three thousand with all of Cadwalader's and Ewing's forces counted as his formation. The Continental Congress had fled to Baltimore, leaving the capital of Philadelphia in Washington's defense. The British outnumbered him and even from their winter quarters, he could sense their strength. He needed a master stroke. The planned attack at Trenton would be the first step, but this Sergeant Mason and his squad could turn the whole course of the war. What things they would know as their history.

He looked at Daniels. "Bring them to me, Vernon. Speak nothing of this to anyone but Colonel Glover. Nathanael? Brief my cousin and his men. Arrange a meeting point far from the camp. I will meet them there and we'll see what they know. I pray it's a fast end to this war and our success, gentlemen. Otherwise, I do not know how long we can fight."

CHAPTER FOURTEEN

An hour after sunset, the cadets left their cabin carrying everything they owned and moved into the forest. They'd agreed to keep the pace almost glacial, moving as silently as possible. Mason put them into a tight Ranger file with Murphy leading the procession. Under fair skies, the nearly full moon cast a weird glow over the land as it rose to the east. The clouds would provide some protection from the moonlight, but they'd need to move quickly before the moon reached full illumination overhead. As long as they moved quietly, it would be okay. The open forest near the farmlands closed in around them as they moved to the east. Even with the moon rising, the forest grew darker than anything Mason had ever seen. When he'd first joined ROTC, he'd wondered about the small rectangular patches sewn to the back of every cadet's patrol cap and helmet bands. The "cat eyes" were universally laughed at because they broke every rule about light discipline being luminous, but making their way through a forest at night, Mason could see Koch immediately to his front and Stratton another five meters away. Their white sheet ponchos helped, too, but if they had to lay down for any reason, Mason hoped they'd be near the sporadic patches of snow so that any interested parties would be challenged to see them at all.

For nearly an hour, they crept through the darkness. A couple of times, Murphy froze them in place. In the ever-lighter forest, there were no voices in the night and once they caught sight of a lighted wagon in the distance. Staying off the roads and near any lower terrain like creek beds worked well as time ticked. By 2200, they were close to their objective and Murphy wisely slowed down even further. As they walked, Mason fingered the pace-count beads his mother had given him for Christmas. The small black plastic beads were designed to slide on a piece of parachute cord to count the tens and hundreds of a traditional pace count. The slow pace and Ranger file were throwing off his traditional pace count. He'd measured it as sixty-six steps with his left foot equaling a hundred meters. Mason had reset his beads at three thousand meters when movement caught his eye.

Koch stopped and raised a fist—the signal to freeze. Mason strained to hear something but couldn't hear anything over his heart thumping in his chest. Koch knelt in the snow, passing back the signal for the squad to do the same. Mason moved forward quietly, his boots crunching the snow underfoot. While he couldn't see Koch's exact footprints, Mason tried to put his boots into the same spaces when they crossed a patch of snow. He snorted and tried not to smile. In his final briefing, they talked about using a tight Ranger file. Traveling single file would hide their numbers, Stratton had said. Mason smiled at the memory because Murphy had immediately started quoting *Star Wars* as a result. The patrol briefing almost spun out of control. But, they'd laughed and smiled as a group for the first time since arriving in 1776. For Mason, it was a start.

As he moved passed Stratton, Mason whispered, "Come on."

They moved past Booker and hunched over as they moved to Murphy, who knelt in the snow at the crest of a small hill. He pointed down the hill.

"Road junction." Mason nodded. "Not bad. We're a little south of the ferry."

Stratton whispered, "You mean that ferry?" He pointed to the darkened face of the river where a solitary boat with two lit lanterns slowly made its way across.

"Yeah." Mason said. He sighed and looked at Stratton. "Set the squad in a cigar-shaped perimeter. One hundred percent security. We're early, so we'll sit here behind this hill and wait. No noise."

Stratton grinned. "You got it." He slapped Mason's shoulder and crept back down the hill toward Booker.

Murphy laid down fully and crawled up the hill so he could see. "I'll let you know when I see something."

Mason looked over his shoulder to see the squad move up tighter to the hill and get into the configuration he'd asked for without much noise at all. He settled into his position, looking off Murphy's right shoulder into the distance and watched the moonrise create strange shadows that moved across the ground until the clouds thickened again. An hour passed quickly. Not long after, Murphy kicked his leg. Mason crawled awkwardly to his left and forward to meet up with Murphy.

"What's up?"

"Two lanterns. All the way across."

Mason looked onto the river and saw the boat crossing swiftly. "Here we go, huh?"

Mason hunched into a sitting position and looked into the squad's formation. He made a "psst" sound and tapped his shoulder, the sign for his team leaders. Higgs and Stratton came forward immediately without a sound. Mason pointed at the river crossing.

Stratton grinned. "Looks like we're crossing the river."

"Meeting George Fucking Washington." Murphy smiled.

Mason nodded and smiled himself. "We can stop giggling like little kids any time now, guys."

They all giggled. "This is so wild," Murphy said.

Higgs cleared her throat quietly. "Game faces, guys. They may be Americans, but they're just as likely to kill us. We are an armed, unknown quantity. Got it?"

The smiles disappeared in a heartbeat. Mason studied the path of the boat. It was coming in north of their position—to their collective right. "We need to move that direction. Stay on the backside of the hill, Murphy, but keep track of where we are. Once we get to the ferry, we'll stop and wait for the signal. Got it?"

"Roger that," Murphy said and stood.

"Move out," Mason said. He and Stratton nodded at each other as they changed direction and the patrol slid to the north. Not more than three minutes later, Murphy halted them again and gave the signal for assault position. They'd not come up with anything different and the assault position was typically very near the objective, so it worked. Mason brought up Higgs' fireteam and watched them form a tight perimeter in the snow. He knelt in the center and waited for Stratton and Higgs to meet him there.

"Okay, we made it, Mason," Stratton said. "Now we just wait for the signal."

"That's your job, Stratton," Mason said. "When Daniels whistles the all clear, you move down the slope first. If all is good, then we'll join you."

"Why me?" Stratton squinted at him.

"You're white, Stratton. They'll think I'm a freedman and it will complicate things. We need to get into the boat and get moving. As little distraction as possible, right?"

Stratton chewed on his lower lip. "Makes sense, I guess."

Murphy gave a soft *psst* from his position on the crest of the embankment. Mason looked at them. "The boat's docked. Here we go, guys."

Stratton moved away to join Murphy, leaving Higgs and Mason alone. She leaned over and whispered, "You're doing great, Mason."

"Tell me that in a couple of hours." Mason shrugged. "I hope I'm right."

"We all hope you're right," Higgs said. He could see her smile at him. "You do realize you made a patrol four or five times longer than you've ever done without getting lost and arriving at the objective on time, right?"

Mason hadn't thought about it until that moment. A sense of pride sprung up in his chest. "Guess I can do this after all."

Higgs put a hand on his shoulder. "Don't forget that."

From the far side of the hill, they heard a soft warbling whistle. "All clear," Mason said. Stratton was already up and moving.

Mason looked around at the small group nearby. "Everybody up," he said softly. "Follow me."

Mason strode past Murphy and down the slope with the rest of the squad behind him. In the lantern light of the low Durham boat, he could see Stratton, Mister Daniels, and a man in an ornate Continental uniform. Behind them were at least a dozen armed soldiers with their rifles on Stratton.

The ornately dressed man gestured the rifles down as Mason approached. Stratton turned to him. "Mason, this is Colonel John Glover."

Mason came to attention and saluted with the musket. "Sir, Cadet Sergeant Jameel Mason in command of a squad of eight."

Glover nodded, but he eyed Stratton for a split second before returning the salute formally. "Sergeant Mason, I am here with this armed guard to escort you across the Delaware to General Washington. Your men will—" He stopped. Mason realized that

Higgs had come up to just behind his left shoulder. "Your men will hand over their muskets until General Washington clears you."

"Yes, sir," Mason said. "Collect the muskets." Higgs and Stratton turned away to do just that. In thirty seconds, Stratton held all of them like firewood in his arms. Mason knew Glover was staring at them, just like the soldiers were. A mix of incredulous wonder and deep suspicion covered the colonel's face.

"Sergeant Mason? You're a freedman?"

How many times am I gonna be asked this?

Mason pushed his shoulders back. "No, sir. I was born and raised in Pittsburgh, Pennsylvania."

Glover nodded. "We must get going. Get your squad aboard."

"Yes, sir."

Glover gestured and two young men came forward. "Captain Washington and his deputy will safeguard your weapons."

Mason watched Stratton hand over his team's muskets to Washington. For a second, Mason wondered if the young captain and General Washington were related. *Have to ask Murphy*, he thought. Higgs stepped forward and the young deputy smiled at her. Even in the low light of the lanterns, Mason could see her blush and return the smile.

"Board the boat," Mason stage-whispered to the rest of the squad. They moved to the middle of the boat with the armed men around them. For an army without a whole lot of professionalism, they understood security pretty damned well. Mason turned to Daniels.

"Thank you, Mister Daniels. For everything."

Daniels extended a hand. "Be safe, Mason."

"You, too."

Glover's men extinguished the lanterns as Mason stepped aboard. With Glover at his shoulder, Mason joined his squad at the center of the boat and shrugged out of his rucksack.

"I'm to understand you are a cadet?" Glover asked quietly. "But a sergeant as well?"

"I'm a cadet, sir." He paused. "We have ranks for each class of cadet to better learn the system."

How much should I say?

"And you were raised in Pennsylvania? What did you pay for your commission?"

Mason shook his head. "I'm not commissioned yet. A cadet is an officer in training, Colonel."

"I am aware what a cadet is, Sergeant," Glover stiffened. "I'm trying to discern if you are friend or foe. I'll take one to the far shore. The other, I'm willing to execute and dump your body in the river for the British to find downstream."

Jesus Christ!

Mason squared his shoulders to Glover. "If you'll permit me to reach under this sheet, Colonel?"

Glover squinted. "A weapon gets you killed, Mason."

Trying not to tremble, Mason reached up under the white poncho to his right shoulder pocket and grasped the corner of the Velcro-backed American flag there. He tore it off slowly, minimizing the sound as much as he could until it came free. He pulled his hand down slowly and opened his palm with the flag in the center.

Glover's eyes widened. "A friend, then."

Mason took a breath and tried to relax. "A friend, sir."

"Well met," Glover extended a hand. "It will take us a quarter hour to cross the river with the current here. From there, we'll march to your designated meeting point with General Washington."

Mason nodded, immediately understanding. They'd go nowhere near the actual position of the army and Mason doubted that Washington would be alone. This security contingent would follow them everywhere. He glanced at Higgs in the starlight, but couldn't immediately discern her face or the young officer responsible for her blushing.

At least one of us is having fun.

"May I ask you one thing, Sergeant Mason?"

Mason turned back to Glover. "Yes, sir?"

"Where did you come from?"

Mason sighed. "It's hard to explain, sir."

Glover looked him over from head to toe. "Your uniform notwithstanding, a colored man is not a leader of men."

Mason licked his lips and took a long slow breath. "Where I come from, Colonel, the color of a man's skin does not matter when it comes to leading soldiers. All that matters is that the leader accomplishes the mission first and always takes care of their people. That's my job."

Glover said nothing in response and they stood in the gently rocking boat. For a moment, near the center of the river, Mason considered sitting down because of rising nausea, but decided he would not give Glover, or any of them for that matter, the satisfaction of seeing him in a moment of weakness. The queasy feeling passed and as the Durham boat slid to a stop against the Pennsylvania shoreline, Mason felt like an enormous weight had been lifted off his shoulders. They were finally on friendly ground.

"Arrange your squad single file. My men will walk on either side of you until we get to the meeting point. You will march in complete silence. Is that clear, Sergeant?" Glover asked. There was something about the man's voice Mason recognized. Authority and command were tone as much as anything.

"Yes, sir." Mason turned to Higgs and Stratton. "Ranger file, on me. Not a fucking word."

"Captain Sutton? Can I get you anything?"

Slumped down in a chair by the dwindling fire, he pushed himself to a sitting position. The damned brandy had run out. "Yes. More wine if you please."

As much as he knew it was a bad idea to drink more, it was perhaps the only way to handle Rall's idiocy. The dragoons would be sent out on patrol again at dawn to wander up and down the roads around Trenton looking for an enemy who was likely sleeping late and praying for warmer weather. A turn in the weather was coming by the sound of the freshening wind outside. He could hear Selena rustling through the adjoining kitchen for another bottle. There was the distinct tinkle of another glass coming down from the cabinets.

She'll have a drink with me. Will wonders never cease?

The door opened and Selena came with a glass and the dark green bottle. She poured a healthy portion into his glass and matched it with her own. She sat opposite him in an ornate chair he surmised she'd not sat in since her husband's death a year ago.

"Ian is asleep?" he asked with a smile he hoped was warm and genuine.

Selena returned the smile. "Yes, he went to sleep without a fight this evening."

"He's a rambunctious boy," Sutton said.

"Aren't they all?" she replied and looked for a long moment into the fire. He couldn't help but think her mind was on her departed husband and how much the boy must take after him and not her.

Selena said nothing for a long moment. He waited for her to speak of the war. Of some type of lasting peace, some desperate dream of a person far from the Crown who tasted a vestige of difference and liked it, but longed for home at the same time. She said nothing until she surprised him. "You are attending the colonel's dinner tomorrow at the Potts residence?"

"Certainly," he said. "And you?"

"Miss Potts asked me to be there, so I will be," Selena said. "And the colonel has requested all of his officers, no?"

Sutton nodded. "He has. But His Majesty's dragoons are not his, Missus Christensen."

"Of course not." She smiled. "Yet, he makes you patrol endlessly and his troops are ragged with fatigue."

Sutton snorted and nodded. "Rall does not know how to command or how to defend. Not that it matters."

"You don't feel there is danger here?"

"No," Sutton said and took another deep swallow of wine. "The only danger here is for those who deny what His Majesty's forces want." He locked eyes with her and saw the small bit of confidence in her pretty face disappear. "Isn't that right, Missus Christensen?"

Selena licked her lips nervously and looked back into the fire. She stood without warning and nodded at him. "Good night, Captain Sutton."

His hand shot out and caught her sleeve in a powerful grip. "What are you playing at, Selena? You've ignored me for weeks and suddenly have an interest in my affairs. What do you want?"

"My apologies. I merely wanted to have a conversation and—"

"And what? Report to Colonel Rall? Or maybe even to Washington?" He grinned and chuckled at her, but made no attempt to lessen his grip. "Are you spying on His Majesty's forces, Selena?"

"How dare you accuse me of such a thing!" Anger appeared in her face and he almost laughed at the absurdity of it. "My husband died in His Majesty's army and you have the gall to accuse me of spying for the rebels?" She snatched her dress above his hand and tore it away, leaving a handful of lace in Sutton's palm. "Good night, Captain Sutton."

Sutton laughed and waved her away with his fingers splayed. "Run along, Missus Christensen. Remember that those who deny our king will one day beg for his forgiveness and mercy."

CHAPTER FIFTEEN

The headquarters of the 4th Virginia Regiment were a cold, dismal affair compared to the fancier homes that Washington and his inner circle enjoyed. Under the command of Colonel Adam Stephen, the regiment arrived earlier in the month to join with General Washington's Continental Army and none of the men, or their leaders, had been happy about it. The long walk north had been one of misery as lengthened supply lines left the men with ragged uniforms and ill-fitted supplies for the brutal New England winter. Captain George Wallis made his way through the bevy of small campfires and clusters of men huddled over them to the Regimental Headquarters—a small drafty cabin that belonged to a family whose names Wallis couldn't remember.

At the rickety porch, a lone guard snapped to attention and opened the door. As he stepped inside, General Adam Stephen sat reclined in a chair and studying maps by candlelight. A bottle of amber liquid and an accompanying glass rested by his trembling hands.

"Wallis," Stephen said. "Come in."

"You asked to see me, sir?" Wallis stood in front of the table, watching his commander fingering the glass of whiskey. For a moment, he hoped the general would share it. "You have an assignment?"

"I do," Stephen said and pointed at the river. "Since those Jägers shot us up the other night, I've decided we should repay their damage in full. Nobody kills my men without retribution. Private Conley was from your company, was he not?"

Wallis nodded. "A good man, too, sir."

"Then you would be interested in such a mission of great importance?"

"Yes, sir."

Stephen nodded and stood. "Come here, George. I want you to look at this."

Wallis stepped closer and saw that Stephen's map was of the Delaware River at Trenton. It was the first time he'd seen the network of roads up close. "Trenton, sir?"

"Yes." Stephen pointed at a spot in the river just north of the small falls where Conley caught a lucky musket ball. "Here's where they shot at you, right?"

"About there, sir."

"Then where, Captain?"

Walling stiffly pointed a little farther north and closer to the known Hessian position along the River Road. "There, sir."

"Fine." Stephen waved away the interruption. "I want you to get a measure of revenge, Captain Wallis. I want you to take fifty men, crossing here"—he tapped the map at Yardley's Ferry barely two miles from the edge of Trenton—"and rile up the Hessians as you see fit."

Wallis brightened. Sitting around puny fires marking time hadn't sat well with him. "Sir, you want me to simply attack the Hessian positions and retreat?"

"I want you to harass them, Wallis. Drive them crazy with quick actions and double-quick retreats. Use the night for your cover and harass them at every turn. Supposedly they are already exhausted from constant fear. I want you to do more than tire them, Captain. I want you to engage them and take revenge for Conley before our fearless leader bungles his opportunity and loses this bloody war."

Wallis said nothing. General Washington was not the butt of sarcasm often. He knew that General Stephen had served under Washington during the French and Indian Wars and they'd tangled in the Virginia legislature for years. "Sir, does General Washington know—"

"Of course not!" Stephen glared. "I don't want him to know! He expects us to sit here and wait out the winter while the Hessian bastards pick us off one by one or we die of dysentery in these awful conditions! He gets a big, warm farmhouse and we get a goddamned shanty!" Stephen reached for the empty glass, fiddled with it for a moment as if pondering another drink, and set it aside with a thump.

Wallis shifted uncomfortably from side to side. "Fifty men you said, sir? And we'll have the provisions ordered?"

"Of course," Stephen said. "I'm not stupid, Wallis. You'll have what you need. You'll return to McKonkey's Ferry for retrieval twenty-four hours later. I'll arrange your transportation. You"— he paused and wiped at his mouth—"have to simply aggravate the Hessians and avenge the loss of Private Conley to General Washington's ineptitude. Are we clear?"

Wallis nodded. "Yes, sir. I'll see the quartermaster to set aside the rations and ammunition for my men. We'll be ready to leave in an hour."

"Not that fast," Stephen said. "Tomorrow. Tomorrow evening, to be specific. After a day of lounging around in preparation for holiday meals and the like, neither the Hessians nor General Washington will expect anyone to cross the river. You'll be able to get across without detection and conduct a proper raid with minimal casualties and return to McKonkey's Ferry for extraction." The general's fingers returned to the glass and poured the whiskey. Stephen stared at it for a second and then drained the glass before pointing roughly at Wallis. "I am told you are the right man for the job, Wallis. A bit wild at the edges, but a good man? The kind who just needs to be set free?"

Wallis nodded. "Conley deserved better than to be shot riding in a damned boat, sir."

"Of course he did, Wallis." Stephen grinned. "We all deserve better than this. Our fearless leader feels it's best to sit and wait on the Congress to help us with supplies and pay chests. They've run for Virginia, leaving Philadelphia at the first sight of the British army across the bloody river. He's too weak to make them support us."

Wallis said nothing as Stephen stared silently into space for a long moment.

"You know, Captain Wallis, I served with General Washington many years ago against the French. He hasn't changed at all. Willing to let others take their shots at us while he waits for a miracle. Well, I'm not about to sit and wait. The bloody Hessians and the Sassenach have taken the last of my men without a god-damned fight! You're going to go over and make them pay for it."

Wallis grinned. The proposition beat sitting around trying not to get dysentery. "Fifty men and provisions?"

Stephen nodded and set his glass down with a thud. "Yes. I will have your weapons, powder, and rations ready by tomorrow at noon. As soon as night falls, you'll dispatch up to McKonkey's Ferry. I'll arrange your passing with Colonel Glover. You're carrying an important message on a critical mission, but say no more than that. No one outside this room needs to know what your real mission is."

Wallis nodded. There was no message. All he was meant to do was bring chaos on the Hessian encampments around Trenton. The fire in his stomach lit from boredom and stoked itself into a fresh, roaring rage. "I can do that, General."

"Splendid." Stephen grinned in response. "You're dismissed, Captain Wallis. I'll see you in a couple of days."

"Sir." Wallis straightened and saluted. As Stephen returned the gesture, Wallis spun on his heels and moved to the door. Immediately outside, he met the expectant eyes of his regimental commander, Lieutenant Colonel Robert Lawson.

"Well?" Lawson asked. "Any issue with your orders, Captain?"

Wallis shook his head. "No, sir. You're aware—"

"No," Lawson said and leaned closer. "General Stephen was adamant that your orders are meant for no one else. All I know is that tomorrow, you'll take fifty men and cross the river on an urgent mission for our commander. That's all."

Wallis nodded. *What have I gotten myself into?*

"If something happens to us, at least you'll know where we went, right?"

Lawson nodded. "Messages have to get through, Wallis. Whether we send them once successfully or it takes a dozen times, the message must get through."

"Yes, sir," Wallis said. As they parted and Wallis stepped again into the cold December night, he looked up through a ragged tear in the low clouds and saw the stars. The Hessians were going to get his message the first time.

And maybe, a second or third message as well. Of that he was damned certain.

☆   ☆   ☆

Lord General Charles Cornwallis stood looking out the thin glass window of his bedroom. The streets of New York teemed with people celebrating Christmas Eve. Occasional choruses of familiar hymns floated down the alleys and reverberated into his quarters. Cradling a glass of wine, he looked back into the maelstrom of his personal belongings being prepared for travel. *Three more days*, he thought. With the army in garrison for the winter, and Washington out there running around Pennsylvania with his wisp of an enemy force, Sir William Howe's guidance had been clear.

"Go home, Charles." Howe smiled up at him. "I cannot promise you'll be home for Christmas, but sometime closely thereafter. You'll spend two or three months at home and return vibrant and ready to wipe Washington's army from the face of the earth."

Cornwallis hadn't been listening after hearing the word *home*. His heart thumped and threatened to beat out of his chest. His beloved Jemima had been ill most of the fall. Her letters were hopeful and cheered him, yet the unspoken worry of her fragile health penetrated his every thought of her. Since returning to New York, he'd written her daily letters and dogged his aides to place them on any ship headed for England. With the word of his leave, he'd written exultantly to her that they would be together soon. Every passing day seemed to take forever and he found himself hating the reality of an army of war in garrison.

His days were spent in paperwork that made his temples throb until it was time to consult those delinquent in their duties from the night before. Many were simply drunk and had either not returned for morning muster or had chosen to spend their evenings, and a copious amount of their salaries from the coffers of His Majesty, in the awful brothels of New York. Entering the names in the record, doling out their punishments, and seeing their reactions only exacerbated the pain in his head. Most nights, he retired early and lay upon his bed with a wet rag on his face and tried not to think of his command. That only left him thinking of Jemima.

Amongst the chests filled with his uniforms and equipment were presents for her he'd purchased from local vendors. Dresses and bonnets so extravagant that no colonist would ever wear them lay between presents for his children and a few trinkets for their home. He'd decorated their home with items from Greece and

France as tokens and reminders of his service to the Crown. The urge to do the same with their certain victory in America had been too strong not to complete before victory had been achieved.

It's a matter of time, he thought. The near thirty years of his service taught him that certain things were inevitable. Victory would occur soon after an enemy had lost their main route of supply. The capture of New York dealt a massive blow to Washington and the quick advance through New Jersey panicked the Continental Congress and pushed public opinion of the war lower. Intelligence operatives reported that the bulk of the Continental Army enlistments ended at the turn of the new year. As few as 800 men would be left in Washington's command.

Victory was as inevitable as duty. Cornwallis looked past the chests to where his dress uniform coat hung. Sometimes duty meant standing around and looking pleased and interested in the people around him. Sometimes it meant leading troops into a volley of musket and cannon fire thick enough to stand on. More often than not, Cornwallis would have chosen the latter.

There was a knock at the door. His butler's voice came muted from the other side. "My Lord? Your carriage has arrived."

Cornwallis did not move, except to sip his wine. Soon, he wouldn't have to answer the door for anyone. No one would be allowed to disturb his leave. He could sit and sip wine with Jemima until dawn and enjoy every lasting moment. As a conversationalist, his beloved wife was unparalleled. Every minute spent in her company was far better than even the best situations inherent of his service. The needs and calls of Sir William Howe or any other general placed in command over him could then wait.

Why not leave the service now?

The thought surprised him for a moment, and then he laughed at his own impetuousness. The price of his commission had seemed so great when he was a boy. And yet, its importance had grown to take hold of his heart. He could not leave the army behind so easily. There were many things to do. One, though, was what he wanted more than anything in his illustrious career. *Washington.*

The orders given to him by Lord General Howe were clear and he felt only half-sated in their completion. The expectation was that Cornwallis would find Washington and destroy him before the weather changed. Across New Jersey, the British army and their Hessian mercenaries succeeded in driving out and driving back the rebels. Washington hid somewhere across the Delaware River near Philadelphia. Rather than tempt the weather gods, Howe instructed Cornwallis to garrison the army for the winter. Cornwallis had objected, at first, until he realized that his commanders no longer felt that Washington's army was a threat. With the Continental Congress currently disbanded, the rebel logistical support channels were strained. In a harsh climate, Washington's army would dissolve itself, leaving little for the British to defeat as soon as the weather turned warm. Still, Cornwallis wanted the thrill of the chase to never end. Even as he learned that Washington's army dwindled and hid to lick their wounds and survive the winter, Cornwallis craved closure.

Cornwallis looked out into the night and as far west as he could see. "Where are you, old man?"

He laughed. At forty-five, and Washington only a few years older than himself, they were hardly old men. Washington, though, presented a unique challenge. He understood terrain and subterfuge more than any American commander Cornwallis had opposed since the war began. Washington used information to his advantage and, more importantly, was a charismatic leader of men. It was too bad he served on the wrong side of the war, Cornwallis believed. Washington would have been a tremendous ally for His Majesty's army instead of a pointed thorn in the side of the British army.

There was only one thing to do. Washington had to be found, drawn out to fight, and eliminated. No other recourse would do. Whether it was on the New Jersey frontier or someplace else, Cornwallis knew it would be his destiny to dispel the rebel army and return America to the monarchy. Short of defeating Washington in open combat, there were other practical ways to destroy the resistance within the colonies. Splitting them from each other, isolating the metropolitan areas, and targeting the general populace would all reap benefits by drawing Washington out. For his misgivings, Washington was an honorable man and the suffering of his people, or those whom he felt he defended, would never do. Still, the older man was not prone to rash decisions, so anything Cornwallis would choose to do had to work toward an end result that even Washington's shrewd planning and aversion to combat would have to face.

Maybe then this war will end.

Maybe then he could spend the rest of his life in England seeing to the growth of his children and the tenuous health of his beautiful wife.

Maybe then. As long as Washington did not do something stupid and jeopardize Cornwallis' leave, there would be time to prepare for the inevitability of American surrender. Cornwallis shook away the thought and sat down the wineglass to put on his uniform and make it presentable. Leaving his spacious room, Cornwallis looked back at the collection of chests ready for departure in a few days' time and smiled. All too soon, he'd be back in England regardless of what Washington did.

Jemima waited.

The silly thing wasn't where it was supposed to have been. At the end of the summer, just before the weather cooled, Emily had washed all of her dresses and hung them outside to dry in a warm western breeze. She'd mended a hem and resewed lace trimmings on another while they dried in the sun. All of them were packed safely away in her mother's old traveling chest save for one. At first, finding the missing dress was a trivial concern. After she'd torn the house apart, she'd even risked looking in the secret compartment in the barn floor only to come up empty-handed. Her father would have chastised her digging around in their cherished belongings for the dress, but he would have understood that the pursuit of the missing dress helped to quell her frayed nerves.

A loaded pistol rested by her thigh as she sat in the parlor waiting for her father to return. The rustle of breeze outside kept her awake and when it failed and her eyes became heavy, she walked the floor of their small home until her feet ached from the effort. At half past three in the morning as she sat in the chair, her father walked into the house and shook off his coat and stood before the fire.

"I was worried about you," she said.

"Nothing to worry about," her father said. "Mason and the squad are across the river with General Washington as we speak." He sighed suddenly. "I'm glad they are. Here, they could be a danger to us and themselves."

"They are better than that," she said. "Mason is a good leader and he has good leaders with him. They can help General Washington win this war."

Daniels nodded. "I'm more worried about the next few days. If what Mason says is true actually takes place, the war will turn a corner. The British will come with all their might."

There was something unsaid behind his countenance that left his face puzzled and calm at the same time. If the British came, they'd be further at risk. Their identities and allegiances would certainly come under increased scrutiny. "You believe we'll have to move from here."

"I don't want that to be the case, but it may be best for us," he said. "Now, get some sleep. Let an old man sit by his fire and think for a bit, please."

"Yes, Father." She gathered her candle and book and was all the way to the top of the central staircase when she remembered the dress. "Father?" she called down the rickety stairs. "Have you opened Mother's chest again?"

"No. Why?"

"My red dress isn't there." She frowned. "Mother's dress?"

She heard his footfalls through the small kitchen and he appeared at the narrow foyer. "It's missing?"

"It's certainly not here."

Daniels walked up the stairs. He turned into his daughter's room and looked into the chest with her. After a long moment, he slid the chest a few feet across the floor and pried up a board with his fingernails. A small notebook lay hidden underneath. He took a deep breath and released it. Their most important secret remained safe.

"You think someone took it?" she asked. "That they were looking for your book and took my dress as some type of warning?"

"No," Daniels said. "The only people who've been here with us are Mason and his squad. One of them came up here and took it, most likely. The same person who took my old boots from inside the front stoop."

Emily nodded. A flurry of thoughts came together. "Dunaway. The shy one."

"She's not shy." Daniels looked at his daughter. "Try again, love."

The game wasn't easy, but she'd grown more comfortable with it over time. Since the beginning of the war, they'd tiptoed around both sides with the grace of dancers. Now, things were getting serious. His trust in her soared even as the danger increased.

Emily took a breath, composed her thoughts, and spoke slowly. "She doesn't want to be a soldier. She's going through the motions."

"And?" Daniels smiled in agreement. "What else?"

"You heard her talking, Father. That's not fair to me."

Daniels shook his head. "I need your wits about you tomorrow, Emily. Tell me."

The shy girl studied everything. Only two types of people study others so intently. "She's an actress, or at least believes herself to be one. She's no spy."

"I think"—Daniels slid the trunk over the concealed notebook—"you are correct. She has your dress and, most likely at the most inopportune moment, she'll leave Mason and the others behind."

"Why would she do something like that?"

"Opportunity. She sees a way out and believes she can pull it off." Daniels put his hands on his daughter's shoulders. "She doesn't see the risk as being hers to bear, unlike you. You're walking into a den of lions tomorrow, Daughter. Do you understand the risk?"

"I wouldn't go if I didn't, Father," Emily said. Her voice was strong and more confident than she felt inside, but it was correct. "I can gather as much information as you can in half the time."

Daniels laughed and it made her smile. Since her mother's death the summer before, he'd not smiled much. He'd supported the rebellion ever since, using his contacts and reputation with the British and the somewhat reformed Hessians in the Trenton area to spy on the enemy for Washington. As he'd repaired the British and Hessian weapons, he'd tinkered with them and tried to make them less accurate and more likely to fail. If there was a major battle and Washington's forces did not prevail, they'd come for them both.

"Only get what we need." Daniels lowered his chin and looked into her eyes. "When the time is right, encourage Captain Sutton to bring you home. Do not stay later than is necessary."

"I won't, Father." She smiled at him. "The rumors are clear that Rall is afraid. I cannot see this party lasting beyond ten o'clock. Their men are tired."

Daniels grinned. "And just where did you hear that?"

"From you," she said. "You spoke the other day of endless alerts and pauses. That has to be exhausting, even to a professional soldier. You've said as much from your time in the war, too. Even Captain Sutton looked tired—well, as tired as that man could look."

Daniels released her shoulders and nodded at her. "The Hessians are constantly on alert. The strain on the men alone will cause confusion if an attack were to come. We saw the same things under French artillery fire in the war. The longer a man goes without sleep, the simpler tasks become difficult. When a man cannot buckle his pants correctly, he can hardly be expected to muster and fire a weapon with any degree of accuracy."

Emily snorted. "What is that, Father?"

"Mason never asked me to reload their ammunition. I think it's time I tried to make it work."

"Didn't he take all of the cartridges?"

"When they cleaned their weapons? Dunaway left a cartridge on the floor."

"That girl is going to get them killed. Maybe it will be for the best if she leaves them soon."

Daniels nodded and reached into his pocket. The brass cartridge with the funny crimped end gleamed in the firelight. "I have to try, I think. Especially if they do not find their missing one. The redcoats will certainly use it to their advantage. We have to beat them to it."

Emily moved her stance to be in his line of sight. She hated it when he stared into space. "You believe you can?"

Daniels shrugged. "If I can't, then no one can. I believe that I have to try."

Emily recoiled. "What could that girl be thinking?"

"She's thinking about a warm bed and good night's sleep at all costs, Daughter."

"As should we, for now. Tomorrow will be a difficult day for both of us."

They said their good nights and Emily turned to her bed. It was a long time before she slept.

CHAPTER SIXTEEN

For the better part of an hour, they sat in the darkness of a small glade with nothing but starlight above them. Captain Washington's men surrounded them in a loose perimeter. No one spoke. Mason glanced around every once in a while, but their guards barely moved except to change positions from guard to warming stations. They huddled around small fires while Mason and the cadets stamped their feet and tried to stay warm. Stratton suggested push-ups and sit-ups before Mason told them to build a damned fire, except that Washington's men stopped them from gathering wood. Mason believed the intent was simple. He sat on his rucksack next to Higgs.

"They want us to sit here and get cold. They think we're not telling them the truth and they're watching us to make a false move."

Higgs was barely visible in the darkness. "I've never seen a sky this dark."

Mason looked up and stared. In the city lights of Philadelphia, he'd maybe see a tenth as many stars in this sky on a good night. "My family went to the Grand Canyon a few years ago. We bought this Winnebago." He chuckled. "My dad wants to just drive around when he retires, so they bought the RV and we headed out there. We camped in Williams, out to the west of Flagstaff. The sky there was like this, and it was a new moon, too. I'd never seen a sky without city lights before. I couldn't see ten feet in front of my face. Never seen anything like it."

The memory was clear and vibrant, but felt a lifetime ago. He lowered his head and stared at the dark ground between his feet for a long moment.

"You know," Higgs said, "they're keeping their distance because they don't trust us. We don't look like they do, talk like they do, or act like they do. We're strangers to them. The way we're dressed? Our snowsuits? They think we're ghosts, Mason. Don't take their distance personally. Or the whole thing about being next to their shitty little fires. The time will come."

"For what—"

A ripple of slight noise came from the perimeter and Mason startled. By the light of Captain Washington's small fire he saw a tall man on a horse approach. "Holy..."

Higgs whirled in that direction. They stared silently for a few seconds. General Washington, there was no question it was him, stared back for a moment. "He's younger than I thought he'd be," Higgs said.

Murphy whispered. "He's in his mid-forties—like Lieutenant Colonel Graves."

Except this man is the Commander in Chief.

The other cadets were silent now, all looking at the father of their country. The first President of the United States. Washington passed the reins to one of his cousin's men and slid down from the stirrups. He was much taller than the others and he walked into the circle a few steps before they heard a voice from behind him.

"General. An escort?"

Washington looked at the cadets and shook his head. "Unnecessary. If they are friends, we'll have a fine conversation. If they strike, you know what to do." He looked up at Mason intently and there was a hint of a smile on his face.

"I can't believe this is happening," Murphy whispered. No one moved as Washington approached them. He was five meters away when Mason stood slowly and whispered harshly.

"Squad, attention!"

Washington froze in place and for a split second Mason was sure the guards would shoot them all down. There was silence as the squad stood to the position of attention as a group and Mason raised a parade-ground salute.

"Good evening, sir."

Washington nodded. After a moment, he answered Mason's salute in a similar, though different fashion. "Good evening. You must be Sergeant Mason."

Mason took a deep breath. "I am, sir."

"Good." Washington stood silent before him for a moment. The general reached out a hand. His grip was firm and warm. Mason had the idiotic thought of never washing his hand again.

"Introduce me to your squad and then let them rest, Mason. We have much to talk about."

They sat in a ring, Washington on Kennedy's rucksack. They'd finished their story with Mason and Stratton handling most of the details from their arrival until their meeting. No one mentioned being lost on the training lane and Mason was grateful. Washington took it all with a poker face. When they were finished, the general fingered the nylon straps and camouflage material for a long moment. He looked up at them appraisingly. "Vernon Daniels and I served together against the French not that long ago. There are few men whose word I take at face value, but he is one. He tells me you're from a time far different than this and hearing your story, I am inclined to believe you. He also says that you have specific knowledge of this war and what is about to take place. Something that no more than fifteen men know fully at this point. Given the circumstances, I suggest you tell me everything you know about my plan and we'll go from there."

Mason looked at Murphy. "Sir, Cadet Murphy is—"

"Cadet?" Washington squinted. "Are you all cadets then?"

"Yes, sir." From the look on Washington's face, Mason wasn't sure that was a good or a bad revelation. "Our ranks are immaterial and really for training purposes. We're all officers in training. Cadet Murphy is the most familiar with this period of history."

Washington looked at Murphy. "Where are you from, Murphy?"

"Salt Lake City, Utah, sir," Murphy said. "It's a couple of thousand miles to the west." He shrugged. "The continent is much larger than you currently believe. We won't do much exploring out there for a few more years."

Washington chuckled. "I have much to learn. What does your history say about the coming days, Murphy?"

Murphy beamed. "Sir, tomorrow is Christmas Day. You've ordered the men to be ready to muster starting in the afternoon with the intent to cross the Delaware and attack Trenton at first light. Over the last two days, you've had two councils of war to determine and plan an attack on Trenton."

"Anyone could surmise that, Murphy. You're not convincing me."

Murphy nodded as if to clear his mind. Mason was about to speak when Murphy continued. "Your attack is three-pronged, sir. You have General Cadwalader to the south who is to cross and harass the enemy at Burlington. This is designed to keep Colonel Von Donop from making a quick attack in support of your operation at Trenton. You've just this evening sent Doctor Benjamin Rush on a mission to determine if Von Donop is still in the Mount Holly area. He is still there, sir. Colonel Von Donop has found a lady friend and is lingering for the holiday there. His troops will be drunk tomorrow evening and unable to mount a quick response."

Mason leaned in. "Murphy? Remember—"

"No, Mason," Murphy said. "This is the Commander in Chief of our army. He needs to know everything."

"We can't change history."

"If I may," Washington said. "You already have. You are correct, Cadet Murphy. I am glad to know that Von Donop will not have an effect on the outcome of our attack."

"The weather will have a significant effect, sir. General Cadwalader will not be able to cross the Delaware, sir. Neither will General Ewing at Trenton proper." Murphy took a breath. "A storm is coming, sir. What we call a nor'easter. The winds will pick up, temperatures will plummet and the river will start to freeze. You'll make it across the river later than planned and run into issues crossing Jacob's Creek. The weather will protect your late arrival into Trenton. Colonel Rall brings his men in from the weather, which relaxes their alert posture. They're all tired from constant harassment and by the time you get there, they won't have stirred. Even two hours past daylight you maintain the element of surprise."

Washington nodded. "We will adjust our muster time and cross earlier to compensate."

"Not much more, sir," Murphy said. "Nightfall is still your friend. And staying out in the elements for a longer time will have an adverse effect on your troops. You'll lose more than you do."

"How many are lost on the march?"

"Two," Murphy said. "But no one dies in your plan during

the attack. There are ... some injuries but no one is killed in the attack. It's quite stunning."

Washington sat for a moment, staring again at the braided nylon strap in his fingers. "And your weapon? The one you lost?"

Mason frowned. Things had been going so well. "That's why we're here, sir. We haven't been able to mount a search being behind enemy lines. If the British get it and study it, their whole culture could accelerate. Industry could develop and create different, more deadly weapons faster than you could retaliate. The war you win would establish this country, but the British would be back with better weapons of war. We didn't want that to happen."

"Vernon told me that the Hessian was wounded. Could he have made it back to Trenton alone?"

Mason shrugged. "We don't know, sir."

Higgs piped up. "If he did, sir, we can at least even out the effects. We have our rifles and more."

Washington looked at her for a long moment. For the first time, his poker face cracked a little. "And you are?"

"Ashley Higgs, General."

"And you're a cadet as well?" Washington rubbed his chin. "Women serve openly in your time?"

"Yes, sir," Higgs said.

The general turned to Murphy. "Women are our cooks. You know this is true?"

"Yes, sir," Murphy replied. "Over the course of the next year, you'll realize on your own that women can be of real service to the army as camp followers—doing laundry, cooking, taking care of the filthy habits of men. The result will cut dysentery and keep your army fighting. There are other isolated cases where women will help on the battlefield and in hospitals."

"Really?" Washington's eyebrows rose.

"But, we can do more than that," Higgs said. "Women are equally capable as men, sir."

Washington took a breath. "We'll see about that, Miss Higgs. I commend your enthusiasm, but facing a wall of muskets has petrified men."

"And where I'm from," Higgs said, her eyes blazing, "women have saved petrified men from the battlefield and lost their lives just as honorably, sir."

Washington almost smiled. "You make a formidable argument,

Miss Higgs. Your very presence, along with Mason and Booker, have me thinking many things, but I do not have the time, nor the ability, to focus on them now. We will revisit this in a few days' time. There is one more thing I need to know about this plan."

Murphy replied, "Yes, sir?"

"When the Hessians strike their colors, what happens next?"

Mason looked at Murphy. *We're really going to change history now.*

"Four hundred Hessians and the British dragoons escape over the bridge south of town. They warn Von Donop to the south and the British garrison at Princeton. Believing that they will attack you, you move east and attack Princeton, though not with the intent to take the town. As you retreat back to Trenton, Lord General Howe sends a message. Lord General Cornwallis is recalled from his leave—he is about to board a ship for England right now—and they march on Trenton. There is a series of skirmishes north of town. Realizing you can't fight the full garrison in the open or in the town itself, you retreat across the river. Then, your entire army slips away in the night and the British return to Princeton. You'll seek winter quarters farther north and have a terrible winter. But spring will bring reinforcements and new enlistments. You'll have a new army."

Washington looked at Mason for a long moment. "Your uniforms? Do you wear white all the time?"

"No, sir." Mason shook his head. "It's all about concealment. Protecting ourselves by blending into the environment makes it harder for an enemy to see us. What they can't see, they don't expect."

"The French and their allies fought us the same way. The British officers believed it was cowardice to hide behind rocks and trees while they deployed their lines and went through their tedious commands. It was no wonder they hurt us so badly." Washington shook his head. "Your army teaches you to fight that way?"

"Surprise is one of the major tenets we fight under, sir. Your example at Trenton is taught as a prime example. Surprise, the massing of troops, the application of them in synchronicity with each other. War is meant to be won, General. The players set the field."

"Indeed," Washington said. "Then the plan stays as it is, save for starting to cross the river earlier."

"What about Ewing and Cadwalader?"

Washington stared into space for a minute. "Their orders will stand. Just in case something has happened across the river that changes things. Your very presence could have that effect, Mason. If your rifle is in the Hessian garrison, their alerts have a purpose beyond an irrational fear that our army is going to come and attack them at a moment's notice."

Mason looked at Higgs and then at Stratton. "We hadn't thought of that, sir."

"And nothing may happen differently than what you've suggested," Washington said. "But there is a hole that must be plugged and your concealments are well suited for the task."

Mason blinked. "You want us in the fight, sir?"

Washington nodded. "The bridge over the Assunpink Creek. Your squad will hold it. The high ground to the south of it is full of deep snow. It is a perfect place to hide you until the attack. Once we fall upon Trenton, you will prevent the Hessian and British escape as best you can."

Mason looked at Murphy. "Didn't you say the dragoons use their horses to cross?"

"Yeah," Murphy replied. "The Hessians cross by the road, though."

"How is the terrain around the bridge?" Stratton asked.

"The creek is wide but not terribly deep. Your position will be good for observation," Washington said. "Until you're needed."

Mason looked at his watch. "We'll have to start moving right now if we want to get—"

Washington nodded. "Colonel Glover is ready to move you down the river. You'll stop on this side just before the falls and transfer to a second boat that will take you across. From there, simply move north until you can observe the bridge. Move onto the high ground and camp there. You will wait for our attack. More importantly—" Washington paused. Any levity drained from his features. "You will stay out of the attack until such time as you engage the escaping troops."

Mason frowned. "You're afraid we'll do something wrong?"

Washington smiled again. Mason decided it was warm and friendly. "I've known a few cadets in my time, Mason." He stood and they all stood with him. "That brings me to this," he said. "If you're going to serve in my army, I do not want you serving as cadets. For now, you answer only to me."

Washington reached into his jacket and handed two documents to Mason.

"One of these are your orders and the other is a specific commission in case you run into friendly commanders who wish not to listen to your story." Washington curled one side of his mouth under. "I doubt you'll find that, but it's hard to say. Keep the seals intact, nonetheless."

"When the Hessians strike their colors, you'll want us to report to you in Trenton?"

Washington nodded. "Yes, we'll determine what should happen after we secure the town. For now, get back to the river and make your way south. I expect to see you in Trenton once the attack is complete."

Stratton leaned in. "Sir? General Washington? You're expecting us to fail, aren't you?"

Washington's expression was blank. "You're questioning me?"

"Yeah," Stratton said. As much as Mason wanted his stomach to turn, he couldn't help thinking that Stratton might actually be right. "You're expecting us to fail and those papers are false intelligence, aren't they?"

Washington frowned. "In case you are caught, yes."

"Then keep us here on this side of the river," Mason said. "You already know the attack is going to succeed."

"Or let us march with your army," Stratton said. "Having us defend the bridge is tactically stupid, sir. It amounts to sitting us in a corner and then trying to have us plug a hole in your dike. If you want us there, give us what we'd need. More troops and supplies."

"I cannot risk my army," Washington said.

"We're expendable," Mason said. He looked at Stratton and they nodded at each other. "If we get there undetected, we plug a hole and keep some of the surprise factor longer. That changes how the British respond. If we get caught, or get killed in the process, we're a deflection."

Washington nodded. "Like your duplicitous camouflage, deception is a necessary evil, Mason."

"So is trusting your troops, General." Mason bent down and shouldered his rucksack. "If seeing us in Trenton is the only way you're going to trust us, General, then we'll see you at Rall's headquarters. It's in Mister Potts' home, sir. You might have heard of it."

"Your tone is disrespectful, Mason," Washington said. "You forget you're surrounded by my soldiers who can fire on you at a moment's notice."

"You said if we were friends that we'd have a nice conversation. You're not going to kill us. Your intention is for the Hessians or the British to do it for you if we don't succeed." Mason raised the half sleeve of his snowsuit on his right shoulder. "That flag means your men trusted you, sir. Your battle at Trenton is the start of something that will change history. If you want us there, fine. We'll be there. But you've got to give us what we need and not some half-assed plan to infiltrate Trenton."

Washington looked at Mason for a long moment, snorted once, and finally let a smile break out on his face. "Half-assed plan? I doubt Colonel Glover and his Marblehead men will agree, Mason."

"Then prove me wrong, sir," Mason said. "We'll give you everything we have, sir. Do us the courtesy of returning the favor."

Washington stepped forward, towering over Mason. He extended his hand again and they shook again. It took a moment, but Washington did the same with all of them, even kissing the hands of Higgs and Dunaway, who curtsied.

"Colonel Glover?" Washington's voice was clear and firm.

"Aye, sir?"

"Ready your boats and provide rations and cartridges to this squad. Anything that they need, see to it that they have it. You'll conduct them to Trenton for infiltration immediately."

"Yes, sir."

They heard Glover giving secondary orders and Washington turned toward his horse and walked away. A few paces away, he stopped and looked over his shoulder. "Mason? If this half-assed plan works, we'll have much more to discuss, I gather."

"Yes, sir." Mason smiled. "Victory or death, then, sir?"

Washington nodded. "Well said, Sergeant Mason. Victory or death. See you in Trenton on the morrow."

You bet your ass we will. Mason turned to the squad, all watching George Washington walk away from them. "You heard the general's orders. Ruck up, people. Team leaders on me for movement."

Stratton and Higgs were in front of him in seconds. The pause was just long enough for him to gather his thoughts. "What's the plan?"

Mason nodded in the direction of Colonel Glover's voice. "I'll see where Glover is going to put us in. We move north, like Washington said, and they get into the high ground above Trenton. From there, we see what's going on."

"You think we'll find cover and concealment up there?" Higgs said.

Mason shrugged. "I don't know. If there's trees and snow, I think we'll be concealed enough to recon the area when the sun comes up. All we have to do is stay warm and be ready when the army comes rolling along."

Stratton chuckled. "Terrible pun, man."

Mason realized he'd quoted the official army song. "That's pretty terrible, huh?"

Higgs looked at them with a smile. "Can we get moving? Miles to go before we sleep and all that."

Mason grinned. "No shit. Let's go, people. Stratton, your team in front, ranger file. Head back to the river. Move out."

Washington motioned to Glover as he took the reins of his horse. "Colonel? A word?"

Glover stepped closer so they could whisper. "I'm not to dispatch them, sir?"

"No," Washington said. "Get them south of the falls and put them in where they can move on foot into Trenton from the south."

Glover nodded. "I'll need a runner to the Trenton ferry."

"You have it," Washington said. "Tell General Ewing's men to put them in safely—like their raids or better."

"You trust them, sir?"

Washington nodded. "I'm not about to question divine providence, Colonel Glover. Those young men and women are here for a reason. I intend to figure out what that reason is. For now, that means you place them as good as any soldiers under my command. We'll see how they do on the battlefield."

"Because they're young and this is new to them, sir?"

Washington shook his head. "To teach them that knowledge is only a portion of the equation when it comes to combat, Colonel Glover. It's a lesson they need to learn now, rather than later."

CHAPTER SEVENTEEN

The silent hike back to McKonkey's Ferry seemed an out-of-body experience to Mason. He'd spoken, actually spoken, with General George Washington. Two days before, he'd failed a simple tactical exercise and questioned everything he'd carefully constructed about his collegiate career. All of the careful preparation, the intense preparation for exams, and sacrificing summer fun for clerking experience went out the window. No amount of academic pressure ever amounted to knowing that the "father of his country" and its first president expected him to successfully cross a river and establish a patrol base in enemy territory. Doing so with a bunch of cadets like himself seemed impossible.

Except that since they'd left the abandoned farmhouse the previous morning, Mason noticed that all of them, even the chronically late and out of shape Martinez, were . . . good. They moved silently and communicated with hand and arm signals. There was no question Mason was the squad leader. What made it better was that Stratton and Higgs seemed to have established a rhythm to their duties and responsibilities. They worked together better than Mason thought possible. Their quiet confidence in him, and each other, resonated with Mason. He was determined to be just as good, if not better.

The dark, sleek river appeared around a bend. Mason felt a brush at his shoulder and he turned to see the pale face of Colonel Glover.

"You seem lost in thought," the older man said. There was a hint of a smile on his face.

Mason knew the look well. His freshman year, clerking during the summer for an appellate court judge in Pennsylvania, he'd seen the same judgment from the grizzled old man's face. *You think I can't handle this.* Mason took a deep breath and summoned as much command presence as he could.

"I'm fine, sir," Mason said. "Reviewing my orders and making a plan."

Glover harrumphed. "A full day behind Hessian lines would seem to make you a bit scared. Unsure. A lesser man might run."

"We've been behind that line for two days, sir. And we're still here." Mason bit his tongue and realized that Glover baited him. "I have my orders, Colonel. You have yours. If you please, sir, put my squad in at a place where we have more than a slim chance of survival. From there, we'll handle the rest."

Glover snorted, but looked at Mason with a glint in his eye. "I have a spot for you. The Hessians patrol the road on the hour. It takes them twenty minutes from their southern post at the Assunpink Bridge to reach the lower ferry. When they turn north, we'll put you in behind them. You'll have forty minutes to get into the higher ground. Is that enough?"

"Plenty," Mason said. The wide Durham boat that had carried the squad across from the Delaware side waited. Unlike their last trip, there were no armed guards. Six oarsmen waited and Colonel Glover stepped inside alongside Mason. "You're going, too?"

"Aye," Glover said. "To the point that I'm not even allowing General Ewing's men to put you in. I take my job seriously, Mason."

"Senior officers shouldn't be ferrying men on a dangerous river, sir." Even as he said it, Mason realized the stark truth that true leadership was more often leadership by example.

"Boy, I've been up and down this river twenty times in the last week. Knowing it like the back of my hand is my job." Glover took a breath. "There's a set of falls above the lower ferry. With so much riding on these boats tomorrow, I can't risk my men scuttling one in the river. I'll be fine. You ... you take care of those young men and women."

"I'm trying, sir," Mason replied as the boat shoved off from the darkened bank. "Everyone seems to think I can't do that."

Glover shook his head. "You're missing the point, lad. The general wants to believe the tale you tell is true. You told him about the one place on the battlefield where Hessians escape. He wants you to be right. He wants you to plug that hole and complete the envelopment. In order to do that, from this moment until then, you have to ensure your soldiers are ready. That means taking care of them. Ensuring that they have what they need and being prepared for action at a moment's notice."

Mason nodded. "We'll be ready, sir. All of us."

Glover extended a hand, which Mason shook in his own. "Godspeed to you, Mason. We'll see you in Trenton."

"Thank you, sir."

"Now, get down and keep quiet. Once we're through the shoals, we'll start looking for the Hessians. If all is well, we'll put in. The rest will be up to you."

"Got it." Mason nodded. He moved to the center of the boat and knelt on one knee between Stratton and Higgs. "Okay. Be ready. Once we get through the shoals, start looking for the Hessians on the far shore. We'll have a window, based on the way they patrol. If it's good, we'll jump and go."

Stratton nodded. "Alpha team will lead, ranger file. We'll get across the road about ten meters and circle up. From there, we can head uphill and find a good spot."

"That's my job," Higgs said. "Alpha team will provide security while we look for a good position that can see the town and the bridge but give us some concealment. As long as there's snow on that hillside, we should be fine."

"That part of the hill faces north. Should be plenty of snow," Mason said. "Once we're there, we tighten up and hit fifty percent security. I want everyone to eat and sleep while they're not on watch."

Higgs nodded and Stratton gave a thumbs-up. Mason clapped each of them on the shoulder and was about to say something when a light in the distance caught his eye.

"Trenton," Mason said. The oarsmen knelt along the gunwales of the boat and gently pushed off the bottom. As they glided through the water, Mason realized that the far bank was getting closer by the moment.

Oh, shit!

Even kneeling, their white snow ponchos stood out in the starlight. Mason whispered to them, "Prone position. Everybody get flat on the bottom of the boat."

They shuffled into position, the Durham boat rocking gently as they did.

"Be still," Glover hissed.

Mason froze and tried to breathe quietly. After a few moments, they slid past a large barnlike structure along the riverbank with lanterns burning in its windows. He could hear voices above them barking in their guttural tongue.

Any second, they're going to look out the window! We're so fucked!

But nothing happened. After another minute, the barn was behind them and the boat rocked gently through what had to be the shoals Glover had spoken of. The lights of Trenton were farther away now; the oarsmen stood and resumed their smooth pushing. The boat picked up speed.

"Mason?" Glover's voice was soft but urgent.

"Sir?"

"See the guards? With the lantern? They're just coming back from patrol. We're going straight to the lower ferry."

"Roger that, sir."

"What did you say?"

Murphy rolled over to Mason. "Roger is another word for 'fuck' in this time period, Mason."

Mason tried not to laugh. "Sorry, sir. We're good to go."

Glover signaled to the oarsmen to pick up the pace. "Be ready when I tell you."

"Everybody up on one knee. Get ready to move," Mason said. The squad moved into position. Stratton turned to Mason and smiled. In the dim starlight, his teeth were eerily white. Mason smiled in return.

The bow of the Durham boat squared to the Delaware shore. Mason watched as the oarsmen accelerated their pushing, but still kept the smooth, quiet rhythm.

Here we go.

"Alpha team, get ready," Mason whispered.

Stratton said, "Brace yourselves for hitting the shore."

No sooner had Mason moved to steady himself than they felt the bow brushing across the river bottom and climbing the bank.

"Go, Mason!" Glover said.

The squad shot to their feet as one and vaulted over the bow of the boat. Alpha team moved in a fast, tight ranger file. Onto the road. Mason took his position in the center and ensured that Higgs and her team were there behind him.

"Move out," he whispered to Stratton and they were off. Across the road, the thicker vegetation pushed the squad closer together. Mason could reach out and touch Koch's shoulder if he wanted to. Through what had to be a summer thicket, they moved at a snail's pace for what felt like an eternity. Mason stepped through and into a clearer, sparse forest floor as they started to move up a hillside. He was about to tap Koch on the shoulder and pass the signal to stop when the signal came back from the front. They knelt slowly. Koch took off his helmet and sat listening to the quiet wind.

Nice. A perfect transition. Mason smiled to himself. The squad immediately moved into a cigar-shaped perimeter, narrow on both ends and wide enough in the middle that Mason could consult with Stratton and Higgs. Weapons out, completely silent, Mason reached up and removed his Kevlar helmet and let the cold air bite into the thin layer of sweat on his scalp. The rest of the squad did the same—a listening halt. Mason closed his eyes and listened to the sounds of the quiet forest. What passed for normal in the darkness was what they had to not exceed. After two minutes, give or take, Mason slipped his helmet on and adjusted his chin strap. Stratton and Higgs did the same before tapping the nearest members of their team.

Mason looked out to the north at the edge of Trenton in the distance. A small hill blocked their view just to the north and east. Given its proximity to Assunpink Creek, and the edge of the lighted, noisy town, Mason thought it was the perfect place to look for an objective rally point.

Stratton leaned over. "Which way, boss?"

"Thinking over there." Mason pointed. "Set up at the hilltop."

"This side," Higgs said. "We put two people on the top and observe the town, everyone else on the backside. Looks like there is a deep little cut there. It would give us protection and a faster way out."

Mason squinted. "Long as we can see the bridge. If we can find the right position on this side of that hilltop, we'll set up there." He looked up into the partially clouded sky. The moon wasn't visible and the woods were dark without much starlight. "Stay close. Arm's length, okay? Make sure you can see the person in front and behind you."

"What if we think we're separated?"

Mason nodded. "Yeah. Stop. Whisper first. Then try to whistle. Just don't start screaming."

"We'll be fine. Just make sure we stay together," Stratton said. "Can't be but a few hundred meters."

"Nice and slow, Stratton," Mason said. "As silent as we can go."

Stratton slapped him on the shoulder. "You got it. Ready?"

Mason took a deep breath and glanced again at the distant lights of Trenton. Hessian soldiers, armed to the teeth and capable of wielding their firepower, were close enough to see. With real ammunition in their M16s, Mason and his squad would have had effective range from their target hilltop. The blanks in their rifles would serve a purpose—making the Hessians believe Mason's squad was more like a regiment. Their muskets would be the real weaponry. There were pyrotechnics, too. The artillery simulators could have great effect to confuse and stop the Hessians. There were a lot of variables he'd have to consider. The weather and the terrain, though, were on their side. In the cold night with a solid blanket of snow on the ground, cover and concealment were good enough that the full moon poking through sporadic clouds couldn't hinder. They could do this.

"Brief your teams and move out in one minute," Mason said. "Nice and silent."

Stratton and Higgs turned to their teams. Mason watched them brief a cadet and then have the cadet turn to the next. A memory came of he and fellow Boy Scouts standing in two long lines, each Scout holding a miniature Snickers bar. The scoutmaster, his father, whispered something in each boy's ear and then counted them down from three. The first person then ate the Snickers bar and attempted to pass the message to the next Scout as fast as possible. When it got to Mason, the message was unintelligible gibberish. The lesson, however, was clear. Time doesn't matter if the message is garbled. Instead of standing up after sixty seconds, he watched and ensured that everyone had the message he'd given. When Stratton and Higgs turned back to him, Mason stood.

"Let's go."

They moved as one, quiet and slow for the better part of an hour before they reached the hill. The farthest western spur of the minor ridge was a perfect place to wait, shielded by a rock outcropping about a meter and a half tall with a small, rounded overhang where at least two squad members could sleep fully stretched out. There was even room for a small fire, but Mason did not want to risk it. Koch and Murphy took the first watch up top. Mason and Higgs took the first watch below. Stratton, Dunaway, Booker, and Martinez shook out their sleeping bags and lay down without a word.

Higgs sat next to Mason on the dirt just outside the outcropping. "It's not as cold as I thought it would be."

"Really?" Mason asked. He hadn't thought about any effect the weather would have.

"Yeah," Higgs said. "Murphy says the real storm is tomorrow night, but if I remember right Washington and the army are in for a brutal winter in our timeline."

Mason snorted, but nodded his head in understanding. "With our gear, a night like this is uncomfortable, but survivable without a fire, huh?"

"Exactly. Its already three in the morning. Not much sleep tonight."

"We can alternate sleeping all day tomorrow."

"I suppose." Higgs laid her musket down and hugged her knees to her chest. It didn't take a rocket science degree to believe something was wrong.

"Wanna talk about it?"

"Not really," she said. After a moment, he saw her shoulders quiver. Her breathing hitched once and he could almost hear the tears cascade down her cheeks. For a moment, Mason struggled with all of the mandatory Army training he and the others had to endure with regard to sexual harassment and sexual assault. The goal of the training had been to support others, just don't touch them. After a long moment, Mason scooted closer to his friend and simply wrapped an arm around her shivering shoulders. Being a soldier was more than learning what not to do.

It was doing what was right.

"We're going to be okay, Ashley."

She nodded her head but didn't respond for two minutes. He heard and felt her cry without a sound and wondered if he could perform that feat and decided that he couldn't. When tears came from him, they were ugly noisy things. Higgs was made of something far sterner than himself. As quickly as her tears came, she wiped at her face.

"Sorry, Mason. It's Christmas morning and I miss my family, that's all."

Mason nodded but said nothing. He hadn't even thought of Christmas or his family. After Higgs had her fit of tears, it was something he would not do. He kept his arm around her shoulders though and for several minutes, they simply sat there as friends. No words were exchanged and he knew that they might never speak of it again, and that didn't matter. For a moment, she'd needed help and for the first time he realized that as a leader he could do that in many ways.

Even in the ways others said didn't work.

Christmas Day, 1776

At precisely 7:00 A.M., the Hessian artillery corps fired a single cannon shot into the predawn sky to welcome Christmas. Over the cold, perfectly paraded troops, the sky was filled with low clouds and an ominous red smear of light at the horizon. Sutton sat astride his horse at the front of his platoon of dragoons with a frown on his face. Two of his men were sick enough to miss the mandatory parade. While not as gross a violation as some of his peer Hessian units, their inability to parade was something he took personally. Dysentery or not, a proper British dragoon did not miss a parade. No sooner had the parade ended than he'd called for a private formation at the stables. He intended to discipline them as a group for the shortcomings of the sick.

The Hessians shifted positions, something between attention and parade rest, but Sutton did not change his unit's posture. They remained at attention, stiff as frozen boards on the frigid morning. Rall was talking now, but his Hessian dialect was almost inhuman to Sutton's ears. The fat colonel would ramble about nothing for ten or twelve minutes, call the brigade to attention, and then saunter off to the godawful music of his personal band. The parade was a standard, unchanging beast that Sutton loathed above all things. Yet, on Christmas morning, his thoughts were elsewhere.

The surprise, as it were, would be perfect. Vernon Daniels was almost certainly a liar and a traitor to the Crown. Without a doubt, the weapons he'd serviced for the Hunterdon men and Washington's army itself would be there in his modest cabin alongside the Hessian rifles he'd seen a few days before. Sutton's promise to apprehend the men on Christmas morning, ill-timed as it was, still served a purpose. Daniels' daughter would be brought to Trenton soon after. The daughter would attend Colonel Rall's holiday ball on Sutton's arm, but her father should be under armed guard and questioned at Sutton's leisure. Except that it was almost better to leave the man in place and more keenly observe him. There was no doubt that Washington and the Continental armies benefited from spies like Daniels on the British side of the line. Sutton intended to capture him, and with the proper form of persuasion, might actually get workable intelligence on the whereabouts of Washington's army. Daniels might have that information, and he might not. All it would take for Sutton to know for certain was to place the girl in a modicum of harm and the old man would crack. Sutton had seen it before and the quality of the information received was never in question.

It was so close he could almost taste the accolades from General Grant and maybe even Lord General Howe himself. *Patience*, he told himself. *Gather the daughter first and then squeeze the traitor as necessary.*

The parade ended with Rall abruptly stopping his speech and screaming at one of his battalions. His cannoneers fired a single empty shot that echoed thunder through the valley. The Hessians scattered in every direction. Sutton saw Lieutenant Sturm turn and look at him with a sour face.

"Another alert for nothing." Sutton smiled in return. He spun on his horse and surveyed the seventeen men in his formation for a long moment.

A smattering of rifle fire to the northeast caught his attention, but there was nothing more. Startled Hessians. He wanted to shake his head with disgust. They'd be firing at ghosts before long.

He turned to his men. The gunfire stripped away his plan for discipline. But it was just as well. "Standard patrols this morning, gentlemen. Three rounds instead of two. First section will converge on the Daniels home with a wagon at no later than ten o'clock this morning and seize all weapons—friend or foe. When she is ready, bring the daughter to my quarters. Let me be clear, gentlemen, no Hessian order will supersede my order. Are my orders clear?"

There was no response. Then again, there seldom was with

his commands. Questions meant additional duties or involuntary transfers.

"Good," Sutton said. "You are released to your patrol routes immediately. Complete this task by two this afternoon and you will have the afternoon to reflect upon your good fortune. Dismissed."

The platoon broke apart into one eight-man section and a nine-man section. The first rode in the direction of the River Road to start their long patrol north. The second arced toward the Burlington Road. They would have the longest ride, to proceed south and then north along the Pennington Road, but both would easily make the gunsmith's home by ten and return by noon. There would be much to do at his quarters to get ready for them.

He lingered for a moment, watching the last of his men start on their patrols without him. They had their orders and would succeed in doing what he'd commanded them to do. In order for him to do his part, and subvert Rall's incompetent command by finding Washington for the British commanders to destroy, there were some preparations to complete.

Washington and his ragtag army were close. There were eyes watching the Hessians and their stupid parades even now. What would those spies report to Washington? Would he see an opportunity? No, Sutton decided. Washington would do the prudent thing and shelter his troops as long as possible in the hopes his Congress would come to their aid. A fallacy, yes, because a Congress was nothing more than a group of individuals looking out for themselves under the guise of service. Sutton nudged his mount toward the dragoon's stable. A warm breakfast awaited at the hands of his hostess, and from there he could determine the best way to get what he wanted under the guise of service, too.

CHAPTER EIGHTEEN

Tucked down inside his sleeping bag system, Mason rolled over so his nose stuck out of the almost closed hole. Cold bit into his exposed skin and snapped him awake. He lay there quietly, not wanting to move for a moment before giving in to the urge to check his watch. He opened his eyes and blinked against the low light of the cloudy sunrise.

0700. Watch ain't till 0800.

He closed his eyes for another minute and tried to relax. The warm fuzz of sleep reached out for him again. Mason relaxed and tried to give in. A cannon boomed from the Trenton side of the hill. Mason snatched at the zipper and shot out of his sleeping bag in an almost instantaneous jump and run. Scrambling up the rocks at the center of their patrol base, he saw two sets of boots and then two heads alertly watching the town. Their calm made him slow down and check his momentum. Mason knelt behind them.

Stratton turned and smiled. "Nice wake-up call, huh?" he whispered and shook his head as Mason crawled into position between him and Koch.

"What's going on?" Mason yawned and rested on his elbows.

Koch had a small set of binoculars. "Some kind of formation. They've got a damned band and everything."

"Can I borrow those?" Mason asked. He tried to remember what Higgs had inventoried from the squad but didn't remember seeing binoculars on the list. "Good thing you have them."

Koch handed them over. "Been laying here for the last two

hours wondering what kept stabbing me in the ribs. Forgot I had them in an ammo pocket. Went hunting two weeks ago with my cousin."

Mason nodded and smiled. "Well, thanks for forgetting them." He watched the milling troops in their strange uniforms and found his eyes drawn to the British cavalry on the northern end of the formation as they left in two groups. There were nineteen in their formation. "How many are there?"

Stratton shrugged. "We tried to count them. Thinking nine hundred, maybe a thousand."

Washington has the numerical advantage and surprise in his favor. Not bad.

"We wrote down some questions to ask Murphy this morning," Koch said. "That's one of them."

Mason traced a line down the main street. "Shit, I wish we had a map."

Stratton pointed at the long north-south street where the formation had been. "That's Queen Street. The one to the left of it is King Street. The Hessian headquarters is there. Murphy was working on a map from memory last night—he'll make up a sand table once everyone's up and around."

Mason nodded. "The cannon woke everyone up, at least."

Stratton chuckled. "We've got another half hour up here. Who's relieving us?"

"Martinez and Dunaway," Koch said.

"I'll get them up here early," Mason said. "Good work, guys."

"No worries," Koch said.

Mason backed out of the position slowly, crawling on his knees and elbows until his boots hit the exposed rocks at the top of the outcropping. From there, he turned and looked down on their makeshift patrol base. Koch and Stratton's position was by far the most important, having more than one hundred eighty degrees of vision from the top of the knoll. Below, the central sleeping area had been watched by two guards through the night, one to the east and west. Mason made sure that he'd rotated the watch positions as well. Amazingly, he'd been able to get almost six hours of sleep and actually felt rested for a change. They'd really lucked out with their choice of fighting position in the dark. Mason crawled down the rocks and found Higgs huddled over an MRE tucked into its water-activated heating bag.

"Morning," he said.

Higgs looked up at him. "I figured it was just reveille or something like that. No other cannons or gunfire."

"A formation." Mason grinned. "Probably set off the cannon to celebrate Christmas. Glad to know that nothing changed for more than two hundred and thirty years."

"I bet they had first sergeants telling them to form up thirty minutes before the actual formation, too. Maybe an endless safety brief, too?"

Mason laughed. "We'll have to ask Stratton when they come down in a bit." He glanced over and saw that Martinez and Dunaway were both packing their sleeping systems into their nylon "stuff sacks" and pulling out MREs of their own. They'd be ready to assume their watch without his having to say a thing. Murphy sat a few feet away on his rucksack with a small notebook in one hand and a package of MRE crackers in the other. Deep in thought, Mason decided. Having someone who'd just written a paper on the battle of Trenton was a godsend, but Murphy looked too serious.

He's trying to remember every little detail.

Mason snorted and shook his head. *Every little detail could save a life.*

Mason went through the routine of stuffing his sleep system away and getting ready for the day. Satisfied that his gear was set for the day and ready to move on a moment's notice, Mason dug into the side pocket of his rucksack for an MRE and grimaced when he pulled out the vegetarian cheese pasta. Still, it was better than the breakfast omelet and he could save the spaghetti with meat sauce for that night to be prepared for the battle itself. It was a good trade-off. He removed a canteen from his load-bearing vest and drank the remainder of the good, fluorinated water he'd had from Fort Dix a few days before. The other canteen was from the natural supply at the Daniels home and they'd have to get more sooner rather than later. Mason looked at the snow and realized that a considerable amount lay on the hillside across from their position. Building a fire was not something he wanted to do and it would take an impressive amount of snow to fill their canteens with water.

Higgs stepped into his view. "You thinking about water supplies?"

"Yeah."

Higgs pointed down at the creek. "We can refill them tonight."

What? Mason shook his head. "That's too dangerous. We can melt snow or—"

"That will take forever, Mason. We should all have at least one canteen plus the extras from Kennedy and Porter that Booker is carrying. We can make it until sundown." Higgs tilted her head in the direction of Trenton. "There may be a spring nearby, too. We'll have to look around a bit today."

"We should stay put—keep watch." Mason reached to his belt and removed a multi-tool. He flicked out the knife blade and sliced open his MRE pouch. "We don't need to attract attention."

"I'm talking in this little valley, Mason. Not marching into Trenton. We can stay out of sight and see what's around. If there's anything we can use. And, we can gather snow to melt if we have to. I have a pot Emily sent along with me for that reason, okay?"

Mason blinked. "When were you going to tell me about that?"

"We have the priorities of work together, Mason. Your job is getting us in position and doing what General Washington ordered you to do. Stratton and I can take care of the rest, okay?"

Mason sighed and tore open his spoon and then the entree packet. The pasta was cold, but edible. He pushed down the taste as much as he could. Calories would be important, almost as important as water. A tiny bottle of hot sauce thumped into the ground between his feet. He looked up at Higgs and realized that she was exactly right. All he had to do was get his shit together, starting right then and there. "Thanks. Let's go ahead and get the water going. Get your pot and let's start melting snow. Build a small fire up by the rocks—nothing huge, like a few inches high at most. The wind is moving it away from Trenton. We should be okay."

Higgs stepped over to her rucksack and withdrew a small pewter pot. She tapped Booker on the shoulder and they moved quickly across the ten-meter-wide valley to the snow on the far side and began to scoop. They returned in a moment with the pot and handfuls of twigs. Booker set to work on the fire as Higgs urged Martinez and Dunaway to finish so they could relieve Koch and Stratton on the top of their position. She moved to Mason and sat down.

"I think there's a spring farther up the draw. See that dark spot in the snow?"

Mason looked where she pointed. He couldn't make out anything other than snow and mud in the small, narrow valley. "Yeah?"

"Just looks like a spring I remember seeing one time. We'll check it out as soon as Stratton and Koch come down. If we can get water replenished, then we're good to spend the day here," Higgs said. "Gives us time to plan."

"There's not much to plan," Mason said around a mouthful of food. "There's a bridge down there. We're supposed to hold it."

"You know what I mean, Mason."

Do I? Mason shook his head at the thought. "A plan never survives first contact, right?"

"We'll have to ask Murphy. He's trying to remember if the Continental Army crosses the bridge to envelop the Hessians after they try to counterattack."

Mason squinted. "They counterattack? I always thought it was a complete rout."

"It was," Murphy said from behind them. "You're talking about me like I can't hear you, Mason. I am trying to remember everything I read, okay? I can tell you Washington's attack was late, and the surprise was perfect. But the Hessians attempted to get their shit together and counterattack. Twice. Remember we talked about this the other day?"

"I forgot, man. A lot of stuff going on." Mason pointed with his spoon over his shoulder toward Trenton. "And the bridge?"

"I think the army crossed it to take away the escape route. But it was after the Hessians tried to counterattack the first time. That's when some of them tried to get away. The British dragoons do get away. They realize pretty quick that the Hessians are going to lose." Murphy covered a yawn with a gloved hand.

Mason nodded. "How many?"

"I don't know. I didn't get that detailed, man," Murphy said.

"It's good, Murphy," Mason said. "You're going to make a sand table?"

"Soon as I finish my chow, yeah. Give me an hour?"

"That's good," Mason said. As soon as Murphy briefed them, the kid was going to sleep. Mason glanced at Higgs and could tell that she was thinking the same thing. Curiosity overwhelmed him for a moment. He hadn't really been thinking about the rest of them. He looked over his shoulder and saw Booker bent over a small fire blowing gently on the flame. Mason watched him for a long moment as his friend nurtured the flame into a small, warming fire.

Mason understood that he and his squad were plugging a hole. What they were really about to do was not much different than Booker bringing a fire to life from kindling and a heat source. Once they defended the Assunpink Bridge and rendezvoused with Washington in Trenton, all bets were off. The American Revolution would come down to what he and his friends knew and how the founding fathers would listen and implement their recommendations.

Higgs handed him a piece of paper. "Rest plan."

He looked it over. They'd go down to one person on security from midday to seventeen hundred hours. With a howling storm on the horizon, Mason believed they should try to rest as much as possible before the battle. Knowing the outcome wouldn't change his plan, but he believed it helped to make his squad more prepared. Knowledge really would be power. Mason smiled to himself. His parents would be proud that he'd recognized that fact even if it took an unexplainable trip back in time to do so. For now, they'd walk through the battle of Trenton on Murphy's sand table and get some rest. Once the storm would start later, Mason doubted any of them would be able to rest.

The lunch of chicken and potatoes sat untouched on Washington's plate as he looked over the hand-drawn maps of Princeton. As promised by Mason and his cadets, the winds had turned with enough force that his experienced fishermen in the ranks were whispering about a brewing storm. As much as he wanted to trust them, their news that Ewing and Cadwalader would be unable to cross the Delaware where they were needed unsettled him. His army set to muster, Washington glanced at the uneaten food and scowled. He knew nourishment would be his friend on the long, cold night ahead and he reached for the plate and ate silently, contemplating the plan for the hundredth time in the last two days. The timeline was critical, even as Cadet Murphy had sketched his plan in the Pennsylvania dirt and told him repeatedly that time would not be his friend, but the weather would be.

His watch lay open on the table. Forty-two minutes remained until the first regiments would form up and march the five miles to McKonkey's Ferry. Sunset would be 4:41 P.M. and given the rising storm, darkness would come earlier and give them more time.

Would Ewing, or Cadwalader, be able to cross if they moved out now?

Washington chewed on a piece of chicken, plucked a thin, sharp bone from his teeth and set it aside on the pewter plate. *No. I must accept that they will not be able to assist. Get the army across and take advantage of the weather to conceal our approach.*

There was a soft knock at the door. "General?"

"Yes, Mister Lee?"

"Messenger coming," Lee said without a hint of emotion. "Should I hold him?"

Washington took a bite of the barely warm potatoes. Time had certainly not been his personal friend that morning. "From our forces to the south, yes. I will deal with them after I eat. From the Congress, let them pass."

He finished the potatoes and chicken, wiped his hands on a towel, and poured himself a cup of water just as the door opened. Lee stood there with a bemused smile on his face. "The messenger? Sir? He comes from General Gates."

"I will meet him outside. Prepare my horse as well."

"Yes, sir."

Lee stepped to one side as Washington stepped outside into the cold, blustery day. His horse waited, fully saddled and ready for the muster to start. They were alone in the side yard as Major Wilkinson rode up.

"General Washington?"

Washington turned to the man. His uniform was disheveled and filthy from long days of riding and little food. His eyes met Washington's for a moment. "Sir, Major Wilkinson reporting with a message from General Gates."

"What a time this is to hand me a letter, Major."

Wilkinson blanched. "Sir, I am acting on orders from General Gates himself."

Gates. Washington felt the scowl deepening on his face. *Is he now too sick to pester the Congress so he has to message me? Or has he finally decided to tell me of his treason against me to the Congress themselves?*

Horatio Gates was a solid commander, but over the past two months and the retreat from New York, he'd vocally opposed

Washington's plans. Speaking to other generals gave Gates no foothold in his own plans to lead the army, so the man had the gall to approach Congress directly, circumventing Washington's command of the army. Asked by Washington to command a regiment just days before, Gates had begged off to Philadelphia on account of poor health. Washington agreed, then asked Gates to check on Cadwalader to the south but Gates refused and took his leave to recover.

"General Gates! Where is he?"

Wilkinson stammered. "I-I left him in Philadelphia this morning, sir."

Heat rose along Washington's collar. "And what was he doing there?"

"He said he was on his way to Congress."

"On his way to Congress," Washington repeated. He took the letter and heard Wilkinson make some quiet form of communication, but stood his ground. Washington tore open the note and read quietly. He realized he'd held his breath for the latter half of the note as he saw red infringing on the edges of his vision. He stood and whirled toward Major Wilkinson. "What is the meaning of this? To usurp my command? Inform the Congress I sit here doing nothing while the British make plans to capture Philadelphia from their warm winter garrisons?"

"Sir?" Wilkinson gaped like a child.

Washington forced himself to take a breath and closed his eyes for a moment. Wilkinson would not be the target of his anger. Gates intended to force Congress to remove Washington based on irrational, boundless claims. Gates had been too sick to check on Cadwalader, but was well enough to ride a hundred miles to find a warm bed in Philadelphia?

"You are dismissed, Major," Washington said and turned away. He looked out the window into the roiling gray clouds and felt his anger turning dangerously toward pride.

I'll show Gates and the rest of them if we have no plan, no chance to succeed against the British. Washington flew past his silent staff and back into his quarters. He consulted the maps once more, tracing the nine miles from McKonkey's Ferry to the outskirts of Trenton with his finger. Mason had been right and he must attack with every man he could.

"Lieutenant Tilghman!" Washington called. The young man

burst through the door a moment later. Washington looked at his watch. It would only be thirty minutes earlier than the original plan, and he decided to risk it. "Order the muster and have the first regiments move as soon as they are ready."

"Yes, sir," Tilghman said. "Are you quite all right, sir?"

Washington smiled. "I am. Tonight, we take this fight to the British and let them know they cannot defeat us. Send for General Greene, my compliments of course, and have him report here before his regiment departs for the ferry."

It would be good to see his friend and let Greene's quiet competence quell the emotion in his chest. Seldom did Washington let his emotions get the better of his bearing, but given Horatio Gates and his meddling in affairs that were not his to challenge, anger would prove necessary at some point. That place needed to be at Washington's choosing, that was clear.

"Anything else, sir?" Tilghman asked.

Washington looked up with a smile. "Bring my horse to the porch, please. I would ride out to confer with General Knox before he starts the crossing."

Tilghman departed, leaving Washington to his thoughts and preparations to go out into the rapidly cooling afternoon. He pulled on his coat and reached for his tricorne hat. An arc of silver on the table, under the street maps of Trenton, caught his eye. He moved the edge of the paper and recognized the coin from Mason's pocket. The impossible dates and imagery suggesting a long-preserved victory.

A victory that starts tonight, he thought. He studied the coin and flipped it again to the side with his profile.

Was I ever that young?

He snorted and placed the coin into the pocket of his coat without a thought and strode out of his private office and quarters into the outer room. His staff looked at him expectantly. They wanted a final word. Something meant only for them in the midst of their preparations.

"Be prepared to strike the headquarters at first light. I believe we may push back into New Jersey to stay with victory tomorrow." Washington nodded at them. "Know that we are prepared because of your hard work and diligence to this great cause. Let's see this attack off appropriately, gentlemen."

By the time he'd reached the door, his staff applauded him.

He turned, wanting to quiet them, but saw the exultant joy in their eyes. Something he'd not seen since they'd fled New York with the British army nipping at their heels. Their passion was a weapon. Mason's promise that victory steeled the Continentals into joining Washington's army and pushing the redcoats from their lands made sense in that brief moment. Washington set his hat upon his head and walked onto the porch. The first regiments were formed just down the road from his headquarters at the Merrick home. He took the reins from Mister Lee, swung his lanky frame onto the horse, and made his way past the soldiers. They, too, cheered, and Washington smiled at them warmly and tipped his cap to them. A great cheer erupted as he moved down the road to Knox's staging point.

His adjutant rode behind him, far enough back to give him privacy and security. The icy breeze worked under his collar, chilling him. Such weather would be hard on the men, he knew. He thought of those with rags for shoes, and those without even rags, waiting to march to the river and John Glover's sturdy boats. Their sense of patriotism and duty made him proud.

Henry Knox stood in the middle of the road with a pair of his colonels. From a distance, Washington could hear the general speaking in his bombastic, clear voice. If there were any voice he'd choose to have lead a crossing in a storm, it would be Knox.

Knox looked up and met Washington's eyes at a hundred yards. He sent the colonels running and strode confidently down the muddy road and closed the distance quickly. He saluted with precision and Washington nodded in response.

"Henry."

"Sir," Knox said. "Colonel Glover is prepared to move. I am to understand you want the crossing to commence as early as I dare? There must be something you know that I do not."

Washington met the man's smile with one of his own. "Time will be of the essence, General. With the storm approaching, I believe we'll be dealing with ice on the river and along the banks. The more men we can get across at the outset of the storm will have us across and on time to attack at daybreak."

Knox looked up into the clouds. "It certainly looks like a storm. Will it stop us from crossing?"

Washington shook his head. "Nothing is going to stop us,

Henry. You will keep the men moving with purpose, I am sure. We will cross safely with your guidance and leadership."

For a moment, Washington thought he saw a slight bit of color in Knox's cheeks at the compliment. Knox cleared his throat and nodded solemnly. "It is an honor to have this command, sir."

Washington looked down the road. The ferry lay beyond a curve. "Glover's men are a godsend."

"That man is an incredible sailor, sir. Given river or ocean, I trust him with every man or woman in our territories," Knox said.

Washington kept his gaze down the road for a long minute as to memorize the road so he could find his way in the coming darkness. Any degree of familiarity would be welcome in the stormy night. He looked back to Knox and gave a friendly nod. "The first regiments are on their way, Henry. Get them across at your discretion. I trust you'll make the right decision."

Knox smiled. "Begging your pardon, sir, but once we push off we have no other choice. This attack is everything."

Washington nodded. Mason had said something along those lines when they'd parted the previous night. For a brief moment, Washington tried to visualize Mason and his fellow cadets tucked into the high ground south of the Assunpink Creek. Nothing from General Ewing's men suggested their capture and Colonel Glover's swift and silent delivery was far better than Washington could have hoped. How the young ones would perform was anyone's guess, but Washington remembered Mason's words and the conviction of his voice.

Washington set his hand on Knox's shoulder. "For this operation, we will use a password. Spread it to your men and I'll spread it to the others. All officers will carry a piece of white paper in their hats. At the request of 'who goes there' they will respond with 'Victory or Death.' Is that clear?"

Knox smiled. "Any other response brings engagement, sir."

"Indeed, Henry." Washington allowed a grim smile to cross his face. "Victory or Death."

CHAPTER NINETEEN

December 25, 1776
Trenton, New Jersey

Rall's Christmas dinner was cut short by musket fire on the northern side of Trenton. Fearing an attack, the colonel ordered the civilians out of his headquarters before riding out himself to check the perimeter. Sutton watched Selena Christensen depart on the arm of Colonel Knyphausen, allowing the regimental commander into her home. His men arrived with a commandeered wagon, as he'd ordered. He stepped back into the headquarters and caught Emily Daniels' eye.

"Your carriage has arrived," he said, smiling. "I trust you'll allow my dragoons to escort you home?"

"Thank you, Captain Sutton."

She returned the smile and made a polite but unnecessary goodbye to Stacy Potts and made her way through the dining room. They walked to the front door, her hand grasping his left elbow. Sutton looked down at her and smiled.

"I'm sorry our evening was cut short. My men will get you home quickly and safely."

Emily smiled. "I'm sorry, too, and thank you for seeing me home."

Sutton shook his head. "My orders are to stay and secure the Princeton Road."

"In this weather?" Emily asked. "A storm is coming, I believe."

Sutton shrugged. "Then perhaps you should stay here? I could house you at my quarters."

Emily shook her head. "I must get home. Father is leaving in two days to hunt in the north. If I'm not there to help him pack, he'll forget his very clothes."

She laughed and he loved the sound of it. "Then, when he's gone, perhaps I can visit you?"

"I would like that very much."

"Then let's get you home," he said and escorted her down the steps. Heat rose in his face and his heart thumped in expectation. In three days' time, she would be his. At the wagon's step, she turned and kissed him gently on the cheek.

"Be well, Captain Sutton," she said. He could barely keep his attention on helping her safely onto the seat.

He looked up at the driver and nodded. With an escort of four dragoons, the wagon trundled into the breezy, overcast afternoon. His mind on the kiss, Sutton called for his horse with the intention of riding out to see what Rall and his army of idiots had accomplished in the brief fight.

He turned and saw Lieutenant Sturm looking at him with a sly grin.

"Something funny, Lieutenant?" They stood beside the deck of the Potts home in what little shelter it provided from the rising wind.

Sturm shook his head. "The good captain smiling like a schoolboy is a sight to see, sir."

"Ha," Sutton snorted. The laughter felt good. "I suppose I am intrigued as to the possibilities."

A fierce gust of wind tore through the treetops at the edge of town and dropped the temperature several degrees. The smell was familiar—a cold crisp scent of snow. The darkening sky to the south gave the storm an ominous tint.

"Will the colonel keep his troops on alert in such a storm, Lieutenant?"

Sturm shook his head. "Doubtful, sir. Such a storm means finding a warm fire and a glass of brandy. The good colonel will certainly do both this evening. Perhaps a game of cards. Will you be joining us?"

He looked down the street toward his quarters. Colonel Knyphausen had not emerged. There was no point in going home.

With the prospect of Emily Daniels in his immediate future, his interest in Selena Christensen turned cold in an instant. She would have her fun and he could have his. "I believe I shall."

"Thank you, Sergeant," Emily said. "Ride quickly and get out of this weather."

The dragoon sergeant saluted crisply and the wagon, with its escorts, shot down the road toward Trenton. She closed the door against the breeze and twisted the simple wooden latches to hold it closed. She ducked into the kitchen and found her father at the kitchen table with the strange rifle in pieces on an oil cloth. He glanced up at her.

"Have a nice time?"

She shivered. "That man is appalling, Father. I see you did not give them all the weapons."

Daniels laughed. "Of course I didn't. Distract them with fresh tea and food and they'll respond to hospitality. You know that all too well, just like I'm sure you kissed the good captain's cheek and made him feel like a king, Daughter."

"I did," she smiled. "I felt like a fox in a hen house. Being that close to him for that long makes me want a bath."

Daniels nodded. "If they'd only known. Now, tell me what you saw. Is there anything that differs from what Mason and his friends told us?"

She sat down and poured herself a splash of wine into a cup. "All of the senior commanders were there. Sutton told me that the forces number thirteen hundred or so capable soldiers. Colonel Von Donop has not returned from Mount Holly and Rall has kept the regiments on an almost constant alert status for days. Everything that Mason and Murphy said rings true, Father."

Daniels wiped at the barrel of the strange rifle. "Do the Hessians suspect anything?"

Emily shrugged. "A man came in. They said his name was Wahl but I did not recognize him. He told Rall that Washington was coming."

Daniels stopped rubbing the rifle and his eyebrows rose. "What did Rall say?"

"He said, 'Let them come,' and they all laughed. Poured more wine," Emily replied. "They do not believe Washington is coming. At least the Hessians."

"And Sutton? What was his response?"

She shrugged. "He wants to have the river freeze deep enough that the entire British army marches across and destroys Washington's army once and for all. He doesn't believe Washington would cross the river even in that eventuality. He thinks Washington a coward with a failing army under his command."

"The weather is certainly doing what our friends predicted," Daniels said. "I believe they were telling the truth."

Emily nodded. "A nor'easter to be sure. Mason and his friends are patriots, Father."

"Aye," Daniels said. "Look at this."

He sat the rifle down and retrieved a single brass casing from his tool kit. He twirled it in his fingers and she could see that the crimped tip of the round was wide and held a small pointed projectile.

"You reloaded it?"

"I think so. Added more powder to the cartridge. Tried to fashion a projectile, but it's hard to say if it will work at all. We won't know until we test it."

Emily grinned. "I thought you would have already."

"No." Daniels smiled in return. "Mason and his friends know how this thing works. I'll let them test it before I do anything else."

"They'll be encouraged you were able to reload it anyway, Father."

Daniels smiled. "What else can you tell me about the party?"

"Plenty," she said. "But the perimeter is lightly defended and if the storm does worsen, I don't expect they'll put up much of a fight. Just like Murphy said."

"We'll see," Daniels replied. He sat down the round and reached for his cup. He held it out for a toast. "You did well, Emily. Your mother would have been proud."

"I want to do more, Father. Especially against those bastards."

Her father stood and gathered six rifles from the far wall. "Then, you can help me load these rifles. When the battle is over, and if the dragoons escape like Murphy said, they'll be coming for us. We have two choices. We can stay here and fight them, or we can run. Whichever you choose, that choice must be made now, Daughter."

"What about you, Father? What would you do?" Emily said

and dabbed at a tear threatening to run down her cheek. She knew the answer before he even started to speak. "You want to stay here and fight, if it comes to that."

"I do," he said. "If it comes to that, I will. However, our young friends might have something to say about whether we'll need to."

Emily smiled. "You think so?"

She reached for one of the rifles in front of her father. With practiced skill she readied it for loading and retrieved a cartridge from the flat wooden box on the table. Loading the rifle took only a few seconds because of long practice, and she looked up at her father as she checked the flint and rested the rifle next to her on the floor.

Father and daughter smiled at each other and sat loading the collected weapons for a stand neither hoped to make. As they worked, the first wisps of snow began to fall from the dark sky. When they finished, their thoughts turned to dinner even though neither was hungry. The sun set and the snow slowly piled up on the road outside. She paused at the window for a long moment.

They're coming. They're coming tonight in this awful storm to change history.

Washington waited as long as possible before mounting his horse and moving to the river for the final time. On the roads to either side of the ferry, his army huddled in clumps around tiny fires trying to stay warm. The winds turned from occasional gusts to a powerful, steady blast. Snow and ice pellets fell at such a rate he could barely see a quarter mile. Still, his army was in good spirits and ready. Along the bank, a flurry of activity began. The steady Durham boats were making their way back empty and ready for another load. Above the excited voices, he could hear Henry Knox's distinctive voice calling for the next units in line. Men turned from their fires with longing glances before stepping into the wide-bottomed boats.

Ice clung to the shoreline and made it difficult for the men to climb aboard. He watched them in their tattered shoes and bare feet. Some stepped into the river before boarding, exposing their feet to the frigid water. *Such dedication. To conduct this attack so shoddily clothed. These are the men our Congress forsake.*

As soon as the boats had appeared, they were loaded and quickly pushed away from the banks with full loads bound for the New Jersey shore. A soft cheer came up as the men saw him now, riding huddled against the storm. He nodded and tried to put a smile on his face while his mind worked to estimate their numbers.

General Knox approached with a frown that confirmed Washington's own dark thoughts. Their numbers weren't even half across the river and time was mounting against them.

"General." Knox saluted. "The army is forty percent across. We're fighting ice in the river, sir, but the boys are making good time now. The far side is deserted and we have security pickets out a half mile down each road."

Washington nodded. "Thank you, Henry. This crossing would not be possible without your stentorian lungs rousing the men to their tasks. I could hear you in camp, almost."

Knox beamed in the starlight. "I do my best, General."

"That you do," Washington said as he swung a leg up and dismounted. No sooner had his feet hit the ground than the cold seeped through his boots. "Have you sent the artillery across?"

"No, sir," Knox said. "I'm hoping to break up this shore ice with the men a bit before we try to load the cannon. Maybe three loads from now, sir. An hour or two at most."

Two hours. Washington tried not to frown. They were behind their timeline. He placed his hands into his pockets and his right hand found the coin. Rubbing it seemed to warm him. "A little off schedule, Henry."

"Yes, sir, but we're making up for it now. Glover's men are leaning into their work, sir. I'll have them across as quickly as I can."

"I know you will, Henry. Don't let me keep you."

Knox turned and called for the next regiments to stand by. As he waited, Washington saw Greene moving his way. Waiting in the cold was not his idea of how to spend a December evening, but it would pass better with a good friend.

Greene approached and stood next to Washington watching the ice floes drift in the gray-black water. "Fine evening for a boat ride, General."

Washington snorted. A bit of levity in a moment of stress always did him wonders. "Against the French, we were ready to march one day when one of my battalion commanders left his post and ran into the woods. Seemed he'd eaten too many cherries and hadn't bothered to take care of himself."

"Did you chastise him accordingly?"

"I didn't have to," Washington said. "Embarrassment is a strong tool."

Greene nodded but did not look his way. "Is that what you're standing here worrying about?"

"You know me too well," Washington said. "Ewing cannot cross. Neither can Cadwalader. Just like the cadets said. Even the weather has turned the way they said it would. I have no reason to doubt what they've told me, that we'll take the town quickly, and yet I stand here thinking terrible thoughts of failure instead of thoughts of possibilities. The ones far beyond tomorrow. Do you understand?"

"They have many possibilities to share with us, General. From their dress to their weapons, there is much we can learn from them and much they can change." Greene cleared his throat. "Ending this war is, if you'll pardon the expression, the tip of the iceberg."

Washington snorted. "You could have waited until we were across to make that joke, Nathanael."

"And ruin the timing?" Greene replied.

Washington sighed and shrugged against an icy gust of wind. "I shouldn't have sent them to guard the Assunpink. I should have just relied on Sullivan's brigades to take it quickly. Mason believes he can hold the bridge, but I am not certain."

"He will, sir. Belief is a powerful tool. Those young men and... women will make a difference there," Greene said. "You haven't put them there to die, if that's what you're thinking. They'll do what you ask and prove, like you want them to, their worth."

"You're right," Washington said. "I know you are."

Greene chuckled. "Then what is it?"

Washington withdrew the quarter from his pocket. "This."

"What about it?"

"Why me?" Washington asked. "Because I command this army? That's hardly reason to stamp my handsome profile on a coin."

"Did you say handsome profile?" Greene grinned. "You were never that good-looking, sir."

Washington snorted. "Only emperors had coins in Rome, Nathanael. What does that say about me? Two hundred and more years from now. What does that say?"

Greene sighed. "I don't know, sir. If it concerns you, do something about it. Make a wish, perhaps."

A wish? Washington chuckled. He flipped the coin into his fingers and prepared to throw the distraction into the river and maybe have a measure of good luck in the process. "Then, we shall make a wish."

Let us prevail.

He reared back and threw the coin as hard as he could. Pausing at the end of the throw, he held the finish for a long moment as if straining to hear the impact. Try as he might, there was nothing to hear.

Greene said in a loud voice. "I think you threw it all the way across, General."

The men in close proximity cheered and Washington shuffled back to his guarded position next to Greene looking over the river. "There's no way that coin made it all the way across," he said with a smile.

"Maybe," Greene said. "But the men don't need to know that, do they?"

Martinez shook him awake. "Mason? You wanted me to get you up, right?"

"What time is it?" He struggled to move in the tight, warm sleeping bag.

"You said get you up ten minutes early. It's 0150," Martinez said. "It's cold as fuck out here, man."

Mason laughed. "Just like Murphy said."

"I hate that guy," Martinez laughed. "He and Dunaway are awake and getting ready to replace me and Koch. He knows you want to talk to him."

"Thanks, Mark," Mason said. "Hope you can get some sleep."

Martinez chuckled, but Mason couldn't see his face. "You should see how hard it's snowing, man. I'm not gonna sleep worth a shit."

"Go get relieved. Tell Murphy I'll be up there in a few minutes."

"You got it, boss."

By the sound of Martinez's boots crunching through the snow, the storm was in full effect. From what Murphy had said, Washington's army was not completely across the river. They wouldn't be able to march until 0400 or so. A lot was still meant to happen. He sat upright with the bag around him and unzipped it. The frigid wind cut into him immediately as he dug for his jacket and snowsuit in the bottom of the bag. A warm jacket made the weather passable. He tied up the hasty snowsuit and reached back into the bag for the musket that had poked him in the back for the last few hours. Before leaving to Murphy and Dunaway's post, he zipped up his bag. With any luck it would still be warm when he came back in a few minutes.

From the base of the rock outcropping, he climbed and crawled to the hasty fighting position at the top. Martinez and Koch met him along the way.

"Get some sleep, guys," Mason said.

Martinez replied, "Definitely." Koch said nothing but clapped him on the shoulder with a heavy gloved hand. Mason knelt on the ground behind Murphy and Dunaway and crawled slowly up between them.

"Halt." Murphy whirled around. "Who goes there?"

"Mason."

"Advance and be recognized."

Mason crawled up until he and Murphy were a few feet apart. Murphy whispered, "Wrinkle."

"Bait," Mason gave the password. He saw Murphy close a knife as he crawled closer.

"Howdy," Murphy said. "Martinez said you wanted to talk with me."

"Yeah. What's going on out there?"

Murphy took a deep breath. "Right now? Washington is across the river and they're trying to move the cannons. It takes them a while. The rest of the army gets across by around 0330 and they're prepared to march by 0400."

Mason nodded. "What then?"

"They'll run into trouble when they try to cross Jacob's Creek. Really hurts moving the cannon through the ravine, but they'll be on track for arriving at the edge of Trenton around 0800."

"It's just the march then?"

"Yeah," Murphy said and pointed down into Trenton. Mason couldn't see anything because of the blowing snow. "Down there, Rall and his men are sleeping. Even the guys on the perimeter have found some shelter from the storm. It's giving them a false sense of security and, honestly, they all need sleep."

Mason chuckled. The squad had rotated through guard duty all day and rested thoroughly. "Just like us?"

"No better place to spend a storm like this than in our sleeping bags," Murphy said.

"Yeah, wish we could have brought them up here," Dunaway said. It was the first time he'd heard her say anything all day.

"You warm enough, Dunaway?"

"I suppose," she said. "It's only a two-hour watch."

Mason smiled whether she could see it or not. Maybe she'd hear it in his voice. "You're right, Dunaway. You can do this standing on your head."

"I was never good at gymnastics, Mason."

Murphy chuckled. "She's a drama minor, Mason. Don't let her fool you."

Drama, huh. That fits.

"I'll try not to," Mason said. The information made him feel better. There was nothing they could do until they all woke up and ate around 0600. From there, they'd move into position around 0730 and wait for Washington's attack to commence. Combat was a few hours away and there was nothing he could do to stop it even if he wanted to. The course of a nation was about to be decided. "What happens after this?"

"After Trenton?"

"Yeah. When do the British come?"

Murphy scratched his chin. "Not immediately. It takes them a couple of days to gather at Princeton and march this way. They're here on January 2. That's when Washington runs on them, attacking Princeton first and then makes them believe he's just across the river while slipping away in the night. Really pisses General Cornwallis off."

Cornwallis. Mason stretched his neck and rubbed his temple. "He eventually takes command of the whole army, right? Who Washington and the French defeat at Yorktown?"

"Precisely," Murphy said. "It would be nice to change that, too."

Mason sighed. "We haven't changed anything yet."

"If that rifle's down there, or if it is already on its way to England, then we have, Mason," Dunaway said. "The industrial revolution a hundred years early? Maybe a World War before electricity makes it all the way around the world? We have to find that rifle. If not, everything gets screwy much faster than in our time. Who knows what this world would be like in 2008 if that happens. It's like the butterfly effect gone crazy."

Mason screwed under one side of his mouth. He'd heard the term before, but didn't understand it. It was science fiction or something like that. "We'll find that rifle, Murphy," Mason said. He didn't know if anyone could hear that he didn't really believe that. "There's a few things we gotta do before that, though. You guys stay warm up here. Yell if you need anything."

Murphy chuckled. "Well, we won't yell..."

"You know what I meant. Good night." Mason crawled away. He moved around the rocks and descended into the small circle of sleeping soldiers. He unzipped his bag and climbed inside without taking off his jacket. That would save him a few minutes when it was time to get up. Being awake and ready would be critical for him and be good for the rest of them to see. Calm was contagious, as his father would have said. Mason looked one last time at his watch, 0205, and closed his eyes not believing he'd be able to sleep a wink until after the battle was over.

CHAPTER TWENTY

December 26, 1776
0415

Captain Wallis signaled for the men to halt. The Scotch Road was almost impassable in the heavy snow. He withdrew his watch and tried to discern the hands in the heavy darkness. A quarter past four in the morning. Fuming at their lateness for rendezvous at McKonkey's Ferry, Wallis shook his head and decided they could slow down a bit. His patrol stood surrounded by swirling snow on the edges of the road. He stepped off to the side of the road to relieve his bladder. Two steps off the road, his boot slipped and he fell and slid down the small embankment. At the bottom, thoroughly wet and cold, Wallis realized that nothing was broken or strained except for his pride.

"Captain? You okay?" a near whisper came from his party. Lanterns appeared and shone down into his predicament.

Wallis replied. "I think—" Next to him was a snow-white face lying on the ground. Wallis startled and backed away before his senses took over. The man lay on his back, frozen stiff in the near darkness. His fingers curled in frozen agony, the man's face was peaceful in death. As Wallis dusted himself off his fingers hit something cold and hard in the snow next to the man. He dug and felt cold metal under his fingertips. It took only a moment to sweep enough snow away to see a thin metal handle. Curious, he picked it up.

"What in the hell?"

A black shape came up from the snow and it looked like a rifle, but not like any type of musket or rifle he'd ever seen. He glanced back at the dead man's face and tried to sweep snow away from the frozen torso. The man's white shirt bore a ruffled collar and there was a small regimental pin attached to it. There were dark patches of frozen blood on the corpse's shoulder and chest.

Hessian.

"Sir? Are you okay?"

Wallis stood, carrying the rifle by the handle. His bladder temporarily forgotten, he walked back to the center of the party.

"What is that?" one of his soldiers asked.

Wallis said nothing. "Who has the lantern?"

"I do," another called.

"Is it still lit in the shield?"

"Yes, sir."

"Bring it," Wallis ordered. The man approached and opened the thin metal shield from the lantern a sliver. Wallis knelt to the ground and set the lantern into the snow. He carefully aimed the shaft of light at the strange rifle and examined it. The barrel stuck out below a strange triangular piece. Inside the barrel was a squared piece of red metal with a strange screw built inside. Behind it was a cold metal handhold with circles cut into the top of the strange device. Under the handle, a small rectangular door was open. Below it, a rectangular piece protruded from the weapon just in front of the trigger and what looked like a handle of some type. The dull black stock was unlike anything he'd ever seen. It wasn't wood or iron, but something hard and strangely soft at the same time. He turned the rifle over in his hands and saw lettering. He could easily make out three small words.

SAFE

AUTO

SEMI

"What is it?" one of the men whispered.

Wallis rubbed his face. "This is like nothing I've ever seen."

No one spoke for a long moment. Wallis looked up. "Bring me a blanket."

A blanket appeared and he wrapped the rifle inside. "This has to get to General Washington."

"Our orders were to stay here and wreak havoc until our rendezvous, sir."

Wallis looked up at the man whose face he could not see. "This takes priority. Are we closer to McKonkey's or Howard's Ferry?"

"McKonkey's, sir. About six miles."

Wallis stood. "Then let's go. Move out."

The fifty soldiers moved silently along the road. Wallis carried his musket in one hand and the hastily wrapped weapon in the other. Where did the Hessians get such a thing? Who possibly could have made it? Muskets were wooden stocked and metal barreled. The strange black rifle was metal and something smooth to his touch. General Stephen would not be happy, but from McKonkey's Ferry they could signal for a boat and make their way back to the Continental Army. Washington needed to see what he'd found. Perhaps it would even be a way for Wallis to leave the 4th Virginia and General Stephen behind.

Wallis couldn't help but wonder, as he carried the strange weapon, whether Stephen would even care about such a thing. He knew Washington would, though. That was enough to quicken his step toward McKonkey's Ferry.

Dunaway checked her watch and glanced at Murphy across from her. His chin had rested on the stock of his rifle for the last fifteen minutes. Just as she was about to ask him if he was awake, she heard a soft snore. It came again, and again. Watching him, she crept backward out of their position and crawled to the rocks. As quickly as she dared, she made her way down the slight hill to her rucksack and sleeping bag. Working quickly and quietly, she opened the upper sack and found the parcel she'd packed at the Daniels home. She would return the dress to Emily, somehow. Stealing it didn't seem right and her intention was merely to borrow it long enough to get to New York and find a measure of fortune. The dress and ill-fitting shoes were necessary. She couldn't waltz into New York City looking like a ghost. Cradling it to her chest, Dunaway laid her musket atop the rucksack. She looked at the sleeping figures for a long moment.

There wasn't a sense of duty. They wanted to go to war, and she didn't. Her parents wanted the Army to pay for her education and wouldn't take no for an answer. They'd never bothered to listen to what she wanted to do. There was nothing to stop her from walking away from playing soldier.

I can do this, she told herself. Still, in her modern gear and warm against the storm, she considered the simple clothing in the satchel and the life it promised.

I can do better than that, she mused. *This could be the role of a lifetime.*

She removed her helmet and set it on the ground beside her rucksack. Leaving it here was the right thing to do. Mason and the others might need it. Maybe it would save someone's life one day, but it wouldn't be hers. She'd take her chances with whatever colonial America could throw at her. She withdrew her compass and looked at the slightly glowing dial.

She moved west, toward the river, until she found a tree large enough to break the wind. She shrugged out of her snow-suit top and out of her uniform and boots. She pulled on the simple leather shoes and settled the colonial dress over her long underwear. There was a thin jacket/shawl that she pulled over her shoulders as well as a kerchief for her head.

Satisfied, she looked at the pile of clothes and walked away without looking back. At the Bordentown Road, she turned to the north. She crossed the Assunpink Bridge holding her breath and scurrying as fast as she could into the town. She kept straight, scurrying with her head down as she moved through the center of Trenton. There were no voices, no lights in many of the windows, and no one on the street. At the north end of the town, she startled when a wagon came into the street from the west.

"Ah!" She jumped and slapped a hand over her mouth.

"Miss? What are you doing out on a night like this?" a man whispered just above the wind. He wasn't dressed like a Hessian or a dragoon.

She shivered. "Leaving."

He smiled. "Me too. Would you care for a ride?"

"Please." She climbed aboard. "Where are you headed?"

"New York. I believe I've had quite enough of New Jersey. My brother works with the theater there and needs a handyman. I've fixed my last wagon of war. The Sassenach are no friends of mine and I won't live in their favor any longer than I can stand it. The storm is a perfect chance to leave."

Dunaway grinned. "The theater?" She scrunched closer to the man. "Then, we'll be fast friends."

The older man smiled at her. "I don't believe I've seen you before. In Trenton, I mean."

"Been making my way to New York from Burlington. Slept in an empty barn by the river this afternoon as the weather changed and the Hessians fled inside. The storm coaxed me to get out of this town once and for all, when no one could stop me."

"My name is Charles Muir. And you are?"

She smiled. "Diana. Diana... Dunaway."

"It is a pleasure to make your acquaintance, Diana." They shook hands briefly and she made every effort to keep her wrist limp like a lady of the time. "Do you have family in New York? What's waiting for you there?"

"I fancy doing something very different there. You see, I want to be an actress. I was hoping to find a theater company once I got there and now I've found you, Charles."

"Quite the opportune moment, Miss Dunaway. Wouldn't you say?"

"Serendipitous, Charles. Almost like it was meant to be."

Under gray skies, Washington realized that sunrise was approaching. The storm continued to blow. Visibility was as bad as ever and the snow gathered in impressive amounts in the forest around them. He looked down at his soldiers.

"Stay with your officers, men! For God's sake, stay with your officers."

The men moved as one, heads down and focused on the ground in front of them, through the storm. Not more than thirty minutes ago, they'd separated the army into two prongs to attack. Sullivan and his brigades charged straight down the River Road. Washington moved with Greene's brigades to the east and onto the Scotch Road. They would turn south and charge into Trenton from the high ground to the north. From the middle of the column, Washington could see them stretching along the Scotch Road. They were closing in on Trenton.

"Press on, men! Press on!"

He turned in the saddle and looked back on the rest of the march. The regiments were tight together and no one lagged behind. Word came an hour earlier that two men had died on the march, exposure it was said. There would be no turning back now.

"General Washington!" a cry came from the front. Several men echoed it. "To the front, sir!"

Washington nudged his mount into a trot. The forward elements of the march had stopped. He reached the front of the column and saw his commanders standing with a group of men, maybe forty, who were on the road.

"What is the meaning of this?" Washington asked. "Who are you men?"

A young man carrying a blanket spoke. "Sir, Captain Wallis, 4th Virginia Regiment."

4th Virginia, Washington thought. *Adam Stephen.* "What is the meaning of this? How did you get across the river before the army?"

Wallis shifted from side to side. "Sir, we crossed the river several days ago. On Christmas Eve, sir."

Washington swallowed hard to keep from screaming at the man. "On whose orders, Captain?"

"General Stephen ordered us, sir."

Of course he did. Washington felt a fresh wave of heat in his face. "To do what, Captain?"

"Our orders were to probe and harass the enemy, sir."

Washington bit the inside of his lower lip. His fists clenched at his sides and he realized he was holding his breath. He let it out slowly, enunciating the words carefully. "I see."

"We hit the Trenton outposts yesterday afternoon—"

"Lieutenant Tilghman!" Washington hissed into the wind.

His aide-de-camp was ten feet away having followed him forward. "Sir?"

"Get me General Stephen. Get him here now," Washington said. He took a long, slow breath and looked back at Captain Wallis. "You hit the Hessian outposts? Yesterday?"

"Sir, we attacked one of their outposts at sunset. Killed four and wounded eleven, we think, sir," Wallis said. "The whole Hessian regiment turned out. Some mounted folks, dragoons we think, gave chase but they lost us in the dark."

Washington nodded, half listening. Adam Stephen was a drunkard and had been a thorn in his side since they'd served together against the French. He'd lost to Washington politically, been unable to be promoted because of Washington in the army, and now had obviously made it a personal vendetta to upset Washington's plans, much worse than Horatio Gates had done.

Incompetence I could stand, he thought. *Insubordination, though, never.* The secrecy and the careful planning for the assault were likely ruined. The Hessians would be on their guard because of Stephen's actions and inability to comprehend patience. Vengeance, misplaced and ill-guided, had ruined many an operation.

Stephen came forward on his horse and saluted. Washington thought there was a faint stench of whiskey on the man's breath. "General Stephen. What is the meaning of this?" he pointed at the fifty men halted in the center of the road.

"Sir?" The man's tone was bemused.

"Captain Wallis tells me that you ordered him to cross the Delaware and harass the Hessians a few days before. Is that correct?"

Stephen nodded. "It is. I believed we weren't doing enough to—"

"You, sir!" Washington raised a gloved hand and pointed at Stephen's chest in rage. "You, sir, may have ruined our plans and put them on their guard!"

Stephen stammered. "I did a great service to the army! I took the fight to the enemy while you sat and planned and planned for nothing!"

"Get out of my sight, General Stephen. When this battle is over, we will speak again and the consequences will not be fair." Washington waited until Stephen clomped away before he turned back to Wallis and set his tone again. "Captain Wallis?"

"Yes, sir?"

"You'll fall into our march with your regiment. I—"

"Sir, if you'll forgive me?" Wallis stammered and held up the blanket. "We found something you need to see." He unwrapped the blanket, and Washington blinked in recognition.

"Wrap it back up." Washington turned to Tilghman. "Summon Mister Lee and a rider immediately."

"What is it, sir?" Wallis asked.

"Nothing, Captain Wallis. Do you understand? It was nothing. Something odd and we don't know what it was. Is that clear?" Washington lowered his chin and fixed his gaze on the young officer.

"I understand, sir." Wallis looked at his men. "The men do, too."

"Good. Speak no more of it, lest your lives depend on it." Washington straightened in the saddle. "Now, fall your men in on your regiment. We march on Trenton and must move now. Go, now. The rest of you? Move out!"

Washington rode back two regiments and allowed his horse to fall in step with the army. Tilghman and Mister Lee appeared at his side a few moments later. A young boy, no more than eighteen, rode up a moment later on an officer's horse.

"General?" Lee said.

"Mister Lee, I believe I have something our friends were looking for," Washington said. He passed over the blanket-wrapped rifle.

"I'm sure they'll be glad to have it back," Lee said.

Washington shook his head. He looked at the young man. "You're familiar with this area, son?"

"I know every road between here and Baltimore, sir."

"Good," Washington said. "You are to go to the Congress and bring Mister Jefferson at once with my compliments. Do you understand?"

"Yes, sir," the boy said. He and the horse headed back the way they'd come.

Lee looked at Tilghman and then at Washington. "You're bringing Jefferson here, sir?"

"He's the smartest man I know," Washington said. "Make sure he gets that weapon, Mister Lee."

"And our friends?" Lee asked. "What do we tell them, General?"

He thought about it for a long moment. Advantages were hard to come by, especially at war with a superior enemy force. "Nothing, Mister Lee. Our friends do not need to know what we found just yet. When Jefferson arrives, we'll collect what they have as well and send it back to Virginia. From there, we can see about these weapons. I believe they're just as important as the knowledge in our friends' heads."

"They'd be better off knowing this is in friendly hands."

Washington nodded. "So they might, Mister Lee. But a little fear could keep them sharp and I need them sharp. Wouldn't you agree?"

Lee nodded. "I'll see that Mister Jefferson gets the rifle when he arrives, sir. Speak no more of it."

"Now then, we have a battle to win," Washington said. "Press on, men! On to Trenton!"

At the Pennington Road, Greene turned east and spread his regiments. As quickly as they formed, they stepped south into the wood line. Washington dismounted and drew his sword. Three columns, with Washington leading from the front center, pushed deeper into the screen of woods. The walk became a trot as he could feel the swelling rage of the army at his side. Heavy rain fell as they pressed forward. Washington loped through the woods, almost running as they pushed toward the north end of town. In the distance, he could see the shape of the cooper shop, the building farthest to the north of the town and their first assault objective. Another gust of wind shook them. Washington shielded his eyes against the sleet and saw the shop's front door open and a lone Hessian soldier stepped into the snow.

A musket shot rang out to Washington's right and the army charged as one. Hessians exploded out of the cooper shop, some tugging on their equipment. A volley came from Washington's right. Two more followed in rapid succession. With the storm howling around them, the Hessians formed a firing line and returned fire. Washington saw his commanders taking charge of the attack and moving to envelop the Hessian outpost. Overwhelmed, the Hessians turned as one and fled toward town. In the distance, toward the River Road, Washington heard the low rumble of artillery.

Sullivan!

Against the weather and all of the conceivable odds in front of them, both divisions of the army reached their attack positions at the exact same time. Startled German kettledrums began to beat the Hessians to quarters.

"Tilghman!"

"Yes, sir." His aide was right there as always.

"Send my compliments to Captain Hamilton. Ensure the artillery has their targets. Make sure they hit that stable first," Washington said. Mason's greatest concern was something he could assuage with the right field commanders in play. The dragoon's would have escaped to the south and risked Mason's position. Taking away that possibility seemed the least Washington could do.

"Right away, sir."

Washington grinned as they moved into the outskirts of

Trenton. Sullivan's arm of the attack was precisely where they should have been at the proper time. Washington ensured that Tilghman was nearby and ready to help facilitate communications with his commanders. For now, they were in the right place, with a considerable advantage, and Washington's heart soared.

The battle was on.

CHAPTER TWENTY-ONE

Mason jerked upright at the sound of thunder. Murphy hadn't said it was going to thunder snow. He looked at his watch as he rolled his face up. The sun was up. His watch said 0805. Another rumble sounded from below the town.

Not thunder. Artillery! Fuck!

"Everybody up!" he cried. "Get up! Get up!"

The ring of sleeping people all jumped to their feet as one. Jackets and snowsuits came on, muskets were grabbed. The sounds of muskets firing in the distance and another volley of artillery washed over them. Murphy scrambled down from their watch position.

"Mason! Dunaway is gone!" he said. "I fell asleep, I'm sorry—"

Mason grabbed Murphy by the collar. "Where is Dunaway? Why didn't you guys wake up the next watch?"

"I fell asleep. She's gone, Mason," Murphy sputtered. "I don't know!"

"Her gear is here." Higgs pointed down.

"Fuck her!" Stratton yelled. "We've got to go!"

Mason whirled toward the voice and realized that Stratton was right. "Get us down there, but don't cross the bridge. Stay out of sight—the Hessians are going to guard that bridge. When the first ones approach the bridge, use an artillery simulator. Scare the fuck out of them!"

Stratton tapped his vest and nodded. "Red star cluster is un-ass, retreat, and run. I've got it. Let's go, Alpha Team. On me!"

Fuck. Mason shook his head. *We're out of position and late!*

Higgs brushed past. "Focus, Mason. We've got time. Get us into position."

Mason nodded. "Yeah. Thanks." He pointed at Stratton, who started moving through the heavy falling snow. With their white suits on, they looked like ghosts moving through the forest and winter underbrush. Mason fell into his position at the middle of the squad as they moved out. A minute later, they passed a pile of clothing. Dunaway's uniform, boots, and snowsuit. Her long underwear wasn't there, so she'd at least had the presence of mind to try and protect herself.

Goddammit.

Where is she? Just as quickly as the thought came and went, another did. *Does it matter?*

Mason shook off the thought and kept walking. They'd have to come back and retrieve all of their gear eventually. The pile of Dunaway's gear was just something else they'd have to carry. Fresh anger surfaced and he raged at himself for failing to see that she was going to run. Now they'd lost a rifle and a human being. The rifle would take time for the enemy to reverse engineer. Dunaway had knowledge of the future, which was just as dangerous. He thought she'd been a liability before leaving, and now she'd crossed the line to all-out risk. Maybe she was in the town telling Rall and his Hessians about the attack. Maybe she'd run and died of exposure somewhere nearby.

Does it matter? Mason took a deep breath and ran after his squad.

Around the small spur of terrain, they turned north and headed down into the brush at the edge of Assunpink Creek. Across the way, Hessian soldiers ran to and fro. In the distance, Mason could make out the vanguard elements of Sullivan's brigades moving fast down the River Road. A sizable portion of Hessians formed up and moved toward the river and their bridge. Stratton waved the squad down into concealment and they found their way to the ground. Mason looked at Stratton and signaled that this was their assault position. Should they have to attack, Stratton's team would provide covering fire while Higgs moved her team across the bridge. They'd repeat the bounding maneuver until everyone was across the bridge.

Mason watched the Hessians form up along the far bank as chaos descended on them from the north. As one they turned and moved north up the River Road to confront the charging rebels. As another rumble of American artillery roared to life, Mason couldn't help but smile. History was being made right in front of them!

Focus, Jameel. Hold that bridge for thirty minutes.
All we have to do is hold the bridge.

North of Trenton, on a spot of high ground suitable to deploy his artillery and observe the town below, Washington saw Rall's regiment form and attempt to flank Greene's division from the east. His Pennsylvania infantry were there and ready for a fight. He turned to Tilghman and a collection of messengers.

"Lieutenant, send my compliments to Colonel Hand and Colonel Haussegger. Have them shift east and take that far high ground and lay fire into the Hessian counterattack." Washington didn't wait for the riders to leave before turning back to the battle. Hessian regiments had formed and drifted back to the center of town. He could see Sullivan's division marching down the River Road and making a swift advance into the enemy's rear. The bridge was secure. Mason had only to hold another precious few moments before Sullivan would arrive.

Washington's artillery laid fire into the town and carnage ensued. Horses went down in spectacular, awful woundings. Hessian guns brought to fire were silenced by sheer volume. Washington strained to see into Sullivan's division for action against the exposed Hessian guns on King Street. If they were to take them, the Hessians would have no other choice than to abandon the town itself and try to reconsolidate in the orchards to the east.

No sooner had Washington thought about the course of action than he saw men from what he assumed were Henry Knox's command split off and charge into the town.

Washington looked to the east and saw Hand's regiment had indeed cut off the Hessian advance with a steady stream of rifle and cannon fire. *If we can take the Hessian cannon,* he mused, *the rout will be complete.* The Hessians continued to retreat house to house in an orderly manner. More ran toward the orchard, exactly where Mason said they would in order to launch a second attack. With Sullivan behind them, there was no place to run except to cross the creek itself, which was where Mason and his squad came in. If they held, there would be no advance warning to General Grant.

If they held.

Musket fire caught Mason's attention to their front. To the northwest, Sullivan's division came down the River Road headed straight for the old stone bridge. He looked to his left and right, saw the faces of his friends behind their muskets, and cleared his throat.

"Give each other time to load. Murphy and Koch. Use your M16s. Semiauto. Keep up a steady rate of fire. Everybody else, muskets until I say switch." The Hessians lined up to fire at the advancing division. Their attention elsewhere, Mason saw an opening. He got Stratton's attention and tapped his chest. His counterpart grinned and withdrew the artillery simulator. Mason watched Stratton unpack it slowly, withdrawing the ignition string. Stratton moved up to his knees, pulled the string, and threw the simulator to the west on their side of the creek. Stratton fell to the prone position. The ignition took a few seconds, but the simulator smoked and began to whistle, replicating the sound of a large, falling artillery shell. Mason closed his eyes and put his fingers in his ears. The simulator detonated and shook snow from the trees above them.

Mason rolled up to a firing position. "Open fire!"

Their first shots dropped two Hessian soldiers at the rear of the enemy formation. The next volley took down two more and Mason saw them pointing and yelling in the cadets' direction. *They can't see us!* Another volley, this one from Higgs and Martinez, dropped an officer and wounded another man. The Hessians looked over their collective shoulders and back at Sullivan's division descending upon them. To a man, they turned and fled toward the east.

A man on horseback raced across the bridge. He rode almost up onto their position before Mason stood in the snow and removed his hood. In the helmet band of his Kevlar was a white piece of paper. The man on horseback grinned. "Washington's bloody ghosts!"

Mason saluted. "General Sullivan."

"Well done, lads," Sullivan said. "We'll take the bridge and this shoreline." He pointed at the center of town. "Move that direction toward General Greene's division with General St. Clair."

"Yes, sir." Mason turned to the squad. "Let's go!"

As one, they stood and ran for the bridge. Mason looked back at the trees where Dunaway's gear lay. They'd recover it later and worry about her whereabouts. Across the bridge, he heard a cheer from King Street and saw a contingent of rebels overrunning the Hessian cannons. Two men, both officers, were down. One of them was bleeding profusely from his shoulder.

Eyes on General St. Clair's horse, Mason moved that direction when he heard Stratton screaming.

"Higgs! Higgs! Get back here!"

Horrified, Mason watched Ashley Higgs sprinting toward King Street with her Combat Life Saver bag in hand.

"Go!" he screamed at them. "Follow Higgs!"

Higgs ran toward the cannons, flinging back her hood to reveal her helmet and piece of paper. A few confused troops spun toward her with rifles ready and stopped. She never broke stride and slid to the ground next to the wounded young officer. He looked up at her with wide eyes.

"It's you," he said. His skin was white and his hands shook as he raised them at her. "From the boat."

She remembered him then. Digging into her first aid kit, her mind was already on his wound. "You're hit."

"Hit?"

"Shot," she said and withdrew emergency shears from the bag. "Going to cut your uniform."

"Shouldn't you wait for a doctor?" the young man asked. There was a hint of a smile on his face.

She looked at his eyes. He was too cute to die. "I'm better than a doctor."

"I hope so." He was a lieutenant, if Murphy's lesson on rank and dress served her right.

"What's your name, Lieutenant?" She cut his coat and pulled it away from the wound. The ball had penetrated his arm and shoulder before exiting. There was too much blood for a clean wound. An artery had been damaged. Maybe even severed. His eyes fluttered and his mouth moved but no sound came out. She looked up at the soldiers around her. "Move this man to a house with a table."

No one moved. A man stepped through the interested ring. "Who are you?"

"Cadet Sergeant Higgs. I'm an EMT."

"Excuse me?"

"A ..." She paused. *How can I explain it*? "I'm a medic."

"What?"

"I'm a doctor!" she growled at the man.

"You're a woman!" the man exclaimed. "I'm Doctor Riker. That man is bleeding to death. Stand aside, young lady."

Higgs looked up at the nearest soldier. "You! Pick three men and move this lieutenant inside that building! Do it right now or he's going to die!"

Thunderstruck, the soldiers did exactly what she said. Inside the small house, they cleared a table and set the lieutenant on it. By the light of the open door, she could see the damage more clearly. She dug into her kit for a clamp. "The artery has been hit."

Riker leaned in. "We'll need to—"

Higgs moved the clamp past Riker and dug into the lieutenant's wound. She clamped it once, but there was no difference in the volume of blood. She tried again and the flow ceased. As she ripped open gauze packets, she looked up at Riker. "Help me clean this wound. We need to look for fragments."

Riker nodded. "Infection. Right."

They dabbed the wound. The lieutenant stirred a little, his skin more colorful and vibrant than it had been mere minutes before. "What happened?"

"You took a ball to the shoulder and it damaged an artery," Riker said. "This young woman found it and has clamped it down. We're cleaning your wound. Everything is going to be fine."

Higgs looked up from his wound and smiled. "We're going to raise your legs, first."

"Why?" Riker demanded. "The blood will move faster through the wound."

"I'm treating him for shock," Higgs said.

"Shock?"

Higgs stared at him. "And you're a doctor? Loss of blood? Loss of consciousness? Any of that sound familiar?"

Riker nodded but said nothing. His incredulous eyes fell over her bloody hands and the bag at her side.

"Good," she said. "Now. I'm going to suture that artery, Lieutenant. You're going to lay still. I'll get you something for the pain." She fingered the ampoule of morphine and a syringe. A small dose loaded, she injected him near the wound. "Now, just relax. What's your name?"

"James," he said. "Yours?"

"Ashley."

The man smiled. "Ashley. I like that very much."

He closed his eyes and leaned back. His body relaxed with the morphine in his system, she leaned in with her suture kit and got to work. Riker watched her, fascinated. As she finished, the older man shook his head.

"I've never seen anything like that. Where did you get your training?" Riker asked. "And that uniform! Just who are you?"

She smiled and shrugged. "One of Washington's bloody ghosts."

The sound of gunfire diminished outside. The door opened and a white-clad soldier stepped into the room. Mason pointed at her patient. "He okay?"

"He's going to be fine," Higgs said. "What's going on out there?"

"Sullivan has the far side of the creek. The Hessians didn't get out." Mason paused. "Three dragoons did. Including the captain."

Oh no. She bit her bottom lip. "They'll go after the Danielses."

"I think so. We're going to tell Washington and go back to protect them, if we can. We have to hurry."

Higgs nodded. "I should stay here in case his suture opens."

Mason looked past her for a second. "Yeah. We can handle this."

"Mason!" Murphy ran through the door. "General Washington is coming down into town. The Hessians have struck their colors!"

Murphy looked at Higgs and her bloody hands before he looked at the young man on the table. "Who's your patient?"

"He said his name was James," she said. "I gave him some morphine before he could tell me more."

Murphy's mouth was agape for a long moment. He looked up at Mason, then Doctor Riker, and back to her. His mouth worked silently. "James. James Monroe."

Mason flinched. "No shit?"

"Yeah." Murphy smiled at her. "How's that feel, Higgs?"

She looked down at her patient asleep on the table, a small smile on his face in the morphine-induced dream. A future President of the United States. Monroe hadn't died before, so Riker obviously got the job done, she thought. *A President!*

A cute one at that.

She looked up at Murphy, unashamed of the tears in her eyes. "Pretty damned good."

"They're struck, sir."

Washington stared toward the orchard. "What did you say?"

"Sir. Their colors have been struck."

That can't be right.

"Struck?"

"Yes, sir."

Washington looked down King Street and saw the flagpole outside of Rall's headquarters was indeed bare. "So they are."

He moved forward without another word, aware that the artillerymen had left their guns and followed him. In the town below, the defeated Hessians mingled with the American troops. A fresh smattering of musket fire erupted near the Assunpink Creek bridge and then fell silent. Washington approached Rall's headquarters aware of his men's adulation only vaguely. A young man sprinted in his direction and Washington took a moment to realize it was General Sullivan's aide. He was talking, but Washington could not hear him.

My God! Mason was right. We're nearly unscathed!

"—regiment has surrendered to a man, sir. Victory is complete."

Washington smiled and extended a hand. "Major Wilkinson? This is a glorious day for our country."

"Indeed it is, sir," Wilkinson said.

Over the young major's shoulder, seven figures dressed in white with greenish helmets and white pieces of paper flapping ran toward him. Washington dismounted and strode forward, smiling. The cadets slowed to a walk and then stopped to salute him. He returned it in their manner, not the open palm salute of the British.

"Mason. You were right."

Mason nodded. "Sir, three dragoons escaped after General Sullivan relieved us. They jumped the creek on horseback."

"Where are they headed?" He glanced at Murphy.

"Princeton, sir," Murphy said. "We're afraid that they might go after Mister Daniels on their way. Their officer harassed the Danielses a lot. We think they are a target."

Washington felt his smile fade. "I see."

"With your permission, sir, we want to go protect—"

A scream came from behind Washington and he barely had time to turn before being knocked to the cold, muddy street. There was a flash and bang at the same time. Washington turned on his side and saw a Hessian grenadier standing in an open doorway with a musket pointing in his direction. For a split second, he checked his body mentally for injury and found none. More rifle fire rang out and the Hessian went down. Washington turned his head and saw the larger, dark-skinned cadet writhing in pain on the ground.

Tilghman helped him to his feet. "Sir?"

His eyes were on the young man. His left arm bled from a wound below the shoulder. Washington brushed off his coat and stepped closer. "Is he all right?" he asked Mason.

Mason turned. "Looks like a flesh wound, sir. I'm going to have Higgs check him out. She's taking care of Lieutenant Monroe."

Washington nodded through his shock. He knelt down to the young man. "What's your name?"

"Booker, sir."

"And you pushed me down to protect me?"

Booker grimaced as they pulled him to a sitting position. Contrasted against the sheer white cloak was the young man's bright red blood.

"I'm deeply indebted to you," Washington said, his mouth suddenly dry. Mason and Koch hauled Booker to his feet and passed him to Martinez and Murphy. Washington followed them with his eyes for a moment.

"We need to go, General." Mason's urgent voice broke his concentration.

"Refit and resupply, Mason," Washington said.

"There's no time, General," Mason said. "If we run, we can be there in a half hour."

Vernon Daniels was a hell of a shot and a tremendous gunsmith. But he was only one man against three dragoons. Mason and his squad could at least provide protection. "Go, Mason. You'll have support as soon as I can get a company there."

"Thank you, sir." Mason saluted and the cadets ran. Washington could hear the men calling them ghosts as they watched the scene. Into the howling maw of the storm, went six young men. The two young women were missing. Mason stopped. "Cadet

Higgs is with Lieutenant Monroe. We don't know where Cadet Dunaway is."

"Go, Mason. We can figure that out later." Washington pointed. "Return by nightfall."

"Yes, sir!"

He watched them for a long moment. *What else did they know? What was to come next?* Lieutenant Tilghman's voice broke through his thoughts.

"Sir? What of their rifle? Are you going to tell them?"

Washington turned and looked at his adjutant. Aside from Mister Lee, there was no one he trusted more. The rifle, safely in Mister Lee's care and awaiting the keen eye of Jefferson, hadn't been on his mind at all. Watching the cadets in action, knowing what they knew and not shying away from their devotion to the country, filled his heart with pride. Yet they were a limited resource. If they died, their equipment and uniforms might not affect anything. Some would serve, but others would be called upon for other duties. Jefferson, he believed, could help discern that while he examined the weapon himself. For that, the cadets did not need to know the missing rifle had been acquired. Passion and purpose were valuable motivators.

"No, Tench," Washington said. "They do not need to know about the rifle."

"And the Virginians? What will you tell them?"

Washington nodded. "The men have been told that it was nothing. Given my impending discussion with General Stephen, I believe they'll keep their mouths shut. However"—he paused and pasted a grim smile on his face—"General Stephen and I will have a most spirited discussion with the full knowledge of the Congress. To be sure."

Another aide appeared. "Sir, Colonel Rall has been gravely wounded."

Washington nodded. "I will see him to pay my respects."

"He's being brought to his headquarters now, sir."

"Very well," Washington said. A few moments later, a grim procession climbed up the shallow hill from the orchards. Hessian soldiers carried their commander slowly. The man's ashen face twisted in agony and the side of his uniform was soaked with blood. Beyond a doubt, he would not survive his wounds. He lay upon a ragged bench with a lieutenant keeping step. The young man looked up at him.

"Colonel Rall, sir," the young lieutenant said. He touched a scar on his cheek and dabbed at teary eyes.

Washington nodded and leaned down. "Colonel."

The man spoke in a harsh whisper. The lieutenant translated. "The colonel asks that his men keep their possessions, General."

Washington nodded and touched Rall gently on the arm. "Of course."

The procession moved on to Rall's headquarters and the colonel was carried inside. By now, his commanders had started to appear in the crowd. Washington turned to Tilghman.

"Treat all prisoners with dignity. Find and inventory all stores and provisions. Send for General Greene and we'll establish a defense."

"Anything else, sir?"

"Assemble the commanders in two hours in the church." Washington pointed. "It's time we do something about this war."

"And those cadets, General?" Tilghman raised an eyebrow.

Washington looked in the direction the white-cloaked young men had gone. "Send a company of men to support them."

"Anything else, sir?"

Washington nodded. Mason and his men had disappeared into the storm in their white camouflage. The soldiers of the future fought much like the enemies of Washington's own past. *You cannot fight what you cannot see.*

"Secure every white sheet in the town, every town we come upon. Ensure that the quartermaster general is aware that white sheets are the highest priority during winter operations. As long as winter howls, we have an advantage to press, Tilghman," Washington said. "Advantages change history."

CHAPTER TWENTY-TWO

The Hessian drums woke Sutton instantly and he leapt from the bed and reached for his clothes in one smooth motion. Wind and rain lashed the home as the first cannon fire rumbled through the valley around the town. He could hear the Hessians screaming that the enemy was coming. For a brief moment, he wondered if it wasn't one of Rall's strange alerts until the clear snaps of a musket volley cleared the thought from his mind. They sounded to the north and Sutton reached for his weapons with his mind racing on how to get behind the enemy and destroy them.

We merely have to—

A thunderous ripple of artillery fire rumbled from the west, by the river. He paused for a moment, his racing mind wondering if Washington had dared to attack in two columns to envelop the town.

Victory was out of the question. If Washington's army had indeed spread their attack, survival would be all that mattered. Dying in Trenton as a part of Rall's ultimate failure was not his wish. Sutton tore from the house, past a visibly frightened Selena Christensen and out into the chaos of the storm and Washington's attack. Another ripple of musket fire, this one sounding much closer, urged him to run to the stables. There he found his men in various states of dishevelment preparing to mount their horses.

His sergeant at arms caught his eye. "Orders, sir?"

"Get what you can carry and get across the Assunpink Creek

231

bridge before the rebels take the town." He found Jack, quickly worked his saddle over the big gelding's back, and mounted. "I'll check the situation to the north and return. Now, go!"

He rode out, turning north along Queen Street at a full gallop. At the north end of town, he could barely see the rebel army approaching through the wind and heavy sleet falling. The Hessians, the ones fighting at least, were holding the rebels back and retreating slowly into town. Cannons fired again from the high ground not more than a quarter mile away. Several of them arced over his position by the sound. He whirled in his saddle and saw a cluster of cannonballs fall into and around the stables.

Bastards!

He nudged Jack as a second volley fired from the cannons and the stables again received the brunt of the attack. A large fire spread and Sutton heard the unearthly squealing of the royal mounts. Two of his men and their horses managed to get through the burning structure and into the street.

"Go! Get to the Princeton Road!" The men were off like a shot and Sutton followed them. He glanced over his shoulder, hoping to see others break from the burning stables and saw nothing. He charged east, out of the town and just south of the apple orchard. To his left, he could see and hear the rebel muskets and cannon. Hessians ran and gathered in the orchard.

To hell with Rall.

Sutton turned more to the southeast as he breached the wood line. For fifteen minutes, he trotted Jack through the woods and stayed north of Assunpink Creek before turning north.

When they reached the Princeton Road, it was quiet. In the distance, a few cannons fired and Sutton felt as if he could hear the rebels celebrating their victory. There was no other possible outcome. He slapped at the pommel of Jack's saddle and shook his head angrily. Washington, whether through luck or God's will, had completely surprised them. In the space of an hour, maybe less, Trenton had fallen. His soldiers, good men to the very last, were either captured or killed in the rout. Of the two soldiers still with him, one had run for his horse without boots or a weapon and the other one shivered in the cold without his tunic. Still, they were away from the rebel army and the stunning surprise attack. Waiting for any other escapees for an hour left them all chilled and growing ever angrier. Rall's incompetence had been on full display. In the midst of a howling storm, Washington and his men had attacked and taken the town with hardly a shot fired.

His men murmured amongst themselves. As if hearing the disgust in their voices, Sutton felt his cheeks flush with fresh anger at Colonel Rall. *Damn that man! His want of cards and fancy dinners instead of redoubts and tactical responses!*

Sutton exhaled explosively and turned his face to the breeze. *Why would Washington attack in a storm? Had he known the weather would change?*

Had he known of Rall's party and love of cards?

His raging mind calmed in a flash. The party. Only one thing had been different at the party.

Emily Daniels.

The weapons in her father's shed. His late-night hunting expeditions. All of the indicators flickered to life.

Sutton turned in the saddle. "Stand ready and prepare to ride."

The one without his boots maneuvered his mount next to Sutton's. "Orders, sir?"

"Princeton," Sutton said. "Ride for Princeton and warn General Grant. Tell him that I will bring a full report when I join you there. I must depart from you to address..."

"Sir, should we not stay together?"

Sutton smiled. "I have business that must be attended to personally, Sergeant. You'll carry the message of his attack to General Grant. I will join you presently."

"Yes, sir." He and the other soldier rode off.

Sutton nudged his mount into a fast trot toward the Daniels home. His mind raced. Daniels' smug face and thin smile came to his mind and his anger at the Hessian defeat turned to rage. The girl possessed the gall to kiss his cheek and take his arm while spying on Rall and his generals. Their exhaustion and frustration had been all over their faces! The rising storm should have been a clue and he had missed it. Perhaps no one could have seen the attack coming, but he felt the shame of missing the signs like a yoke around his neck.

Yet, because of the attack's success, Washington and his army lay exposed in Trenton and if the storm raged on, the ice-filled river could trap the cowards in Trenton while the British army and Colonel Von Donop's forces fell inward to end the rebellion once and for all. His shame, his very honor, could be cleared by bringing justice to the spy Vernon Daniels and his daughter as well. At the Pennington Road, he turned and left his dragoons to their ride to Princeton. He nudged the horse into a gallop and set his mind to the task at hand.

The cabin appeared in the distance amidst the swirling snow. Sutton slowed the horse to a walk and studied the terrain. All was quiet. He smiled and stopped fifty yards away from the door. In a moment's time he lashed his horse to a small tree below a slight embankment. Withdrawing the pistol from his belt he grasped the hilt of his sword and strode to the door of the cabin. Instead of a knock, he kicked at the door and knocked it from his hinges. Daniels appeared around the corner with a musket. Sutton swung the pistol and reveled in the dull, wet sound it made when it hit the man's head. The gunsmith fell in a heap at the door.

Emily screamed from the kitchen and tried to run for the staircase. Sutton closed the distance and grasped her by the neck.

"Spy!" he hissed into her face. "You came to dinner not for me but for your whore's cause and disgraced His Majesty's army!"

She struggled, red-faced and kicking, against his grasp. He tossed her to the floor and waved the pistol in her face.

"Now. Tell me what you know about Washington's army and their plans." He grinned like a jackal. Standing over her, he pressed the barrel of the pistol against her forehead. "Tell me everything."

The path Mason chose to the Danielses' home led them through the eastern end of the forest where they'd appeared in this now different past. Across the field where they'd carried Kennedy's body, they ran almost as one. Martinez lagged behind a couple of hundred meters. Mason glanced over his shoulder and saw the big kid sweating and puffing but his pace never changed. He might have never made it as a cadet, but Martinez had heart like no one Mason had ever known. They'd stopped three times to wait for Martinez. At the last stop, a half mile short of the cabin, Martinez wheezed and puffed as he stopped and bent over next to Mason.

"You okay?" Mason had asked.

"Yeah," Martinez huffed. "Go on without me."

"We're not leaving you, Martinez," Stratton said. He had glanced at Mason and almost smiled. The change in their relationship was welcome, if weird. The disappearance of Dunaway in the middle of the night made them all the more vulnerable and dependent upon each other.

"He's right, Mark. Get to the barn," Mason said. "We're going to attack from there. They can't see us approach from there."

"No windows," Martinez huffed. "The one on the east side of the house is too filthy to see anything, either."

Mason slapped Martinez on the back. The kid was more observant than he'd realized. Mason stood and watched his fellow cadets. They were now just five. Stratton and Murphy were fifty meters ahead and pushing hard through the snow. Mason and Koch were next with Martinez trailing. Ahead, Mason saw the outline of the cabin appear in the snow. The wind howled. Without cover, they'd all freeze to death from the sweat running down their bodies from their six-mile run. If the British were there expecting them, a brief fight or a long pause in the snow was not something he looked forward to.

Stratton turned, still moving forward, and pointed at the barn. Mason nodded and waved them that direction. Stratton reached the back door first and slipped inside. Murphy followed. By the time Mason and Koch arrived, Stratton and Murphy were already out of their rucksacks. Mason paused at the door, waved Koch inside, and stopped to look for Martinez.

"He coming?" Stratton asked.

Mason nodded. He strained but could not see through the storm. Another blast of wind chilled him to the bone as he watched. Martinez was there, still moving forward at a shuffle. "There he is."

Stratton moved to the side of the barn to peer through the slats. "I don't see anything."

"There's a horse down there," Koch said. "Left side of the road. Just down the side."

"I don't see it." Stratton pressed his face against the wood. Mason turned and watched Martinez shuffle ever closer.

"It's there," Koch replied. "Look closer."

"Yeah, yeah, I see it," Stratton said. Mason chuckled to himself.

No, you don't see it, Stratton. I can't see it, either.

"What color is the horse?" Murphy asked.

"White. I think it's that officer's horse," Koch said. "Sure looks like it."

Fuck.

Come on, Martinez.

Three minutes later, Martinez shuffled through the door and dropped to his knees. "Holy...shit...I've never ran that far before."

Mason touched him on the shoulder. In a microsecond, a plan formed. "Martinez, you stay here and guard our gear. Stratton? Murphy? Come here."

They gathered as Mason sketched out a rough rectangle on the ground approximating the Danielses' cabin. "We'll stack against the door. Stratton on point, Murphy in the middle taking right and I'll take the left. We'll clear the kitchen first—that's where he'll be. Koch, you've got the rear."

Murphy swallowed. "Are we weapons free?"

Mason looked at Stratton. "Yeah. Kill him."

"Okay," Murphy said. "I'm ready."

"Me, too." Stratton nodded. "Let's go get him."

Mason turned to Martinez. Doctrine said he was to leave a GOTWA report with the stay-behind element. Like all good army techniques, the mnemonic device was simple. A leader was to state where they were going, others they were taking, what time frame for success or failure, and actions if either the reconnaissance party or the stay-behind party were engaged. "We're going in there, Martinez. We're going to take him out. If he comes out of that cabin, and not us, fire at him. Try to take him out. If you can't, run. Get back to Trenton and General Washington."

Martinez wiped his face with a gloved hand. "Okay. Yeah."

Mason knelt down to look the big sophomore in the face. "Hey. We're going to be okay. Stay here, catch your breath, but be ready to help us out, all right?"

"Got it, Mason," Martinez said. "Be careful."

I hope so.

He looked up at Stratton and Murphy. "Your muskets loaded?"

Both of them nodded. Stratton pointed at Martinez. "You loaded?"

"Yeah."

Mason looked up at them and met each of their stares with his own. Every sensation seemed clear as if his body was aware of everything necessary for survival. He took a deep breath through his nose and exhaled slowly through his mouth. A sudden thought made him snort and grin at them. "The movies all say we're supposed to say something epic right now."

Stratton grinned. "I was thinking about that, too."

"It's a bit more serious than that," Martinez said. "It has been since Kennedy died, man."

Mason nodded and their smiles disappeared. "You're right, Martinez. We all know what's about to go down. I think it's time we go and do it."

"Fuck the British, man," Koch said. They all grinned a little.

Stratton moved to the door. "Follow me."

"Be careful," Martinez said again. "See you in a few minutes."

Mason nodded and followed Stratton through the barn door. They sprinted across the snow toward the cabin. With no window looking out at them, Mason, Stratton, and Murphy reached the ragged wall and pressed their backs into it. Stratton moved to the corner with Murphy sandwiched in the middle. Mason could feel Koch's shoulder against his. They were ready.

"Move," Mason whispered and Stratton slid around the corner with his shoulder against the frame. The wind braced them as they moved to the door. Stratton peeked in and turned to Murphy.

A second later, Murphy turned and whispered, "Door is down."

Fuck. Mason replied immediately. "Kitchen. Go."

Stratton rushed inside and they followed behind him. Mason blinked against the near darkness as they rounded the corner into the kitchen—

BAMM!

Stratton went down to the floor. Murphy screamed and came up with his rifle. The British officer, his powdered wig askew on his head and a pistol in each hand, whipped Murphy aside with relative ease. The pistol in the officer's left hand smoked from the shot that felled Stratton. The other wasn't smoking and it was pointed at Mason.

"Well." The man smiled. "Look at you! Drop your rifle or I kill your friends."

Mason glanced at the red pool of blood circling around Stratton's head. The wound looked bad but head wounds always bled a lot—and he could see the young man's chest moving. Stratton was still breathing, clearly enough.

Murphy lay against the hearth, eyes closed. But he was breathing also.

Mason shook his head. "You don't have to do that."

"Actually, I do." The man's thin smile seemed fixed in place. "Now, put your rifle on the floor."

Mason did. As he knelt, he tried to listen for sound behind him. There was nothing. Koch was still in the foyer, which was what Mason was counting on. "Fine. My rifle is down. Put your own weapon down."

The man laughed and centered the pistol on Mason's forehead. "You're a stupid bastard."

He pulled the trigger and there was a loud click. Mason flinched and instantly realized the weapon had misfired. Movement around his right shoulder caught his eye. The barrel of a musket appeared and there was a crash with a flash of light so intense he moved away.

The British officer's chest exploded with the shot. Eyes wide, he looked past Mason toward Koch. His mouth moved, but no sound came out. A heartbeat later, the officer fell to the ground over Stratton's form.

Mason looked at Emily. "Where's your father?"

"In the parlor." She stood. Her face was strained but she moved quickly to Stratton and leaned over, examining him. "I don't think the bullet pierced his skull. It's just a flesh wound."

She made a face. "Nasty one, though. He'll have quite a scar." She turned away and reached for a cloth hanging from a hook, in order to stop the bleeding.

Mason glanced at Murphy and Koch. "Help me with Daniels." Emily's father was breathing but unconscious with a vicious cut on the side of his face. They rolled him up and carried him into the kitchen also.

"What do we do now?" Murphy asked.

"Go get Martinez in here," Mason said. "And get the horses and wagon hooked up. We have to get back to Trenton and tell General Washington that the British are going to come in a few days."

Murphy nodded. "They'll take Trenton easily. They come down and Washington counterattacks to Princeton. They fight at Trenton again and it's costly as hell. Washington runs across the river and they head to northern New Jersey for the winter and—"

Mason shook his head. "Not this time, Murphy."

"What do you mean? The British will bring almost eight thousand soldiers. They'll push Washington back across the Delaware and—"

"We're not going to let that happen," Mason said. "We know

where they're coming from. We know their strength and intent. We're going to hit them when they're not expecting it and send the British back to New York. That's what we're going to do."

December 28, 1776

Footsteps from the lower floor shook Cornwallis from his daydream. Assuming the courier had arrived, he sealed the letter for Jemima with his customary red wax and blew gently on it. With any luck, the letter would reach England a week before he would. Imagining her smiling face in the window of their home as he arrived made him smile. He pressed his seal to the wax just as a knock came at his bedroom door.

"Enter."

"Sir." It was Jenkins, his aide-de-camp. The young man's eyes were wide and in his hands was a familiar parchment bearing the obvious, overblown seal of General Lord Howe. "A letter, sir. And news."

"News?" Cornwallis stood from his desk and walked toward the young man.

"Sir, the rebels have taken Trenton from the Hessians. Almost a thousand captured and all of the Hessian artillery."

Cornwallis blinked. *Washington had attacked?*

"When?"

"Two days ago," Jenkins said. "Reports are that they've fortified the town and stand prepared to repel an attack from both directions. Colonel Rall's command was decimated. Colonel Von Donop was south in Mount Holly quelling a rebellion. They attacked at the perfect time."

"In the bloody storm?" Cornwallis gaped. "Washington barely had an army a week ago, how could he have crossed the Delaware much less taken an entire Hessian garrison? There must be more to this story, Jenkins. A barely capable army cannot simply destroy a Hessian unit by surprise."

Jenkins did not immediately respond. Instead, he sputtered and extended the letter. "Orders, sir."

Cornwallis looked at the dull envelope. An awful, twisting feeling rumbled through his gut. A good aide knew the contents of any package before it was opened. "I'm to return to the garrison immediately?"

"Yes, sir."

"I see," he said and turned to the window. Disappointment turned to anger. "My leave has been postponed or canceled?"

Jenkins swallowed again. "Canceled, sir. General Grant requests your presence at the garrison with haste."

Cornwallis looked out into the snow-covered street below. The storm had passed and left an icy coating across the sleepy city. "Recall my bags from the *Bristol* and summon my horse. Prepare to move the staff forward. I imagine we'll have one very clear order to follow. Dismissed."

Jenkins' footfalls on the stairs sounded like a coming thunderstorm. The noise and rhythm was not lost on Cornwallis. Washington's bravado in crossing the river would be met with a crushing response. Once and for all. With forces to his north and south, Washington would most likely retreat across the river before any attack could march, but the chance to destroy the rebel army and their increasingly aggravating leader called to him.

March the army. No, the entire garrison. We'll outnumber them three to one.

He'd also send riders to the Hessian forces at Mount Holly. Move them up from the south to join forces. They'd close down on Washington like a vise and put down this rebellion.

Cornwallis fingered his own letter, forgotten for a long moment, and frowned. He tore it into two pieces and set it aside. To make the next ship, he would not have time to draft a full letter professing his love. A short note, hastily written, would alarm Jemima and coupled with the news of Washington's attack, she would worry more than normal.

It was best not to send anything. After putting down Washington's army, he would haul the traitorous bastard across the ocean and present him to His Majesty personally. After that, he could leave the army behind and live the rest of his life in quiet retirement in the favor of his king.

Cornwallis tossed aside his more formal tunic and outer coat. In the top of the battered trunk he thought of as his war chest, Cornwallis found his traditional tunic and cloak. After a moment, he decided to wait before putting it on and rushing off unkempt to see General Howe. Cornwallis gathered the pieces of the letter to his beloved Jemima and walked to his desk. For a moment, he considered burning them. Instead, he sat them atop a bunch of administrative documents he would leave right where they sat. The same would go for most of his belongings. Washington would be a fool to leave Trenton. Intelligence reported that Washington's supply lines verged on disaster even with a great victory. It would take weeks for the rebel Congress and Washington's army to right the ship.

Weeks they don't have.

Cornwallis made a mental note to have Jenkins pack only the war chest and leave the rest here for his triumphant return. If his mission lasted more than two weeks, he would send for the rest of his belongings. Two weeks, however, should be more than enough time to end this war once and for all.

CHAPTER TWENTY-THREE

December 30, 1776

Mason woke well after dawn. The floor of the Anglican Church made a warm, suitable place for the squad to bed down together for the first time in days. Koch snored in one corner and no one else moved as Mason stirred upright in his sleeping bag and rubbed his eyes. His watch read 0830 and for a moment, he could hear nothing from outside. One sleeping bag, the one where Higgs had neatly laid out her gear, was flat and empty. Mason quietly unzipped his bag and considered changing his socks for a moment before realizing that digging in his bag would wake the others and he didn't want that. They all needed sleep.

For the past forty-eight hours, they'd helped Washington and his generals learn the principles of modern defensive positions, clandestine-movement operations, and ambush techniques to the point of exhaustion. Washington would meet with them again at 1100 to discuss his plan for the arrival of the British army on January 2. So far, there was no indication that the British army knew anything different regarding the situation and Murphy's knowledge of the timeline would soon expire. His term paper had been through January 1777 and Washington's movement to the higher ground of northern New Jersey. After that, the histori-cal knowledge in the squad lagged. They knew that Cornwallis would take the war effort south and that many battles would be waged over the next several years. Congress would occasionally succeed, but Washington's logistical operations would need a serious boost. The French would eventually come to the Continental's assistance, which could be good or bad. Lastly, they knew simply that Washington and the French were able to box in the British army at Yorktown. Murphy, to his credit, had left the French out of things so far. Mason knew it was for the best. They, like the British, were coming and it was just a matter of time.

It was also a matter of time to see if the British or the Hessians had the missing rifle. A complete search of the town revealed nothing, even in the shattered stables where the dragoons were killed. Washington tried to reassure Mason and the others, but it felt like a nagging, awful fear looking over his shoulder everywhere they went. Washington vowed to use his intelligence network and the army itself to track it down. Without having his hands on the rifle, Washington's promise was more than enough for Mason. That feeling, though, of being responsible for the eventual end of America, would not go away.

Mason slipped on his boots and stood slowly, collecting his jacket and musket. Their M16s were stacked into pyramids along one side of the church, waiting for ammunition that might never come. Next to the rifles were the extra gear from Kennedy, Porter, and Dunaway. The empty helmets and laid-out clothing tugged at his emotions. Fresh anger at Dunaway, sadness for Kennedy, and regret for the loss of Porter all crashed in upon him at the same time and instead of weighing him down, he held them up with a glance at the sleeping forms around him. His people lived. It was no small accomplishment.

Mason pushed through the door and nodded to the posted guard. Washington had made it clear that the cadets were not to be bothered. Down the street to the south he could see the weeds where they'd positioned themselves before the battle began. He walked that way, keenly aware of the eyes on him, and found the cabins where the hospital had been created. Inside the first one, he found Higgs sitting at Monroe's bedside.

"Hey," he said softly to avoid waking her patient. The future President of the United States was asleep.

Higgs looked up. "Morning. Did General Washington find you?"

Mason shook his head. "I just woke up."

"He told the men to let you guys sleep." Higgs smiled. "I think the father of our country likes you."

Mason chuckled. Three days before, he'd been a failure of a cadet and hardly someone that George Washington should trust.

"How's he doing?" Mason asked. "Where's Booker and Stratton?"

"Both asleep," Higgs said. "Their wounds will hurt for a while, but they'll both heal up nicely. Stratton got lucky and Booker was so damned brave."

Mason nodded at the sleeping Monroe. "And your patient?"

"He's going to be fine."

Mason sat down next to her on a thin wooden bench. "Murphy says he gets evacuated to Virginia. I'd imagine somewhat soon."

"Yeah," she said, now looking at Monroe. "I'm wondering if I should go with him. I know more about medicine than any of the so-called doctors in this day and age."

Mason shrugged. "Washington's not going to let you stay here with the army, anyway. Welcome to the eighteenth century and all that."

Higgs made a face but she didn't argue the point. Women in the military in the year 1776 were camp followers, not soldiers—and that battle was probably a bridge too far, at least for the moment. The Continental Army just wasn't ready for Ashley Higgs.

"I think Virginia sounds good," Mason said. "You could do a lot more for us there than you can here."

Higgs exhaled, clearly relieved. "You're sure?"

"You think I need your help?" Mason felt a smile creep over his face.

"No, you don't." She touched his arm. "You've always been a good leader, Mason. Now you believe in yourself. You never did that before."

"I don't know about that," he said and looked away.

"Hey! You are a good leader, Mason. You guys are about to change the world." Higgs shook her head and pointed a finger at his chest. "Don't think you're not. The British army are going to march down that road and you all are going to be there to meet them. What we know changes history."

Responsibility tightened its hands around his neck. "It's too much. I mean, slavery? Discrimination? All of that is still coming, Higgs."

Higgs smiled and patted his arm. "Or is it? Have faith, Mason. You changed the Battle of Trenton. What's next?"

☆   ☆   ☆

Mason walked across the street to the home of businessman Stacy Potts, now Washington's headquarters, and climbed the steps. The posted guard there snapped a salute, which Mason returned in pure astonishment.

He pushed into Washington's office and found the general alone at his writing desk. "You asked to see me, sir?"

"I went looking for you, yes. You and your squad needed rest, so I've endeavored to handle the copious needs of the army." Washington did not look up from his writing. "Our army grows with every passing minute, Mason. Men have come from miles around at the news of our victory. We number nearly three thousand."

Mason nodded. "They'll continue to come in, sir."

"Likely, yes." Washington looked up. His eyes were bright and sharp. "They strain our ability to feed and clothe them, though. But that's not why I wanted to see you. I expect to get another intelligence briefing from Murphy today. You're certain his detailed knowledge is only for the next few weeks?"

"That's what he said, sir. From there we know the eventual outcome, but the events of the campaign from now until then we don't." Mason shrugged. "Murphy told me that we have a few chances to really change the outcome of the war, though."

"As in a faster resolution?" Washington asked. "When does this war end?"

"1781, sir."

"Four more years." He shook his head. "Even with the significant advantages you and your men provide, this army will not last four years without a renewed vigor in the government. The Congress must be made aware of your men, too. Perhaps I might even send one of you there."

Mason squinted. "That would mean splitting us up."

"Indeed, but it cannot be helped, Mason. Your collective knowledge is something this country cannot lose in battle. I would rather have your talents equally distributed in the disciplines this country will need," Washington said and held out a piece of paper. "Some of you will most certainly stay with the army."

Mason took the piece of paper and read it. "A captain's commission, sir?"

Washington nodded. "Yes, Mason. Contingent upon the approval of the Congress. I wanted you to know before I sent it off with the day's dispatches."

"Sir? I don't know what to say."

"You'll command a company of regular troops I will employ for specific missions. Your first will be training the others to move in small units, not unlike your squad. Your use of camouflage intrigues me, as well. I've ordered all white sheets to be conscripted for the army's use. Given the snow cover, we would have a clear advantage against the British during the winter months."

"Sir, I still don't think it's a good idea to split us up."

"And I do, Mason." Washington enunciated the words carefully. The argument was over. "I will, however, take your recommendations on where some of your squad would go. Do they have any specialties? Murphy, for example, seems to have a grasp of the history and is adept with people. I see him working with Congress, perhaps with Mister Franklin abroad in France."

Murphy with Ben Franklin? Mason blinked. "Cadet Higgs wishes to remain with Lieutenant Monroe."

Washington nodded. "That suits me well enough. Cadet Booker will be staying with the army, as will you and Stratton. I'm not sure yet where Koch and Martinez might best be of use."

Mason thought for a moment. Koch's training in agriculture wasn't particularly critical, certainly not in the short run. Martinez, though...

"Martinez was a civil engineering student," he said. "I think he'd best be suited—do you have a corps of engineers, sir?"

"Yes. Colonel Richard Gridley is in charge of it. You think I should assign Martinez to him?"

"Yes, sir. Koch can stay with the rest of us."

Washington nodded with a finality Mason could sense without another word said. "We could easily defend this town from the south. Maybe even counterattack them with great success." Washington paused for a moment, and then added: "Bring Murphy and let us plan the next phase of this campaign before winter closes in on us. The Congress granted me the authority to fight this war autonomously as Commander in Chief and I sense an opportunity that cannot be wasted."

On the floor of the Anglican Church, their temporary barracks, Mason watched his squad carefully reassembling and cleaning their M16 rifles. Their orders were to turn over the weapons to the Congress for examination. Higgs would take Lieutenant

Monroe to Baltimore and deliver their modern weapons into the hands of "strong-minded men," in Washington's words. He met her eyes. She sat amongst them in period dress.

"You look the part," Mason said.

Higgs frowned and slapped at the folds of her dress. "I'd rather be staying in uniform, dammit."

"You have a mission," Mason said. "We all do."

"I know," Higgs said. "I'm to take care of Lieutenant Monroe and turn over our weapons and the extra gear from Kennedy and Porter for examination. It's just..."

"Just what?" Martinez asked. "Do you not trust General Washington?"

The group laughed, albeit a bit nervously. Higgs smiled. "I do, but we're really talking about messing with history now."

"We have to win the war, first," Murphy said. "Granted, we could split off to the four winds after that, but that's not what Washington wants us to do. He has a plan."

Mason looked at him. "So what do we do?"

"You said it yourself, Mason. We know where they are and where they're coming from. Cornwallis is with them. We take him out and the war..."

"The war what?" Higgs asked.

Murphy chuckled. "I almost said the war should end. We don't know that for a fact. I mean, what if killing Cornwallis makes things worse?"

Mason sat back. He hadn't taken that thought seriously. Turning the bolt assembly in his hands, Mason watched the low lights of the lanterns flicker on the dull metal. "Courses of action."

"What?" Martinez asked.

Mason looked up at them. All eyes were on him. "C'mon people. Military Decision Making Process, right? MDMP? Captain Branson taught us all that, right? Courses of action. We need to think this through. All of those boring lectures from Colonel Graves? Yeah, we need to think about everything we know. How can we change the situation?"

Murphy took a deep breath and shrugged. "Let's say we kill off Cornwallis. The British under General Grant will likely hole up until spring in Princeton. That makes them a huge target."

"What about the regular garrison in New York?" Mason asked.

"Howe will stay there. His brother is commanding the British fleet in New York harbor. He'll elect to stay in New York if New Jersey is lost," Murphy said. "He'll send for reinforcements, of course, but he'll sit the winter out."

"Getting reinforcements will take some time," Higgs said. "A couple of weeks? A month?"

"Maybe longer," Murphy replied. "There's no guarantee they'd come to New York, either. King George will attempt to divide the colonies. Remember, he goes after the south."

"So, taking New York doesn't accomplish anything?" Mason asked.

"Not exactly. I'd say that we could take New York, but the British would still come after the south," Murphy said. "That does, however, bring France into the war."

"This is a good thing?" Martinez smiled.

Mason nodded. "Without them and their naval actions, we likely wouldn't have won the war anyway." The ideas crystallized in Mason's head. Washington wanted Murphy to go to Paris with Franklin to bring about a better partnership. One that could even take the fight to England's door.

"Any luck finding Dunaway?" Koch asked.

Mason looked at Higgs, who answered for them both. "No. No one has seen her. She's not anywhere in Trenton nor have any of Washington's spies found her."

"What if she's captured?" Murphy said. "She could compromise a lot of things."

"We have to assume that." Mason shrugged. "The only good thing in our favor is that she left almost all of her gear and clothes when she ran away. Had she taken her weapon..." He let the thought trail off. If Dunaway was still alive, and captured, she could certainly change the outcome of potential actions.

I wonder how much she really knows about history.

"She's more interested in drama than anything else. Her mother wouldn't let her major in it, so she wanted to double major in drama and art." Higgs stared at the floor. "I don't know how much of an impact she could have."

"Any impact can be substantial," Mason said. "We just don't know."

"And that means we have to assume the worst," Murphy said. "We can hope for the best, but we have to plan for the worst."

"That changes the fight," Mason said. "We can't be sure that Cornwallis will even attack."

"Your buddy Washington has a pretty good intelligence network, right?" Martinez grinned. "I'll bet we find out pretty quick whether Cornwallis arrives at Princeton and sets his sights on Trenton. If they come down the Princeton Road like Murphy says they do, we can hit them there."

Mason nodded. The road curved through dense forests with plenty of snow still on the ground. In their snowsuits, much of the Continental Army would be invisible, but still outnumbered two to one. They would need more than camouflaged infantry. "When they march, Murphy, is it fast or slow?"

"Slow," Murphy said. A slow smile appeared on his face. "They run into a lot of mud."

"Then we still have the advantage," Mason said. "So, the most likely course of action is that Cornwallis marches on Trenton like we know. The least likely is that they don't based on their own intelligence. The most dangerous course of action is that Dunaway has been captured and is spilling our secrets along with telling them how that missing rifle works. Does that about cover it?"

The group nodded, almost in unison. After a few seconds, Higgs spoke up. "You know what those COAs change, Mason?"

"What?"

"Absolutely nothing," Higgs said. "We're still here, we're still at war, and we still have a chance to change the course of history. If Dunaway is telling the British everything she knows, she's one person. How much can a drama major change the world, guys?"

CHAPTER TWENTY-FOUR

January 2, 1777
Princeton Road

His eight thousand troops spread over nearly two miles of muddy New Jersey roads, General Cornwallis paused his horse to one side as the army trudged on. The uncharacteristic warmth of the winter sun felt good on his face. He imagined Jemima sitting in the solarium in a similar warm light, the kind that so greatly affirmed her health. A groan rose from the ranks to the front of the column. They had been marching since before dawn in their hurried push for Trenton. Cornwallis meant to dispatch Washington's army by nightfall. Cornwallis frowned at the groaning troops as he turned in the saddle. The army, again, stood still. Forward cannons, specifically placed to lead the attack on Cornwallis' order, stood mired in ankle-deep mud. Officers roared at weary soldiers and Cornwallis glanced again at the sun.

Noon. We should have taken Trenton by now.

He shook his head and walked his horse alongside the eastern edge of the road. The deep forest on the east side was full of snow as far as he could see. On the west side, high grasses and scrub forest stretched toward the Pennington Road. The southern-exposed faces of the surrounding terrain had warmed enough to begin melting, adding to the water along the road and slowing the army. The heavily traveled Princeton Road proved treacherous, but he'd known the risk the moment General Grant ordered him to retake Trenton from the colonials. Washington was still there by all reports, fortifying the town through the days and nights. Word amongst the colonists was that the newly reinvigorated army would establish a northern headquarters in Trenton for the winter and resolve to take New York in the spring.

No, Cornwallis thought. Washington would run back across the Delaware to the Pennsylvania hills and dare the British to cross the semi-frozen river. He wouldn't dare attack New York and he certainly would not attempt to maintain a headquarters when virtually surrounded by the enemy with an often impassable river at his back.

What are you doing, old man? Where are you planning to fight? It's not Trenton. Maybe not New Jersey. Where do you think you're going? Cornwallis looked to the lead and trail elements of his army, as they slid out of view in the gentle bowing curve of the Princeton Road. Field captains rested their men in place because there was nothing else to do.

"Sir!"

Cornwallis turned to the voice. A young artilleryman with mud up to his knees ran up alongside and saluted. "Sir, the forward battery is almost clear. Another hundred yards and the ground is firm enough for the cannons."

"How long?"

"Ten minutes, sir. Maybe less."

Cornwallis frowned and spun in his saddle, looking to his staff in the center of the column. In the breeze, he smelled something burning. There was a pop and a hiss in the eastern tree line. He whipped his head around to see a full battery of guns erupt from behind massive snowbanks in perfect camouflage. The first cannons fired in the direction of his forward elements. By the sound of the detonation, they were firing canister at fairly close range. The shotgun-like rounds shredded his lines and soldiers fell in droves.

Another battery fired, and then another rippling canister fired down the column's length. The overlapping fires cut great swathes through his forward forces. He heard his officers, the ones that lived, yelling orders for the men to form up and fire. Another battery, and then another, fired from the wood line in rapid succession. Their interlocked fires made their way through the first half of the army. In the brief pause, Cornwallis waved to his staff to form up around him. Another series of cannons froze his arm mid-gesture as they tore into the rear of his formation firing one after the other. As soon as their firing ceased, Cornwallis drew his sword and pointed into the trees. He couldn't quite make out the positions of the rebel cannon, but that didn't matter. His army would cut the rebel cannon to shreds with well-aimed and controlled fires.

He turned to scream at the nearest regiment and a thunderclap of musket fire erupted from the grasses to the western side. A young cannoneer reeled to one side and fell into the mud. Blood covered the man's face. Like the cannon, muskets raked his column from south to north for what appeared to cover the entire force. Cornwallis heard his officers responding to the ambush. Calling the men to arms, forming them into their firing lines. Smoke obscured the road in many areas. He could hear the injured moaning and screaming from the road in both directions. Many of the units nearest to him stood and prepared to fire. They could still seize the day, Cornwallis believed.

Another volley of canister came from the forest and seemed to reach as far as Cornwallis could see in both directions. Even more men fell into the mud. A line of infantry managed to fire a ragged volley before they were cut down. In the quick silence after the cannon fusillade, he heard rebel commanders calling to their troops in the grasses.

"Ready, up!" A line of infantry dressed in white jackets and hoods leapt to their feet like ghosts in the smoke. "Fire!" At such close range, his men could easily defeat Washington's ragged army. Their shots whizzed harmlessly through the air around him.

"To your rifles!" Cornwallis commanded. A few of the men who could hear him looked incredulously up at him. He brandished his sword and pointed into the nearby grasses. If the rebels wanted to fight like the cursed French, then he could take the fight to them. "On me! On me!"

He nudged the horse into a trot and felt his tricorne hat torn away by a musket ball. Another clutched at his coat as he crossed the road. Cornwallis raised the sword high over his head and prepared to scream an order to attack. Something smacked his right leg. Another struck him and he watched a fine red mist erupt from his chest. He looked down at the gaping wound, saw the gray, bloody shards of his ribs, and grasped for the pommel of his saddle to steady himself. Arms failing to move, the sword fell from his hand and bounced harmlessly off his mount's back and into the mud.

A moment later, his vision swimming with blackness at the edges, Lord General Charles Cornwallis fell from his saddle mortally injured. He lay in the mud, gasping for breath, and saw white-covered figures running like ghosts toward the road and screaming incoherently. Hundreds of them raced toward his men, and the remains of his army ran like scalded dogs. Cornwallis turned his head slowly toward the wood line and the hidden artillery. A moment later, Cornwallis saw a horse come through the forest toward them.

There you are, old man.

There you are.

Mason came up from his position after the final volley. "Assault through! Assault through!"

Five meters from the edge of the road, the majority of the hidden army could have thrown rocks at the British and accomplished a similar victory. The broken English soldiers, the ones who were alive or injured with a degree of common sense, tried to run or surrendered en masse. Around him, soldiers cheered as they pushed through the shredded British units. Redcoats lay everywhere. The victory had been sudden and swift. Mason looked up and saw Washington approaching on horseback.

Martinez stood on the road's edge. "Take all weapons and magazines! Leave the personal effects! Take all weapons and magazines! Leave the personal effects! Secure the cannons!"

Mason slapped his friend on the shoulder and turned to see Koch running his way. "Central cannons are in good shape. The forward ones are pretty mired. Should we leave them?"

"Can you get them out?"

Koch grinned. "Of course we can."

Mason shook his head. "Get as many men as you need. Get those cannons out and fall back to Trenton. You're in charge of collecting and inventorying the captured artillery."

"You got it." Koch grinned and saluted.

Mason returned it with parade-ground precision. "Get going. The general wants to be back in Trenton by nightfall."

Koch glanced over Mason's right shoulder and then ran toward the front of what had been the British column. Mason turned to see Washington's familiar long strides coming toward him. The general had dismounted to observe the carnage firsthand. Mason came to attention. "Sir, we've defeated the enemy march."

"So you have, Captain Mason." Washington kept walking. "Come with me."

Halfway up the column, Mason followed Washington through a weaving journey to find a man lying in the mud by his sword. Wig askew on his head, the man's face was a calm mask of death. Washington knelt next to the man, grasped the dead man's hand, and looked up at Mason.

"Do you know who this is, Mason?"

"Sir?" Mason knelt in the mud and stared at the British officer whose hand Washington held.

"This is Lord General Charles Cornwallis, Mason. Tell me about him from your time."

Mason took a deep breath. "General Cornwallis, four years from now, would have been the supreme commander of all British forces in the colonies. He surrendered to your forces in 1781 at Yorktown, sir."

"That shall never happen, now." Washington stood and looked down the massacred British column. His eyes were suddenly soft and concerned. "Is this honorable, Mason? To fight from behind cover and surprise the enemy in this manner?"

Mason stood and let his eyes wander over the scene. While technically he was a veteran of Trenton and had seen the carnage waged by modern weapons of war up close, he'd never seen a battlefield torn asunder. The decimated British corpses lay in the rows where they'd marched, oblivious to the army hidden along the road. They never saw their fate coming. "You're worried they never had a chance to fight?"

Washington snorted and still watched the army clear the site with a haste and drive that had waned in the months up to Trenton. Mason could see it, too. The army, and the nation, needed a victory like this. But, with history changed and the future now uncertain, advantages were to be pressed. "I fight to win, Mason. It never occurred to me that I had to let the enemy set the time and place of the battle."

"We need every advantage to end this war faster, and with far fewer casualties, sir."

"Speed is not an advantage in war, Mason. I could do many things quickly, but only a very few things correctly." Washington looked up and down the road. "And what of this?"

"A great victory, sir," Mason said. "One that changes the future in ways we cannot see."

Washington took a slow breath. "I wish I could share your optimism, Mason. Somehow I feel this will simply bring the full measure of His Majesty's army to our shores come springtime. We must be ready to fight them here, but in other places as well."

Mason nodded. Thankfully, he knew the right people for the job.

The march back to Trenton passed quickly. Boisterous troops sang and yelled the entire way. Mason walked at the head of the column with his fellow cadets in tow. Their final mission together had been a rousing success and would likely change the course of the war. He'd not told them of their next duties. They would agree, perhaps with the notable exception of Martinez, who'd unexpectedly blossomed into a quality combat leader. As tight a unit as they'd become, the young officers simply could not stay together.

"You okay?" Murphy asked from his left shoulder. "Seems like something is on your mind."

"Yeah, lots. Sorry."

Murphy touched his shoulder. "You know it's okay, right? We came back, survived, and didn't mess up. Everything is going to be all right, Mason."

"I wish I believed that, Murphy." Mason shrugged. "We can't get home, either."

"Maybe we're not supposed to," Koch said from Mason's right shoulder. "Maybe we're supposed to do all those things we can dream of, you know?"

They walked in silence for almost a minute. Mason wondered if their minds were on the possibilities in front of them or the ones they'd collectively left behind. Martinez jogged up to walk with them. His thinner face was just a shadow of the fact that he was a greatly changed young man over the last week. "Time is going to move a lot slower than we're used to, I think."

Mason laughed and tugged at the left shoulder pocket of his ACUs. "Like our phones don't work, right? I haven't even looked at it in days. I guess I can charge it—look at the pictures and shit—but it's worthless now, huh? Especially if Kennedy's charger ever shits the bed."

"Right now it is," Koch said. "We need to make sure all of that stuff goes with Higgs, too."

"I want my music, man." Martinez grinned.

"Learn to sing," Koch grunted.

"This new world ain't ready for me, brother!" Martinez guffawed and Mason found himself laughing for the first time in days. It felt really good. They walked with their heads up, muskets held at the low ready, in their field-made snow ponchos at the front of a very different American army. A few days before, Washington pleaded with them for six more weeks of service at a bounty of ten dollars per man. Most of the army stayed. Joined by the southern elements of Cadwalader and Ewing, Washington's army now sported more than three thousand men. After taking nearly eight hundred Hessian prisoners in Trenton and with the trail elements escorting more than three thousand redcoats and leaving lots of them on the Princeton Road, Washington could expect the press to influence men across the country to join his forces in the coming weeks.

"Are we going to be able to feed these prisoners?" Martinez asked. "I thought our supplies were running low. A few thousand prisoners will suck that up quick."

Koch cleared his throat. "This army's logistics suck, man."

"We'll figure that out," Mason replied. "We'll also have to figure out how to stay in touch with each other."

Murphy exclaimed. "Hey! When was Alexander Graham Bell born?"

Mason shrugged and the group remained silent.

"We need to hurry up and establish the phone system so we can text and email each other." Murphy grinned. "My handwriting is too terrible for letters."

Mason laughed. "I think that makes you a great candidate to be a politician in this day and age."

January 4, 1777
Trenton

Murphy would leave for Baltimore in two days' time to work with the Congress. His hope to work with Franklin crushed, Murphy reveled at the chance to be with the founding fathers.

Washington hadn't eliminated the possibility of moving Murphy to Paris, but the young man didn't need to know that just yet. He had work to do. Martinez was headed to Baltimore as well, but he would team up with Colonel Richard Gridley.

There was one final request from Washington to administer—which was an order, really, just put out very politely. As they sat down, Mason took a deep breath and said, "We have to turn over all of our technology."

"Like our phones?" Martinez said. "They're worthless to anyone else."

"And without our power source," Koch said, "they're going to die anyway. You can have mine."

"The solar panels go too," Mason said. "All of the phones, our radios, our weapons, all of that goes. Everything extra from... the salvaged gear. Higgs has been instructed to keep it secured and everything quiet and get it to Virginia for safekeeping."

"Virginia?" Murphy asked. "The Congress is in Baltimore."

"Our stuff isn't going to the Congress, Murphy," Higgs said. "You'll have to keep your mouth shut until we can develop ways to manufacture more of it."

"The technology doesn't even exist to manufacture inter-changeable parts," Martinez said. "Unless that's part of what you're doing?"

"Wait. Our stuff is going with you, but to who specifically?" Murphy squinted at Higgs.

Higgs nodded. "Everything is coming with me, that much I know. I just don't know who'll be spearheading this effort."

"Anybody want to go find a quiet place in California?" Booker asked with a grin.

Mason nodded. The urge to run and find a quiet corner of the country was still there, but muted. There was a mission to complete. Porter and Kennedy would have wanted them to complete the mission. "Make sure and hand over all of your magazines and ammunition to Higgs. The weapons are the most critical. Keep your boots. We'll use the extras to see if someone can manufacture something similar in the next few years. We don't know how long this war will go. We might have changed it for the worse by killing Cornwallis."

"And we may have changed it for the better," Higgs said. "What matters is that before us the English came back in thirty or forty years and try it all again. The War of 1812, remember? We'll have to be ready for them. With what we're going to do, we can defeat them and anyone else."

"Could we invade England?" Koch asked. The group looked at him incredulously.

"Would we want to?" Murphy asked.

"Maybe," Martinez said around a mouthful of peanut butter and crackers. "But we're a long way from that decision, right?"

Mason nodded and conversation lulled. Theorizing beyond the next few days overwhelmed them. The squad ate silently, out in their own thoughts. Mason believed there was so much at stake that a nascent American government could be taught ways to avoid conflict for the next several hundred years. Eliminating slavery was just the first step. Uniting the southern states to the glorious cause would be next. The French were still in play and, should the war continue, they would come to the aid of the United States.

So much at stake and so much left to do.

There was a knock at the church door. "I got it," Martinez said. He rolled to his feet and strode to the door. Mason hoped it was information on Stratton. Shot in the head at point-blank range, the round had merely chipped the skull and torn away a considerable amount of scalp, yet Stratton would live to fight another day.

"Can we help you?" Martinez asked and jarred Mason's thoughts back to the present.

A vibrant voice carried into the church. "Good morning, I'm looking for a Miss Higgs. Please inform her that her carriage has arrived."

"Come in," Martinez said.

A tall man walked in and looked them over. Mason stood. The smiling man's eyes lingered over all of them and their weapons for a long moment. He wore an open coat with ruffled collared shirt. Under his arm was a walking stick. He turned to Mason. "You must be Mason."

"I am," Mason said. "You've been cleared by General Washington?"

"I should say so," he said. "I have come to personally escort Miss Higgs and Lieutenant Monroe to parts unknown, but likely in Virginia. General Washington has most certainly given me all

of the information I need. But, I believe you have more information for me still."

Mason scratched his head. He'd seen the man before, he was
certain. "You look very familiar to me, sir."

"That makes me feel rather good," the man said. "Being known
by a man from two hundred years in the future says I managed
to leave a small, lasting legacy through my work."

"And what kind of work is that?" Mason asked.

The man squatted down and fingered the barrel of Martinez's
disassembled rifle. "Making sense of things from a scientific per-
spective and other things. To be fair, I work in politics and the
like, but I'm also concerned with how things work and finding
ways to do them better. Things like this that have little meaning
but could change everything. Like every single bit of equipment
you've brought from the future, I'm told."

"I know I've seen you before," Martinez said. "Who are you,
sir?"

The man stood and stepped forward to Mason with his hand
extended. "My name is Thomas Jefferson and I'm very pleased
to make your acquaintance. Now, show me these otherworldly
rifles from another time. In fact, show me everything. Leave no
stitch unraveled, so to speak."

Mason shook Jefferson's hand. "A pleasure, sir."

Jefferson looked them over with a quizzical eye that Mason
saw was only half as lackadaisical as it seemed. When Jefferson
faced him, the look in the older man's eyes was almost wicked.
"No, my new young friend. The pleasure is all mine."

CHAPTER TWENTY-FIVE

January 4, 1777
Trenton

The wagon containing the squad's rifles and extra gear stood in front of Washington's headquarters. Lieutenant Monroe was already aboard and a platoon of cavalry stood ready to escort the wagon and its occupants to Baltimore. A second wagon, one fitted with seats like a coach, sat in front of the supplies. Washington and Jefferson stood on the porch talking quietly. Mason strained to hear them but could not. A hand grabbed his arm and he turned. Higgs stood there with tears in her eyes.

"Hey, it's okay," Mason said.

Higgs wrapped her arms around his neck and pulled them together. Her breathing hitched once but she did not sob. The strength of her embrace surprised him, and he squeezed back as much as he dared. She needed to know it would be okay. He needed to know it would be okay, too. He could feel his own eyes filling with tears and he let them come.

"This isn't goodbye, Ashley," he whispered into her ear.

"I know—" She paused. He could feel her swallow the sob threatening to come out.

"We'll see each other again. Very soon. I promise."

She nodded her head against his collarbone, but did not speak. For a long moment, they stood there in each other's arms. Two friends, two peers, a man and a woman of different skin tones locked in a fierce embrace of support. Mason could feel a thousand eyes on them, but he didn't care. Moreover, the whole damned continent needed to see it. A man embracing his sister-in-arms with their different skin color be damned. She needed his support and he would be damned not to give it to her. He knew that all of them felt the same way. They'd buried Kennedy and Porter along the way. Maybe none of them would survive the next year—it didn't matter. They were much more than friends or family could ever understand.

Higgs snuck a hand up to her face and wiped her tears. They pulled apart slowly, Mason looking down at her to make sure she was okay. "You okay now?"

"No. I'm not, and I might never be. But I have all of you guys. You're just a letter away."

Mason nodded. "And we'll come running if you need us."

Martinez was the closest to them. "Damn straight," he answered. "You call, I'm there. Even from Philadelphia or wherever I'm supposed to go."

Higgs nodded with tears in her eyes. "Okay."

Mason touched her arm. "You need to know something. These men may not consider you a soldier, they may not believe that a woman can make a difference in the fight, but we do. You saved a future President of the United States by charging into the middle of a firefight. Nobody here thinks you don't have what it takes to be a soldier. You are a warrior, Higgs. A damned fine one at that. Don't forget that."

Fresh tears squirted down her cheeks. "Thank you, Mason."

They hugged again for a long moment until Washington's voice cut them apart.

"Before Miss Higgs makes her goodbyes with Mister Jefferson and Lieutenant Monroe, there is something I need to do," the general said. He looked at Mason. "From the moment I met you, Mason, and you told me the story of who you were and where you came from, I could sense an enormous patriotism in you and your squad. You wanted to serve your country. And all of you have, honorably. For that, I will see you are all decorated appropriately, but as that depends on the Congress it will take time that we do not have. They have, however, acquiesced to my request from a few days ago. I do believe there is something you all would want and appreciate for what it is. Something that I can do for you as the commander of this army. But, all of you should be present."

Washington turned to his right and nodded. Out of the rough home the army used as a hospital came a stretcher born by four uniformed men from the Pennsylvania regiments. Propped up on the stretcher, bandaged about his head, was a smiling Stratton.

They rushed him at once, each of them hugging their friend. There were a few fresh tears in the group, Martinez leading the way. Mason approached last and looked down with a smile. "About time you woke up."

Stratton chuckled. "Could say the same to you, Mason."

Heat flushed Mason's face. Tears threatened his own eyes as Stratton reached up with a hand, which Mason took, and they wrapped each other's hands with their own in a clasp of brotherhood. "I'm glad you're okay, Stratton. You're a hell of a soldier and exactly what this army needs."

A tear ran out of Stratton's right eye. "So are you, brother."

Booker stepped in and hugged Stratton silently. The young man cried openly. When he released Stratton, he grabbed Mason in a fierce embrace.

"We'll follow you to hell, Mason."

Let's hope it doesn't come to that.

Washington stepped forward and put a hand on Stratton's shoulder; the stretcher separated him from Mason and the others. He looked down and nodded at Stratton with a smile and his eye twinkled. "As the commander of this army, I have certain powers and authorities which I take seriously. Over the course of the last weeks, I have seen your bravery, your commitment, and your duty charge this army with spirits unimaginable just weeks before. Our winter will be hard and the British will not leave this continent without a fight. I cannot do anything about that at the present time. I can, however, grant something that will mean as much to you as it does to me.

"This is for all of you, including Miss Higgs. I understand there are some necessary modifications to what you would be accustomed to hearing, but this oath will be taken henceforth by all new officers in the Continental Army. Each of you shall raise your right hand and repeat after me. Mason, you'll say your appointed rank to be captain instead."

Mason shivered. *I still can't believe this is real.* He raised his right hand, wishing his parents could see him standing there to receive what he never thought he'd receive and from a man whose honor was beyond reproach. The father of the United States of America.

As Washington spoke, the cadets echoed him in strong voices. "I, state your name, having been appointed an officer, in the Army of the United States, in the rank of lieutenant, do solemnly swear that I will support and defend the United States of America, against all enemies foreign and domestic. That I will bear true faith and allegiance to the same. That I take this obligation freely, without mental reservation or purpose of evasion, and that I will well and faithfully discharge the duties of the office upon which I am about to enter. So help me God."

Washington smiled at them. "Congratulations, lady and gentlemen."

Mason turned to Higgs and they hugged again. In a moment, Martinez joined them. As did Koch, Murphy, and Booker. Together they pulled up Stratton into as much of an embrace as they could muster and simply held each other.

Someone in the crowd, it may have been Jefferson, clapped loudly. It was joined in a chorus of applause that rang out around them. Not a word was said as they clutched each other like brothers and sisters. Undaunted by their assignments and ready for their challenges, they held each other as long as possible before standing tall in their commissions.

CHAPTER TWENTY-SIX

February 2, 1777
New York

Silas Connor beamed as the audience broke into a storm of applause for the seventeenth night in a row. His actors took their places for their bows amidst shouts and whistles. At the center, his relatively unknown Juliet stood on the brink of becoming a phenomenon. He'd never seen an actress take to her role so flawlessly. In only three days of rehearsals she'd bypassed all of his usual stable of actresses and taken her place in the lead. As if recognizing his casting choice, the audiences swooned as one for Diana Dunaway, his new sensation. She smiled and curtsied to the crowd again and again. The Loyalist crowd and bevy of British officers cheered her every move. The ovation threatened to go on forever, but his cast took their cues and moved backward through the curtain, leaving the beautiful Diana alone for a moment to bask in a resounding crescendo of applause that was both louder and more prolonged than the other.

Working his way through the crowded passages in the backstage area, Silas catered to the officers, many of whom asked to privately meet the young actress. Silas begged them away, as he had for many nights, saying that she needed her rest. More gifts of wine and perfumes showed up at the backstage door with poetic noted from would-be suitors. All of them would be collected and sold to benefit the company, as was his policy. He inspected the collection and saw that a handful of general officers had sent their admirations. It was to be expected. The British army was in winter quarters and bored. As such, the generals wanted to play at new distractions, and the age-old game of who could bed the newest darling of the New York theater scene would serve to fill his audiences and bolster the coffers of his troupe. For a week, the theater had been standing-room only with more than a few wealthy officer and Loyalists offering fifty pounds or more per seat.

Life was good and getting better every day for the New York Theater Company.

Tonight, though, there was more reason to push the crowd away and for smiled reassurances that their desires would be met.

He moved backstage, through the invigorated company of actors. Two weeks before, they'd been only slightly competent. When Diana entered the picture, everything changed. Brought by a weary coach from the snowy battlefields of New Jersey, she was a measure of determination and grit in a captivating package. She coached the troupe through their rehearsals and test performances with intent and purpose. Now, their every movement crackled with authenticity. Their lines flowed like conversation and a depth of emotion Silas hadn't imagined possible. His long-suffering troupe warmed quickly to the tasks and performed beautifully, taking their cues from Diana. Her perfection was enthusiasm for the others and they excelled together.

Silas patted the reassuring fold of paper inside his vest. He'd make an announcement to the whole cast momentarily, but he wanted her to know first. She'd changed the very prospect of his theater company and she deserved the news.

He found her being hugged by the cast and passed from one quick embrace to the next. The crowd dispersing, she sat at a table and let down her long, curled black hair. Her eyes were down, studying a folded newspaper on her table with keen interest. Her hands found her brush without a glance and she brushed out her hair and read. She'd taken every interest in the papers, he believed, to find news of her family in the aftermath of the rebel victory at Trenton.

Silas frowned at what Diana had called a headline. There were obviously no ghosts in the service of the rebel army and yet, the change of Washington's tactics gave the news credence. After his attacks on Trenton and Princeton, Washington and the bulk of his army had disappeared. Some said they'd gone into the wilderness of northern New Jersey, while the fervent rumors of the townspeople said Washington had made a deal with the devil and his ghosts were summoned back to hell to rest and recuperate.

The British leadership, stunned at the losses of Trenton and Princeton as well as the decimation of their New York garrison under the command of the late General Cornwallis, sent a request to His Majesty for additional troops. Content to let the war effort rest until spring, they waited in banquet halls and theater performances to revel in the distraction from fear. They didn't know where Washington was and instead of trying to find him in the fierce winter showering down upon them, the generals and admirals did nothing.

On the front page of the paper, there was a small article that said colonial forces were growing by leaps and bounds over the previous months. Having heard of the victories and spurred by the promise of freedom, colonials and freedmen reportedly poured into Washington's ranks. Undoubtedly, she would write her family of the news as she'd done every other day for the last two weeks. A loving sister and her brother missed her, but their encouragements of her career in the handful of letters she'd received had steeled her heart in these troubled times.

Silas looked back up to Diana's face and saw a faint smile on her lips. Done with her read, she studied herself in a mirror for a moment, and her eyes flitted to meet Silas'. He walked forward and withdrew the paper from his vest.

"Flawless, love," he said and placed a hand on her shoulder. "You have quite a crowd of suitors outside those doors and twice as many gifts as last night or the night before."

She blushed. "Silas, please. You know the only performance I want to give is on your stage. They can fawn over me all they want, but this company is my home. No gifts or handsome suitors will ever take me away."

"Love, I'm so glad you walked into our lives. Had Charles not found you cold and alone, making your way here, I do not know what would have become of us."

"You flatter me, love," she said. They'd shared a bed for the last two weeks and while he couldn't see it lasting, because she was too perfect, he enjoyed their time. Being the director had certain advantages. "It was divine intervention, if nothing else."

"Indeed," Silas replied. "Three weeks ago, I was ready to close down the company. Our accounts were in arrears and my debts insurmountable. Today, I was summoned by Lord General Howe for lunch and conversation. He watched your performance three nights ago and said he could hardly blink without seeing your elegance."

Diana blushed. "So very touching."

"Our favor with his command has grown. So much that today, I received this." He unfolded the paper. "We have been summoned by General Grant to perform at his garrison for three evenings. I believe we may even have the honor of performing for Lord General Howe and his entire staff, as well."

Diana beamed. "How splendid."

Silas nodded at her. "I would imagine, love, that you might find favor with Lord Admiral Howe. He has expressed a desire to make your acquaintance and be dazzled by your performance as you've won over his military commanders despite the dreadful turn of events with the rebels."

Diana looked up at him for a moment. "Do you believe the stories of Washington's ghosts? Figures dressed in white? Unseen and deadly in the snow?"

Silas shrugged. "I'm not a military man, love. I know not what to believe."

"Do you think His Majesty's forces will win?"

"Of course I do." Silas smiled. "Ghosts or not, Washington and his army will fail. Come spring, the full might of the army, under Lord General Howe I might add, will succeed where so many others have failed."

Diana grinned up at him. "It fills my heart to hear you say that, love. Performing for the brothers Howe is an honor that we cannot afford to miss. In their garrison, no less? What a splendid location for a performance."

Silas smiled. "I believe Lord General Howe might even ask you for a more intimate performance. I fear that given a chance you will accept his offers and affections."

Diana smiled at him and turned to the mirror. Everything about her was beautiful. In her smile was an innocence that died in her uncommonly solemn eyes. Silas believed it to be her actress's perfection, the challenge of the role, coming through. Her determination to make a good impression, in his mind, shrouded all other possibilities. Her silence he attributed to nervousness.

"Are you quite all right?" he asked.

She smiled up at him in the mirror. "Of course, love. As you said, ours is a business relationship and what better way to expand our company than through the favors of a smitten general and his men? So, yes, I gladly would accept his advances to further this company, love. If he truly is smitten with me and asks for an intimate performance?" she replied in her slightly curious accent. "I can think of nothing I'd like more."